LOVE, DEATH & PARANOIA

Asian Misadventures

By William Bennett Foulk

Published by Foulk Creations, 301 South Fifth Avenue, Suite B, Arcadia, California, 91006
(wfoulk@gmail.com), with technical assistance from Create Space.

ISBN—13: 9780615915722
ISBN—10: 0615915728

Library of Congress Control Number: 2014907355
William B. Foulk, Arcadia, CA

Acknowledgements

Many *thanks* to the numerous unscrupulous *characters* I met during my fifteen years of living in Asia. Without endorsing their actions—particularly when it comes to fathering children—they inspired me to write this novel.

In a more benign sense, I am indebted to the following: Thom Steinhoff for his work on the cover; my daughter, Melody Manwaring, for contributing the Epigraph and for helping me with the Spanish phrases; Laura Shimizu, in Brazil, for some preliminary editing contributions; Richard Manwaring for his "About the Author" recommendations; my son, James, for his plot suggestions; my son, Thomas, for his moral support; and, my wife, Yalin, for being very patient during the two years I worked on this book; she never pressured me for time or attention.

Lastly, I must acknowledge the unnamed man who planted the prime seed for this tome, a Eurasian man missing both hands and his arms between his wrists and elbows. I only spoke with him once, that during a rainy day on a main thoroughfare in Kunming, China. When I ask him how he lost his hands and arms, he told me, in near perfect English, "I am a grown-up *beggar-baby*. My mother cut my arms off soon after I was born so I could be a beggar to support my family. My father was an American who left China before Mother had me."

Disclaimer

All characters appearing in this work are fictitious. Any resemblance to real persons, living or dead, is purely coincidental.

Dedication

This book is dedicated to those thousands of children born in Asia to Caucasian or Black fathers and Asian mothers. Most of those men deserted their children—and their mothers—never to see them again. *Out of sight, out of mind.* Usually, the mothers never received a penny for child support.

Epigraph

I look for my father's face,
In every man I see,
As if in finding him,
I will find light,
To illuminate the dark places inside of me.
— Melody Manwaring

Table of Contents

Introduction

How could a man who killed over forty human beings, had three wives, and deserted three children while accumulating billions of dollars in personal wealth, be considered—at the time of his death—a compassionate man, a loyal man, a benevolent man, and a loving father?

PART I

Finding the Man

Hello, Brother! Hello, Sister!

When thirty imminently successful attorneys entered the seminar hall at Harvard Law School, none expected they were about to witness a near mathematical impossibility.

October 31, 2002: "Good Morning ladies and gentlemen. Welcome to Harvard Law School's seminar for attorneys advising and litigating in international trade law. You represent six of the seven continents—only Antarctica didn't accept the invitation *(laughter)*, and you came from eleven different countries.

"All of you invited to this event have distinguished yourselves by writing, teaching, or practicing international trade law. We want you to share your experience and knowledge. Call this a brain picking seminar, or if you choose, an idea stealing colloquium. *(more laughter)*

"First, we need to get to know each other. Most of us probably know most of you only from your writing and reputations; now we will put faces with names, and please tell us where you practice.

Thirty brief introductions, and I emphasize brief, should not take too long. I will go first."

After Professor Sloan introduced himself, Twenty-nine introductions followed. For the purposes of this work, we will only consider three.

At the far end of the massive table, a trimly built man with Eurasian features, moderately tinted skin and dark eyes, wearing a brown tweed sports coat with a solid green tie, brown horn rimmed glasses, and owning a full head of neatly trimmed black hair spoke:

"Hello. I am *Timothy Rogers*. My office is here in Boston. I received my early education in Hong Kong. My undergraduate degree in Accounting is from the University of California at Berkeley, and I earned an MBA from the Stanford School of International Finance. I also attended law school at Stanford. I'm married with one son."

At that moment two others at the table, both with similar Eurasian features—and last names of Rogers—snapped their heads to look at the speaker.

A short time later, *Sara Rogers-Givens*, the most comely of the three females in the room, lightly made up, wearing a navy, knee length business suit and light-blue hose, with eyes that emphatically suggested her genetic connection to Asia, introduced herself:

"I am Sara Rogers-Givens. Until I was seventeen, I went to school in Thailand. Then I attended Cambridge in the United Kingdom for an undergraduate degree in Philosophy. After Cambridge I studied law at Yale. My office is in Cupertino, California. My husband, Jonathan, also practices law, and we have two girls, Julie six, and Margaret, four."

Fifteen introductions and ten minutes later, the seminar attendees broke into unabated but good natured laughter when *Lawrence Rogers*, dressed as the quintessential attorney, dark suit, a red tie, and highly shinned black shoes, introduced himself:

"Good Morning. No joke, meet *Rogers* Number Three, *Lawrence Rogers*, and believe it or not, I have never met numbers One and Two, but I hope to do so soon. Through high school, I was educated in Cebu, Philippines. I went to Colorado State University for pre-law, then to the University of Chicago for my Law degree. My practice is in New York City. My wife and I have a son, Resile, and a daughter, Aneta."

After the introductions were completed, the two *Rogers* and one *Rogers-Givens,* quickly migrated to each other, shook hands and decided to have dinner together that evening. Timothy, who knew the Boston area well since he lived there, volunteered, "There are many good restaurants near here, but I will treat you to my favorite, the Blue Ginger; it's in Wellesley, only a fifteen minute drive. How is 7:30? I can pick you up at your hotels."

After exchanging hotel and cellphone information, the three *Rogers* diligently attended and contributed to their seminar workshops, somewhat distracted, thinking about the evening to come. What revelations, if any, would be discovered? Was it possible that the three Rogers had something in common other than the *Rogers* name and Asian childhoods?

While on their way to dinner, the inquisitions and exchange of information began. By the time their food arrived at their secluded corner table, they learned that they did have a lot in common: all three had been born in the United States, in Los Angeles; their *fathers* were American, but all, they were told, died when the Attorneys Rogers were infants. Sara's and Timothy's mothers remarried, so they had step-fathers. Lawrence, however, was raised by an aunt and uncle.

As they picked at their food making small talk, all were preoccupied with questions yet to be asked. Finally, they lapsed into silence, gifted minds working in high gear. When the conversation resumed, it became more pointed. Timothy, the eldest of the three— two years senior to Lawrence and four years older than Sara—spoke: "You know, there are too many similarities between us for this to be totally happenstance."

Sara added, "I agree. At about age five, when I started to a private school in Chung Rai, I became aware that my last name, *Rogers,* didn't match my father's, *Gulfrey.* When I asked about that, Mother told me, 'Your real father died when you were three. Rogers was your name when you were born.' Later, when I asked Mother to tell me about my real father, she described him as, 'A very kind, handsome man, who died of malaria.' She showed me some pictures of him holding me, and she gave me one I still have."

Timothy added, "My experience with the name thing was similar, but Mother didn't have any pictures to show me. She never actually said he was dead, but she always implied so when I tried to get more information about him. One time she did say, 'I know your father was seriously ill years ago; I assume he didn't survive.'"

Lawrence chimed in, "I knew early on that the people I called 'Mother' and 'Father' were actually my aunt and uncle. Mother simply told me that my real father visited once when I was very young but never returned. If I asked more, she would simply say, 'He's gone.' She too described him as handsome, kind, intelligent, and she showed me a few pictures of him and my real mother; she died giving birth to me."

Timothy, in a more emotional tone, "I don't know about the two of you, but this is going to drive me insane until I know what our connection is, or is not. Do either of you have quick access to your birth certificate?"

Sara answered, "I can get the information from mine in a couple of minutes. My husband will still be awake and our personal documents file is in our bedroom. Give me a few minutes. To show you what kind of an attorney I am, I don't even have a pen. May I borrow one?"

Timothy accommodated Sara, and she walked to the restaurant's front porch. Ten minutes later she hurried back, her forehead furled as if under intense strain. In her absence, Lawrence called his wife and was still talking as Sara took her seat. When his conversation ended, he said, "This is going to be interesting; you go first."

Referring to the back of the business card she had written her birth certificate details on, Sara took a deep breath and said, "I was born at *Cedars Sinai Medical Center* in Los Angeles, on February 28, 1966, to Silsuch Buakhieo Rogers, my mother, and Theodore Ruiz Rogers.

Suddenly the color drained from Lawrence's face, and he muttered, "I don't believe this; this really can't be true". After pausing and shaking his head, "I too was born at *Cedars Sinai Medical Center* in Los Angeles, on October 9, 1963, to Charlita Sabino Rogers and, a man with the same name as Sara's father, Theodore Ruiz Rogers."

"Jesus Christ!" Timothy almost snatched his pen from Sara's hand and walked to the porch. Five minutes later he came back, "My wife can't find my birth certificate. She thinks it is in our safety deposit box at our bank, but I have a copy in my office. Shall we go there?"

After a simultaneous, emphatic, "YES!" the three *Rogers* departed the restaurant, leaving more cash on the table than needed, most of their food untouched.

The ride to Timothy's office near the Boston Common grew eerily quiet. After answering some security questions from the building's security officer and an elevator ride up thirty-five stories to a penthouse office suite, the trio entered Timothy's office. After two faulty attempts at entering the security code for the door leading to his personal office, the third try finally opened it, and the three marched in.

"Please have a seat; this might take me a few minutes."

Timothy hurriedly rummaged through a file cabinet and then picked up the phone, "I have got to call my secretary; she will know where she filed that material."

"Rachel, Tim here. I am at the office looking for my personal papers file. Can you point me in the right direction?"

Pause! "Ok, let me check."

After unlocking the middle drawer of his desk with one key, and removing another key that opened the top drawer of an oak file cabinet sitting next to an adjacent wall, he rummaged until, "Ah! Here it is. Thank you Rachael."

Timothy silently read before exclaiming, "We all need to sit down for this: I was also born at Cedars Sinai Medical Center in Los Angeles, on February 7, 1961, to Yalin Wong Rogers and, believe it or not, to Theodore Ruiz Rogers.

Hello, Brother! Hello, Sister!"

2

The Search

The impenetrable silence abruptly ended when Sara said, "Wow! Where do we go from here?"

Timothy probed, "Who was our father; why were we never told about him? Mother told me he died shortly after my birth, but he obviously lived at least four more years when he fathered the two of you. If he wasn't dead then, maybe he isn't dead now, but how do we find out?"

After another period of silence, Timothy suggested, "For lack of an alternative at this moment, why don't we do a Google search on his name?"

"Good idea," responded Sara.

"Let's do it," Timothy chimed as he punched his oversized Macintosh's *on* button; two minutes later, "This is interesting; Google has a *Wikipedia* link for that name."

The three attorneys, newly found brothers and sisters, crowded around the computer as the *Wikipedia* page came up, and each gasp as a picture of a very young looking Marine standing with former

President Harry S. Truman highlighted the page under the title, *Theodore Ruiz Rogers—America's Youngest Medal of Honor Winner with President Harry S. Truman (July, 1951.)*

Sara returned to the leather couch, leaned forward and put her face in her hands while chocking up, "This is too much; I don't know if I can take this."

Timothy read the article out loud:

At a White House ceremony on July 2nd, 1951, Corporal Theodore Ruiz Rogers received the Medal of Honor from President Harry S. Truman 'for heroic deeds in combat near the Chosen Reservoir in North Korea on November 29th, 1950. Although seriously wounded himself, he saved the life of his critically wounded commanding officer while inflicting heavy casualties on the enemy.'

Rogers was discharged from the Marine Corps in August, 1951, and later, enrolled at Montana State University where he studied English and Mathematics. Prior to his graduation in 1955, he won 170 million dollars in the Northern Hemisphere International Lottery. During the summer of 1955, Rogers disappeared; rumors circulated that he relocated to Asia.

Theodore Ruiz Rogers, the son of a migrant Mexican farm laborer, Hector Ruiz, and Christina Rogers, the daughter of a socially elite Denver bank president, was born on July 4th, 1932. When Theodore's parents married, at his father's insistence, they took Christina's family name—Rogers.

After being disowned by her family—in 1931 it was socially taboo for Caucasian women to marry Mexican men, especially migrant workers—Hector and Christina retreated to Valle Hermosa in Mexico near Brownsville, Texas. Theodore was born in Brownsville because Hector wanted to insure that his son would be an American citizen.

Seven years after his birth, Theodore was orphaned when his mother, father, and three-year-old sister were killed in a fiery traffic accident while traveling to a citrus harvesting job near Riverside, California. A California highway patrolman, Jerome Glover, and his wife adopted Theodore—raising him until he joined the Marine Corps in 1949 at the age of 17.

Timothy was the first to speak, "I'll be god-damn! This man was our father?"

"Maybe he still is," chimed in Lawrence.

While dabbing the tears still rolling from her eyes, Sara added, "I guess it's possible."

The three attorneys retreated to leather, office chairs before Timothy spoke again, "Well, we know where he went: to China, the Philippines, and Thailand to have three babies, and his lottery money explains how we got educated and our mothers lived comfortably while they were raising us. I wonder if he is, indeed, still alive, and if so, where is he?

"Tomorrow I will have my Investigations Office try to track him down; they are very good at that," said Timothy.

"One thing for sure, this has been one hell-of-a night, and apparently we had, or have, one extraordinary man for a father, and I don't know if this *extraordinary* is positive or negative; more than likely it's some of both. In any case, if he is still alive, I hope he will tell us his side of the story."

3

AKA—Jackson Ruiz—Meets an Investigator

When Richard Tomlinson, a private investigator working for Timothy Rogers, drove onto the Marine Corps Veteran's Retirement Home (MCVRH) grounds in Alexandria, Virginia, he had a positive feeling for the first time in his two week-long search for Theodore Ruiz Rogers. Obtaining a Freedom of Information Act access order from a federal judge in Virginia, the Honorable Jason R. Campbell, accounted for most of that time.

Prior to Judge Campbell's ruling, the Marine Corps cited privacy concerns for denying Tomlinson access to the Medal of Honor winner's records, although they did confirm that Theodore R. Rogers was alive and receiving the monthly stipend given to all Medal of Honor recipients. More significantly, after finally gaining access, those records revealed Rogers's current address and an AKA[1], *Jackson Ruiz.*

---

1 also known as...

Jackson Ruiz was sitting at his favorite reading spot under a large magnolia tree on the immaculately groomed, park-like lawn surrounding MCVRH. Reading at this spot from 9:30 a.m. until 10:30 every fair-weather day for thirty years—reading the *Washington Post, The Wall Street Journal*, and sometimes one of the numerous books about Asia from his personal library—gave *Jackson's* life predictability and serenity.

It had been twenty-eight years since his last visit to Asia and then only for ten days, but that part of the world still held sway over him. On the other hand, his home at MCVRH was a better fit; it was his sanctuary from the world. Nevertheless, when memories of his past invaded his psyche—a phenomena that happened periodically—intense loneliness tested his sanity and his decision to live alone.

Unlike other residents, *Jackson Ruiz* had no need for the subsidized housing provided at MCVRH. His affinity for the place was based on a profound desire to live in a peaceful, immaculately clean environment, and most importantly, one with absolute privacy, away from prying eyes and queries, particularly those of military historians and financial investment gurus.

Jackson's quarters didn't follow the design of the other residents. Theirs were well-appointed, 800 square feet, comfortable apartments with small kitchenettes, a community laundry, cafeteria meals, and twice weekly maid service. Conversely, due to *Jackson's* $500,000 annual contribution to MCVRH's general fund, the home's Board of Directors approved construction, at *Jackson's* expense, of a unique apartment exclusively for his use, one containing: 1,200 square feet of living space, Japanese cherry hardwood floors throughout, an office-library, his own laundry room, fully equipped kitchen, a large bathroom with a Peruvian tiled floor and an oversized bathtub. Other conveniences included phone, fax lines, and a cable television link. His wall-to-wall, floor-to-ceiling, bay windows gave him travel poster like views of Arlington Nation Cemetery, the Washington Monument, and the Capital Building.

Jackson didn't own a car. Long ago his driver's license expired, and he never bothered to renew it. On those infrequent occasions when he left MCVRH for trips into Washington, D.C., or rarer, journeys to New York for a Broadway play, he used limousine service, but he never rode in long, ostentatious limousines, always in sedans.

Other residence of MCVRH considered *Jackson* eccentric, mostly based on their laconic conversations. However, from his point of view, he was simply a measured man.

Jackson lived a series of routines: after getting out of bed precisely at 4:00 a.m. each morning—seven days a week—he washed his face in cold water, brushed his teeth, then dampened his thick hair in preparation for brushing. After putting on a t-shirt and under-shorts, he brushed his hair with a stiff, boar's hair brush, exactly sixty times with his right hand, followed by sixty with his left.

Jackson ran, rain or shine, for three miles along the Potomac River at exactly 5:00 each morning, six days a week; on Saturdays he walked. If the weather was decent, he stopped at the Potomac River Park workout area and did twenty-five minutes of exercises including: 100 sit-ups, 25 push-ups, 65 pull-ups in 5 sets, and 13 dips on parallel bars. During inclement weather, he exercised in his apartment.

After his workout, Jackson soaked in the 110° water that filled his oversized tub, a ritual that often brought back memories of weeks without a shower or bath during his time as a Marine in Korea. Before dressing, he brushed his hair again, this time thirty strokes with each hand. After his evening bath, he repeated the hair brushing ritual a third time, but only fifteen repetitions with each hand.

After dressing in immaculately clean and precisely ironed clothes—he did his own laundry including ironing his underwear and sox—CNN International News became his companion as he prepared and ate breakfast.

Jackson's breakfast always consisting of: three-quarters cup of steal cut oatmeal, cooked at *High Power* in his microwave oven for ten minutes; one slice of dry, whole-wheat toast adorned with two tablespoons of Greek, non-fat yogurt; an orange, the meat of one walnut, and thirty-six raisins.

At 09:00 a.m. he knapped for twenty minutes before walking to the magnolia tree to read. The rest of his day was less regimented with the exception that each Sunday[2] and Thursday, precisely at 6:45 p.m.[3], he consulted by phone with the Investments Management Branch of the British Royal Bank of Hong Kong (BRBHK), the largest of his three investments entities. The other two were in Singapore and Shanghai; he met by phone with his Singapore surrogate on Mondays and the one in Shanghai on Wednesdays. At night he always went to bed at 7:30, read for thirty minutes and then fell asleep at about 8:00.

Jackson had no real friends. He did play chess with the MCVRH Chess Club on Wednesday evenings. Other than chess, in which he was highly competitive, there was no stress in his life, with one caveat: the lingering paranoia caused by his perceived mystical influence over the deaths of those he had loved.

Was *Jackson* a private person given to diffidence? Definitely! But he was also an astute Asian historian and a highly capable investor. However, perhaps, his most utilitarian philosophical attribute—an axiom embedded by his natural mother—continuously served him well: *I have always wanted to know more than I know.*

Studying history and participating in financial markets—mostly Asian—were his passions. By initially investing most of his 170 million dollars in lottery winnings in Hong Kong and Singapore real-estate, in less than 10 years his portfolio grew to 950 million dollars. Then in the 1980's he rolled the dice and invested in two fledgling American companies—Apple Computer in 1980 and Microsoft in 1986. He purchased one-million shares of each at their pre IPO[4] prices, approximately $10 per share for both companies. In less than ten years, those transactions alone turned *Jackson* into a billionaire. The only other investments he delved into were Asian real estate and precious metals, those on a dollar-cost-averaging[5] basis.

---

2 Monday in Hong Kong
3 9:45 AM in Hong Kong
4 Initial public offering
5 Investing in the same amount each week, month, or year, often in the same stock or mutual fund

In total, by the year 2010 his net worth exceeded 16 billion U.S. dollars, at the time making him one of the richest—and by far the most reclusive—private investor in the United States. Ironically, by the year 2000, he had quit looking at the *bottom line* on his quarterly statements; he simply accepted the fact that it was substantial. It goes without saying, that *Jackson* had more than enough money to make any man feel at ease; that, however, wasn't his circumstance on this day.

Suddenly *Jackson* had the uncomfortable feeling of being watched. He swiveled his head, scanned the lawn, and quickly found the source of his uneasiness, one of the blue-uniformed MCVRH escorts walking across the lawn with a man dressed in a dark business suit. Immediately *Jackson* thought, "That guy looks like an FBI agent."

As they walked in his direction, their eyes glancing at him, *Jackson* had the urge to get up and run; he sensed trouble approaching.

"Hello," the sleuth looking man said in a too friendly voice, "You must be *Jackson* Ruiz."

With unenthusiastic flaccidity, *Jackson* shook the extended hand, and nodded his head.

"Can I talk with you for a few minutes?" Tomlinson asked.

Ignoring the question while more intensely sensing a threat to his peace and tranquility, *Jackson* replied, "You know who I am, but who are you? Do you have a card?"

"Certainly!" Tomlinson fished in his wallet and handed *Jackson* a card.

Two words on the card immediately caught *Jackson's* attention: *Rogers* and *Investigator*. Reflexively he tensed up and assumed a defensive body-language posture, uncrossing his legs and sitting up straight in his chair, visually giving away his subterfuge.

Tomlinson exclaimed, "Please don't let the title Investigator alarm you. I am only here in hopes that you can help me find a man whom you may have served with in Korea, Theodore Ruiz Rogers, a man who won the Medal of Honor for heroism in that war."

Jackson hesitated. Staring at Tomlinson's card, he turned it over, looked at the blank back for a few seconds before speaking quietly but quickly: "No, I don't know him, and I don't want to talk with you. Please leave!"

Tomlinson took a step back and replied, "All right, but please listen to me for a moment. I am here on behalf of three attorneys, two with the last name of Rogers and their sister with the middle name of Rogers; they are looking for their father. In fact, I work directly for one of those attorneys, Timothy Rogers. If you are ever inclined to talk about a man named Theodore Ruiz Rogers, please give me a call."

When Tomlinson turned and walked away without glancing back, he was flushed with success. He knew he had found Theodore Ruiz Rogers, but he also knew he could not force a window open into this man's life. On the other hand, if his gut feeling was correct, Theodore Ruiz Rogers would soon open that window himself.

4

Crossing the Rubicon

Jackson had a knot in his stomach as he watched Tomlinson go, and he started shaking. The intrusion by the investigator killed his desire to read, so he left his refuge and walked, and walked, and walked; thinking, thinking, thinking; wondering about his children and their mothers. He knew the three Rogers Tomlinson referred to were his children, and it stunned him they were looking for him after so many years, years when he thought of them often, wondering where they were, wondering what their lives were like.

Jackson didn't sleep that night. At 2:00 a.m., he retrieved a manila folder marked *Important Photographs* from his file cabinet and emptied the contents onto his desk. Methodically he studied all the pictures: a faded picture of his family when he was five; another washed out picture of his biological mother and father taken on the day they were married; one of his Mother and Father Glover who raised him after his parents were killed; one photo of him and his deceased fiancé, Jane, in the mountain meadow where he proposed to her; a picture with Yalin—his first wife—propped up in a hospital bed holding their infant son, Timothy. In that picture *Jackson* sat on the edge of that bed with his right arm around mother and baby. He looked at a similar picture with Suchanat—his third wife—holding Sara; and one of his second wife Charlita. An Apo Island picture showed Jackson and his second son, Lawrence. He put all of the pictures back in the folder except three small ones.

Jackson placed the three pictures side-by-side; each showing the face of an infant with its eyes open. After turning them facedown, he read the inscriptions on the back of each out loud: "Timothy Wong Rogers, born February 7, 1961; Lawrence Sabino Rogers, born October 9, 1963; Sara Buakhieo Rogers, born February 28, 1965."

Jackson turned the pictures over and looked at the precious little faces; he studied each for an emotional connection, and he found that link. All had their unseeing eyes open, staring inquisitively, directly into their father's eyes as if they were interrogating him, each asking the same question: "Why did you abandon me? Why did you abandon me? Why did you abandon me?

Those mythical demands brought his emotions to a boil as tears started spotting the desk; finally, he gave in to the sentiment, put his head down on the desk and sobbed.

Two hours of restless sleep didn't ease *Jackson's* emotional distress, but running three miles—the first mile in a mental fog — cleared his thinking, and following a tasteless breakfast, he called the number on Mr. Tomlinson's card only to hear a message: "You have reached the office of Mr. Richard Tomlinson. Our office opens at 9:30, but you can leave a message. Please include your full name and telephone number."

Although the temperature in Theo's room was a comfortable 72 degrees, he started sweating as he talked into the phone, "Hello, my phone number is 571-627-4637. Please ask Mr. Tomlinson to call me." Then he crossed the emotional Rubicon: "Tell him Theodore Ruiz Rogers called."

While waiting in his living room for the phone to ring, he went through the motions of watching the morning news on NBC, ABC, and FOX, nervously switching from channel to channel, occasionally glancing at the phone, picking it up twice to make sure it had a dial tone. At 9:45 he jumped to his feet when the phone rang: "Hello."

"Hi, this is Richard Tomlinson returning your call."

Theo paused, speechless.

Finally Tomlinson said, "Are you there Mr. Ruiz.., I mean Mr. Rogers.?

"Yes, I'm here," replied Theodore, "Thank you for calling me back. We need to talk."

"Great," Tomlinson said. "I am back in Boston, but I can return to your place later today if you want me to."

Theodore took a deep breath and replied, "I don't want to cause you a lot of trouble, but I want you to know you have found the man you are looking for; I am Theodore Ruiz Rogers."

"Should I call you Theodore or Jackson?"

"I don't know. At this moment I am very confused.

Tomlinson responded, "That's alright. I understand. I know this is very difficult for you, but believe me, we can work it out. I will catch the shuttle to Washington, rent a car, and be in Alexandria as soon as I can, probably by 2:00 p.m.; if I'm lucky, maybe a little earlier."

Theodore spent the next hour trying to read, an exercise in futility, his ability to concentrate gone. Instead he walked the pedestrian path along the Potomac River until after 1:15 p.m. As he approached his apartment, he could see Mr. Tomlinson sitting in the atrium in front of the building.

Theodore walked up to the investigator with his eyes down, shoulders slumped. "Mr. Tomlinson, I am sorry for the way I treated you yesterday. You touched a nerve I buried years ago, but now it is exposed—raw, and throbbing."

"Please, call me Richard.

"Ok. You can call me Theo."

"Have you talked to my children about finding me?"

"No," Richard replied, "but I must talk with them soon, as early as late today. Out of respect for you, however, I want us to discuss how best to do that. They are going to pose some difficult questions, questions only you can answer."

After a long period of silence as Theo first stared at the surrounding lawn; then walked out of the atrium and stared across the Virginia country-side before walking back to Tomlinson and saying:

"Do you really think that is a good idea? You know the old axiom, 'Let sleeping dogs lie.'"

"In this case, Theo, I don't think that axiom applies."

"I guess my children hate me, don't they?"

"I don't think so, Theo. In fact, they don't know if you are dead or alive. Timothy's and Sara's mothers implied to them you were dead. Lawrence knows his mother died while giving birth to him, and his aunt and uncle told him, ambiguously, you were 'gone,' which he thought meant dead.

"Your children didn't even discover each other until two weeks ago at an attorneys' seminar at Harvard University. They are all successful lawyers, and all three specialize in international trade law, mostly with firms dealing with Asian companies, and they have families of their own."

"It's good to know their mothers, and Lawrence's aunt and uncle, used the money wisely I set aside for their care and education. How are their mothers?"

"Timothy's and Sara's mothers are still alive, but at this point, I don't know about Lawrence's aunt and uncle."

"I am afraid if they learn I am alive, it will disrupt their lives; I don't want to do that. How terrible I treated those women; how terrible I treated my children. I was a coward; I was a liar, lying to myself, rationalizing I was doing the right thing when I abandoned them. Don't you think it would be better if you told them you couldn't find me, or that you learned I am indeed dead?"

"No Theo, I can't do that. I have a professional and moral obligation to tell them the truth, that their father is alive and doing well. At least you certainly look like you are healthy and contented; that's what I see."

"Richard, I am 70 now. I have been living here for over 30 years, and the last twenty-five have been mostly tranquil and comfortable physically, but I am often dead emotionally. I read a lot, study my investments, and do a little writing; I run or walk every day, and, on rare occasions, I listen to the other former Marines living here tell war stories, mostly lies, but often interesting lies. I use some of their fantasies in short stories I sporadically write.

"For the last twenty-four hours, since meeting you, I have been going crazy. Down deep, Richard, I want to see my children, but I don't want to hurt them any more than I already have; I don't think it would be good for them—or me."

"Let me tell you a story, Theo. When I was eleven years old, the man I assumed was my father told me, 'Son, we adopted you.' I spent the next fifteen years of my life trying to find out who my birth parents were. It wasn't that the couple that adopted me at birth weren't great parents; they were. But the inherent urge to know where I came from constantly drove me to try to find the man and woman who brought me into this world. When I was twenty-five, after getting a court order giving me access to my mother's name, I found her. Maybe that was the happiest day of my life. The fact that she had given me up for adoption because at sixteen, and unmarried, she didn't think she could provide for me, did not distract from our meeting at all; nor, did it matter much that my birth father, married to a different woman, had died in a car accident. To this day, I still consider my adopted parents who raised me my mother and father, but also, to this day my birth mother is part of my life. I talk with her frequently on the phone, and at least twice each year we see each other. I care deeply for all three of my parents."

"Thanks for telling me about your mother, Richard. That is a very positive story, a touching story. Yes, I guess I should see my children."

"Well, Theo, that's a good start. We know what you want to do, see your children, but maybe we should make some preparations for those meetings so you are ready to answer the questions they are going to have. You need to be ready to share their pent up pain and combine it with your own, so all of you can get on with your lives."

With emotion and tear filled eyes, "I still don't know! I still don't know! How can I explain my life to them, be honest, and still not have them hate me?"

"Look, Theo, your children are all highly intelligent adults, not adolescence. They have children of their own; they have made mistakes in their lives as we all have. If my gut feeling is correct, they just want to know who their father is—just the truth! I don't think you will find an element of hate in their attitude toward you, but again, certainly they will have a lot of pointed questions. They may even be anxious to share the stories of their lives with you."

Suddenly Theo remembered: ten years previously he spent a few weeks writing what was tantamount to an autobiography. Somewhere in his closet, he still had all of those handwritten pages; maybe they would be useful now.

"Richard, several years ago, I hand-wrote a one draft chronicle about my life, simply for the purpose of venting during one of my unhappy periods, one of those times when depression and guilt overcame me. But I think it might be too accurate and too graphic for my children to read; on the other hand, it is truthful. Maybe you should read it and see what you think."

Richard's face broke out in a wide smile, "Great idea!"

"Give me a couple of minutes; I think I can find it quickly."

It only took a minute for Theo to dig in a closet and find the envelope with his one draft, unedited, *autobiography*—written on both sides of school-lined, three-hole paper—a document written for therapeutic purposes only.

"Here it is Richard. *(with a smile)* Now you will know more about me than I really want to know about myself."

Richard took a few minutes to browse through the manuscript before saying, "I will start reading this on my way back to Boston, and with your permission, I will have my secretary photocopy it so we can FAX a copy to each of your children—if you decide to do that. You can make that decision tomorrow.

Theo responded, "Right now, I don't want anyone but you to see this."

"Whether we send them a copy of this or not, should I give them your phone number?"

Theo was suddenly faced with a frightening decision: he had never really talked with his children, only a little baby-talk with Sara which she couldn't possibly remember. Thirty-three years had passed since he last held her in his arms and kissed her. He hadn't seen any of them since they were very young. Now, the prospect of talking with them terrified him. Theo froze to speechlessness, to inaction, to indecision.

Richard could see the indecisiveness in Theo, and he admonished him with: "Theo, I know you received the Medal of Honor for courage. I think it is time for you to show some of that courage again. Give them your number. Maybe they will not want to talk with you, but let them make that decision. Give them the opportunity to know their father."

After a short pause, "Alright, do it! Give them my number."

5

Hello Dad

A s soon as Richard Tomlinson left his apartment, Theo started feeling nauseous, followed by numbness in his arms and legs; then heavy breathing led to hyperventilation—all signals of a panic attack. He wanted to burst out of his room and run; run from who he was; run from where he had been hiding for over thirty-years, run from facing his children who he deserted when they were infants; run from the phone that might ring any moment delivering voices he wanted to hear but gravely feared.

As he headed for the door, the room started spinning. His vision distorted, he dropped to his knees, crawled to a nearby couch, pulled himself up, and passed out. In that unconscious state his breathing returned to normal, his body relaxed to an almost comatose state resulting in deep sleep, his panic attack over.

When the phone rang, it took Theo several seconds to connect the ringing to reality and not the dream he was experiencing: three smiling faces, three mouths moving, two men and one woman, Theo's children, all talking without sound.

Out of long habit he answered, "Hello, this is Jackson Ruiz."

"I'm sorry. I am trying to reach Theodore Rogers. Does he, perhaps, live with you?"

Theo was stunned. His first impulse was to hang up, but he took a deep breath and said, "This is Theo Rogers. I am a man with two names. Who is this?"

"This is your son, Timothy." After a few seconds of silence, "Are you still there?"

With building emotion, "Ah, Ah, Yes, I am, sorry. Timothy! Hearing your voice is a wonderful shock. Thank you for calling."

"When Richard Tomlinson told me about finding you, I had to call. How are you? Are you in good health?"

"Yes, I believe so, but when you are seventy-years-old, good health is relative. Maybe it can be defined as simply being alive." Both men laughed.

"Gosh, it is good to know you have a sense of humor; that is a sign of excellent health," responded Timothy. "Can I call you Dad?"

"Ah, oh, yes! Please do. The pleasure will be mine."

"Well Dad, I have a thousand questions, but they can all wait; most of all I want you to know I am very happy you are still alive."

"Mr. Tomlinson told me you recently discovered your brother and sister. That must have been a shock for all of you."

"Oh, yes! How true! The unlikelihood of that discovery is almost too ironic to be believed," said Timothy.

"Did Richard tell you that I wrote an autobiography of sorts?"

"Yes, and he said his secretary is going to make copies of it; at this moment it is probably being scanned, and it will be faxed to Sara, Lawrence, and me, but only if you approve. Will you?" Please!"

After a short pause, "Umm, Yes. I guess I have gone too far to stop now."

"Great! I will start reading it tonight, and I will finish reading it tomorrow no matter how much time it takes. I'm sure Lawrence will do the same. Sara hasn't made up her mind about reading it, but I believe that after she thinks about it, she won't be able not to.

"Well, Timothy, it is not a pretty story, but it is the truth. When I wrote it, I never imagined my children would read it one day, certainly not while I am still alive.

PART II

Theodore's Autobiography

Introduction

T o whoever might read this, most likely after I am long dead:
Much of what I will write about my parent's lives—before I
was born and up until I was four or five—is based on conversations I had with my mother's closest confident, Alondra Lopez. She was
my mother's wet nurse and the Rogers family's housekeeper in Denver,
Colorado. Also, when I was between five and seven, Grandmother and
Grandfather Ruiz told me a lot about my father's life.

I am going to write dialogues as I think they might have occurred;
some came from Alondra's memory.

By the time I was four, I had started asking questions about why
Mama had blond hair, blue eyes, and fair skin while Papá's hair was
black, his eyes dark, and his skin terracotta brown. Also, I wondered
why Mother spoke both English and Spanish fluently—just as my
little sister, Rachel, and I did—but Papá only spoke Spanish. Later
my curiosity morphed into, "Mama, where did you meet Papá?"

Mother, who otherwise always answered my questions, said, "You should talk with Aunty Alondra about that; she'll remember more than I do."

Aunty Alondra lived with us—I thought she was Papá's sister—and I always called her "Aunty"; however, she wasn't really my aunt but the woman who wet nursed Mama when she was a baby.

I often went in the kitchen where Aunty Alondra and Grandma Ruiz were cooking and endlessly ask them questions about my family's history and that part of my life up until I was about four years old. (Then I started remembering almost everything, often more than I wanted to remember.)

When I returned to Valle Hermosa, a nineteen year old Marine veteran, supposedly a Korean War hero—with a combat damaged body and a mind in the early stages of paranoia—I was more inquisitive about my family's history. Aunty Alondra gave me an incredible amount of information, some included dates and specific scenarios. I took notes on much of that information, notes I have to this day, but I must confess, in this piece of writing, I will fill in some details, particularly those related to times, dates, and dialogues, with approximations and my imagination.

My Mother and Father Meet

Naturally, the provenance for all people is their mother and father; nevertheless, I think, much to my advantage, my origin was unique and my parents exceptional.

My mother, born Christina Farina Rogers, came into this world with an axiomatic *silver spoon in her mouth*, but early on—actually when she was an infant—she became the benefactor of being exposed to less affluent people, particularly to the Hispanic domestic who worked in the Rogers mansion, Alondra Lopez, an undocumented alien, who became Mama's wet nurse and surrogate mother.

When she was an infant, mother's stomach could not tolerate the milk formulas available in the 1920s, and since my grandmother didn't want to be a slave to the time-consuming process of nursing a baby—she belonged to two bridge clubs, was President of the Methodist Church Social Committee, played golf in the summer and indoor tennis in the winter— after Alondra nursed Mother on a trial bases for a few days, she became her primary source of nutrition. She obviously provided Mother with wholesome nourishment because she grew into a fine-looking, healthy child, and later, into an incredibly beautiful woman.

In contrast, my father, Hector Ruiz, was born the fifth son of a semi-penurious Mexican family that lived in Valle Hermosa, Mexico. Like his father and brothers before him, he became a migrant farm worker in the United States.

Upon on their return to Valle Hermosa from laboring for the *norte americanos in de Ustados Unidos* (North Americans in the United States)—with *gringo* silver dollars jingling in their pockets—Papá and his friends no longer felt poor like they did when they swam the Rio Grande River into Texas months earlier. Also, now their neighbors considered them rich. As a matter of fact, compared to their friends and neighbors in Valle Hermosa, a village of 1,500 persons, they were, indeed, in the upper economic class; each owned two pairs of shoes, a mark of prosperity in Valle Hermosa.

The morning fate selected my mother and father to be the prime players in the drama that became my life—a life filled with romance, adventure, fear, *love, death and paranoia*, but finally relative tranquility—Mother, seventeen at the time, woke-up rested and unhurried in her cozy, French canopied bed.

Only two miles away, Papá, at the age of twenty-one, lifted his head from a blanket spread on the dirt floor of a migrant workers shack, unrested but realizing he had to rise and start working when the sun came up.

After lying in bed and contemplating the equestrian activity scheduled with her father, Mother toileted in her perfume scented lavatory suite—even the toilet paper was fragrant—a lavatory equipped with imported Italian ironstone fixtures, including an oversized tub. Near the same time, Papá, using a stinking privy—a one holler with dry corncobs for wiping—contemplated his work for the day. He would earn $2.00 for twelve hours of labor, thrashing wheat with a hand scythe.

After bathing and washing her hair, Alondra rinsed it for her, Mother sat before an ornate French mirror while Alondra towel dried and brushed Mother's locks. She and Alondra sang Mexican ballads in espanól during that process.

At the well near the shack, Papá washed his hands with lye soap before splashing cold water on his face. While looking into a small piece of broken mirror, one precariously balanced on two nails driven into a water-drawing post[6], he ran his fingers through his thick black hair. Finally, he brushed his teeth with a small piece of sassafras wood, looked into the mirror again, bared his clean, perfectly white teeth, and smiled; thinking how lucky he was to have a roof over his head, food to eat, and a *well-paying* job.

Later, Mother descended the spiral staircase leading to the first floor of the Rogers mansion. There she enjoyed a delicious breakfast: two crepe suzettes, a chorizo omelet, toast with strawberry jam, and a glass of fresh squeezed orange juice, all prepared and served by Alondra.

When her parents were absent, which was frequently, Mother enjoyed spending time in the kitchen with Alondra learning how to cook. She also enjoyed helping her clean the house, something she did for entertainment when she was a child. When she turned ten, however, her father absolutely forbad his daughter from doing the activities of a domestic. Nevertheless, she still did, but never when her parents were home.

Papá quickly ate breakfast with the other *Los trabajadores agrícolas* (farm workers), cold black beans spread over stale, unrefined wheat bread, the remains of last night's dinner. Ten minutes later, he headed for the fields to harvest wheat.

On Saturday mornings Mother often rode her flaxen-colored Arabian mare with her father—an accomplished polo player with a stable of six ponies—who always mounted his pure white Arabian stallion for the Saturday rides. Both horses, and a third for Grandmother Rogers, had been gifts from the Saudi Arabia royal family, a gratuity to Grandfather for a successful mountain real estate transaction he managed for them: the purchase of 3,000

---

6 Two posts with an adjoining beam, rope and bucket attached, are used to draw water from a well.

picturesque acres near the obscure, Colorado, mountain village of Aspen.

On this crisp September morning, with the sun reflecting off the first snow of the season highlighting the Rocky Mountain Peaks to the west, and with a gentle breeze undulating the ripe wheat to the east—like waves in the ocean—Mother and Grandfather cantered their horses south on a section-line trail.

"Father, I want to run Juno."

"OK, but for no more than five minutes; you don't want to strain your horse."

In an instant Mother's steed started galloping; her long blond hair flowed parallel to Juno's flaxen flowing mane. Framed by the mountains and waving wheat, she became an exquisite moving portrait of a young woman racing her horse and enjoying life. Little did she know that in a few minutes her life would drastically change; she would meet the one and only love of her life—Papá.

After going a minute or two beyond her father's requisite five minutes, she brought Juno to a cantor at a dirt road intersection where perpendicular section lines met. No more than twenty meters away, five Hispanic men, stripped to the waist, worked together cutting wheat with hand-scythes. One, taller and more muscular than the others, perspiration highlighting his statuesque physique, lifted his head, looked directly at Mother and smiled.

Returning the smile, she said in the perfect espanól she learned from Alondra, *"Buenos días, Señor."* (Good morning, Sir.)

Papá responded, *"Buenos dias, señorita hermosa. ¿Cómo se llama usted?"* (Good morning, beautiful young lady. What is your name?)

"Mi nombre es Christina Rogers. ¿Cómo se llama usted?" Qué es el suyo, para Cuánto tiempo llevas trigo de corte?" ("My name is Christina Rogers. What is your name, and how long have you been cutting wheat?")

"Mi nombre es Hector Ruiz. Des de los catorce años, durante siete años, ("My name is Hector Ruiz, and I have been cutting wheat since I was fourteen, for seven years.")

"Ha! Ha! No cuántos años; ¿Cuánto tiempo has estado trabaja-ndo hoy?" ("Ha! Ha! Not how many years; how long have you been working today?")

With a smile that highlighted his perfect teeth, *"No sé, desde la luz del día; tal vez cuatro o cinco horas."* ("I don't know, since sunrise, maybe four or five hours.")

During this short conversation their eyes never strayed; some undefinable magnetism glued their individual gazes into one.

Too soon, Grandfather Rogers rode up and immediately stated, loudly and scornfully, "Christina, why are you talking with this man. Never talk with wet-back workers. Let's go home."

As a young boy, it never burdened me that Mother came from a rich Denver family and had a father who thought negatively about Mexican farm workers like Papá. Things like that didn't matter to me; my Mama and Papá were simply two people I loved as dearly as they loved me. And, thankfully, I never had to suffer through hearing my Grandfather Rogers call my father a "Mexican wet back," nor was I privy to him and Grandmother Rogers admonishing Mother for marrying Papá.

8

Smitten Lovers

On the last Friday morning in September 1930, Mother, a high school senior, was working as a subaltern—part of her Business Finance class—at the 6ᵗʰ Avenue Branch of Freedom Savings Bank of Denver, one of the two banks her father owned and directed. She wore an institutional like full-length, navy blue dress, black shoes with medium heals, and above her left breast a name-tag reading "Christina."

Mother's long blond hair rested easily on her upper back as she watched two Hispanic men, obviously still in their work clothes, walk in the main entrance of the bank. They were stopped by the bank's armed guard. Mother immediately recognized one of the men, the same handsome man she spoke to three weeks earlier when she and her father were riding their horses, the same man she sometimes fantasized about.

The men tried to explain something in español to the guard, but he couldn't understand. Denied entrance, the men started to leave, but Mother, determined not to let them get away without talking with her, went to help, but by the time she reached the door they had exited. Mother followed them out and shouted, *"¡Espere! ¡Por favor espere! Tal vez le puedo ayudar."* (Wait! Please Wait! Maybe I can help you.)

Immediately the taller of the two men, Hector Ruiz, who would be my Papá two years later, turned and faced Mother. In a repeat of the wheat-field meeting, in another electrifying, enchanting instant, azure blue eye locked with dark brown. Two silent seconds, bordering on faux pas, went by before Mother said, *"¿Te puedo ayudar?"* ("Can I help you?")

Papá smiled, surprised and delighted to hear the Gringo beauty speaking espanól again, replied, *"Quizás."* (Maybe.)

After a short conversation, Mother understood the banking problem Papá and his friend faced: They had been working in the wheat fields near Denver for a month, earning two dollars a day for twelve hours of work. Since thirty cents was deducted each day for food and lodging, they were usually paid in coins; consequently, Papá and his friend had their pockets bloated with change. They wanted to convert that cumbersome cash into lighter and larger values, five and ten-dollar bills, before moving on to their next thrashing job in Wyoming.

Mother led Papá and his friend back into the bank, to a cashier who changed their money, and while Papá stood in front of the cashier waiting for the transaction to be completed, Mother had the opportunity to see him more closely.

Papá had obviously been working hard earlier that day since white flecks of salt—dried heavy sweat—dusted his black hair. With his sun painted face and muscular arms—unblemished sepia brown—perfect white teeth and flashing dark eyes, he looked as if he had just stepped off of a Hollywood set. The sight of him took Mother's breath away.

When they finished with the cashier, Mother led the men back to the bank's entrance as the female cashiers and clerks tried not to look at Papá, but they were compelled by primordial instincts to do so.

Mother heard the second man, who turned out to be Pedro Martínez, say to Papá, *"Tengo hambre. Yo vi un restaurante mexicano en la calle. Vamos tratar nosotros mismos."* ("I am hungry. I saw a Mexican restaurant down the street. Let's treat ourselves.")

Papá replied, *"Esa es una buena idea."* ("That's a good idea.")

While Papá fumbled to fold his money neatly, inquisitive eyes met again. Mama blushed, and Papá nervously looked away as he told her, *"Muchas gracias, señorita."* ("Thank you so much.") Then the men walked away.

Ten minutes later, Mother had an hour lunch break. She spent the first five minutes in the ladies room refreshing her make-up and hair; then, with quick steps she left the bank so she could, hopefully, find the Mexican restaurant where the two men would be eating.

One block down 6th Avenue was the best—by Gringo standards—Mexican restaurant in Denver, the Mexicali Gardens. As she approached the door she realized that the men would not be there; undoubtedly, they would not be able to get in the front door. The Mexicali Gardens only served Caucasians; the only Mexicans allowed were employees and then only by the back door.

Immediately Mother remembered a small, Mexican owned place, *Francisco's Tortilla Restaurante*, located in an alley-like street, three blocks away. As a child, she visited there with Alondra a few times. It was a popular place for Hispanics to eat and socialize, in fact the only place for those cooks, dishwashers, janitors, street cleaners, garbage collectors and any other Mexicans who did the mundane *heavy lifting* in downtown Denver.

As soon as Mother stepped into Francisco's she spotted the two men sitting at a table close to the door eating chili-black beans enchiladas; Papá saw Mother at the same time she saw him, but neither knew what to say. It was an exciting but uncomfortable moment for both, and they just gawked. Speechless to the point of embarrassment, Mother turned and left. Walking quickly, she headed back to the bank, but after a short distance she heard running steps behind her; she turned and saw Papá who smiled and said, "Buenos Dias, Senorita Christina."

"*Buenos Dias, Senior Ruiz,*" Mother replied. Mother was delighted they remembered each other's names; Papá was too.

After silently scrutinizing each other for a few seconds, they began conversing. Papá asked if she was hungry; Mother lied and said she wasn't, but she would like to talk. Since they were only one block from Veteran's Park, Mother suggested they go there. Papá, acutely aware of the attention they would attract walking down the street together, suggested she go first; he would follow several paces behind. A Caucasian girl walking or talking with a Mexican man in downtown Denver—actually in any part of Colorado and most other states— in the 1920's was socially taboo.

Mother led Papá deep into the park. Under a stand of shielding evergreens, away from inquisitive eyes, and there they sat an appropriate, benign, distance apart on a stone bench. Intriguing, romantic minutes passed quickly.

First, Papá wanted to know where Mother learned to speak *español* so well. Mother explained how her mother was too busy to nurse her, and neither cow's milk nor formulas agreed with her, so Alondra, the family housekeeper, who only spoke a little English, became her wet nurse and surrogate mother. Mother told Papá she suckled Alondra until she was four, but only surreptitiously after she was two, because in the 1920's people of means thought it profane for children to nurse beyond that age.

She told Papá her earliest memories were of Alondra singing to her in *español* as she nursed. By the age of three Mother could sing and converse in Alondra's patois. Mother explained, "I didn't realize that English and *español* were different languages until I started to school."

Mother went on to tell Papá that her father, the president of the bank where she worked part time as an intern in conjunction with her high school Business class, would not be happy if he knew she visited with a bank customer. She didn't tell him that if her father knew she was with Papá, a Mexican migrant worker, he would have exploded.

Grandfather Rogers had profound, adamant disdain for Mexicans, unless they worked as domestics in his home. They were all in his words, "dirty Wetbacks." He used that epitaph frequently when speaking about Hispanics.

As the minutes ticked by, Mother developed an aching desire to sit closer to Papá but restraining herself, and instead she asked him where he was from and how long he would be in the Denver area.

Papá explained that his home was in the small town of Valle Hermosa, Mexico, a few miles south of Brownsville, Texas. He looked down as he said, "I swam the *Rio Bravo del Norte* (Rio Grande River) with my friend, Pedro, and we rode railroad freight cars north; eventually to Denver." He added, "Pedro and I will leave Denver tomorrow for Cheyenne, Wyoming where there are many wheat harvesting jobs for Mexican workers." He went on to say that they planned to work in Wyoming for three weeks before moving north with the wheat harvest, to Montana, South Dakota, North Dakota, and maybe even into Canada,.

Disappointed to learn Papá would be leaving, Mother asked, "Would you send me a letter?"

Papá took a deep breath, one suggesting disbelief, smiled, touched Mother's arm, and nodded twice before saying, "*Sí! Sí! Señorita Christina.*"

It took them a few minutes to straighten out the logistics for exchanging mail. Mother gave Papá the address where Alondra's sister lived. While she printed that address in large, block letters, Papá moved closer so he could see. She felt his nearness: she could smell the odor of a man who had been working for hours in a wheat field, but it was not unpleasant. She could feel his breath on her neck as he leaned closer; and, she became acutely aware of the energy that resonated between them. As she later told Alondra, "I wanted to close the gap between us so much, but I controlled myself."

With Mother's lunch hour already expired, the clock forced them to say good-bye. Before they parted, Papá asked, "Va a ser mi amiga? (Are you my friend?) With misty eyes, Mother, smiled and nodded. Papá stuck out a brown, labor worn, calloused hand with broken fingernails, and Mother took it in her, white, soft, coddled hands with perfectly manicured fingernails and kissed his. They took a long, last look into each other's eyes and parted with pounding hearts. Mother left the park going east; Papá went north.

As soon as she arrived home that afternoon, Mother told Alondra about meeting Papá and their letter writing scheme. After receiving serious words of concern and caution from Alondra, Mother pleaded, "Please don't mention this or any letters I receive from Hector to my mother or father." Alondra pledged her secrecy. That night, Mother dreamed she was in bed with Papá; when she awoke she was happy they held each other—if only in fantasy.

Mother didn't wonder if she would receive a letter from Papá; she knew she would, but it would take time. She counted each day, and twelve days later Papá's first letter arrived from Worland, Wyoming. Written in Spanish, of course, it started "Dear Senorita, Christina. Even though I have only seen you two times, I miss you. How can that be? I don't know, but it is true. I think about you all of the time...."

For the next four months, they exchanged letters filled with romance and getting-to-know each other information, and when Papá came back through Denver, on his way to Mexico, in October, they shared their first kiss. Six months later, after Mother turned eighteen and Papá twenty-two, they were covertly married.

Alondra and Pedro went with them to a justice of the peace in Boulder, Colorado. Knowing her parents would never approve beforehand, Mama decided to inform Grandma and Grandpa Rogers after the fact of her marriage that evening.

On the way back to Denver, Alondra told Mama, "You know your mother and father are going to be shocked and very angry, especially your father"

"They will get over it. I am their only child, and they both love me very much."

Before Mama and Papá even entered the Rogers mansion both her parents were already upset. Mama had missed dinner and was arriving well passed her father's mandate, "Always be home by 6 p.m. unless you have permission to arrive later." Now, after 8 p.m., trauma waited.

When Mama unlocked the front door and entered the foyer to the massive house, she shouted, "Hello, I'm home, and I have a surprise for you."

While not being able to see his daughter and her *surprise* from his seat at the dining room table, Grandfather shouted, "Young lady where in the hell have you been? Get in here right now."

Papá cringed, pointed to the door, indicating he thought he should leave, but Mama grabbed his arm and pulled him with her.

The sight of mother in her white wedding dress, with a pink rose pinned to it, and Papá in a dark suit and a red rose on his lapel, caused the eruption Alondra predicted, and at this point Mama hadn't even made the big announcement—that she and Papá were married. Maybe her parents thought they had been to a dance or some other social event. Even that possibility, however, clashed with a long-standing taboo in Denver at that time: a Hispanic man having a date with a Caucasian woman—absolutely unheard of.

Then Mama dropped the bombshell "I want you to meet my husband, Hector Ruiz Rogers." She didn't have time to explain: for logistical reasons at the U.S. Mexican border, they decided to use Rogers as their family name.

Grandmother collapsed, and Grandfather—mouth agape, face flushed, eyes bulging—jumped to his feet, at that instant unable to speak.

Mama and Papá were only a few feet from Grandfather. Papá stepped forward with a forced smile on his face and his right hand extended. Grandfather took two quick steps back, thrust both hands in the air, and screamed, "No! No! Never! Never! This cannot be true!"

After refusing to shake Papá's hand, followed by telling Mother she was no longer a member of their family and would be disinherited, he continued his tirade with, "I will not! I will never! NEVER, accept this idiotic marriage. Get that Mexican out of my house, NOW!"

Two hours later he fired Alondra for her admitted duplicity in the marriage, and the next day he instructed his attorney to "Get that stupid marriage annulled." He was unaware that the age for marriage consent in Colorado in 1930 was sixteen.

The next morning Mother withdrew $2,000 from her savings account, money she had accumulated over the years from birthday gifts and part time work at her father's bank. That same day the newlyweds purchased a good, used pickup truck for $750—*in 1930, a similar new truck would cost about $1,500*—and headed for Mexico, Alondra and Pedro with them. Alondra would remain a member of the Ruiz-Rogers clan for the next twenty-five years.

For a few months, Mother missed her parents, and since her letters to them went unanswered, she felt totally rejected. She also missed the Rogers's mansion and her horse, her French bed, her Italian bathroom, and her friends. Finally, however, with the help of the mother-daughter relationship she had with Alondra, her total literacy in espanól, new friends in Valle Hermosa, but most importantly, never wavering from the fact that she and Papá truly loved each other and reveled in being together—Valle Hermosa became her home. Mother's and Papá's romance, one initially inspired by elemental instincts, developed into deep appreciation and love for each other. As far as Mother was concerned, Papá was the best man in the world for her—the only man. They were happy with each other, and even more happy when she realized she was going to have a baby—me!

As the incubation months passed the Ruiz family and Alondra doted over Mother continuously, talking every day about baby names and where I should be born. Papá insisted that I be born in Brownsville, Texas—in the United States—so I would have an American birth certificate, proof of citizenship, and as I grew, the freedom to travel between the U.S. and Mexico uninhibited—no swimming of the Rio Grande for his son.

Finally, all agreed that if I turned out to be a boy, I would be: *Theodore Ruiz Rogers*. *Theodore* after former U.S. President Theodore Roosevelt, an American many Valle Hermosians revered because as a U.S. Army colonel he once rested there for two days with his cavalry troop and bestowed a lasting gift on the city—ten purebred cattle, one a bull. *Ruiz* represented Papá's family, and *Rogers* to make passing to and from the United States perfunctory. Also, the *Rogers* name might remind my grandparents, on my mother's side of the family, they had a grandchild. If a girl, I would have become *Rachael Ruiz Rogers*, the name eventually given to my little sister who followed me by two years.

The months prior to my birth passed quickly. Papá worked in cotton fields on the Ruiz family farm so he could stay close to Mother. Up until a week before I was born, Mother spent a lot of time teaching English, mostly to children in Valle Hermosa but sometimes to the migrant workers who traveled back and forth to the United States.

People in the village constantly lauded Mother, giving her confidence as a teacher, and by all indications she became an excellent one. Soon after she started teaching them, many of the children in the village were singing everything from *Take Me out to the Ball Game* to *Jingle Bells,* and some used English greetings and phrases without being prompted to do so.

Twice Mother visited a doctor in Brownsville who told her she seemed to be doing well with her pregnancy, and that he would try to be with her when she delivered. He wasn't; however, on July 4th, 1932, I was born in the Emergency Room of the Brownsville Community Hospital. I came quickly. Two days later, my birth was recorded at the City Hall in Brownsville before the Ruiz-Rogers family traveled back to Valle Hermosa.

9

Back to Denver

When I was about four and a half, the Ruiz-Rogers family traveled to Denver so Papá could thrash wheat and Mother could introduce me to my grandparents. For two weeks the thrashing went well, but the reconciliation only half succeeded; Grandfather Rogers refused to see Mother or me. On the other hand, Grandmother was happy to see us. On two days, Mother and I—Papá was working—spent several hours with her.

Grandmother hugged, kissed me, and bounced me on her knees while she repeated, several times, "What a beautiful boy; he is going to be a very handsome man." She even asked about Papá in a seemingly concerned and civil way.

On our second visit, two days after the first, Grandmother showered me with toys and clothes, some clothes several sizes too large. When mother asked about the large sizes, Grandmother remarked, "This boy is going to grow faster than you can imagine." Three years later, when my family had a terrible, tragic accident, I was wearing the blue jeans Grandmother Rogers gave me.

Mother didn't expect us to stay in the Rogers mansion during our short stay in Denver, but she wanted to be invited so she could graciously decline. The invitation never came, and as we were driving away from that second visit with Grandmother, Mother started crying. She stopped the truck and pulled me close to her. Sobbing, "Theo, never forget your mother and father will always love you no matter what you do."

On our last day in Denver, Mother visited the 23rd floor of Freedom Savings Bank; with me in tow, she walked into her father's outer office, and his secretary announced our arrival, but Grandfather refused to see us. No reason was given except, "Your father does not want to see you."

After leaving Grandfather's office with Mother in tears, we retreated to the bank below, and almost as a whim, Mother checked to see if her bank account was still active, and to her surprise, she had a balance of about $1,200. She closed the account and pocketed the money. Later, that money provided our family with some comforts we otherwise would not have enjoyed: new tires for the truck, new shoes and clothes for Papá, books Mother had been craving, toys for our extended family in Valle Hermosa, and she saved $600.

From the bank we went to tell Grandmother, "Good bye." During that short visit we didn't feel welcome; Grandmother's cold demeanor suggested Grandfather had called and discouraged her from seeing us. Sadly, that day was the last time Mother would see Grandmother Rogers. The next time the Ruiz-Rogers family stopped in Denver, we learned that Mother's parents died in an airplane accident while vacationing in Kenya, only a month before we arrived.

Later that day, after we packed our truck for travel, and at Mother's request, Papá slowly drove by the Freedom Savings Bank of Denver—she probably sensed she would never see that building again.

Next, we stopped near Veterans' Park, the place Mama and Papá had their first extended conversation. We walked into the center of the park where there were a lot of big trees, and the three of us sat on the very bench where Mama and Papá flirted five years before. As soon as she sat down mother started weeping again. Papá took her in his strong arms and asked, "Are you OK? Why are you crying?"

"I am fine now. My father would not see me, but his bank had over one thousand dollars of my money, so I got it. Let's try to forget my father. More importantly, I want to give you something that I wanted to give you the first time we sat on this bench."

She sat me on Papá's lap, pulled us both close, and gave Papá a full, prolonged kiss on the mouth, and she planted one on my cheek. Finally, Papá said, "We better go. It is a long drive to Wyoming."

But Mother had something else in mind: "There is one more thing we must do before we leave Denver." Mother took our hands, and led us two blocks to the Mexicali Garden, the restaurant exclusively for Gringos. We brazenly walked in the front entrance, the place Mexicans never enter. When the maître de glared at Papá, Mother quickly said, "Do you know my husband?" When the man shook his head, she added, "We would like a nice table by the windows." Heads turned, but no one tried to stop us.

We ate an expensive meal in splendor: fruit salsa and cinnamon chips, guacamole, spicy chicken soup, chili rellenos, bean salad, sweet corn, tortillas with beef chili, and sopapilla cheesecake for desert. When we finished, Mother left an appropriate tip, and carrying a box of leftovers, led her family, as other patrons gawked, the long way out of the Mexicali Garden; it was a parade of defiance.

10

The Blissful Life

Our family really enjoyed that summer and fall; jobs for migrant workers were plentiful, so we felt rich: our stomachs were full, our truck ran well, our travels were adventurous, and our stays in migrant workers' camps were usually more pleasure than tedium, and absolutely nothing could diminish our joy of traveling together.

For the five weeks we lived near Laramie, Wyoming; there Mother organized and taught English classes for the workers' children during the day and for the adults at night. Wheat and potato harvests took us through Wyoming, South Dakota, North Dakota, and Montana before we headed back to Mexico, traveling through Utah, Nevada, Arizona, and Texas; we crossed the border at Brownsville.

During that long sojourn, we sang songs, some many times, first in espanól, then in English; consequently, by the time we arrived home in Valle Hermosa, I could sing numerous songs bilingually.

Our extended Ruiz family and others in the village were happy to see us return, and the gifts we brought made our arrival more exciting, as did the news that Mother was going to have another baby.

Rachel Ruiz Rogers—soon we were calling her RR—was born in Brownsville, Texas in the same hospital, Alamo Regional Hospital, where I was born. Again, Mother gave birth easily, and getting RR's United States birth certificate was also uncomplicated. Papá insisted that he pay the extra five dollars to get three copies of RR's and two more of my birth certificate, because he wanted our births as American citizens to be well documented. To him, three birth certificates meant you were two times more documented than you would be with just one.

That process was one I replicated years later to substantiate the American citizenship of my own three children, all of whom were conceived in Asia—China, Philippines, and Thailand—but born in the United States, hopefully, to their distinct advantage.

When RR was born, I was almost five and a blossoming boy. Like my mother, I spoke English and espanól as if they were one language, giving credibility to Noam Chomsky's linguistic theory that the *language acquisition device* imbedded in the brains of children is incredibly adaptive and permeable, allowing them to learn two or more languages as if they were one; the only requirement being for both languages to be continuously used by the child's family.

Before she was two RR would regurgitate English and espanól words and phrases every waking moment, and her aberrations in pronunciation were entertaining. The whole family laughed when she called me "Tee O," rather than Theodore, and within a few months that deviation stuck. By the time I was five and Rachel three, "Theodore" had morphed to "Theo," and people called me "Theo" for the next forty-five years, until I added the pseudonym *Jackson Ruiz* to hide from the public in 1977— explanation to follow.

As I grew I had my father's dark hair and my mother's blue eyes. When my playmates in Valle Hermosa, particularly my best friend Rico, teased me about my slightly brown skin and blue eyes— all of the other children in the village had skin much darker than mine with dark brown eyes—Mother would tell me, "Your skin is a beautiful blend of brown and white, because God in Heaven made you a perfect mixture of brown people and white people."

Rachel had her mother's blond hair, fair skin, and her father's dark eyes. Both of us blushed when people told Mother or Papá, "What astonishingly beautiful children you have." Visually, maybe we were a perfect amalgam of a Latino father and a Caucasian mother.

During my first five years, I became the epitome of a happy little boy, up until the time I experienced my first tragedy in life. It happened shortly after we returned from the previously mentioned trip to the United States.

My closest friend, Rico, and I were like brothers; we played endlessly together, often roaming the countryside near our homes and along the banks of the Matamoros River. We never thought of the river as dangerous. In the summer we frequently waded in its shallow water looking for tinny fish and tadpoles, and often we would lie in pools of clean water, letting it flow over our young bodies while we played splashing games. We never knew—actually we were too young to know—just how dangerous the Matamoros could be during the spring; then the river was much deeper and faster flowing.

On a day in May of 1937, Rico and I were playing along the banks of the Matamoros watching the debris: tree trunks, boxes, and even one car, dashing toward the Gulf of Mexico. As Rico and I stood viewing the angry torrent, suddenly the ground started moving, and a big piece of the river bank crashed into the water. I jumped back, but Rico fell into the surge as I shouted, "Rico! Rico! Swim! Swim!" I only got one short look at him before his head disappeared, swallowed by the angry river.

I ran screaming to the field where my father labored, "¡Ayudar a Papá! ¡Ayuda a Papá! Rico cayó en el río." ("Help Papá! Help Papá, Rico fell in the river.")

My father and two other men, one of them Rico's uncle, dashed to the river, but there was no sign of him. Two days later his body appeared, wedged near a bridge buttress in a tangle of rubbish. The day after that, I saw his black body before it was wrapped in a white sheet and lowered into the ground as his mother, father, brothers, and sisters grieved. By that time, I was all cried out; all I could do was stand in depressed silence holding my mother's hand.

As we left the graveyard, Rico's mother looked directly into my eyes for several seconds in a way that told me she blamed me for his death. For some inexplicable reason, I indelibly absorbed and believed that message—and I still do.

Even though Rico had not uttered a single word when the river swept him away, in my nightmares I clearly hear him screaming for my help. I hear the refrain: "¡Ayúdame, Theo! ¡Ayúdame, Theo!" (*"Help me Theo! Help me Theo!"*) Still, I don't know what I could have done.

Unfortunately, Rico's death would not be the last I would be associated with at a young age; many more came later, and in most of those incidents, I saw, heard, and even smelled, the people dying. With each death an additional layer of emergent paranoia developed. I came to accept as fact: *I contribute to the premature death of people I love.* After more than seventy years, I still *feel* that stare from Rico's mother, and the knowledge of that incident—along with the death of others—has taken me to the brink of suicide more than once.

After Rico died, I slipped into the first of many melancholy periods in my life. I quit playing with the other children in the village; I only apathetically played with Rachel and spent more time with Grandpa Ruiz, often helping him in the rice and corn fields. My family never asked me questions about Rico and that terrible day, but others in the village did—with their eyes.

I did, however, get support from my family: when I walked through our neighborhood with RR, she always held my hand, and Grandpa often put his strong, callused hand on my shoulder when I walked with him from the fields; also, he often planted a comforting pat on my back. When I needed more support, I went to our kitchen where Grandma Ruiz and Auntie Alondra were usually busy, but when they saw me, they knew what I was there for, and they always gave me a hug and kiss and offered me something to eat. Those were healing therapies, at least on the surface, but they didn't burnish the subliminal turmoil churning in my mind.

By the time I was seven, I knew my family was the *ship* I wanted to sail through life on, and Mama and Papá were its anchors, always giving RR and me more love than most children receive, always insuring our security, our education, and our future.

Education was mother's focus. She made sure we attended the village school—a parochial Catholic school—punctually every day, well dressed, well fed, well rested, and well-motivated to learn. During my first two years of elementary school I never missed a single day, and each day when I got home Mother required me to tell her three things I had learned. If I couldn't remember them, she had me sit in silence—not as punishment but teaching me to concentrate—until I thought of all three. In addition, Mother gave me more instruction at home, often teaching me geography and science. Before I was seven, I knew the names of all the states, and their capital cities, both those in Mexico and in the United States, and I knew the location of all major rivers and mountains. In addition, I could explain how H_2O transformed from one state—liquid, solid, or gas—to the others.

As a child, I knew the best mother, father, sister, and grandparents—my Ruiz grandparents—in the world were mine. No seven year old boy ever received more love and returned more love than I did.

11

The Fateful Trip

When I was seven and Rachel five, I often asked Mama and Papá, "When are we going on another family trip?"

I remembered the trip Mother and Papá took me on years earlier, and more clearly I remembered sitting on a strange lady's lap as she squeezed and kissed me; that, of course, was Grandmother Rogers. Most of all, however, I recalled riding in the truck with Mother and Papá singing songs—a song in Spanish followed by the same song in English—and all of us laughing. I wanted my family to do that again, this time with my adorable little sister, RR, contributing; she had an endearing singing voice enhanced by an intriguing lisp.

I was acutely aware that Papá went on many trips; he would be gone for as long as three months. During those times Mother, RR, and I missed him terribly from the day he left until he returned. Too frequently RR and I asked Mother, "When is Papá coming home?"

Papá wrote Mother a letter every week, and with it he always wrote a note to me and one to RR, usually telling me to be the man-of-the-house, "Take care of the ladies, and, and give your mother and Rachael a kiss for me." He would tell Rachel to help Mother cook and clean, and, "Give your mother and Theo a big hug for me." As soon as Mother finished reading those letters the hugging and kissing game started, always with laughter and chasing; over sixty years later, the memory of that joyful ritual is still sweet.

At last, Papá came home after a long absence. One morning, after he had been home for a month, he announced a family meeting for that evening. Rachel and I were sad that entire day because "family meeting" usually meant Papá would be leaving soon on another long trip, but this meeting was different.

After we were seated around the kitchen table, Papá said in a subdued, deceptive tone and manner:

"Please, pay attention; I have an announcement. Next week I am going on a long trip, through Denver, into Montana and Flathead Lake for the cherry harvest; after that to Rexburg, Idaho to dig potatoes; followed by Utah, for that state's watermelon, fruit, wheat, and hay harvests, and last, to San Bernardino, California to pick oranges."

He paused and looked at three sad faces, all of us had concluded it would be a long trip, and Papá would be gone for many months. Then he added, "Does anyone want to come with me?"

"¡Hago! ¡Hago! ¡Hago! (I do! I do! I do!")" followed by cheers and hugs.

"OK! We will leave next Wednesday, and we will be gone for four months, maybe longer if I can find enough work in California." More cheers.

Immediately we started planning, making lists of things we needed to take: clothes, food, extra oil for the truck, and an extra tire .... I had to write the lists, and Mother made me spell each word correctly. Also, Papá insisted that we take the metal box with our family papers in it: Mother's and Papá's wedding certificate, our birth certificates, and some family photos. That box would be stored in the back of the truck near where RR and I would sleep.

Mother went to the school and met with my teacher to find out what my class would be studying while I was gone. She borrowed copies of all of the books my class used because for the next few months Mother would be my teacher.

In those years, crossing the border in our truck had been easy; it hadn't required showing any documents. Mother, the obvious Gringo, always drove it across into Brownsville, and there she turned it over to Papá . Then she walked back across the border unchallenged and caught a bus for the one hour trip back to Valle Hermosa. At that time a Mexican returning to Mexico did so unchallenged, and an American—if familiar to the border officers as Mother was—received a ¡ *Bienvenido a México!* (Welcome to Mexico!) For our family trip, however, it was a good thing we brought the family documents with us.

When a new immigration officer on the American side of the border ask me in Spanish where my home was, I answered him in Spanish, *"Yo vivo en valle Hermosa, señor."* ("I live in Valle Hermosa, sir.") Then he asked Rachel how old she was, and she answered, again in perfect Spanish, "Tengo cinco años, señor." ("I am five-years old, Sir.") The officer instantly had a concerned look on his face; he thought Mother and Papá had possibly bought a couple of children in Mexico to sell in the United States, not an unusual happening in the 1930's. The officer inspected our birth certificates then asked about Papá; mother, waved their wedding license, and simply said, "He is my husband." Then the officer waived us into the United States.

Papá would not be looking for work in Denver; the only reason for stopping there was so Grandmother Rogers could see Rachel and me, but that didn't happen. When we drove up to the Rogers mansion and mother rang the doorbell, an elderly woman came to the door and invited us in. Immediately, she said, "I am afraid I have some terrible news for you." She went on to tell us that Grandma and Grandpa Rogers had been killed in an airplane accident while vacationing in Africa, Mother started sobbing "Oh, no! Oh, no!"

RR and I cried and hugged Mother even though we had never seen our grandfather, but mother was so sad we had to share the grief with her. As our family sat on a large leather couch, the four of us together, the lady—who turned out to be Grandpa's sister who lived in England, an aunt Mother had never met—without being asked, told mother, "I am very sorry, but your father didn't mention you in his will."

Mother simply said, "I know; I expected that."

The bodies of Mother's parents were brought back to Denver and buried in a nearby cemetery. We visited their graves.

Both graves had large, ornate headstones. We all stood in silence facing the graves, RR and I holding Mother's hands—Papá stood behind us—with tears running down our faces, heads bowed, Mother said a prayer. Then she let go of our hands, slowly walked to each grave, got down on her knees and kissed her parents good-bye.

With sadness in our hearts, we drove out of Denver and headed for Montana. We didn't sing at all as we had much of the way from Brownsville to Denver. Still, it was late May, and excellent spring weather made traveling easy.

Once we arrived at Flathead Lake, near Kalispell, Montana, our spirits soared. The migrant workers' camp, only 100 yards from the shore of Flathead Lake—one of the largest and most scenic lakes west of the Mississippi—became a magic spot for the Ruiz-Rogers family as well as for the other migrant workers. Each family had its own clean cabin with a wood floor, running water, beds, a wood burning stove, and a small fireplace. Those men without families were housed three to a cabin.

Flathead Lake looked like an artist's concoction, a perfect fusion of blue paint and water, producing an intoxicating aquatic azure, soothing the human eye and pacifying the soul. Populated with impeccably colored rainbow trout, the lake provided fish daily for Mother's frying pan. We caught them with a tree limb, a piece of string, and a hook holding a struggling grasshopper. Some adept men caught the trout with their hands; Papá caught a couple that way.

The log bungalow, undoubtedly cold in the winter, provided warm, comfortable living for us that spring. It nestled under a stand of giant cedars whose *singing* boughs emanated intoxicating melodies when gentle winds blew. Sleep came easy every night. In the early mornings, we took the chill out of the cabin by burning a never ending supply of dry pine cones in our fireplace.

At night most of the workers and their families sat around a fire, some strumming guitars and singing Mexican folk songs. RR usually sat on Papá's lap and I sat between Mother and Papá. Frequently Mother affectionately squeezed me and kissed my forehead, and a least once each night she told me, "Theo, I love you." For the rest of my life, I would never feel so warm, so secure, so loved.

The cherry orchards were only minutes away from our cabin, so the workers walked to-and-from the fruit trees. We children often accompanied our parents in order to supplement our breakfasts of hot gruel, toast, and fresh milk with a few hands-full of sweet cherries. The orchard owner didn't mind, even when a few of us stuffed our overall pockets full. When we returned to the cabins, some of us drew the wrath of our mothers because of cherry stains on our clothes.

One morning, when I too had stains on my clothes, but Alfonso had more, his mother spanked him until he cried. My mother witnessed this and saw the terror in my eyes. I thought I might get the same punishment, although I couldn't remember Mother or Papá ever spanking me or RR. Mother simply said, "Theo, take your overalls off, and I will wash them; next time take a bag."

Three weeks of storybook-like living at Flathead Lake went by quickly, too quickly for the women and children who would not experience such enjoyable conditions for the rest of the summer nor the fall. Our next stop would be the fields belonging to The East Idaho Potato Company near Rexburg, Idaho.

In Rexburg, poor living conditions and the arduous labor of constantly stooping to dig the tubers from the rich soil, soon became tedious work for the men and much less gratifying for us children; eating bland potatoes turned out to be no substitute for feasting on an unlimited supply of sweet cherries.

After almost two months in Idaho, we drove south to Utah where father worked in wheat fields and fruit orchards. By mid-September the watermelons in southern Utah were ready for picking. We loved those three weeks of eating all the watermelon our bodies could hold, so much so that I often got up three or four times each night to urinate. Papá's last job in Utah was cutting grain.

Finally, when late October came, we loaded up for the destination we had all been looking forward to: *California, here we come!* First, however, we had to navigate the deserts of Western Nevada and Eastern California.

Papá timed our trip so we would travel through the hottest part of the Mojave Desert at night. When we left Las Vegas at about 9:00 p.m., the weather had started to cool. Rachel and I were riding in the back of the truck rolled up in blankets, but when we drove up into the mountains where the temperature turned much cooler, she told me, "Theo, I'm cold."

I should have pulled her close to me, but instead I made a remorseful decision, one I loath to this day: I pounded on the top of the truck cab until Papá pulled off the road and stopped. Mother bundled RR up, and put her in the cab.

With no visible traffic on the road, and no lights from nonexistent nearby towns, under a magnificent cloudless sky—millions of stars seemed only an arm's length away—Papá stopped again. RR still wore a warm blanket as we stood by the truck listening to Mother delivered an astronomy quiz.

"Who can find Orion?" I knew that RR could find that constellation, so I remained quiet until she said excitedly:

"I see it! I see it!" as she pointed her small hand into the intoxicatingly beautiful star flooded sky.

"See the hunter?" Mother asked, and RR found that constellation too.

Then Mother asked me, "How can we count the stars?"

"We can't. We are only seeing most of the stars as they were millions of years ago. It all has to do with the speed of light, and the light from the stars we see now has been traveling a long time."

"Good job, my loveable students. Let's back get in the truck; RR is getting cold." With that, Mother helped me make a sleeping bag out of our blankets, rolled me up in them, put a pillow under my head, and said, "Sleep well, Theo; never forget your mother loves you very much." Those were the last words she spoke me. Then she kissed my nose and got back in the cab of our truck.

I wouldn't know until later, but we were starting up the west side of Cajon Pass. In 1939, when we made our fateful trip, Cajon Pass was a mountainous, narrow, two lane road with thin shoulders—where there were any shoulder at all—and many sharp curves.

Quickly, I fell asleep but soon a blaring horn abruptly woke me. The horn sounded more like a train's horn than that of road vehicle. It terrorized me. Wrapped in my sleeping blankets, I struggled to my knees just in time to see a big gasoline truck, lights flashing, one of its front tires on fire, and obviously without brakes, careening down the opposite side of the road, barreling in our direction. Before I could think about the danger we faced, the truck capsized on the curve, jackknifed, and struck the front of our pickup. At that instant I heard an ear splitting crash; still in my blanket cocoon, I catapulted into the air and flew for more than fifty feet before I struck the cactus strewn desert and rolled. The blankets protected me; I wasn't seriously hurt. As soon as I stopped rolling I heard RR screaming, "Theo, HELP ME! Theo, HELP ME!

I got out of the blankets as quickly as I could and ran up the embankment toward our truck. I couldn't see it, but the smell of gasoline was thick, and when I got to the top of the road bank, I could see the terrible collision from the light of the burning tire. The cab of the gas-truck partially lay on top of our truck, and where the sharp curve caused a depression in the road, gas had accumulated. As I moved toward the truck and Rachel's screams, a tremendous explosion shot fire into the sky, and the blast knocked me back down the bank. Then a second explosion sent the gas filled tank into the air spewing flames. It came down on the wreck of our truck where my mother, father, and my little sister were. The burning pool of gas on the curve instantly engulfed both vehicles, and five human beings, my family, the truck driver and his wife, were trapped in an inferno no one could possibly survive. I felt so helpless, so alone, so lost, so desperate. I knew that my family died; I could smell their bodies burning, and RR's screams had stopped.

After backing away from the fire to a knoll where I could still feel the intense, death rendering heat, I screamed over and over, "Mother, Papá, RR! Mother, Papá, RR..." I wasn't aware that much of my exposed skin was receiving second degree burns.

12

Life with the Glovers

The next morning I woke up in a hospital bed in Barstow, California, bandages covering my hands, ears, nose and chin. A nurse stood over me, and a large man in a policeman's uniform was standing beside her.

The policeman said, "Hello, young man. Can you talk? What is your name?"

"Yes, my name is Theo. Where is my family, Mama, Papá, and RR?"

My question momentarily ignored, "Were you in the pickup truck?"

"Yes, in the back. My mother, father, and little sister were in the front. Where are they?"

"I know this is terrible for you, but they all died in the fire. You have some first and second degree burns, but you will be OK."

I couldn't speak. I couldn't cry. I closed my eyes hoping I would die too—how could I live without Mama, Papá, and RR? How could I live without my family?

The officer turned out to be Officer Jerome Glover, a California Highway Patrolman. When they let me out of the hospital two days later, Officer Glover took me to his house in San Bernardino where he lived with his wife Marcella.

The day after I arrived at the Glover home, I asked Officer Glover if there would be a funeral for my family. He told me, "Theo, I am very sorry but the bodies of your parents and sister were totally incinerated in the fire. We only found what was thrown from the back of the truck with you."

"What does incinerated mean?"

"They were totally consumed by the fire; there is nothing left of them,"

"We did find a metal box with several birth certificates and your parents wedding certificate, also some family pictures. We easily recognized you in one picture and assumed that those with you were your family members. We didn't know how many and who they were until we talked with you in the hospital.

"Even though we have nothing we can bury, we will have a memorial service at the Holy Angeles Catholic Church when you are ready."

Four days later we had that service, and many people from the Holy Angeles Church came. Officer and Mrs. Glover sat on the front row with me. I sat between them and each tried to hold my hand, but I rejected them; I didn't want to hold anyone's hand—I wanted to be dead.

After what seemed like a lifetime, Officer Glover took me to a court house where we talked with a judge. He asked me about my Mexican grandparents. I told him I wanted to see them, and I could live with them, but they didn't know about the accident. As it turned out, however, Officer Glover found their names and address in the box, and sent them a letter telling of the tragedy and letting them know I was OK. It was translated into espanól and mailed the week before we met with the judge.

The judge asked me if I wanted to live with the Glovers, or did I want to live in an orphanage until I could be taken back to Mexico. I didn't know what to say; however, since Officer Glover and his wife were being so kind to me, I told the Judge, "I want to stay with the Glovers."

Then after two more weeks, Officer Glover received a letter from Father Nunez, the priest in Valle Hermosa, one he wrote for my grandparents. In it they expressed their grief for the deaths and said, "Certainly," I should live with them. A week after that, Officer Glover, Mrs. Glover, and I made that 1,500 mile trip, mostly in silence, by car.

Officer Glover told me he and Mrs. Glover were going to stay in Mexico for a week sightseeing; he promised they would see me before they made the long trip back to San Bernardino.

Grandma and Grandpa Ruiz were kind to me, but they certainly weren't happy to see me under the circumstances. They had trouble understanding the accident, how I lived when the rest of my family died, and why their son's body could not be brought back to Valle Hermosa and buried in the village graveyard. As a seven year-old boy, that was hard for me to explain. The strain was terrible; unlike in the past, now when I talked with my grandparents our eyes never met, nor did they touch me; I wanted so much to have a hug from them. Another big disappointment, Auntie Alondra had moved away from Valle Hermosa to live with her ill mother near Mexico City. I wanted to see and talk with her so badly because she understood me better than anyone, other than my parents. (When I returned to Valle Hermosa for three short visits years later, I did see and visit with Auntie; she didn't have trouble looking into my eyes or giving me loving hugs.)

The day after I arrived back in Valle Hermosa, I went to school, the same school I attended previously. Miss Gomez, my teacher, as well as the students, treated me strangely. They were not trying to be cruel; they just didn't know what to say to me. On the second day, when we were having recess in the afternoon, Jorge Gonzales, one of my friends told me, "My mother says you bring people bad luck. Rico died when he was with you and so did your family."

Inexplicably, that was the trigger that released my pent up grief. For the first time since the accident, I started crying, and I attack

Jorge, beating him until his nose bled. Terrified and with blood blotching the front of his shirt, he ran home screaming. Many students saw what happened, but they had no idea what set me off. Actually, Jorge didn't mean any harm; he just repeated what many people in the village undoubtedly were saying. My grandparents were very disappointed in what I had done, and Mr. Rodriquez, the school Master said, "I don't know what caused that fight, you don't seem to want to tell me, but you can't be beating up students in this school. You must stay home tomorrow."

No one except Mr. Rodriquez even asked why I hit Jorge. Had they, at the age of seven, I wouldn't have known how to explain my misplaced aggression. I wasn't beating Jorge; I was lashing out at the world, the cruel world that had destroyed my family.

That evening, I walked down to the river where Rico died; I went there to jump in and kill myself. Now, however, in late September, only a trickle of water flowed down the Matamoros. By stepping on rocks, you could walk from one side to the other without getting your feet wet.

Again, my grandparents were not unkind to me; however, we just didn't know what to say to each other. The next five days were miserable for me; I didn't belong in Valle Hermosa anymore, and I didn't think I ever would.

Finally, Officer and Mrs. Glover came to the Ruiz house. When I saw them exiting their car, I ran to them in tears and hugged both of them. While crying, I told them, "I don't want to stay here; I want to go back to California and live with you."

Officer Glover asked me what was wrong, and I blubbered through the tears, "People hate me here. They say I brought bad luck to my family."

Officer Rogers talked with my grandmother while I interpreted. Grandmother took him to see Father Morales, who spoke English, and they talked for over an hour. Then they called me to the church and the priest asked me if I wanted to live with my grandparents, and I told him, "Yes, but I can't live in Valle Hermosa anymore; I want to live with Officer Glover and his wife in California."

Officer Glover and Father Morales left and returned a couple of hours later with a bilingual, Mexican, lawyer. My grandparents signed some papers before they told me, "Theo, you can live with us anytime you want. The Glovers have agreed to take care of you until you want to come back."

Then everyone in the room—my grandparents and the Glovers—gave me a hug, and I felt better. Less than an hour later, we were on our way back to San Bernardino.

As fate would dictate, a year later the Glovers adopted me and became my surrogate parents, remaining so until they died years later.

13

Elementary School in San Bernardino

After returning to California, Mrs. Glover enrolled me in Lincoln Elementary School in San Bernardino. There, the adobe style building suggested a predominantly Mexican population, but my new classmates only included three Hispanics, just one really fluent in Spanish. Nevertheless, I immediately felt welcome, and my new teacher, Miss Turner, a beautiful lady with long blond hair just like Mother's, gave me an embrace. It was a full hug, her arms holding me tight but very comfortable. While returning her embrace with all my strength—mimicking how I responded to my Mother's cuddles—I had a positive feeling for the first time since the accident. Later, when I looked at Miss Turner, occasionally I started crying, and she would ask, "What is wrong Theo? Can I do something to make you happy?" After three of those incidents, she talked to Mrs. Glover who told her about the death of my family.

When asked about my crying in class, I told Mrs. Glover, "Sometimes when I see Miss Turner's hair, I see my mother, and I am reminded how she died; it makes me so sad."

"Would you like to have another teacher? I can ask the principal to put you in a different class."

"No! I like Miss Turner. I want to stay in her class."

The second week I was at Lincoln Elementary, a man from the principal's office gave me some tests to see how my academic skills matched up with the other second grade students. The next day, Miss Turner told me, "Here is a letter for your mother and father. It tells them you are a very smart boy. You should be one of the best students in our class."

It was the first time that I ever heard the Glovers referred to as my "mother and father," and I really didn't like it, but I didn't say anything. Within a few months, however, I accepted them as my parents, and I addressed them as "Mother Glover" and "Father Glover."

As it turned out, I was a good student, and the other students liked me. Many people at the school seemed to be amazed that I could read, write, speak, and even sing, fluently in both English and Spanish.

Those skills served me well all the way through high school; when I was in the Marine Corps; when I attended Montana State University, and when I became an English teacher in Asia.

The next school year, I skipped third grade and went to the fourth. I loved school: the examinations, academic contests like the spelling bees, math quizzes, running races on the playground, jump rope contests, and writing essays, all challenged me and made me a better student and a happier boy.

In the spring, during my year in the fourth grade, our physical education teacher entered me in the city-wide track meet for elementary students, grades four through six. I ran the one-half-mile race, the longest race, and won third place and a bronze medal. Mother Glover saw me run, and she came down on the track and gave me a hug and kiss after I crossed the finish line. That night, a Saturday, Mother and Father Glover took me to a fancy restaurant, the best Mexican restaurant in San Bernardino, Fiesta de la Comida Mexicana (Mexican Food Fiesta) for a great dinner.

When I was in the fifth grade, I won a silver medal in the half-mile-run and a bronze in the quarter-mile run. That got me another special dinner as did winning the school's spelling bee. During my sixth grade year I won both of those races, and I was selected as the top student in my class. But that year, one terrible thing happened.

A girl who sat next to me in the classroom, Delores Hand—we often teamed together on class projects, and secretly I really "liked" her—had not missed a day of school since she started kindergarten. Then one day Delores didn't show up, and we all wondered what could be wrong with her, not only that day but for the next five. A week later—I remember that day too well—Mr. Hammond, our sixth grade teacher, told us that Delores died of spinal meningitis. That terrible news devastated our entire class, me, perhaps, more than the other students because I had already been around death too often for a young boy. I felt that same guilt when I learned that Delores's died as I had the day Rico drowned and the night my family perished. I wanted to talk with Mother and Father Glover about how I felt, but I couldn't; it was an inner feeling unpresentable to anyone.

Our entire class went to Delores's funeral, and the experience left us subdued for the rest of the school year. For me, guilt lingered in my conscious mind for months, until it finally descended into the darker sanctuaries of my subliminal. Nevertheless, life went on, generally in a spirit of happiness because I loved school and my step parents, the Glovers, treated me with kindness and affection; they were wonderful, and I grew to love them.

(Still, sixty-six years after my friend Pedro's comment in Valle Hermosa after my family died: "My mother says you bring bad luck to people," I am still haunted by that comment. For my entire life, anytime a person dies I am close to, and there have been too many, I feel guilty, and then all of those ruthless death memories stored in my subconscious are dredged up. That is the main reason I have, and will continue, to live as an ascetic recluse here at MCVRH.)

As a thirteen-year-old freshman in high school, my reputation pegged me an excellent student and a good runner. In junior high school and high school, I never received a grade less than an "A," and I won most of the races I ran, even against older runners.

When I was ten through sixteen, I visited Valle Hermosa and my Ruiz grandparents three times. Although seeing and talking extensively with Auntie Alondra, who had returned to Valle Hermosa after her mother died in Mexico City—mostly about my pre-memory life and the history of Mama and Papá—was wonderful. Still, after a few days, I was anxious to get on the train in Brownsville and return to my Glover parents in San Bernardino.

14

I Want To Be A Marine

New Year's Day, 1947, when I was a fifteen year old high school junior, became an epical day in my life. The Glovers took their Mexican-American, adopted son to Pasadena to see the Rose Bowl Parade. We left home early, 4:30 a.m., and arrived in Pasadena about 6:00, in time to find a good observation spot on Colorado Boulevard, not one at the beginning of the parade route—those prime viewing spots were all taken by people who slept on the side walk the night before—one closer to the end. On that famous boulevard, we joined more than 500,000 other spectators.

Assuming someone who might read this has never attended the Rose Bowl Parade, here is a bit about it:

The first Tournament of Roses Parade, now called the Rose Bowl Parade, held on January 1, 1890, didn't have a football game coupled with it; football didn't begin until 1902. Nevertheless, since 1890, except for two years during World War II, both parades and *games*—of some kind—have continued uninterrupted.

However, between 1890 and 1902 the sporting event that followed the parade, chariot racing, attracted large, roaring crowds. In a cloud of dust—Colorado Boulevard wasn't paved in those early years—horses towing chariots and drivers, dashed one mile down the thoroughfare.

The Rose Bowl Parade is much more than a parade; it is a series of one act performances, each lasting for a couple of minutes before the parade and the acts, move further down Colorado Boulevard, about a quarter of a mile, before they stop and the acts perform again. Marching bands, drill teams, equestrian groups, and floats representing cities, major business entities, and some foreign countries, are also on display. For many spectators, the floats are the main attraction. From design to completion, most floats take an entire year to construct. All visible parts of every float are entirely created from roses.

On the day we watched, the first marchers stepped off promptly at 8:00 a.m., but it took the first band almost thirty minutes to reach our observation spot on the corner of Colorado Boulevard and San Marino Avenue. Thanks to our early arrival, we were able to place our folding chairs on the front row for a perfect view.

Since Illinois was playing UCLA in the big game in 1947, Illinois had several floats and bands in the parade, and the University of Illinois's mascot, supposedly an Indian, an *Illini,*7 danced, pranced, and chanted the length of the parade route. When he came to our spot, within a few feet of me, I could see that the man really wasn't an Indian, but simply a well made-up Caucasian—a Mexican, or even part Mexican like me would have looked more authentic—still, he danced well as his band played the Illinois fight song. However, the group of marchers that inspired me that day, one totally authentic, not ersatz like the *Illini* Indian, represented the United States Marine Corps.

At our location, for the first time since the parade began, an inexplicable hush settled over the throng. Suddenly that silence vanished as the clarion call of harmonizing trumpets seized the

---

7 Illinois got its name from that extinct tribe.

attention of the crowd. An inspiring rendition of the Marine Corps Hymn followed: *"From the halls of Montezuma to the shores of Tripoli...,"* sending shivers down my spine.

A drill team of a hundred or more Marines, all shouldering M1 Garand rifles adorned with stainless steel bayonets reflecting flashes of early morning sunlight, followed the band. Dressed in immaculate uniforms—blue trousers with blood-red stripes running the length of each leg, darker blue tunics with gleaming brass buttons, white hats with sparkling black bills, and glistening black shoes—the Marines marched with impeccable precision.

When the drill team stopped in front of us, the Marines in the first rank tossed their weapons high in the air, over their right shoulders, to be caught by the men in the second rank. Then the first rank—now without weapons—split in the middle and marched smartly to each flank and to the rear of the formation; so it went until all ranks had tossed and caught rifles. I never figured how they all had a rifle when they marched away.

Those Marines in the band and the drill team were unerring: drummers never missed a beat; the trumpeters never missed a note; and the marchers never missed a step. Without contemplation or logical explanation, I knew at that moment I wanted to be a Marine, and that contagion didn't go away with the parade.

Conversely, four years later, the blood and gore of combat immunized me from all romantic notions inspired by patriotic, marshal music and spiffy uniforms.

That afternoon, we went to Santa Monica Beach where we walked in the chilly surf then sprawled on blankets in seventy-five degree Southern California weather, the kind of perfect New Year's Day the Los Angeles County Chamber of Commerce likes to brag about.

After lunching in nearby Brentwood—an enclave of Los Angeles adopted by Hollywood's rich and famous—we drove to Hollywood Boulevard and walked the *Walk of Fame*, that thoroughfare bearing the hand prints of legends of the silver screen. Hollywood Boulevard overflowed with people like us: people watching people, who were watching people watching people.

Finally, we started the trek home, only stopping one more time in Mother Glover's hometown, Arcadia. She wanted to show me the park she played in as a child. Under an ancient, giant oak—so old its massive limbs were supported by steel posts—she looked up into the boughs and told me, "Theo, my first memories as a very young child are of my family having pick-necks under this very tree. Aaah, what great memories those are."

As we sat on a stone bench under the tree talking about our activities of the day, the setting sun sent beams of orange light flashing through the trees. It was another enchanting moment on that magical day, a day of profound joy and consequential inspiration.

As daylight started fading into night, Mother Glover asked me, "Theo, what did you enjoy the most today?" I answered without hesitating, "Seeing the Marines march in the parade; I want to be a Marine."

Father Glover laughed and said, "Theo, my boy, there is a lot more to being a Marine than marching down Colorado Boulevard on New Year's Day. We will have Uncle Ned tell you about the Marine Corps."

I didn't respond then, but over the next eighteen months Father Glover, Uncle Ned, and I often talked about the Marine Corps, and I read every book I could find that mentioned the Marines: from their exploits in Cuba during the Spanish American War; their incursions in Tripoli and China; the battles in the Pacific during World War II, every heroic account of Marines in battle inspired me and nurtured the seed planted by the Marine Corps Band and Drill Team during that Rose Bowl Parade.

Uncle Ned had endured the battles of Guadalcanal, Saipan, and Okinawa when he was with the 1st Marine Division during World War II. Wounded twice, once on Guadalcanal when he took mortar shrapnel in his legs, and again on Okinawa when a Japanese sniper shot away two fingers on his left hand, he came home with a phrase on his lips that he repeated many times: "Theo, You are looking at one lucky bastard; I survived the war." For his heroism on Okinawa, Uncle Ned was awarded both the Silver Star and a Bronze Star.

I know that Father Glover asked Uncle Ned to try to dissuade my Marine Corps ambitions, and on several occasions he attempted to do just that; one particular time I remember well.

"Theo, let me tell you my boy, Marine Corps boot camp is not a pleasant experience for anyone; it is twelve weeks of hell,"

He felt that for me to enlist at the age of eighteen was too early. He didn't know that I planned to take the oath shortly after I graduated from high school, on July 5th, two months after graduation, the day after I would be seventeen and old enough to take the Marine Corps oath of office—if, I had my parents' written permission.

Since it looked like I might be offered track athletic scholarships by several universities, Uncle Ned advised, "Get your college degree; then, if you are still interested in being a Marine, go in as an officer. You will get much more pay, wear and even nicer blue uniform, and live a much more comfortable life."

When I won the mile and half-a-mile races at the California State Track & Field Championships, coaches from several schools visited our home. Along with Mother and Father Glover, I listened to them and ate dinners with some of them, but the beat of the drums, the sound of the bugles, and the strides of Marines in immaculate blue uniforms at the Rose Bowl Parade had *infected* me. Consequently, the day after graduating from high school in 1949, I told Mother and Father Glover, and Uncle Ned, "I am determined to be a Marine as soon as possible. I need your signature to do it soon, on July 5th, after I am seventeen. You have been wonderful to me, and I don't want to disappoint you, but I have to do this, and I want your blessing, and I need your permission."

Uncle Ned joined in, surprisingly to support my plan, by stating, "Theo, you know how we feel about you being a Marine at seventeen, but since there probably won't be any wars for Marines to fight in for many, many years, World War II ended only four years ago, now is undoubtedly a safe time to enlist. When you come out, you will be twenty-one, much more mature, and probably better suited for university life."

Uncle Ned's backing did the trick: both Mother and Father Glover agreed to sign the permission papers. On July 5th, 1949 Mother and Father Glover drove me to the Marine Corps Recruiting Station in Ontario where they signed the necessary documents. A captain adorned in that striking blue uniform—one I assumed I would soon be wearing—administered the oath of enlistment to me and seven other recruits:

"Raise your right hands and repeat after me, I, your name...."

"Theodore Ruiz Rogers, do solemnly swear...."

Then he added, "Welcome to the Marine Corps, but you can't call yourself Marines until you have completed twelve rigorous weeks of Boot Camp. Survive that challenge and you can wear Marine Corps blues with the anchor and globe[8]."

Mother Glover cried and Father Glover had tears in his eyes as they gave me one last hug before I boarded the Trailways bus that took me to San Diego, the location of the Marine Corps Recruit Depot (MCRD).

As the bus rolled down Pacific Coast Highway, Uncle Ned's advice played itself over and over in my brain:

"First Theo, be in great condition when you report to San Diego. Be able to do 100 sit-ups in two minutes; fifty push-ups, thirty pull-ups, and run two miles in less than thirteen minutes. Keep all your equipment clean, especially the M1 rifle they will issue you, and learn how to shoot it well. Be prepared for a lot of harassment, both physical and mental, and never lose your temper. Your drill instructors will be playing a cruel game with you, one that will supposedly make you a stronger man; don't let that game get you down. Most of all, remember you have a family that loves you, and we will all be very proud when we see you graduate in that blue uniform."

I took Uncle Ned's advice to heart; I could meet all the physical goals he set for me well ahead of my departure for San Diego, but I had doubts, and they had to do with my mental toughness.

---

8 The symbol all Marines wear on their uniforms.

15

Boot Camp

ervous and wondering if we would be met by a representative of MCRD, we arrived in San Diego at 7:30 on a Saturday evening. As soon as we stepped off the bus, a tall, unsmiling, corporal, shouted, "All Marine recruits, OVER HERE!"

We quickly knotted up around the corporal, expecting the traditional, cordial greeting: "We are glad to see you. How was your trip?" But instead he counted eight heads, and asked, "I count eight. Is that everyone?"

Three or four of us said, "Yes."

"What the hell do you mean, 'Yes'? Do you mean, Yes Corporal?"

"Yes, Corporal."

"Follow me, and stay together," ordered the corporal in an agitated tone.

He led us behind the bus station where a canvas covered truck and driver waited. Contemptuously, he said, "This is your last chance to run away or jump into the ocean. Climb on board you sorry bastards."

Fifteen minutes later we stopped at the entrance to MCRD. A sergeant with an *MP*[9] band on his arm shined a flashlight in our eyes and counted us, followed by, "You'll be sorry. When this gate closes behind you, you will be in Hell."

The truck moved forward, and as I heard the clang of that iron gate, my first inclination was one I would repeat many times over the next twelve weeks, *"What have I got myself into? What the hell am I doing here?"*

Five minutes later we arrived at the MCRD Receiving Barracks. There, another sergeant, this one with the ultimate loud, rude voice, appeared at the back of the truck, dropped the tail gate and gave us our official *welcome* to Boot Camp.

"Get you mangy asses off that truck and fall-in at ATTENTION. You dumb bastards; whatever made you think you can be Marines? I said fall in at ATTENTION! Geesus fucking Christ; you don't even know what ATTENTION is. Get your heels together! Spread your feet at a forty-five degree angle! God damn it, look straight ahead! Quit looken around! Eyes straight ahead! Why are you looken at me, Shithead? Are you in love with me, you dumbass fruitcake!"

Boot Camp would not be impossible to survive, but it did turn out to test of one's sanity, especially that first week when nothing made sense: unbearable short nights with three or four hours of sleep, less if you had guard duty; days with activities that seemingly had no purpose other than to torment us.

Our first barracks inspection, on the very night we arrived, held at 21:00 (9 p.m.) went like this: We were ordered to clean the latrines (toilets); scrub the showers; wash the barrack's ports (windows), and make our sacks (beds) tight enough so you could bounce a coin on them. Once we had completed those tasks, two drill instructors (DIs) inspected while we stood at attention under such stress that two men passed out. Then, we were psychologically crushed when one DI screamed, "This must be the fucken Pig Platoon. I have never seen a filthier barracks. You fail! Now, god-dam it, we will give

---

9 Military police

you something to clean up, and you will have one fuckin hour to get the job done. If you fail again, I am going to run your sorry asses until you puke, pass out, or shit in your pants."

To make the next cleaning cycle impossible to finish in one hour, ten recruits were ordered to fill buckets with dirt and water. Then, the DIs threw the mud on the walls, in the sinks and toilets, and on the floor. Then to top it off, they turned all of our bunks over and stripped off the blankets and sheets.

One hour later we weren't nearly finished cleaning up the mess; we ended up working on the impossible project until 0100 (1 a.m.). After waiting another hour for the DIs to inspect, but they never did, most of us laid on the floor to get some rest—we were afraid to use our ready-for-inspection bunks—and nervously tried to sleep for three hours before starting our next day in Hell.

Even though I questioned it silently, the harassment didn't bother me much, but it tortured many of my comrades. Every night when the lights were turned out that first week, I heard at least two men sobbing. Sad too, but not so much that I cried, in seconds, I slept with Uncle Ned's words redundantly echoing in my mind, "Remember, Theo, the DIs are just playing a game with you. They aren't really serious."

Technical Sergeant Moore, a highly decorated, recruiting-poster-like man became our Head Drill Instructor (HDI). His three assistants, one sergeant and two corporals, were our bane, doing most of the harassment, shouting, and cursing. They were truly the *bad guys*. Sergeant Moore, on the other hand, the *good guy*, always talked to us firmly but logically, sometimes he even listened to us, and he never used profanity. I will never forget the first time he spoke directly to me.

In our first formation with Sergeant Moore, as he moved down each squad, we had been instructed to tell him our rank, first and last name, and serial number:

"Private Donald Smith, 12250222, Sergeant."

"Private Jackson McDonald, 13137655, Sergeant."

"Private *Theodore Ruiz Rogers,* 1180603, Sergeant.

Sergeant Moore quickly asked, "Private Ruiz-Rogers, weren't you ordered to only give me your first and last name?"

"Yes, Sergeant."

"Well, Private, why did you use your middle name?"

"Sergeant, I consider *Ruiz* and *Rogers* my last name."

"Where did the *Ruiz* come from, Private?"

" Sergeant, that was my father's family name. He was Mexican, and I am proud of my Mexican heritage. I am requesting you allow me to use *Theodore Ruiz-Rogers* as my Marine Corps name?"

Sergeant Moore looked at me for a few seconds before saying, "Request approved, Private, but I expect you to be one of the best recruits in this platoon so you can bring honor to your heritage. Do you understand, Private *Ruiz-Rogers?*"

"Yes, Sergeant. I will do my best."

From that moment on, I never had a problem with my full name, or with Sergeant Moore, but on all rosters and official paperwork, the Marine Corps did not join *Ruiz* and *Rogers* together with a hyphen.

Unlike the bad guys, Sergeant Moore often did physical exercises with us, including push-ups.

One day when we were enjoying a seldom, prolonged wait—rarely did we have an inactive minute—to be issued our field equipment: canteens, entrenching tools, ammunition pouches, and first aid kits, Sergeant Moore announced, "Listen up! We are going to have a push-up contest. Anyone who beats me will go to the head of the chow line for one week. Keep your eyes on me and follow my cadence. Drop to the leaning-rest position, and wait for my command."

We all dropped with our heads up, eyes fixed on Sergeant Moore who was in a leaning-rest [10]position on an elevated loading platform in front of the warehouse. He started commanding and exercising, "Down, up, one. You count with me...down, up, two... down, up... three...twenty...thirty...."

We were all completing the push-ups in unison with Sergeant More while counting, but some started straining, and a few dropped out. By "forty" only ten of us were still exercising; at "fifty," three

---

10 Body prone, hands on a surface with arms straight

remained, including Sergeant Moore; at "sixty," he and I were locked in head-to-head competition. At "seventy," he slowed down and so did I. When we finally counted "seventy-eight," Sergeant Moore stood up and said, "Private Ruiz-Rogers, do one more! Well done, Private! I expect you to be able to do 100 before graduation day. You lead the chow line for the next week."

A few days later, when I had the fastest time in the two mile run and did the most pull-ups, Sergeant Moore made me the Right Guide. That meant I no longer marched carrying my M1 Rifle; instead, I carried the platoon flag attached to a seven foot staff. In effect, I led the platoon in all formations, and I often passed on information from the DIs to the platoon. No one seemed to care, or maybe they didn't know, that I was only seventeen. I guess I didn't look my age since I had already started shaving my dark beard, one that popped out before I turned sixteen.

The physical demands of Boot Camp were daunting for our platoon. Not only were the required numbers for push-ups, pull-ups, set-ups, and running beyond the capability of most—at least those first weeks—some still struggled to meet the standards by the end of Boot Camp.

Finally, those days totally devoted to shocking us from civilian life into military life ended, and we started doing more pragmatic activities, including classes on weapons. We learned how to *field strip11* our M1 rifles and reassemble them blindfolded; how to arm and throw hand-grenades; and, how to fire machine guns. However, the live firing of weapons didn't come until we went to the Firing Range at Camp Mathews for two weeks.

We also learned how to administer combat first aide. That class was a real attention-getter: we were taught how to cover the chest of a wounded comrade with cloth and poor water on it—in the absence of water, urine would suffice. Navigation, infantry tactics, Marine Corps history and how to maintain and wear the uniform were also part of the curriculum.

---

11 Take apart

Physical training, which I loved, became more of a scheduled activity rather than a harassing or punitive one, although on occasions individuals, or the entire platoon, were ordered by the DIs to, "Drop and give me thirty."

Nevertheless, eventually, continuity and predictability dominated the program: marching for hours on the MCRD parade ground, sometimes with our rifles carried over our heads; rifle inspections; barracks inspections; footlocker inspections; and uniform inspections, all never declined in frequency.

On Saturday mornings, we always had a formal parade and inspection with several other platoons. Those were the only occasions when we had contact with officers.

An officer—usually a first lieutenant or captain—stood in front of each recruit and inspected his rifle, haircut, uniform, and some officers even got up close and looked into our ears. Usually, the inspecting officer asked one or two questions. Woe be it for any recruit who received a gig—equivalent to a demerit—or couldn't answer a question. That *criminal* marched for two hours for each gig, carrying his rifle at *Right Shoulder Arms,*12back and forth on the MCRD one-half-mile in length parade ground, usually during the hottest part of the day.

As soon as the parade and inspection finished, Sergeant Moore talked to us for several minutes before he disappeared for the rest of the weekend. Then we were at the *mercy* of the Assistant DIs, and they had no *mercy*.

During part of every weekend, the DIs entertained themselves by inflicting physical and mental aggravation on us, sometimes punching our ribs or kicking our legs. Corporal Jennings often ordered us to kneel on our metal buckets—they have a one-eighth inch ridge on the bottom—while holding our rifles over our heads for up to thirty minutes. Our legs would fall asleep; so when he ordered us to ATTENTION, we couldn't stand. He would laugh and kick us as we struggled to gain our balance. "What's wrong with you pussies? Stand at ATTENTION, god damn it!"

---

12   Right Shoulder Arms, Left Shoulder Arms, and Port Arms are the positions a marching Marine must carry his rifle

Corporal Douglas preferred standing us at attention in the hot sun for an hour or more, followed by having us duck-walk for 100 or more yards while he screamed and cursed. I assumed those activities were to harden and temper us—raw, immature privates—into Marines worthy of wearing the coveted blue uniform.

On Sundays we always had the option of going to church, and, Christian or not, we all went to get away from the harassment. Since no DIs were present in the chapel, some of us even took a nap during the service.

A respite from the training routine finally came when we went to Camp Mathews for two weeks for live weapons firing. There we threw live hand grenades, fired machine guns and 45 caliber pistols, but most importantly, we became *one* with our M1 rifles; we were required to qualify with them.

At the end of World War II, Uncle Ned departed the Marine Corps illegally in possession of the M1 he used in combat on several Pacific islands. Many other Marines, and soldiers, did the same thing. They simply field stripped their rifles and hid the many parts in the duffle bags they were allowed to take home.

When Uncle Ned knew I would, indeed, be going into the Corps, he taught me how to fire his M1 when he and Father Glover took me to the San Bernardino Shooting Range, usually once each week. That experience paid off during the firing-range part of Boot Camp. I really had a leg up on the other recruits in my platoon; none of them had ever fired an M1. Also, I practiced shooting Father Glover's service pistol. Near the end of our two weeks at Camp Mathews, when we fired for record, I was the highest scoring marksman in our platoon with both the M1 rifle and the 45 caliber pistol.

Late in the afternoon on the day we finished firing for record[13], one of the DIs ordered me to report to Sergeant Moore. I knocked on the wood door facing of his pyramid-tent.[14]

"ENTER!"

---

13 *Firing for Record* is important for a Marine. His scores become a permanent part of his personnel file and are used for promotion and assignment considerations..

14 The roof of this tent has a pyramid shape. It is used to quarter officers and senior NCOs when a unit is in the field.

After taking two steps inside the tent and snapping to attention, "Private Ruiz-Rogers reporting as ordered, Sergeant."

"Private Ruiz-Rogers, AT EASE! Where did you learn to shoot an M1 and a 45 pistol?"

"My Uncle Ned taught me how to fire the M1, Sergeant."

"Is your Uncle a veteran?"

"Yes, Sergeant. He was a Marine in the Pacific and participated in several island invasions. He brought his M1 home with him when the war ended."

"Who taught you how to fire a 45?"

"My father did, Sergeant. He is a California Highway Patrolman, and he taught me how to fire his service revolver."

"They taught you well, Private Ruiz-Rogers. DISMISSED!"

When we returned to MCRD—two more weeks of Boot Camp remaining—we continued to train diligently, especially for the physical fitness test. One of our graduation requirements: run six miles in less than one hour and fifteen minutes carrying a full combat pack—approximately thirty-five pounds—minus our water canteens but wearing our steel helmets; that run proved to be a challenge for all of us. Those who didn't make the time goal tried again two days later; failure again resulted in the same run in two additional days. Non-qualifiers repeated that run until the day before graduation. When that day came, we still had two men failing; they recycled to another platoon and repeated the torture until they finally passed.

I was confident when the run started, but I didn't think about trying to complete the course before all of my platoon mates, especially when my shoulders started hurting. My backpack harness rubbed blisters on my shoulders; also, after the first two miles, my boots had a lot of irritating sand in them. Still, I did finish the run first, in 39.42 minutes.

The day before graduation Sergeant Moore called me to the front of our morning formation, handed me the chevrons of a PFC[15] and announced I would be the Honor Graduate of our platoon and

---

15 Private first class

have the privilege of carrying our platoon's flag in the graduation ceremony.

At 10:00 a.m. on graduation day, adorned in our newly issued and sanctified dress blue uniforms—with Mother and Father Glover, Uncle Ned, along with other parents and sweethearts looking on— we marched to the strands of John Phillips Sousa's *Stars and Stripes Forever* and *Semper Fideles,* the official march of the Marine Corps. When the ceremony ended with the playing of the Marine Corps Hymn—the music that so affected me during the Rose Bowl Parade almost three years before—my heart swelled, my spine shivered, and my eyes blurred. Shortly after Colonel Netherland handed me my Honor Graduate certificate and I saluted, Sergeant Moore commanded, "DISMISSED!"

Quickly I found Mother and Father Glover, both had tears in their eyes, but Uncle Ned simply smiled; he understood the boot camp process with less emotion but no less pride. We exchanged hugs and handshakes. Mother Glover said, "I am proud of you. Theo, you look so big and strong. The Marine Corps must be giving you a lot of good food."

Father Glover said, "Theo, you did it. You've reached your goal. Now you are a Marine, and I am so proud of you."

Uncle Ned patted my back and simply exclaimed, "Good job, Jarhead[16]."

---

16 A synonym for Marine

Training for Hawaii—Going to Korea

After ten refreshing days of leave at home in San Bernardino, I spent much of it in bed catching up on lost sleep, I reported to Camp Pendleton, only a one hour drive from San Bernardino. Our training at Camp Pendleton, labeled: *Combat Infantry Training*, a misnomer in our way of thinking because combat really didn't seem possible, turned out to be more fun than tedium. Those of us still in our teens, the majority, took the course as playing war, not really preparing for the real thing. After all, World War II ended less than four years before, and very few people in the United States, or even in the world, thought another war possible for many, many years, maybe never in my lifetime. Consequently, from October 1949 until May of 1950, we played war games in the boondocks of Camp Pendleton and the nearby beaches, firing weapons, assaulting make believe enemies on hills, practicing disembarking from transport ships onto amphibious landing craft before storming picturesque California beaches while screaming "Gung-

Ho,[17]" all conducted with a blasé attitude in the moderate climate of Southern California; however, there was no cold weather training, a shortcoming that would lead to the demise of many of my comrades in less than a year.

At least once each month I went home to San Bernardino. Sadly, in January, 1950 Father Glover suffered a heart attack, one first diagnosed as minor and non-life-threatening, but his recovery, slow and complicated, left him a shell of the man who adopted me when I was seven-years-old. After he became ill, I went home at every opportunity. In April he died. Mother Glover and I were devastated and we grieved together, hugging and consoling each other, tears running down both of our faces. When we finally stopped crying, she would hold me at arm's length, look into my eyes and say, "Theo, you're all I have left. I love you so much; please be careful."

"I will Mother; I will."

Father Glover was only sixty, always took care of himself, didn't smoke or drink alcohol, and exercised regularly; he was far too young and outwardly fit to die. At his funeral, those somewhat dormant fears of me being bad luck for people I loved returned. The night after we buried him, I lay in bed thinking, *Why do those I love die unexpectedly, apparently for no good reason, except maybe, they are close to me?*

At Camp Pendleton, I belonged to the 5th Regiment, commanded by Colonel Chesty Puller, a living legend for his combat exploits against the Japanese during World War II.

In one incident he personally led a charge against an enemy stronghold. In the middle of that foray he was wounded twice but refused to be evacuated and continued to lead the thrust to a successful conclusion, one resulting in 150 Japanese Marines, from Japan's most elite infantry fighting force, being killed.

In May we were notified that our regiment would soon be transferred to Hawaii. We were elated with the news; visions of Waikiki, hula girls, and luau parties danced in our heads.

---

17 A Chinese battle cry adopted by Marines in China in the 1920's, meaning "always together"

On June 22, 1950 we sailed from San Diego aboard the *USN General William Wiegel*—bound for Honolulu. The Marine Corps Band serenaded our departure, and many wives, girlfriends, and family members were there to see us off; I could see Mother Glover waving a handkerchief to me and miming, "I love you, Theo; be careful."

As two tug boats pushed our ship away from the dock, the band started playing the Marine Corps Hymn, and electricity ran through those departing as well as those staying. Neither group dreamed we were going to war, but fate has a way of altering dreams, turning them into nightmares of reality, inserting people into places and situations that turn out to be abysmal—nothing like Hawaii.

As soon as we reached the open sea and the ship started rolling with the waves, I became nauseated, and within two more hours, seasickness—a malady I had never experienced—brought me to my knees. Of course, I wasn't the only one vomiting almost endlessly.

Sergeant Prouty called all the seasick together and told us, "Men, I know you think you are seasick, but you really aren't until you feel hair in your throat. When that happens you will know your ass hole has come up. Then, but not until then, you are seasick."

We tried to laugh. Then he told us to drink small amounts of water and to eat a little food. After the second night, those of us still ill, including me, started taking Dramamine, a motion sickness medicine. Unfortunately, it didn't work, and I remained sick until we were one day out of Pearl Harbor. On that day, June 27, 1950, Colonel Puller, came on the ship's *bullhorn18* and announced, "Gentlemen, we will not be landing in Hawaii as planned. This ship and our regiment have been directed to sail west and await further orders. I will give you more information when I have it."

All of us were puzzled, and we turned to our platoon sergeant, Sergeant Prouty, a World War II combat veteran, for an explanation. He told us, "Men, I don't know any more than you do, but I will say this: an abrupt change in orders, especially when you are at sea, is not made without reason. My guess is we are needed somewhere."

---

18 Public address system

Before sunset that same day, Colonel Puller made another announcement. "We are going to be refueled at sea tomorrow. As soon as that is done, we will sail at flank[19] speed for Pusan, Korea. North Korea has invaded South Korea, and the South Koreans need our help, and by God we are going to give it to them.

"All officers and NCOs, you are hereby directed to prepare your men and equipment for combat. We will test fire all weapons from the fantail[20] by a schedule company commander will have in one hour.

"One last thing: We are Marines, and fighting is what we are all about. I am totally confident the 5th Marine Regiment will successfully complete any combat mission we are assigned."

There was total silence in our troop compartment until Sergeant Prouty said, "Since only two of us in this platoon have any combat experience, the rest of you will soon get one of those life-altering experiences that cannot be explained. You will only know what it is like the first time an enemy soldier fires at you and you fire at him. We are going to be ready for that moment. Starting now, we will field strip all of our weapons, check and double check them, clean them better than we ever have before, and apply a light coat of oil to all moveable parts. Let's get to it!"

---

19 Fastest possible speed
20 The most rear part of a ship

17

Combat

On July 6, 1950—two days after my 18ᵗʰ birthday—the *General William Wiegel* dropped anchor near Pusan, and we immediately disembarked via loading nets onto amphibious landing craft for the short ride to shore and into a city in chaos.

Thousands of soldiers from many United Nations (UN) countries were milling about trying to locate their units and assembly points; several bullhorns overrode others as each attempted, simultaneously, to call their troops together. It seemed to be a great place for North Korean agents to gather intelligence and enjoy the bedlam surrounding a confused enemy, us; they probably were doing so.

Pusan is on the extreme southern tip of Korea. The only directions for us to go from there were south, into the Sea of Japan, or north, directly into the front lines of combat.

Once our entire 5ᵗʰ Marine Regiment reached shore, platoons, companies, and battalions chaotically formed. When order was restored, we marched two miles to a soccer field where equipping and organizing us for combat only took one day, a process that would normally take a week.

Early on July 8th we loaded onto Army duce-and-a-half trucks for an all-day, stop-and-go, convoy trip of less than fifty miles. Our destination: as close to the combat as we could get without getting blown up by artillery fire.

Every jam-packed truck carried sixteen Marines—normal load is twelve—all with full combat gear, extra ammunition, extra water, and combat rations. Early in the afternoon our convoy stopped; we were ordered to load our weapons with safeties on, a process referred to as "lock and load." Apparently, from this point on, ambushes were possible.

Just after sundown we reached our destination, a dusty field at the bottom of a long, steep escarpment, the separation line between relative peace and definitive combat.

Strewn with the rubbish of battles past, damaged trucks, jeeps, and one tank, the area looked like a junk yard. Nevertheless, in the center of the pitch sat two connected squad tents with large, red crosses painted on them, obviously a field hospital.

Within minutes, several wounded soldiers—all with bandages on their torsos or heads, some seeping blood—were carried on stretchers out of the hospital tents by medics, and loaded onto the trucks we just emptied for an undoubtedly miserable, but welcome, ride to Pusan and a hospital ship.

As we scrambled out of our vehicle into 90° temperature, humidity to match, the bantering and laughter going on during the trip from Pusan quickly squelched into dramatic silence, a silence only broken when Sergeant Prouty barked, "SECOND PLATOON! You have five minutes to piss, organize your gear, and smoke a cigarette before we climb this fucken hill."

By that time I was getting nervous—a euphemism for scared—but I tried to pile positive thoughts on my increasing fear: I thought of Uncle Ned who endured four years fighting the Japanese on Pacific Islands and survived, followed by a second thought, *Damn!*

I don't want to be wounded like Uncle Ned. Unfortunately, that wish didn't pan out.

As many of us urinated near the trucks, suddenly five or six screaming artillery shells split the air over our heads, presumably friendly fire since they came from the south and went north; still too close to ignore. Every Marine in sight prudently dove to the ground, several of us with our peckers in hand, some spewing urine uncontrollably. That inspired the last laughter we would have for several days.

Soon Sergeant Prouty commanded, "SADDLE UP AND FALL-IN, single file, ten paces between each man; weapons at the ready; safeties on. I will lead, and Corporal Jenkins will bring up the rear.

"Jenkins, don't let anyone get behind you. Let's move out."

The two other platoons in our company were starting up the same hill by different routes; we would link-up on the summit.

Twenty-five minutes of slogging up the mountain—the term *hill* no longer appropriate—with over fifty pounds of equipment, ammunition, and water strapped to each man, resulted in our column spreading out. Many simply couldn't keep up; ten paces between men soon became fifteen, then twenty; faster climbers started passing the slower. When I started huffing and puffing I switched to my running-breathing-rhythm—deep inhaling for two seconds, forceful exhaling for one second. Soon I marched ten paces behind Sergeant Prouty. He turned, looked at me and the column strung out below and commented. "Goddamn, Rogers! Are you and I the only ones in this platoon in battle condition?"

I didn't answer.

After almost an hour of climbing we stopped near the top, waited for the stragglers, and then Sergeant Prouty led us of the left of the crest and about fifty meters down the back side of the mountain. The other arriving platoons took up positions to our right; the company headquarters setup on the reverse slope.

In the now fading light, from our location we could see the other side of the valley where exploding artillery rounds and muzzle flashes from small arms fire were clearly visible. A war was definitely being fought, but from where we observed, it looked more like a war movie. Only the absence of dramatic, orchestrated music negated any theatric ambiance.

Quickly Sergeant Prouty assigned our squad an area to defend and told us in his usual assiduous manner, "Start digging your foxholes now. Dig them at least seven feet long and four and one-half feet deep; be quick about it. Your life may depend on how fast you can get your holes dug and get your asses into them."

With flashing thoughts of my San Bernardino home and my long deceased family, I started digging furiously along with my foxhole mate and close friend, Jim Cordell, a farm boy from Illinois I would get to know and like well—too well. Then Uncle Ned's 1947 remark detonated in my head, "There won't be any wars for many, many years; Theo should be safe for his entire enlistment."

Next the Rose Bowl Parade and the blue uniforms that inspired me to become a Marine came to mind. I thought of my own blue uniform, one I had only worn three times since joining the Marine Corps: once for Boot Camp graduation, at Father Glover's funeral, and once for a picture I gave to Mother Glover on her birthday. Now my combat uniform—dungarees, covered with Korean soil turned into stinking mire from soaking sweat, and a steel helmet—adorned my tired, agitated body.

After we finished digging, for some inexplicable reason, even though I knew serious combat was imminent, the fear left me. That anxiety I felt when I climbed from the truck melted with acceptance of reality, and even though my first year in the Marine Corps had gone well, until this moment I never really felt like a Marine. Now I did!

During combat training at Camp Pendleton, I often thought, *Do I really have the desire and courage to point my rifle at another human being and pull the trigger?* Now I understood: shooting an enemy in combat, an enemy who would not hesitate to shoot me, is not a moral issue to be debated but a matter of survival. Within hours, pulling the trigger would not be a problem.

Just as dusk faded into total darkness, our mortar section started registering their tubes[21] in front of our newly established line. First mortars exploded about 400 meters in front of our foxholes, next 200 meters, and last approximately 100 meters. By this time concertina wire had been strung, claymore mines placed, and unobstructed fields-of-fire[22] cleared. Of course, we were prepared to lay down rifle and machine gun fire and toss hand grenades down the hill on any enemy attempting to come to the top and overrun us. Those preparations comforted us, and we were confident we could repel any attack.

Our foxhole seemed to be in a relatively safe position: approximately thirty meters to our right sat an emplacement contained a 50 caliber machine gun, a weapon capable of inflicting serious damage on any aggressor; and to our left, another foxhole held two more men, one armed with a Browning Automatic Rifle (BAR), sometimes called a light machinegun.

Soon Sergeant Prouty and Private Zwinki appeared at the back of our hole. Zwinki was loaded down with water and ammunition. Prouty gave us the password for the night: "New York," with the response being, "Cardinals." After giving us two boxes of rations, more ammunition and grenades, Zwinki filled our canteens with water. Prouty's final instructions were, "Don't fire unless you have identified your target. Tonight, or early in the morning, the Army unit in front of us will probably withdraw through our lines. They have the password; so don't forget: you challenge them with 'New York,' and their response should be, 'Cardinals'. If they have forgotten the response listen to their voices before you shoot.

"So we don't find you dead in the morning with your throats cut, one of you stay awake all night. Got that? One of you will be awake the entire night!"

With that our sergeant left us—an eighteen-year-old, already with too many death experiences, and a nineteen-year-old with many farm experiences—alone in a foxhole to face combat and the

---

21 checking for the exact amount of propellant necessary to place a mortar round on a specific spot
22 open areas where approaching enemies can be seen and fired on

realities of war for the first time in our young lives, realities only marginally related to the games we played at Camp Pendleton.

That night a few incoming artillery rounds hit near our lines, none close to Jim and me, but some shrapnel did whistle over our heads. Off and on we could hear and see firefights well below us, about 1,000 meters away, and flares illuminated the valley floor much of the night.

At daybreak, after a heavy North Korean artillery barrage targeting the Army positions, we heard the sound of bugles and saw the North Koreans in a frontal assault, running directly at the Army positions. We started firing but too soon; we were too far away to help the soldiers. When the charging North Koreans breached the Army battalion's line in two places, the soldiers started a semi-orderly retreat.

In squad size units, the Americans would lay down coordinated rifle and light machine gun fire, then turn and run about 100 meters before dropping to the ground and firing again. As the battle approached us, our mortars, machine guns, and rifle fire finally provided effective support, and the North Koreans stopped their pursuit. Soon spent and wounded Americans started passing through our positions while Jim and I continued to fire. No passwords were necessary; we could see them clearly.

The North Koreans never came closer than about 100 meters from our position, and I don't know if we hit any of them. Only a few of the enemy's shots came near us, but each time we heard the *zzzip* of a bullet, we ducked our heads, a useless gesture since by the time we heard the round, it had already passed.

The second night turned out to be the last relatively quiet one we enjoyed for six weeks. The period from August 4th to September 18th, 1950—the time the UN forces spent trying to hold the perimeter near Pusan—historians refer to as *The Battle for Pusan*.

During those long weeks, bugles often sounded at night announcing the beginning of a head-on, suicidal assault on our position. Even though our company, Bravo Company, suffered casualties, the North Koreans never penetrated our perimeter, and we inflicted heaving casualties on them. On many mornings fifty or more bodies sprawled in front of the machine gun emplacement near us, many more hung on the concertina wire, and one morning ten lay within twenty meters of our foxhole; Jim and I obviously had killed them. We clearly weren't having any trouble pulling the trigger.

Firing at the enemy and being fired at never became routine, particularly on those occasions when I could see the faces of those I killed, some ironically, obviously younger than me. Still, I never had a unilateral, moral debate about the duties of a Marine in ground combat. Pure and simple: we were there to kill the enemy and, hopefully, survive.

For six weeks we held the line, while on either side of our battalion the line collapsed three times. The Army's 24th Infantry Division—weakened by three months on the front lines and with three times the casualties our division suffered—just could not hold. On those occasions, we withdrew toward Pusan to reestablish an overlapping, defensible front. On September 10, 1950, a contingent of British Royal Marines replaced us and we marched to Pusan, now only three miles from our front lines. From our positions that first night in Korea, we had retreated over forty-five miles.

18

From Inchon to the 38th Parallel

fter a brief rest in Pusan—four days of good food, showers, clean uniforms, and sleep—we boarded a transport ship for an overnight passage to Inchon. There, on the morning of September 15, 1950, we made an amphibious landing over a high, stone seawall southwest of the city; we had to use ladders to scale that obstacle. Heavy bombardment by big guns on battleships and cruisers softened the North Koreans to the point that our landing was lightly opposed, and we suffered few causalities; however, that is not to say that our arrival was totally passive.

One hundred yards before our landing craft ground to a halt against the seawall rocks, machine gun fire raked the front of our LCA[23]. The loud, ringing ping of bullets on steel made us realize how vulnerable we would be when the three-inch-thick metal shield dropped and we charged off the boat.

Near the top of the seawall, I reached up, got a firm grip, vaulted over as quickly as I could and immediately took cover behind a large bolder. Being alive and unscathed, I had landed successfully.

I only heard a few enemy rifles and one machine gun firing during those first nervous minutes ashore. Luckily, the rounds that impacted nearby left me unharmed, and only three men in our platoon were hit, one killed.

Navy fighter planes set a fuel tank farm ablaze resulting in a lot of black smoke and flames. They also dropped napalm on enemy positions, and soon the machine gun emplacement that had been firing on us, along with its occupants, was incinerated. Thirty minutes later when we passed that roofless bunker, the repulsive, but familiar, smell—the same odor I experienced when my family burned eleven years back—of burning bodies filled the air. The charred remains of four North Korean soldiers presented us with one of the uglier realities of war.

That first day after the landing, we slogged through the mostly deserted streets of Inchon City; we spent an uneventful night in our fox holes. Soon, we became complacent, and mistakenly assumed that this operation would be a total cake walk; true for a while.

Three days later, when we were continuously but slowly advancing up and down hills adjacent to the highway that led from Inchon to Seoul, the capitol of South Korea, another paranoia building incident happened.

On a pleasantly cool morning—after a day and night when neither side fired a shot or suffered a casualty—we were tramping in a skirmish line on the side of a hill north of the highway that ran from Kimpo Airfield to Seoul. Jim Cordell and I were enjoying an animated conversation about girls in general and specifically his fiancé. We casually carried our weapons at the ready but not in a firing position, and our safeties were on. Suddenly, Jim stumbled and fell; an instant later we heard the echo of a distant rifle shot. Our patrol, a squad of thirteen Marines, dropped to the ground in defensive firing positions. I called to Jim, but he didn't answer, so I crawled to him. Face down, he still had his helmet on but not moving. As I shook him and rolled him over, his helmet fell away exposing a bean size wound above his left eye, but the bullet left a silver dollar size exit wound behind his right ear.

Jim's eyes stared blankly at the sky. Stunned, I could only say, "Jim, Jim, don't die!" A useless appeal.

We never located the sniper that killed Jim, and soon the Army graves registration unit placed his remains in a black body-bag, a nineteen year old Marine soon to be buried in a military graveyard near Pusan, half a world away from the farm where he was born and grew up; half a world away from his family, friends, and fiancé.

At dusk, for the first time I occupied a foxhole alone. Depressed, my morale at its nether, I pondered the fact that another person I cared for died in my presence. Soon, however, Sergeant Prouty slipped into my hole accompanied by a new man, PFC Tito Gonzales, my new partner. After accurately assessing my frame of mind Sergeant Prouty said, "Look Ruiz-Rogers, Cordell, was a good Marine, and I know you two got along well, but you must remember, in combat you don't have any friends, just acquaintances that are here today and may be gone tomorrow. Pull yourself together and continue to march. Don't dwell on it; that's dangerous. Also, you have to break in Private Gonzales; this is his second day in Korea."

That night I said little to Gonzales, only the necessities like: "One of us has to be awake at all times." However, the next day I got to know Tito, and we started talking, primarily in espanól—what a pleasure—until he too got killed weeks later on Hill 3010.

I spent most of the night Jim died thinking: *How could he die that way?* The bullet that killed him was mysterious, like it fell from the sky, and not fired by a sniper, a sniper who only fired once and then never heard from again. Had some transcendent power killed him, one that had some abstract connection to me? The logical answer, No! But my answer, Yes!

That syllogistic conclusion—Cordell was dead; he was with me when he died; therefore, I became responsible for his death—drenched me with guilt. It didn't hold up to rational scrutiny, but I wasn't rational; I believed it—to this day, I have never totally disbelieved it—and the guilt has never totally subsided.

Seoul, a city mostly flattened by airstrikes and artillery fire, surrendered to us after five days of brutal house to house fighting. After one day of rest, we continued to march north.

On October 1st, we reached the parallel that marks the border between North Korea and South Korea, the 38th Parallel. We stopped and set up camp. Most officers and experienced NCOs thought reaching that point would mark the end of our advance. We had expelled the North Koreans from South Korea and inflicted sever causalities on them, probably ending the war. But that wasn't to be. After only two days of rest, our new orders were to continue moving north as quickly as possible. Obviously, General MacArthur's strategy was to trap and annihilate the entire North Korean Army. Only slowed by occasional pockets of resistance, all quickly neutralized, we progressed up the west coast plain to the twin cities of HamHung and HungNam, deep into North Korea, as it turned out—much too deep.

19

Disaster at the Chosen Reservoir

For five days we rested and refitted near Hungnam before we started trekking northwest, following the seventy-six mile road that led to Chosen Reservoir close to the Yalu River. The Yalu forms the border between China and North Korea.

On 9 November, the temperature was 40° above zero, but overnight it turned brutally cold, dropping to 35° below. Oil thickened in truck and tank motors, and our inadequate summer clothing quickly caused frostbite casualties.

Within a week, winter boots became available; but those rubber soled *winter snow packs* failed to protect our feet; they had been designed for the relatively moderate winter weather of Europe. Days later, most of us still did not have down parkas, but we made do with as many layers of cotton clothes we could find. Some would still be wearing that inadequate garb when the coldest weather—as low as 51° below zero—hit us.

Sergeant Prouty, and many of our combat experienced NCOs, started warning officers of a potential disaster. They emphasized that our supply line from Hungnam stretched too far and relied too much on one unimproved, originally dirt, but now an ice and snow packed road. Those officers didn't have to be told that many of our vehicles would not run, vehicles essential to moving fuel, food, ammunition and other supplies. And, they also had to know that all of our food was now frozen, and food service units, like all others, were critically low on fuel oil for thawing it out. One of my most unpleasant memories of North Korea: eating frozen C-rations, a can of greasy ham and lima beans stuck on the end of a bayonet.

At about the same time we started eating frozen food, the effective air support we had enjoyed since the Inchon invasion became non-existent. Planes were grounded or tied down on aircraft carrier decks because of winter storms and the thick, overcast skies which didn't break for several days. When in trouble, no longer could we radio planes to drop bombs, particularly napalm, and lay down machine gun fire to protect us.

Even the moving mechanisms on our weapons were affected by the cold: machine guns clogged; the bolts on M1 rifles froze and refused to move when Marines breathed on them while sighting to fire; ammunition for artillery pieces didn't function properly, often causing them to fall short, resulting in the death and wounding of UN forces; lastly, but ultimately the most important, rumors that Chinese divisions—their troops equipped for and accustomed to extremely cold conditions—had crossed the Yalu River from mainland China to fight us, turned out to be true.

Our situation was grim; as First Sergeant Grimes put it, "If ever an American fighting force was set up for disaster, it is this one." That turned out to be a most prophetic statement.

By the time we reached Hugaru-ri, the weather had taken its toll on our moral—it sunk with the thermometer. Finally, on one frigid day we had a short reprieve.

Thanksgiving Day, November 23, with a temporary break in the overcast, Marine F7F fighter planes got the enemy off of our backs with napalm, and Air Force C-119s dropped turkey dinners by parachutes. Some companies ate frozen turkey, but we were lucky. Our mess sergeant found some fuel oil and set up a mess tent near the road ahead. A half a mile before we got there, we could smell the turkey. That turned out to be the last hot meal I had in Korea.

While we were eating, Sergeant Prouty came up to me and said, "Congratulations, Ruiz-Rogers. You have been promoted to corporal, so I am making you the fire-team leader of the 2nd Fire Team.[24]"

I really didn't give my promotion much thought. I knew the responsibilities of a fire-team leader: lead the three privates under you, see that they had ammunition, water, and rations, and once combat started, direct their fire. The fact that I was only eighteen didn't fit into any combat equation.

On November 25th, the Army's 8th Infantry Division, supposedly protecting our southwest flank, was attacked by a large force of Chinese and collapsed; entire battalions fled in panic, resulting in thousands of U.S. soldiers being killed, wounded, and captured. As we entered the area the 8th Division had abandoned, bodies of dead Americans greeted us, stacked like cord wood, mouths agape, frozen eyes looking like hardboiled eggs, arms and legs in solid grotesque positions. At that time we never imagined the same thing could happen to any unit of the 1st Marine Division—we were wrong.

On November 26th, we left the road and climbed a series of steep hills until our Company Commander, Captain Doydt Redmond, ordered us to dig in on the crest of Hill 3010[25] and prepare a defensive perimeter. The plan called for us to patrol the nearby mountain ridges looking for signs of Chinese soldiers, and thus, protect the road, our only escape route back to safety of Hungnam. The 1st Marine Division's original mission, reaching the Yalu River—so General McArthur could piss in it as the joke went—no longer seemed possible.

The ground, now too frozen to dig fox holes in, yielded some to TNT charges. While we were chipping and digging, our platoon

---

24 Each squad of thirteen men has three four-man fire teams, each led by corporals; a sergeant usually leads the squad. Each platoon has four squads; a platoon sergeant, and a platoon leader— most often a Lieutenant.

25 The hill number indicates the hill's altitude above sea level.

leader, Lieutenant Timothy Wilson, stood near us looking through binoculars when he pointed to a ridge to our north and exclaimed, "God damn! Look at that."

It didn't take vision assistance to see what captured his attention. On the other side of the valley, maybe three-quarters of a mile away, thousands of Chinese troops were cresting a ridge to our north and massing; their large red flags waving in the icy breeze. Lieutenant Wilson immediately reported to Captain Redmond at the company command post, and soon he and our battalion commander, Major Terrash, stood near us looking at the Chinese units thru their binoculars.

I heard Major Terrash tell the other officers, "We can't stop that horde. I will ask regimental headquarters for permission to withdraw to a position closer to the road."

That request must have been denied, because as night fell, we continued to prepare our defensive perimeter.

With bugles blaring, mortars leading their charge, voices screaming in broken English, "Americans you die," at 01:00 (1 a.m.) thousands of Chinese attacked. They rolled through our mortars and small arms fire, wire, and claymore mines almost without hesitation, even as we were killing hundreds of them.

Scores of Chinese fell from their own mortar fire, but five took the place for each that went down. When they reached our wire, three or four Chinese dove on it, and the others used their bodies as a bridge into our perimeter. What we considered a strong, well prepared defensive barrier only slowed the horde for seconds.

Quickly the Chinese swamped our fortifications and started passing through our lines as they threw hand grenades into our foxholes. Three grenades landed between Tito and me, but we managed to throw them out before they exploded, killing and wounding several Chinese near us. Tito and I were firing in a 360° circle from our foxhole. Two attackers fell into our hole after I shot them, one in the face and the other in the forehead. During this chaos, screams of the wounded and the smell of blood saturated the air—Hell was on Earth.

Suddenly, Tito fell dead against me; he had two bullet holes in the left side of his chest, undoubtedly hitting his heart. A round hit my left shoulder, just under my collar bone, but the projectile didn't hit a bone or sever a major artery. The battle took away the pain; only the blood made me aware of the wound.

Suddenly all was quiet except for the groans and cries of the dying. "Corpsman! Corpsman! I'm hit; oh God; oh Jesus, help me; Mother! Mother! Mother!"

The Chinese had overrun us, but they didn't pause to exterminate us as they easily could have; they rolled over the hill top, like a tsunami wave engulfing a beach, and into the valley below.

After a few minutes, I crawled out of my hole and dashed to the machine gun position. All four Marines manning the 50 caliber machine gun were dead, the lower half of their bodies still in their sleeping bags, trying to keep their feet from freezing. In front of that position over a 100 enemy soldiers lay lifeless or dying. In the distance I could still hear the rattle of Chinese burp guns and the barking of M1 rifles, but soon even those sounds quieted.

Of the 186 Marines and two Navy medics in our company, only thirty-six of us remained alive, all Marines; we had lost our medics. One officer, two buck sergeants[26], four corporals, and twenty-two privates that could still fight, and seven seriously wounded who could not walk or fire a weapon, were all that remained alive. All of our radios had been destroyed, so we had absolutely no way of communicating with other elements of our regiment or the division headquarters.

Sergeant Prouty and Captain Redmond, two supposedly indestructible Marines were both dead; Lieutenant Wilson instantly became the company commander. The burden of getting us out of our dilemma fell on his shoulders. He immediately accepted that responsibility, didn't hesitate, and quickly gave us hope, something we were in dire need of, with an escape plan.

---

26 In 1950, a buck sergeant had three stripes, a staff sergeant four, a technical sergeant five, and a master sergeant six.

"OK, Men. I don't have to tell you we are in a tough situation, but here is the plan: we will bring all of our dead to this area, cover them with snow and mark the spot so they can be retrieved later. (*I don't think they ever were.*) We will make the seriously wounded as comfortable as we can in the company headquarters tent. (*Every officer and man in the company headquarters had been killed by hand grenades.*) I will need four volunteers to stay here to protect the wounded until help arrives. The remaining twenty-four of you will divide into six fire teams, each with a corporal or sergeant in charge. Those teams will take different routes back to the road; if you stay together you will probably be spotted and killed. Your mission is to get to the road and report our situation. Try to find anyone with authority, including high ranking NCOs, tell them we need help immediately. It will take a substantial relief force, at least two platoons, to evacuate our dead, the wounded, and those of us who remain here. Who will volunteer to stay with me? Anyone?"

Eight of us stepped forward; Lieutenant Wilson instantly selected four of us, probably because all of us were wounded but not with life threatening injuries; we were still mobile.

"You men leaving will leave as soon as it is dark, in fifteen minute intervals. The noise from the road should help you navigate, but fire-teams leaders, make sure you take multiple compass readings before you depart. Share them with every man in your team."

Gathering our dead and stacking them four deep was a gruesome task accomplished in silence. Before helping Private Starks carry Captain Redmond's body, I tried to close the captain's mouth and staring eyes, but I was too late; they had already frozen ajar. Of course, it was also difficult to carry Sergeant Prouty's body; he always seemed invincible.

Next Lieutenant Wilson directed all ammunition be brought to a central location where we divided it: Each departing man received six clips of M1 ammunition, eight rounds per clip, and two hand grenades, but no more, because Lieutenant Wilson didn't want them to be weighted down, speed being imperative.

When darkness fell, the first departing fire team slid down the northern tip of the ridge we occupied. Below, flares and fire fights lit up the critical road. By 20:00 (8 p.m.), all six fire teams had departed and only twelve of us, including Lieutenant Wilson and the seven critically wounded, remained on Hill 3010.

The Lieutenant directed us to restore the 50 caliber machine gun position that had been destroyed in the battle and prepare three, widely spaced, 30 caliber machine gun positions. If we were attack—Lieutenant Wilson thought that unlikely since the force that overran us probably had Yudam-ni, the location of the 1st Marine Division Headquarters, as its objective—we could run from position to position firing a long burst before running to another position. That should give the enemy the illusion that we had more men and armament than we actually had. We knew, of course, if we were attached by a force similar to the one that had virtually destroyed our company—we were going to die.

During a cold sleepless night, three of us attended to the wounded while Lieutenant Wilson and PFC Reed stayed on watch in our key position, the 50 caliber machine gun bunker. At 05:30 artillery shells started going overhead from the east, indicating they were ours, but they started impacting dangerously close to our position. I left the medical tent to consult with Lieutenant Wilson; seconds later two artillery rounds hit that tent killing the seven seriously wounded and the two men caring for them.

After the friendly fire barrage lifted, we surveyed the damage, confirming that the only Marines still alive on Hill 3010 were Lieutenant Wilson, PFC Reed, and me. Obviously, we needed to get off of that death trap quickly and head for the evacuation road on the valley floor.

Before we departed, we placed the severely mutilated bodies of our companions killed by the friendly artillery with the other dead Marines and covered them with snow. Then we piled all the remaining weapons and ammunition together around the 50 caliber machine gun, except for a Thompson submachine gun, two M1 rifles, and Lieutenant Wilson's 45 caliber pistol, ammunition for those weapons, and six grenades, all of which we would take with us. A few seconds before we slipped over the crest of Hill 3010, we ignited thermite grenades—devices that generate enough heat to melt metal—and threw them into stack of arms and ammunition.

As we cleared the hill, an explosion sent ammunition flying through the air and cracking like a 4th of July celebration. However, celebration never entered our minds as we preceded quickly but cautiously, each of us a bit confused and disheartened by the events of the past forty-eight hours, wondering about our fate: would we make it to the road, and if we did would it be open so we could withdraw to Yudam-ni, the closest UN bivouac? Another unknown, the strength of the Division and UN Headquarters. Could they withstand hordes of Chinese like the ones that swept us aside and annihilated our company?

Lieutenant Wilson led as we entered a canyon, its walls narrowing as we proceeded through snow above our knees, in temperature of minus 35°. Suddenly there was a sustained burst of machine gun fire, and all of us were hit. PFC Reed took three rounds to the chest and died quickly; Lieutenant Wilson took three bullets to his legs, both femurs were broken, with bone fragments protruding from his left leg as blood spurted. The lobe of his left ear was also shot away; however, he hadn't lost consciousness and cursed our bad luck, but still he hadn't given up hope: "Good damn it, what rotten fucken luck. How in the hell are we going to get out of this? But there is a way, and we have to find it fast."

My new wound, again to the left shoulder, hit a bone this time rendering that arm nearly useless, and causing a lot of pain; it dangled lifeless against my side. Fortunately, again, there wasn't a lot of blood. Quickly, with my good arm and hand, and the thumb and forefinger of my left hand, I cut away part of the lieutenant's fatigues and applied tourniquets above each of the his wounds, using our belts to stem the blood flow. Reed's lifeless eyes starred at us as we struggled.

Raising my head to see where the automatic weapons fire came from, I drew another burst that passed over me, and I dropped again, but I saw the machine gun's position—at the mouth and bottom of the canyon where it narrowed to about twenty meters.

A stand of large pine trees to our right would provide some cover if I could get the lieutenant into them. While laying on my back, legs spread—as he screamed in pain—I rolled the lieutenant onto his back and pulled him up to where his head touched my crotch. With my good arm, while holding onto the hood of his parka, I started dragging him through the deep snow, digging my heels and pushing us forward while leaving a trail of blood. Immediately I knew we were going too slowly. The snow, while giving us cover from the machine gun, built up behind my shoulders making our progress difficult. Just as I thought I would have to risk standing up and trying to carry the lieutenant, we hit a patch of ice near a tree. Quickly we slid under that evergreen, and I partially covered us with the tree's lower limbs. Miraculously, we had made it to some protective cover.

At that point, I was totally exhausted. As I lay gasping for breath, listening to Lieutenant Wilson's raspy, pain filled encouragement:

"Great work Corporal! Great work!"

Since I thought that our only way out was to retreat up the draw we had come down, I looked in that direction. Standing on the skyline, at the top of the canyon, perhaps 400 meters away, about fifty Chinese soldiers were looking down on us, and some started firing. As hopeless as our situation seemed, I pledged to myself I would not give up or surrender as long as blood ran through my veins and my brain worked. Assuming the machine gun that hit us was manned by the only Chinese blocking our exit from the canyon, I gathered four grenades into the pockets of my parka and took Lieutenant Wilson's 45 Pistol. Using the trees for cover, I quickly made my way to a position to the right and slightly above the machine gun nest. With my teeth, I pulled the pens on two grenades, one in each hand, and I squeezed their handles[27] as the best I could. Keeping the one in my left hand down was difficult; I had no feeling. Without my mittens, my hands were getting numbingly cold.

---

27 If the handle on a grenade is allowed to spring off, it will explode within a few seconds

Counting on the element of surprise, about twenty meters from the machine gun nest and its four occupants, I let the handles fly from the grenades activating their fuses; I jumped to my feet screamed, charged at the side of the gun emplacement, ninety-degrees away from where the weapon's muzzle was pointing, and threw the two already primed grenades. One exploded; the other was a dud, but all four men went down seriously wounded. I ripped Lieutenant Wilson's pistol out of my parka, I shot all four in the head and immediately went back into the trees toward Wilson.

As I looked to the top of the canyon again, I could see a Chinese patrol coming down the fall line to finish us off. When I got to the Lieutenant, I quickly burrowed through the snow under him, placed him over my right shoulder—he had passed out from the pain—and stood up. Having made a trip to and from the bunker, the snow was somewhat compacted and I was able to move steadily if not quickly. By the time we got to the now neutralized Chinese machine gun emplacement, the pursuing soldiers were less than 50 meters away. I dumped the unconscious lieutenant on the snow and attempted to activate the machine gun by recycling its breach. It worked! With sustained bursts I stopped the advance on our position by hitting several of those charging, maybe ten. To our advantage, one of the wounded started screaming like I had never heard a wounded man scream before. "Ahh, Yaa! Ahh, Yaa! Ahh, Yaa...!

As fast as I could, I took my remaining hand grenades, pulled their pins threw them as far as I could up the canyon. Then I put my mittens on, placed Lieutenant Wilson over my right should again, and moved as quickly as I could out the rear of the machine gun nest, toward the road.

As soon as we cleared the trees, I could see the road and the vehicles stalled in traffic gridlock. Many Marines and soldiers were lying in firing positions, gun muzzles pointing directly toward us. One fired, but missed, I started screaming, "Marines! We are Marines!"

I kept moving with the Lieutenant on my back, and I could feel him coming to, squirming and mumbling, "Corporal! Corporal! Where are we? Where are we?"

"Hang on Lieutenant! Hang on! We're almost to the road."

With about ten meters to go to the relative safety of the road bank, a Chinese bullet hit me in the back and went through my left kidney. Within seconds I lost consciousness, but, as I learned later, friendly hands dragged Lieutenant Wilson and me to the shelter of a medical truck.

20

Evacuation and Medical Treatment

On December 5, 1950, on a Navy hospital ship, the USS Consolation, anchored off the Hungnam coast, I regained consciousness for the first time in seven days. It took a few days to piece together the details of the scenario that delivered me to that ship.

The Marines that carried us onto the road and placed us in a medical truck on November 28th, didn't think either Lieutenant Wilson nor I would make in to Hugaru-ri alive, let alone to Yudam-ni and the 1st Marine Division Headquarters, certainly not to Hungnam. We were set to be tagged KIA.[28]

The tourniquets I put on the lieutenant's legs only slowed the blood flowing from his body, and even though in critical condition, once he gained consciousness —after passing out during the pain I inflicted on him—he remained conscious until the doctors put him under for surgery. The internal bleeding from my punctured kidney caused my blood pressure to drop to near zero.

The Chinese cut the evacuation road in several places; chaos reigned at those points, but again and again, the road reopened with the help of Marine tanks and courage. The medical van transporting us repeatedly took fire; some wounded occupants were killed lying in their medical stretchers. While unconscious, I received a grazing bullet wound to my left cheek, one later closed with sixteen stiches. *(If you look closely today, you can still see the scar left by that wound.)*

The driver of that medical van is a real hero. Totally on his own volition, he abandoned the road and drove far out onto the ice of Chosen Reservoir, away from the raging battles, and moved parallel to the shore line until he could see the smoke and fires of Hugaru-ri.

There, all wounded went through a triage procedure that separated those with a good chance of survival from those whose chances were not so good—they were expected to die. I was placed in the not-expected-to-live group because of my lack of blood pressure. Thankfully, Lieutenant Wilson was still conscious, and he and I shared adjacent spaces on the ground in the triage tent. So when he saw me being set aside as expected to die, he refused to accept evacuation on a C47 medical aircraft unless I went along. His leg wounds were so serious he was tagged for "probable leg amputation."

Sometime later we landed near Hungnam Harbor and expedited to the hospital ship where I immediately received several blood transfusions along with two surgical procedures in less than four hours, both to seal my lacerated kidney. During this time I remained unconscious and was still not expected to live.

Lieutenant Wilson underwent seven hours of orthopedic surgery in an attempt to save his legs. Before he went under the anesthesia, he told one of the doctors, "If you can't save my legs, let me die."

On that glorious day, December 5th, 1951, a growing circle of bright light woke me, and in the center appeared a face bejeweled with beautiful blue eyes and framed by a nurse's blond hair. Her mouth moved, but at first I could not hear her, but her lips continued to move until I understood, "Are you back with us, Corporal?"

"Have I been sleeping long," I asked?

With a laugh, "Only seven or eight days."

"Where is Lieutenant Wilson? How is he?"

"At the moment he is in the surgery recovery room, but he will be in the bed next to you in an hour or two. By the way, Corporal, you are the first patient I have ever seen with thick black hair and beautiful blue eyes."

I managed a faint smile followed by tears as memories of my father's black hair and my mother's blue eyes came to mind.

Two days later, during another surgery, my left arm and shoulder were put back together with surgical wire and stainless steel screws, only a week after one surgeon recommended amputating that arm.

On December 10, Lieutenant Wilson and I arrived at the Yokohama Naval Hospital in Japan where we underwent two more surgeries each, mine to further repair my kidney and my left shoulder; his to reattach severed arteries.

Prior to our arrival in Japan, Lieutenant Wilson demanded that I be placed in the same medical ward as he. By military protocol, officers and enlisted men are not warded together in Navy hospitals.

On December 19, Lieutenant Wilson and I boarded another hospital ship, the USS Haven, for a fifteen day journey to San Francisco and the U.S. Navy Pacific Fleet Hospital. That hospital—more like a five star resort—provided the best medical care, great food, and a fantastic view of the Golden Gate Bridge. The only reason a wounded or seriously ill person could not recover there: they were already DOA—Dead on Arrival.

By this time I was on my feet and recovering quickly; Lieutenant Wilson's legs were in traction. He would not stand for three more months.

Just before the Navy doctors released me from the hospital on a convalescent leave—several months before the lieutenant got out—the last time we met, I sat by his bed as we talked.

We had already gabbed for many hours during our hospital stays, but strangely we never discussed those fateful forty-eight hours on Hill 3010 and our escape from death. Lieutenant Wilson broached the heretofore forbidden subject by saying, "Theo, it is unbelievable that we are here safe and sound. What a difference a few weeks, a few surgeries, a few good doctors, and a few pretty nurses make. We are two lucky bastards, don't you agree?"

"That's so true, Lieutenant, I wonder what happened after we were evacuated; how much of the 1st Marine Division got out? Do you think Marines will ever try to go to the Yalu again?"

"Well, most of the personnel got out, although many of them were dead. I haven't been able to find out if the bodies from our company were recovered or not. However, very little equipment was salvaged. Ships took everybody, including many Korean refugees, back to Pusan to start all over again. The dead recovered were buried there in a U.N. graveyard.

"As far as going back into North Korea, I don't think that is ever going to happen. President Truman sacked General McArthur, and I think, at least I hope, saner heads are now making the decisions. Probably the status quo at the 38th Parallel is going to be the defining result of this war. There is one word that I think adequately describes this conflict—*internecine*."

"I don't know that word, Lieutenant."

"Well, Theo, as far is this war is concerned, internecine means a lot of death and destruction for nothing. Personally, it is difficult for me to accept, but who am I but a lowly first lieutenant."

"Sir, you are one great first lieutenant. I bet you will be a general someday."

"I don't think so, Theo. They already told me I will probably be put on medical disability and discharged, but I don't want that. So I will just have to wait and see.

By the way, Theo, how do you feel about Hill 3010 and our experiences there?"

After a moment of staring out the window, "Lieutenant, I know those two terrible days happened, but now it seems like a bad dream, a terrible, terrible nightmare, something that happened to someone else, not to you and me. I am so glad you were there; without you, no one would have made it out alive. I understand that all but one of the fire teams you sent off the hill before we left made it. All of us who survived are lucky you were with us."

"Lucky! Theo, without you, I'm dead. You are my hero for the rest of my existence; I owe my life to you.

"I have never mentioned it before, but I have formally made two recommendations concerning you. I put you in for a Silver Star for your actions on the night we were overrun; the way you stayed at your post and kept fighting was incredible. In addition, I have recommended you for the Medal of Honor for the way you got us out of that doomed situation, destroying the machine gun nest, and saving my life even though you were seriously wounded yourself; those were extraordinary acts."

I didn't know what to say, but finally I responded. "Lieutenant, I don't think I deserve any medals; I was trying to keep you alive for my own selfish reasons. During my eighteen years of living, a lot of people, people I cared for deeply, died when I was near them. I didn't want you to be another dead person I would have nightmares about; I didn't want your ghost waking me up in the middle of the night."

"Well, Theo, I just want to tell you: Thank you! If I can ever do anything for you, now, twenty, or fifty years from now, just let me know."

Ten years later, I saw Lieutenant Wilson again; and, on that occasion, he did a lot for me.

21

The Medal of Honor

Two days after my last conversation with Lieutenant Wilson, I started a sixty day medical convalescence leave—one later extended to ninety days—and I returned to San Bernardino and Mother Glover. We were extremely happy to see each other; we exchanged many hugs, kisses, and tears, and for the next month she pampered me as if she had just found her long lost son.

The day after I returned, Uncle Ned came to see me. He is a good man, and I have always cherished the time I spent with him. I wondered which one of us would mention his statement, "There won't be any more wars for many, many years." He did.

"Theo, I am so glad you are home, and I am sorry you collected four Purple Hearts, but I am elated you survived the war, one I said would never happen." We both laughed and talked about the Marine Corps in general, little however, about Korea.

Uncle Ned asked, "Do you still enjoy that blue uniform you wanted to wear so badly?" When I told him I only had it on three times, he quipped, "Gee, Theo, I thought you would sleep in it."

As I savored those weeks at home, I started wondering what the Marine Corps would do with me at the end of my convalescence period. With my damaged shoulder, could I still be a Marine? Considering my experiences in Korea, did I really want to be a Marine? Fantasies inspired by blue uniforms and spine tingling music had been consumed by the realities of war: dirt, mud, snow, and cold; killing the enemy; the odors of exploding ordnance and blood; up-close seeing my comrades have their bodies torn apart, and hearing their screams before they died. My entire Korean experience wasn't pleasant and not a bit like I idealistically imagined it would be.

With two weeks to go on my leave, I received a telegram directing me to immediately call Colonel Nelson in Washington D.C., and, "reverse the charges."

My initial thought, "They are going to discharge me because of my wounds." On the other hand, I didn't think they would have a colonel calling me from Washington about that. I made the call.

"Hello, Marine Corps Awards and Decoration. This is Miss Casey."

The operator said, "You have a collect call for Colonel Nelson from a Corporal Theodore Rogers. Will you accept the charges?"

An enthusiastic voice responded, "Yes! Certainly!"

"Is this Corporal Theodore Ruiz Rogers?"

"Yes, Mam. This is he."

"Colonel Nelson is at a meeting at the moment; however, he is very anxious to talk with you. Please give me the number you are calling from."

"Our number is 909-538-4355."

"Will you be at this number for the next hour or so?"

"Yes, Mam. Can you tell me what this is about?"

"No, I'm sorry, Corporal, I can't; Colonel Nelson will explain everything to you when he calls. Please don't go anywhere. Wait for his call."

"Yes, Mam."

Thirty minutes later the phone rang. "This is Colonel Nelson at Headquarters Marine Corps. Am I speaking with Corporal Theodore Ruiz Rogers?"

"Yes, Sir. This is he."

"Son, I want you to know that the entire nation is proud of you. President Truman is proud of you, and he wants you to visit the White House as soon as we can arrange it."

Him calling me *"Son"* bothered me; he wasn't my father. Maybe it is because only my real father, my Papá, called me "hijo" (son) and always in Spanish.

My response was shock. "Sir, are you sure you have the right man? Why would the President want me to visit the White House?"

"He is going to award you the Medal of Honor for the heroic deeds you performed at the Chosen Reservoir in Korea."

"Wow! You mean to tell me, Sir, that Lieutenant Wilson really did recommend me for that medal?"

"That is correct; he and Colonel Chesty Puller, your regimental commander, both signed the recommendation, as well as two other Marines who saw you carrying Lieutenant Wilson to safety when you both were wounded. By the way Son, how are your wounds healing? "

"My only real problem is with my left shoulder where I was shot twice. The bones were shattered; it seems to be healing but very slowly. I think my kidney is fine, and the other wound I received, the one to my face was not serious. It is completely healed.

"Well, Corporal, the White House wants us to have the ceremony as soon as we can. The news out of Korea has not been all good recently, and this is something positive we can share with the American public and your Marine Corps buddies. We would like to have the ceremony before your 19th birthday, which, of course, is on the 4th of July. You will be the youngest recipient of the Medal Honor in our nation's history. What do you think about that?"

"Really, Sir, I am astounded. I don't really think I deserve that medal, but if Lieutenant Wilson and Colonel Puller recommended me, I guess I have to accept it."

"Excellent! We will plan the ceremony for July 2nd; that's a Monday. You will come to Washington one week before so we can have a closely tailored dress-blue uniform made for you. You and your family will stay in guest rooms at Blair House, across the street from the White House, and all of you will travel on first class airline tickets. During that week we will help you prepare for the press and assist you in writing a short speech. How many are in your family?"

"Just my Mother Glover and Uncle Ned, I was adopted; my real parents are dead."

"I am sorry to hear that, but we are going to see that you, your mother and uncle have one of the most exciting and enjoyable weeks of your lives."

"I don't know what to say, Colonel."

"You don't need to say anything, Son. All of us in the Marine Corps, from General Shepard, the Commandant, to the privates in boot camp, are proud of you, and we are looking forward to honoring your heroism."

"That's very kind of you, Sir."

"Now listen. You have our phone number. When you have questions, and I am sure you will have many, call us. Always call collect.

"Miss Casey, my secretary, will be calling you frequently for information about you and your family. She will also be arranging your transportation and coordinating your stay in Washington. Do you have any questions now?"

"No, Sir."

When I told Mother Glover the news, she couldn't wait to call Uncle Ned. He immediately came to our house to congratulate me in person. The two of them were way more excited than I was.

When I left the house for a walk—as I told them, "I need a little private time."—Uncle Ned apparently started calling everyone he knew, and within a day, I started getting too many calls from people I had never known. Some worked for newspapers or television stations; some wanted me to come to their American Legion or Veterans of Foreign Wars clubs and be a guest of honor; some wanted to give me things. I called Colonel Nelson and asked him for advice. He called Camp Pendleton and had them assign a public relations officer, Lieutenant Jerome, to screen all the calls and requests for me to appear. I told him, "I don't want to give any speeches or attend dinners. I just want to rest here in San Bernardino. Maybe after I have actually received the medal, I can do some of those things." Lieutenant Jerome thought that was a good idea, so Mother Glover referred all calls to him; I quit answering the phone at all, or the knocks at the front door.

The next couple of weeks went by in a blur of activity. Miss Casey called two or three times each week, giving me information and asking for information. For instance, she wanted to know if I, Mother Glover, or Uncle Ned had any special food requests or dietary restrictions the White House kitchen should know about; and, would my mother need a new dress or Uncle Ned a new suit. "Where would you and your family like to visit in Washington?

"Gee, I'm not sure."

"Well, if it is OK with you, I will arrange a very nice tour for you and your family."

"Great! Thank you."

Miss Casey told me that after I received the medal, the Marine Corps Public Relations Office wanted me to stay in Washington until the next Saturday, July 8th so I could be presented at 4th of July events and meet some members of congress, particularly the senators from California and the representative for the San Bernardino Congressional District. None of that struck me as something I wanted to do, but I didn't really think I had a choice. Eventually, it was time to go to Washington.

Our first day in Washington was full of surprises. On our arrival at Blair House we learned that President Truman and his family occupied the majority of the residence because the West Wing of the White House, where the president and his family normally reside, was undergoing extensive renovation. Then they told me that Mother Glover, Uncle Ned and I would be dinner guests of the President and his family. Now I was a long way from a foxhole in Korea.

We ate dinner that Sunday evening with the President, Mrs. Truman, and their daughter, Margaret. We were sitting at a massive dining table talking with Margaret Truman when the President and Mrs. Truman entered. Immediately, we all stood, even Margaret, my family and I nervously and stiffly, but President Truman quickly put us at ease.

"Sit down! Sit down, Corporal! Everybody, have a seat!"

After introductions all around the table, The President said, "I'm sorry we couldn't have this dinner in the White House, but I haven't paid the rent for a while so they kicked me out, and workers are tearing that place apart."

Mrs. Truman, looking at the President and obviously a little irritated, said, "Harry, don't say things like that."

Then looking directly at me, she added, "The White House is being renovated so it will be a better place for the staff to work, and a better place for us to live."

The President smiled and continued to talk, "I have never seen a Marine look so spiffy in a blue uniform. If I join the Corps, will they let me wear one of those?"

"I'm sure they will, Mr. President."

For the next hour, all the table talk was about our families and early childhoods, both the President's and mine. He seemed particularly interested about my years in Mexico. Margaret could speak Spanish quite well, so I think she tested me with a couple of questions in Spanish. After I answered both of them, she exclaimed, "Corporal Rogers speaks Spanish like he was a native of Mexico."

Mrs. Truman, again showing irritation, admonished, "Margaret, weren't you listening? He just told us he spent the first seven years of his life living in Mexico." Everyone at the table smiled.

The President only had one question about Korea: "Corporal Rogers, what do you think about Korea?"

It was such a broad question; I didn't know how to answer it. Consequently, I just said, "It is very hot in the summer, but extremely cold in the winter, Mr. President, as cold as 50° below zero."

"God damn, that's cold," he responded.

On the 2nd of July President Truman hung the Medal of Honor around my neck; he and two other people, one the Commandant of the Marine Corps, General Lemuel C. Shepard, made short speeches, saying things about me that I didn't recognize as being factual. I said a few words of appreciation; then, we spent almost thirty minutes at the mercy of photographers.

Colonel Nelson had briefed me, "When they start taking your picture smile and look at the camera. Then for the VIP pictures, look at the VIP that is shaking your hand and keep smiling."

The only people I knew when posing for all of those pictures, Mother Glover, Uncle Ned, and President Truman, all seemed happier than me; I couldn't help but dwell on those two nights, only eight months before, on Hill 3010.

Finally, President Truman took my hand in a firmer grip than during the previous handshakes we exchanged, looked directly into my eyes and said, very seriously, "Corporal Rogers, thank you for your service and heroism. I am proud to have met you, and I will never forget you."

"Thank you, Mister President, for your kind words and hospitality." Then he left, and that was the last time I saw him.

The rest of the week went slowly, the tours Mrs. Casey arranged wore us out, and by the time we boarded the Pan American flight for Los Angeles, we were all exhausted and happy to be going home; I slept the entire five hour flight.

In San Bernardino, I talked with some newspaper reporters and had some radio and TV interviews, but those requests tapered quickly since I wasn't good at those things, and I refused to talk about the gory details of the Korean War. After another month, my life almost got back to normal, but the uncertainty about my future in the Marine Corps started bothering me; I wasn't sleeping well, and for some no-excuse reason, I wasn't exercising; consequently, I put on about twenty pounds of unwanted weight.

The process of my shoulder healing still had a long way to go, obviously years. The chief orthopedic surgeon at the Navy Hospital in San Diego said, "It may never be totally pain free."

As a result of my Medal of Honor, the Marine Corps extended my convalescence leave another thirty days and left the decision about staying in the Corps up to me: stay on active duty until the end of my enlistment, scheduled for July of 1953, with the option of reenlisting; or, accept a medical discharge with disability benefits. I talked with Mother Glover and Uncle Ned about that decision, and they both advised me to accept the discharge. Even though I still respected the traditions of the Marine Corps, my unconditional enthusiasm for it had deteriorated; I elected to get out.

22

The End of My Rogers Family

For a few weeks after my medical retirement from the Marine Corps, I didn't do much. In fact, I had no inspiration to do anything: when I woke up at 4:00 a.m., disappointed I hadn't slept longer, I always tried to go back to sleep, but it never worked. Maybe an hour later, after reading for a while, I forced myself out of bed and out the door for a walk. Pacing around the neighborhood for an hour failed to give me any motivation, but by this time the newspaper had arrived so I browsed through it. The only articles I really read were those concerning the war. It was still going on without me, and that gave me an uncomfortable feeling, one of abandonment and guilt. Marines and soldiers were still dying in Korea, and I was living a comfortable life with plenty of food, a good bed to sleep in, two hot baths each day, and totally removed from the possibility of some Chinese soldier putting a bullet in my head.

What should I do next in life? *Nothing,* became my only answer to that question. Yet, acutely aware that as a nineteen year old, that option would not work, I half-heartedly attempted to inspire myself by going to the library each day hoping for an epiphany. However, the library environment did not inspire a better answer than—*nothing*.

I talked for many hours with Mother Glover and Uncle Ned. They both suggested I attend a college or university, starting immediately. Although she didn't say it, Mother worried about me hanging around the house doing *nothing* but cutting the yard once each week:

"Theo, get out of this house and go meet some people your own age. I am sure there are a lot of pretty girls in San Bernardino who would like to meet you."

I hadn't had any practice in meeting pretty girls, or even ugly ones. The thought of introducing myself to one of either ilk frightened me. Nevertheless, out of boredom, I finally I took Mother Glover's advice and started going to the San Bernardino Aquatic Center located in the County Park less than a mile from our house. The Olympic size swimming pool at the Aquatic Center, a magnet for people near my age, became my haven. I started going to the pool for two or three hours each day.

I had never been a great swimmer; however, in high school friends told me I had good swimming technique. Now though, my damaged left shoulder made swimming the crawl—better known as freestyle—impossible. On the other hand, I could breast stroke without much pain. So breaststroke I did, up and back, up and back, up and back... Within two weeks I was pain free, and I had also made a friend, a beautiful lifeguard, Charlene.

One day when I crawled out of the pool, lovely long, tan legs were only a few feet from me. I took off my swimming goggles and looked up into a beautiful, smiling face with green eyes enclosed by shinning auburn hair. She stood gazing down at my now tired body and said, "I think I know you. Are you that Marine hero whose picture was in the paper a few weeks ago?"

I avoided the question, "Hi, I'm Theo Ruiz-Rogers. What's your name?"

"I'm Charlene Webb, but you aren't going to get off that easy. Are you that guy or not?"

"If you will go for a walk with me after you get off work, I will tell you. We can walk here in the park."

"OK. I get off in an hour, but I can only walk for thirty minutes. I don't want to miss supper. We eat exactly at five thirty."

"Great! I will take a shower and wait for you outside the main entrance."

"Good, see you then."

As Charlene walked away, then climbed into her lifeguard's chair, the view of her posterior, even more attractive than her anterior, captured me. I thought, *Wow! I want to get to know her.*

We hadn't walked ten yards, when Charlene asked, "Well, are you the hero guy or not?"

I laughed, "Hmm, I don't think I'm a hero, but if you are asking if President Truman gave me a medal, yes, he did."

"Fantastic! Congratulations. I've been watching you swim for several days, and I wondered why you never swam freestyle. Then I noticed those scars from your wounds around your shoulder; that had to be the answer. Is that why?"

"Gee, you are very observant. Yes, you're right. I can't lift my left elbow and hand very well, but I can breaststroke without pain."

Over the next two months, Charlene became the focus of my life. I saw her almost every day at the swimming pool, and when I did, we always went for that same thirty minute walk, chatting and enjoying each other's company. Soon, we were going to movies and sometimes to restaurants, and eventually we started hiking in the national forest on her day off.

Eventually, during one of our mountain hikes, we passionately explored beyond the trails and trees while we whispered words of love. Charlene stole my virginity, but I don't think I took hers; she seemed comfortable with the act and actually led me. That really didn't bother me though because I seemed to be falling in love with her, and that did bother me.

Close relationships had become antithetical to my makeup. I feared them: If I didn't have a close friend, I couldn't be hurt by one, and I wouldn't feel guilty if they should die.

Charlene was two years younger than me, and understandably her parents wanted to meet the ex-Marine their daughter spent so much time with. They invited me to their home for dinner.

The Webb family, devoutly Christian, started every meal with a prayer. When they asked me if I wanted to "say grace," I declined, resulting in a portending frown from Mrs. Webb. A few minutes later Charlene made the mistake of saying, "You have probably seen Theo's name in the news. He is a war hero."

From there, the dinner conversation turned into an inquisition, and my Marine Corps experiences became the subject of all questions. Finally, the big question came from her mother, "Did you ever kill anyone?"

My short, truthful answer, "Yes."

After a period of awkward silence, Charlene's younger brother, Jerry, questioned, "How many?"

I paused. He repeated, "How many?"

My commitment to honesty, mixed with a large dose of naivety, required the fact, "At least forty, but probably more."

End of discussion. End of any real conversation. We started talking about the unusual summer weather; a rare summer rainstorm had blessed San Bernardino the previous week.

Charlene didn't walk me to my car, actually Mother Glover's car; in fact, my farewell, at the front door, totally void of any touching, curt and painful, hurt. "Goodbye, Theo. See you at the pool."

After being brushed off at the pool a few times, "Theo, I'm too busy right now; I can't go for a walk," I called her, and I asked if she wanted to go for a hike in the mountains, an activity we were emotionally and physically married to.

"I can't this week, Theo."

"Charlene, what is wrong? Something has changed between us."

"Theo, I don't know how to tell you this, but both my mother and father say I should not be alone with someone who has killed people. I'm sorry. I will miss you." And, with that I crawled back into my shell to social isolation and turned to Mother Glover for my female companionship.

Mother Glover and I started going to movies together and even an occasional stage show in downtown Los Angeles, and we went to horse races at Santa Anita Racetrack in Arcadia. Interestingly, I couldn't bet on the horse races because I wasn't twenty-one, so Mother Glover placed my two dollar bets for me. The most we ever won was ten dollars.

However, the place we liked going the most was the beach in Santa Monica, and I also enjoyed spending a little money on Mother Glover on Santa Monica's all-cement *boardwalk*, buying her clothes that often didn't fit because she wouldn't try things on until we got home. I also bought her a fancy goldfish bowl with six fish, a watch, beach hat, sunglasses, and an umbrella. I wasn't trying to pay her back for all she and Father Glover had done for me; I just got a good feeling about treating her to a little shopping, although she never let me spend more than about forty-dollars on her.

For the first time in my life I had a bank account, at the Bank of America on Foothill Boulevard in San Bernardino. Both my military disability check, $468 per month, and my Medal of Honor stipend, $150 per month, were deposited there.

Eventually, my life evolved into one hard to define, then and now, but peaceful; my nightmares had gone away; my fixation on the Marine Corps subsided; and, what little contact I now had with the media over my Medal of Honor no longer agitated me. However, as had happened so frequently in my life, the serenity didn't last; in fact, it crashed on another fateful day, in a most unlikely location, the beach at Santa Monica.

Mother Glover and I arrived early that Wednesday morning, early enough to enjoy the transition from a cool, overcast morning, to a sun drenched summer day. After walking the peer and chatting a bit with a fisherman who proudly displayed his catch to us, I bought him and Mother Glover some coffee and a cup of hot chocolate for me. We sipped the chill quenching liquids as the sun struggled to burn through the coastal clouds.

Walking off the peer, we turned north toward Malibu, to our favorite spot about 400 meters up the coast not far from a lifeguard tower. Except on weekends, this part of Santa Monica Beach provided the tranquility that only a deserted beach early in the morning can. On this morning, low tide resulted in a wide shore with hundreds of shellfish trying to survive until the next incoming tide rescued them. As we stroll among the crustaceans, Mother Glover commented, "All these little creatures certainly have a tenacious appetite for life. I wonder what their life expectancy is."

"I don't have any idea, Mother."

After walking for fifteen minutes we spread a large blanket on the still cool sand, covered ourselves with another, intending to doze while the sound of lapping surf and the smell of salt water sedated us. Over the past four months we had repeated this ritual several times, always finding it salubrious both physically and mentally.

After about five minutes of sublime peacefulness, Mother Glover turned to face me and said, "Theo, I have a terrible headache." I put my hand on the back of her neck and started gently massaging. "Ah, thank you; that feels better." Then, her entire body jerked and she became silent. I tried talking with her, "What's wrong, Mother? What's wrong?" But totally unconscious, she couldn't answer.

I saw a lifeguard opening his station nearby, and I ran to him, shouting, "We need an ambulance; my mother is unconscious." He immediately picked up a red phone and within two or three minutes a beach ambulance crew loaded Mother Glover and me and whisked us to Santa Monica Hospital's Emergency Entrance. Immediately, two Emergency Room nurses rushed her into an examination room.

A few minutes later Mother Glover underwent a CAT scan, followed by me signing an authorization for surgery: the CAT scan revealed a ruptured brain aneurysm, a life threatening condition that requires immediate surgery.

In the Family Waiting Room, I sat nervously for over two hours until a doctor in a surgical gown walked in and asked, "Mr. Rogers?"

I immediately stood, and he led me to small room, one sparsely furnished with two comfortable chairs, a floor lamp, and a small table. The doctor spoke, "I am very sorry, but your mother didn't recover; she has expired."

"No! No! It can't be; she was so happy this morning. No! No!"

Three days later, Uncle Ned and I, along with Mother Glover's close friends, sat together on the front row of Holy Angeles Church and grieved. Previously, I suffered losses that devastated me, but only the catastrophic deaths of my original family members, Mother, Father, and my little sister Rachel, impacted me the way Mother Glover's passing did.

That night, I didn't sleep; I lay on my back staring at the dark ceiling thinking: *my curse is back. People I love die when they should not; I am cursed, and I curse those I love.* Those words of Jorge Gonzales, fifteen years earlier in Valle Hermosa, echoed in my brain, *"My mother says you bring people bad luck: Rico died when he was with you and so did your family."*

Now my second mother—one I loved dearly and depended on for emotional stability and unconditional love—was gone. I repeatedly asked myself, *What did I do to cause all of those deaths?*

The night of Mother Glover's funeral, those words echoed off the walls of our house because I repeatedly shrieked, *"What did I do? What did I do? Why! Why!"*

23

Mexican Citizenship

One week after Mother Glover's funeral, Mr. Reynolds, an attorney, called to tell me he needed to have a meeting with me and Uncle Ned to review Mother Glover's will. Not really being familiar with wills, I went to the San Bernardino Public Library and educated myself. When we met that Wednesday, I didn't expect, nor did I want any of my mother's assets; nevertheless, much to my surprise, Mother Glover's desires, as stipulated in her will, were: her mortgage free house and $50,000 in cash from her $250,000 insurance policy became Uncle Ned's; she left me the remainder, $200,000 in cash.

The next week, my continuing remorse over the loss of Mother Glover—exacerbated by me gaining monetarily from her death—left me in complete anguish. At that time, absolutely no joy came with accepting the Prudential Insurance Company's check. Nevertheless, several months later, that money did make my life more comfortable.

Uncle Ned asked me to stay in the Glover house until he decided what to do with it; he wasn't anxious to sell or rent it out. He and his wife were contented in their home, a place they had lived in for twenty-five years. Consequently, I lived as a recluse for several months reading everything from Freud to Einstein, also a particularly interesting book by Edgar Snow, *The Long March,* which gave me some understanding of the Chinese Communist and Mao Tse Tung.

I started running a lot—eventually, up to eighty miles each week—to fight my depression and to shed the extra pounds I had put on in the past six months. Still, I just could not shake the guilt I felt over Mother Glover dying—not a modicum.

During that period, however, the pain from my shoulder wounds subsided significantly; now it didn't seem appropriate that I should be receiving seventy-five percent disability, yet, when I visited the Navy Hospital in San Diego and asked to be taken off the debility list, an orthopedic surgeon, followed by a disability evaluation counselor, told me my disability could not be totally removed. It could, on the other hand, be reduced to fifty percent, with the proviso that in two years I would be reevaluated.

While driving back to San Bernardino, I passed Camp Pendleton where I completed Combat Infantry Training in 1950 before going to Korea. An inclination to drive in and look around came to me, closely followed by the emotion: *I no longer belong on a Marine base; I no longer belong anywhere.*

Struck by a bolt of self-pity, I pulled off the road, parked and wept uncontrollably. After a few minutes the wise words of First Sergeant Merrill H. Pyetzki, a highly decorated Marine, came to me.

In 1950, during one of my periods of extreme sea sickness—I had been lying in my bunk in the bowels of the USS William Wiegel for several hours—Sergeant Pyetzki and an officer came through our compartment on an inspection tour. When they got to where I suffered, I didn't get on my feet and stand at attention as military protocol dictates when an officer enters an enlisted man's area. Sergeant Pyetzki immediately confronted me, "What is wrong with you Private?"

"I am seasick, First Sergeant," I whined in a voice he interpreted as intended to evoke compassion.

Sergeant Pyetzki callously and loudly chided me, "Listen to me, Private! If you are looking for sympathy, look in the dictionary between shit and syphilis. There are hundreds of Marines on this ship who are seasick. You get your ass out of that bunk, go topside and do 100 pushups and 150 set-ups. Then if you don't feel better, jump overboard so I don't have to deal with your sorry ass."

With that recollection, I immediately quit sniveling and started thinking: I had to make some radical changes in my life. I started going through a mental list of possibilities and every contingency included me going to a college or university. My financial situation would be infinitely better than most college freshmen; I had money in the bank and a monthly income, giving me the freedom to attend any institution of higher learning that would accept me.

The next day, I started a pragmatic search for a school. Following a few weeks of submitting applications, I was surprised that all the schools that garnered my interest: USC, UCLA, University California at Berkeley, Stanford, and Montana State University (MSU), in Bozeman, Montana, all accepted me. I included MSU on my short-list because of a brief rest stop my family made in Bozeman when I was seven-years-old, and we were on our way to Flathead Lake.

On that day our family, while we were lying on the grass resting under some massive elm trees on the edge of the MSU campus, our well-traveled truck a few yards away, was approached by a campus policeman.

"Hello, Folks. Are you visiting someone here at MSU?"

"No," mother replied. "We are just getting some rest before we drive up north to Flathead Lake. We are going there so my husband can work picking cherries."

"Great!" the policeman said, "Those Flathead cherries are the best in the world. Bring me some will you?" He laughed, and when he saw a concerned look on Mother's face. "Just joking."

"I am sorry, but we won't be coming back through Bozeman," replied Mother.

The officer laughed again before adding, "Well, then just eat a lot of those cherries for me, ok?"

Then we all laughed, and rather than extricating us from the MSU campus, the officer told us where we could get some water and use a bathroom. The congeniality of that man stuck in my young mind, and I took it as a reflection of all associated with that university.

Another major factor in my decision, the desire to get away from California and the focus I still occasionally received as a Medal of Honor recipient. Also, maybe a complete change in environment would shake me out of my depression. So, Montana State University became my choice for matriculation.

Before going to Bozeman, I decided to reconnect with my Ruiz roots in Valle Hermosa, Mexico. I had not been there since I last visited for five days when I was a senior in high school. My Ruiz grandparents would now be in their eighties and probably didn't have many years remaining. In addition, I had an emotional task to fulfill in Valle Hermosa: I would go to the exact spot on the Matamoras River where my childhood friend, Rico, died—the single tragedy, that foreshadowed my paranoia—and ask for his forgiveness.

Accordingly, I turned the Glover house over to Uncle Ned—he had decided to sell it—loaded my new Buick with my few important possessions and headed for Bozeman, Montana, via Valle Hermosa, Mexico, a journey of almost 3,600 miles.

When I arrived in Valle Hermosa, bad news awaited me: both of my Ruiz grandparents passed away during my first year in the Marine Corps, Grandmother Ruiz at eighty-five and Grandpa at eighty-seven. I don't know why I wasn't notified. None of my extended family members offered an explanation. In all likelihood, they just had no idea of how to contact someone in the U.S. Marine Corps.

The morning after arriving in Valle Hermosa, I walked to the Matamoros River alone. Finding the exact spot where Rico fell into the raging river didn't present a problem; that location, burned into my brain, pulled my feet to it like a magnet.

As I stood looking at that mostly dry river bed in the middle of August, I could hear Rico in my reoccurring dream screaming,

"¡Ayúdame! ¡Theo! "¡Ayúdame! ¡Theo!" ("Help me, Theo! Help me, Theo!") Although he hadn't said those words in real life, they were indelibly printed in my mind. I closed my eyes, stood in my best military posture, cupped my hands, and screamed down the river in the direction Rico had disappeared:

"¡Lo siento, Rico! ¡Lo siento, Rico! ¡Perdóname, porfavor! ¡Rico! "¡Perdóname, porfavor! ¡Rico! "¡Perdóname, porfavor! ¡Rico! ("I'm sorry, Rico! I'm sorry, Rico! Please, forgive me, Rico! Please, forgive me, Rico! Please, forgive me, Rico!"

I stood motionless and silent for several minutes, and then I walked away. Had Rico's ghost been exorcised? No! He still visits me, just not so often as he once did.

To my joy, my extended family and former elementary school classmates seemed genuinely happy to see me. News about my Medal of Honor and my Valle Hermosa connection preceded me; Mexicans knew about it the day of the Washington ceremony. The press release the Marine Corps distributed to all news organizations, a release which mentioned my early childhood in Mexico, became a feature article in many of Mexico's newspapers.

Uncle Ricardo Ruiz, my father's youngest brother, now forty-seven, spent several hours with me; I intensely enjoyed our time together. In one of our discussions he mentioned that the Mexican government recently instituted a policy that allowed foreigners— with at least one Mexico-born-parent—to become Mexican citizens themselves, allowing dual citizenship. The process only required one document: a birth certificate that showed your mother or father as a Mexican citizen; mine did.

I told Uncle Ricardo that I didn't think I would ever have use for such dual citizenship. From the look on his face, he obviously took my decline as a rejection of my Valle Hermosa and Mexican heritage. I felt badly, so I told him, "OK, Uncle Ricardo, if you will go with me to the office that processes those applications, I will apply."

An hour later Uncle Ricardo and I, along with three of my cousins, arrived at the Mexican Department of Naturalization in Matamoros. As soon as we walked in the main office, Uncle

Ricardo, speaking in Spanish of course, told the receptionist, "This is my nephew Theodore Ruiz Rogers. You have read about him in the newspapers. He is the Mexican that received America's Medal of Honor from El Presidente Truman."

Within five minutes, all the executives in that government office were crowded around me; five minutes later the Mayor of Matamoros and the Chief of Police arrived, and they all wanted a picture taken with me.

While the officials summoned their official photographer, Uncle Ricardo led me to a corner and asked:

"Theodore, do you have your Marine uniform and Medal of Honor in your car?"

They were in the trunk of my car, so I retrieved them. Ten minutes later, adorned in wrinkled Marine Corps dress blues, the Medal of Honor around my neck, I faced an unending line of Mexicans—government officials in front—for two hours of posing with various people for pictures and signing autographs. At one point, the photographer ran out of film and sent for more. In the chaos of all this activity, I didn't notice that a mariachi band had assembled and several street vendors had arrived.

On a stage in the heart of Heroica Matamros, the Governor of the State of Tamaulipas, after making a fifteen minute speech in which he told me how proud the people of Mexico were of me, presented me with a Mexican passport and a certificate of citizenship. I gave a short thank you speech, in Spanish, and the assembly roared. I never dreamed I would use that passport one day; how wrong that assumption turned out to be.

That night I went to bed exhausted but happy. I had sacrificed a little privacy so my Mexican family could share my award. The next morning I drove out of Valle Hermosa chaperoned by two Tamaulipas State police cars with lights flashing; they escorted me to the American border. Now the long leg of my trip began, to Bozeman, Montana, 2,025 miles away.

24

Education, Good Luck, and Tragedy

When I started considering the possibility of living in Bozeman, Montana, its weather history almost caused me to reject a fantastically beautiful and tranquil place. Weather records—particularly the lows—told me Bozeman often gets very cold in the winter and sometimes stays that way for several consecutive days. As I contemplated that burden, I came to the realization that I would not be exposed to the elements like I had been in the hills surrounding Chosen Reservoir in North Korea.

Three years later, after I had enjoyed a few seasons of what Bozeman offered, I came to the calculated conclusion it had to be one of the best places in the world to live. The many outdoor activities, and the Bozeman lifestyle in general, suited me perfectly: climbing through high mountain meadows filled with wild flowers, rafting on fast flowing, clean rivers, fly fishing for colorful trout in pristine streams, skiing on over 300 inches of snow, all activities I had never participated in during my years in Mexico and California, rescued me from my chronic mental malaise.

Even though the pursuit of academic goals garnered my attention, my mental health held a higher priority that first year at MSU. I wanted to do things I enjoyed, and I wanted to be around people I liked, and I wanted to sleep well at night without being haunted by ghosts.

During my first academic counseling session, when a new student is asked to select a major and schedule classes, as well as complete forms calling for family information and military experience, my counselor, Mrs. Shannon Burlingame, questioned my veracity, but she never openly did so. After declaring I wanted to study for two majors—English and Mathematics—she informed me that the English curriculum required a foreign language minor, something that challenged most students, and the Mathematics curriculum was even more difficult. She noted from my high school transcript I had never studied a foreign language, and suggested I take an introductory, non-credit language course my freshman year. Disingenuously—since I was already totally fluent in Spanish—I told Mrs. Burlingame I wanted to take Spanish for credit starting my first semester.

Pointing to the class registration sheet I had filled out, she asked, "Are you sure you can handle for-credit Spanish along with the English, Calculus, and the Physics classes you also want to take. Twenty-one credit hours are usually way too many for a first semester freshman."

If she had looked at my middle name, Ruiz, she might have surmised I had a *background* in Spanish.

"Yes, Mam; I definitely want to do that; I have some Spanish experience—*what a fudge*—and I will study hard."

The most uncomfortable part of that interview came when Mrs. Burlingame asked questions about my family and military experience. "Hmm, let's see, you indicate here you are a veteran, but you are only nineteen. Is that correct?"

"Yes, Mam; I spent little more than two years in the Marine Corps."

"I thought Marine enlistments required a four year commitment."

"They do Mam, but I was discharged because of wounds I received in Korea; I could no longer use my left arm normally."

"Oh, I am sorry to hear that, Theodore. What about your home address; you don't list one or name your closest family member."

"Mam, my home address is the dormitory I am living in. All of my immediate family members are dead, and I only have some extended family members alive, and they have absolutely no responsibility for me. You are looking at my family."

"How are you going to pay your out-of-state tuition, Theodore? Your GI Bill stipend will cover some, but not all of it."

I didn't know anything about a GI Bill, but I told her, "I will pay cash; I have the money in my bank account."

Like me, Mrs. Burlingame seemed uncomfortable with my interview. However, she finally approved my class schedule before telling me, "Next, you need to stop at the Veteran's Affairs Office (VAO). It is on the second floor of the Student Union Building."

At the VAO I received good news: As a Korean War veteran, I would receive $475 each month, for forty-eight months, to assist me with my housing, food, and tuition. If I didn't graduate by the end of that period, I could request an extension of the benefits.

As I walked away from the VAO, it struck me just how financially solvent I was for a nineteen year old freshman. I had $180,000 in my bank account, received a Medal of Honor recipient's monthly stipend of $175 each month and a military disability check for $575 each month, and now the VAO was going to give me an additional $475—all to take care of one enthusiastic, but mentally fragile, nineteen year old university freshman.

Obviously, I could afford to rent an apartment, but I opted for a double occupancy room in a dormitory so I would meet people and maybe make some friends. That turned out to be an excellent decision, but ultimately it led to heartbreak.

My roommate, Gilroy Turner, a handsome, confident, eighteen-year-old, bona fide cowboy, from the metropolis of Roundup, Montana—population 475—became my best friend. Gilroy's family had a 2,000 acre ranch ten miles from Roundup where they primarily raised cattle and grew wheat.

Gilroy was a godsend for me, making me laugh, challenging me physically with his distance running ability, introducing me to pretty girls—some he knew, some he had never seen before—and teaching me how to fly fish, ski, and hunt both deer and elk.

In a high meadow in the Bridger Mountains, Gilroy was astounded when, from 800 yards, I dropped the first deer I ever shot at. Earlier that day we spotted four deer, but every time we tried to get close enough to have a reasonable shot they bounded away. Finally, I told Gilroy, "I am tired of chasing those damn deer; I'm going to take a shot."

When the eight point buck fell dead, Gilroy said, "Ga-aud damn, Theo, that is the longest shot I have ever seen." I didn't bother to tell him I had some training and practice with long range marksmanship.

Sunday evenings were *Eat Your Own Game*—animals you had killed—in the dormitory dining room. Whatever you might have bagged on Saturday, you could turn over to the cooks, and they would butcher and cook it for everyone living in the dormitory to enjoy; a traditional, great-eating social event at MSU dormitories.

The names of the successful hunters were displayed on a large white-board; consequently, since Gilroy and I bagged something every Saturday, we received a lot of admiring attention, and we loved it, at least until Jane Hewitson came into the picture.

On a Sunday evening, Jane, a beautiful girl with long auburn hair and probing brown eyes, sat down at the table where Gilroy and I were basking in the acclaim our dorm mates were showering on us. Jane, however, wasn't impressed, at least not in a positive way. She appeared out of nowhere, and sat down sideways in the cafeteria chair next to me. Her sitting posture suggested she would dash away in an instant.

"I hope you guys are proud of yourselves. Killing innocent animals takes a lot of gall and not much courage. I hope you choke on eating them." Then she immediately got up and walked away in a near sprint, leaving us no time to mount a defense or debate the issue.

Stunned, I asked Gilroy, "Who's that?"

"Oh, that's Jane Hewitson; she's some vegetarian nut and the only Buddhist I know of on the campus. The only thing she would kill is a mosquito, and maybe not even that; don't pay any attention to her." But I did.

Two days later, I saw Jane sitting alone in a booth at the Student Center. I watched her from a distance and noticed her frowning over an Algebra book, scribbling numbers furiously, referring back to her book, aggressively scratching out her calculations and starting again. Hoping she wouldn't recognize me from the wild animal feast, I walked up and said, "Hello, Jane, I am Theo Rogers. May I sit down?"

Obviously recognizing me from the previous Sunday, she turned her magnetic brown eyes toward me and in a cold tone said, "I know who you are; I am very busy. What do you want?"

"I don't want anything. Maybe I can help you with your Algebra."

Jane shook her head and started to say "No", but stopped herself and asked, "Do you know anything about quadratic equations?"

"Yes, I think I can help you if you let me sit down."

"OK, please do."

My mother had introduced me to Algebra when I was six, and I could solve quadratic equations by the age ten. For me, quadratic equations had been a rather benign step in my mathematics education.

After an hour, Jane was solving the most difficult quadratic equations in her book, including those that were part of her assignment for her next Algebra class. When certain she understood the math, I got up to leave, primarily as a strategic social move, hoping she would ask me to stay, maybe show the slightest hint of ardor, but she didn't. She simply said, "Thank you, Theo," and not in a beholden manner.

Over the next month, from a distance, I frequently watched Jane when she came to the Student Union, always at 9:00 each morning.

A couple of times, when I it looked like math might be bothering her, I offered my help and she accepted; however, no sparks flew, and it looked like a dead end in the romance game. Then one day one of those life altering events took place.

As I crossed West College Avenue, going from my dormitory to English class, I heard the screech of car brakes and the yelp of a dog; it had just been hit. The car sped off, and the dog, a large mixed breed, lay in the street. Immediately, I put down my book bag and carried the dog out of the traffic. The unconscious animal had blood coming from its mouth, suggesting a bad prognosis.

The MSU School of Veterinary Medicine, only a block away, seemed like the logical place to take the dog, and that is where I headed on the run. Just as I reached the main entrance, Jane exited. Immediately she became very attentive toward the injured canine, and helped me get it into the Emergency Care for Animals Clinic. Miraculously, after nearly two weeks of treatment, the dog recovered and was returned to its owner.

Helping that dog became the seed that germinated into a romance. Jane, a veterinary medicine major, had a soft spot in her heart for all animals and, thankfully, for anyone who helped them. We started visiting each morning at the Student Union, talking about animals, sometimes Algebra, and other things that had nothing to do with Algebra or animals. In addition, soon we were hiking mountain trails and skiing together.

Jane's father, a veterinarian himself, and an avid fly fisherman made the trip from Great Falls to Bozeman every other weekend to spend time with his daughter. I started fly fishing with the two of them regularly. Gilroy had introduced me to the sport earlier, but Dr. Hewitson helped bring my skills with the rod, line, and lure to a much higher level.

The three of us, and sometimes Gilroy came along, explored and fished all of the trout streams between Twin Bridges and Livingston that spring, always catching and releasing because I and

Jane's father knew that if we dressed and ate one of those fish, she would go berserk.

On one fishing trip, when Jane was fishing in shorts, I noticed her skin had a subtle tannish tint to it. I commented, "Wow, you have a perfect tan or did you paint that on?"

Laughing, "No, that is my Burmese heritage showing. My mother is from Burma, and as the little mentioned family story goes, her great-grandmother became the consort of a Norwegian ship captain for a short time. Mother's genes allow me to have a hint of her Burmese skin. From my father—and my great-great- grandmother's lover—I get my brown hair and brown eyes, but not so brown as Mother's."

In an after-fishing dinner at John Bozeman's Bistro, the conversation between the three of us turned to speculating what Jane and I would do after we graduated:

"Jane tells me you are an outstanding student. What do you plan to do after you graduate, Theo?"

"Right now, I plan to become an English and Mathematics teacher, but that could change. I have two more years to think about it."

Dr. Hewitson, a World War II paratrooper who served with the 11th Airborne Division in Europe, participated in two combat jumps, and suffered a nasty chest wound that ended his Army service responded, "Have you ever thought about going into the military?"

Jane, interrupting, speaking with an element of pride in her voice, "He's already done that, Daddy. He's a former Marine."

I remained silent; I had no desire to talk about my military service. Nevertheless, Jane's father became more inquisitive. "How many years were you in the Marine Corps, Theo?"

"A little over two, Sir."

"How did that happen? I thought the Marines required a four year enlistment."

Since I didn't want to get into a discussion about the Marine Corps and my time in Korea, particularly those agonizing days in

North Korea, I answered, "I had some physical problems, so they discharged me early."

Sensing that the military conversation caused tension at the table, Dr. Hewitson quickly changed the subject. "Do you plan to ski more this winter? You probably don't know it, but you have a reputation for being an extraordinary skier for someone with little experience."

"I do enjoy skiing very much, but you know Jane sometimes exaggerates."

Jane punched me in the ribs, "I do not! You know you are good."

"I am comfortable on skis until I get into deep powder, then I tense up and everything goes wrong. I end up with my parka, and my eyes and ears, full of snow."

Jane instructed, "Of course, the key to skiing in really deep powder is sitting back. At first, that is hard to do, since on packed snow you are always pushing forward with your knees."

"I know, Jane. You have told me that many times, but saying it and doing it are two different things."

Over two years later, that conversation would come back to haunt me and send me into another mental tailspin.

Not too long after that discussion, on a weekend when Jane went home and I stayed at MSU, I received a call from Jane's father. Immediately concerned that some misfortune had happened to Jane, I asked, "Is Jane OK?"

Dr. Hewitson laughed and said, "Yes, of course! At the moment she and her mother are out riding horses."

"That's good."

"Theo, I am calling about you."

I thought, *Oh, Oh, he does not want me to see her anymore.*

"As a father with a daughter that is the apple of his eye, I was somewhat concerned when you didn't want to talk about your military service when we were together a couple of weeks ago. I shamefully admit I thought you might be trying to keep a negative military record from me; maybe you had been kicked out of the Marines with a bad conduct discharge, or worse.

"Anyway, since I have a good friend working at a high level in the Defense Department, I asked him to do some snooping for me. I asked Jane if your real name was *Theo Rogers*; she told me it was *Theodore Ruiz Rogers*. As it turned out, there are two other men named *Theodore Rogers* that have been discharged from the military in the last four years, but only one, *Theodore Ruiz Rogers,* spent time in the Marine Corps. Is that you?"

In stunned silence, I tried to think what I should say. Should I lie and say "*No*," or tell the truth and beg for him to keep my military record secret. I chose the latter.

"Yes, Doctor Hewitson, I am Theodore Ruiz Rogers."

"Theo, I remember well when President Truman presented you with the Medal of Honor, and I actually saw a picture of that ceremony on the front page of the Billings Gazette and on the cover of Life Magazine, but I simply didn't recognize you."

"Well, that blue uniform hid a lot of things that day, my torn up body and a jumbled mind."

"I understand. Are you completely recovered from your wounds now?"

"I think so. I have to visit the Navy Hospital in Seattle at the end of this quarter to see if they will take me off medical disability."

"Theo, I can understand why you want to keep your military experiences secret at MSU, particularly you're Medal of Honor, but don't you think you should tell Jane?"

"I've thought a lot about that. I try very hard to be truthful with her, but soon after I came back from Korea, I met a girl I really liked. When her parents found out I had killed more than forty North Korean and Chinese soldiers, they didn't want their daughter spending time alone with someone who, in their words, 'was a killer'. Since Jane loves animals so much, I'm sure she feels the same about humans."

"That's possible; Theo, but I think she will understand you were simply doing your duty in Korea. She really admires and cares for you; and I will guarantee you, her mother and I are not concerned about her safety when she is with you."

"If I tell her, do you think she can keep from talking about it with her friends? I don't want to have to deal with the attention I might get at school if that information became public."

"What do you think, Theo? In some ways you know my daughter better than I do, but it is up to you. Let me add though: Theo, I am very proud of your service, and the fact that you received the Medal of Honor when you were only eighteen is incredible. I admire you very much, my boy, and I am proud that my daughter is your special friend."

Four days later, after turning over in my mind several methods of telling Jane about my military service, we went for a walk up Sourdough Trail. During that two hour stroll, I told Jane about my military history and the entire history of my family. When I told her about the death of my mother, father, and little sister, she cried and I cried with her.

After I finished telling her about Chosen Reservoir, and the death of Mother Glover, we set in silence for several minutes. Then, she took both of my hands in hers, kissed them and said, "I love you, Theo."

Those words went through me like a bolt of lightning, and I barely managed, "I love you too, Jane," before I collapsed in her arms.

A month later, I went to the Navy Hospital in Seattle for a disability evaluation. The orthopedic surgeon said my case, now borderline from a medical point of view, would be decided by a medical board, but since I requested removal from the disability list, something that had never happened in his experience, possibly I would be removed. Six weeks later, I received a document which indicated, "REMOVED FROM MEDICAL DISABILITY AT THE PATIENT'S REQUEST." There was a government seal on the document and the signature of Vice Admiral James J. Stokes, Director of Medical Services.

When I finished reading that certificate, a surge of relief went through me; now my Marine Corps service truly became a memory.

The next two years went by too quickly; it became the most enjoyable time of my life, studying, recreating, and loving Jane more with each passing day. However, during the spring quarter of my senior year, also Jane's senior year, one in which we started talking about marriage, two events—one positive and one tragically negative—distorted my life again.

On a Sunday evening, after a day of skiing at Big Sky near Yellowstone National Park, a car accident clogged the Gallatin Canyon Road. While my Buick ate up gas, Jane, Gilroy, Sharon—Gilroy's girlfriend—and I, spent more than two hours with the engine running to keep warm, telling jokes, and singing stupid songs like *Ninety-nine bottles of beer on the wall, ninety-nine-bottles of beer...* When we finally got out of the traffic jam my car's *Low on Fuel* warning light came on, and we were still fifty miles from Bozeman. I thought I might be able to make it to the campus, but just when we reached Four Corners, still six miles from home, the engine started sputtering; we had run out of gas.

The four of us pushed the car into a small, one pump station as a lady was locking the door; it was a few minutes after closing time, 7:00 p.m. With a smile on her face, she agreed to open the door and turn the pump on. While doing so, she commented, "I won't be able to give you change. My husband took the money sack home."

After filling my Buick with nine dollars worth of gas, and with Jane, Gilroy, and Sharon still in the car, I handed the lady a ten dollar bill. She immediately said, "I'm sorry, but as I told you, I don't have any change."

"What do you have for one dollar?"

"Not much. Maybe some candy, chips, or a lottery ticket."

I had never purchased a lottery ticket before; I didn't even know how to do so. "OK, I'll buy the lottery ticket, but I don't know how to play; will you please put in some numbers for me?"

As I watched, she punched some keys on a machine that looked like a large calculator and said; "This thing will do it for us." Out came a small piece of paper that I immediately stuck into one of the deeper recesses of my wallet.

When passing that same station a few days later, on a Wednesday afternoon after ice fishing with Jane, she noticed a sign nailed to a telephone pole. "If you have lottery ticket numbers 5-24-37-39-44-13, please come in."

Jane asked, "What are the numbers on the ticket you bought here, Theo? Where is it?"

"I don't know, maybe in my wallet, but I don't care. I am not a lucky guy."

"Get the ticket out, Theo. You've got to check."

I handed Jane my wallet and said, "Here, you find it."

We had driven about three miles toward Bozeman before she found the ticket. "Theo, I think you have some of the numbers. I know you have the last one, 13. Go back."

"Are you serious? I'm hungry. It is just a waste of time and gas for us to go back to that station."

"If you don't go back Theodore Ruiz Rogers, I will never speak to you again."

Jane only used my full name when she was impatient or angry with me, a rarity. When we returned to the station, I stopped in front of the sign. Jane read, "5, 24, 37, 39, 44, 13," then screamed, "You won, Theo! You won! Really, Theo, you won!"

When we walked into the station, the lady who sold me the ticket looked at me with excitement in her eyes when she saw I had a ticket in my hand. I handed the ticket to her and asked, "Is this worth anything?"

After looking at the ticket, she grabbed me, and kissed my cheek, "Yes! Yes! You are a rich man now," she screamed. "You have won 250 million dollars, and our station two million. Don't lose that ticket. Here! Here!" Handing me a pen she added, "Sign and date the back of it right now, and make darn sure you don't lose it."

That lady, Cecelia Cushing, took my name, phone number and dormitory address before we left. Still hungry, I insisted we go to John Bozeman's Bistro for a celebration dinner. With excitement starting to build but still skeptical, I told Jane, "This might just be a sick joke. Let's give it some time."

"I know it is true, Theo; I know it! I feel it!

Jane demonstrated her excitement by eating faster than usual, talking faster than usual, and overly anxious to get back to my dorm. When we arrived, we decided that Jane would come to my room and visit until the lottery question got totally resolved.

As soon as we walked into the lobby, the floor monitor on duty jumped from behind the counter, "Theo, a lot of people have been looking for you, and I have a telegram for you." She handed me the Western Union envelope, and I sat down on an overstuffed couch in the lobby with Jane by my side.

TO: MR. THEODORE R. ROGERS

FROM: NORTHER HEMISPHERE INTERNATIONAL LOTTERY DISBURSEMENTS OFFICE—NEW YORK—MICHAEL M. JEFFERS, DIRECTOR.

CONGRATULATIONS MR. ROGERS. IT HAS BEEN REPORTED THAT YOU HOLD THE WINNING TICKET FROM THE DRAWING OF APRIL 7. I RECOMMEND THAT YOU IMMEDIATELY SECURE YOUR WINNING TICKET IN A BANK SAFETY DEPOSIT BOX OR OTHER SECURE FACILITY. YOU SHOULD SIGN AND DATE THE BACK OF IT IMMEDIATELY. YOU WILL BE REQUIRED TO GIVE THAT TICKET TO OUR AGENT BEFORE YOU ARE PRESENTED WITH THE CASHIER'S CHECK IN THE AMOUNT OF YOUR WINNINGS, MINUS FEDERAL TAXES AND ADJUSTMENTS. PLEASE CALL MY OFFICE TOMORROW, APRIL 26, SO WE CAN ASCERTAIN YOUR DEDUCTIONS AND DISBURSEMENT DESIRES. AGAIN, CONGRATULATIONS,

MICHAEL M. JEFFERS, DIRECTOR

I handed the telegram to Jane, but she already knew the contents; she had been reading over my shoulder.

When I got to my room two men and a lady were standing in the hallway. Immediately, they started bombarding me with questions as I tried to unlock my door.

"Mr. Rogers, did you really win the lottery?"

"What are you going to do with all of that money?"

"When will you get it?'

"Do you have a bank account?"

"Theodore, did you really win the Northern Hemisphere Lottery?"

Since they were all talking at the same time, I only said "I don't know, maybe."

Jane and I forced our way into my room and locked the door, but immediately people started knocking, and they would not top. Finally, Jane made a sign that she taped to the door. "Theo is not answering any questions tonight. He will have something to say tomorrow." But people—mostly students—were still gathered in the hallway, some started chanting: "Theo, Theo, Theo."

Dumbfounded by the sudden chaos, I told Jane, "I don't know what to do. How long will this go on?"

"Why don't we call my father? He has a cool head in times of stress. He will know what to do."

It was good to hear her father's usually calm voice, but it wasn't calm now; I could tell he was already excited. "Is what Jane just told me true, or is this a late April fool's joke?

"I'm not positive, Mister Hewitson, but it is beginning look like it's the real thing. The lady at the gas station where I bought the ticket was very convincing when I showed it to her, and I have a telegram from a lottery executive that seems to be confirmation. To be honest though, I am still not 100% convinced, maybe 90%. What should I do? Everyone is asking me questions. There is a group of people, some might be from the Bozeman newspaper and radio station, but there are a lot of students out there too, banging on my door and shouting. Jane is with me, and I don't feel we are safe in my own room. I thought about going to a hotel, but it might be even worse there."

"Well, the first thing you need to do is call Campus Security and the Bozeman Police Department, and let them know about your problem. No! Don't you call; I will call them now. Let me talk to Jane for a minute."

Dr. Hewitson dictated to Jane for a couple of minutes, and that resulted in the following notice being taped to my door, and it worked like a charm.

If the preliminary report that Theo Rogers has won the lottery is confirmed, he will hold a news conference on Friday, time and place to be determined. Please respect Theo's right to privacy. Jane Hewitson, Information Agent.

Within fifteen minutes a campus policeman and two Bozeman policemen were in my room.

"Congratulation," said the police sergeant. "We will get everyone off your back." Campus Security agreed to keep a guard at my door until everything quitted down. He only needed stay about an hour.

Jane stayed with me until midnight, and she read the notice over the phone several times before she left. Then I took the phone off the hook.

As it turned out I did win the Northern Hemisphere Lottery with a value of 250 million dollars. However, when I opted for an immediate cash payment, coupled with federal taxes, I received a cashier's check for 175 million 250 thousand. I immediately deposited the money into two joint accounts at the Bozeman Bank of the Rockies, under the names of Theodore Ruiz Rogers and Jane Hewitson, 160 million into a jumbo money market certificate account, and fifteen million plus into a joint checking account. Jane protested vigorously, but I harangued her until she signed the signature cards.

That of course wasn't the end of my problems connected with having that amount of money dumped on me. Three hours after the news conference at 1:00 pm on Friday, one in which a Northern Hemisphere International Lottery's agent presented me with the cashier's check, the Bozeman Daily Journal's headlines read: "MSU STUDENT, THEO ROGERS WINS N.H. LOTTERY—250 MILLION."

The accompanying article went on to explain that I had opted for an immediate payment, reducing my actual winnings to 175 million.

That same article, and others similar, hit newspapers, radio and TV shows on Sunday. Then the crusher came the next

Wednesday, when both the New York Times and Washington Herald announced: MEDAL OF HONOR WINNER RECEIVES HIS DUE: MEGA DOLLARS. Articles accompanying those headlines focused on the details of my Medal of Honor award by President Truman and a recount of the action that took place at Chosen Reservoir.

My tranquil life as a Montana State University student was over, and my sudden notoriety had a negative effect on my studies; it cluttered my mind. And, I could no longer walk from my dormitory to a class without being stopped multiple times by people wanting an autograph, asking unwanted questions, or making irritating comments. One particularly aggravating comment really got under my skin, "Man, your girlfriend is lucky; she must be happy with all that money."

The following is an example of the irritating notes left under my door: "Good job in killing all those Gooks; you should have shot a few thousand more."

I thought about getting off the MSU campus. Obviously, I could buy a nice home quickly and move out of the dormitory; that's what everyone expected me to do. But Jane and I only had a few weeks until graduation, and we hadn't really decided exactly what we wanted to do afterwards or where we wanted to live. We continued to talk about getting married. We both liked the idea, and we were constantly fighting a strong sexual attraction.

Out of respect for her father, at sixteen, Jane gave her father a pledge that on the day she married, she would still be a virgin, and we never totally crossed that *forbidden* line. Her Buddhist mother, less concerned about her daughter acting on her primal instincts, said nothing on the subject.

Early on the first Sunday in May, only one month before our graduation, we drove to the end of Sypes Canyon Road and hiked up a trail into a high mountain meadow, one filled with purple and yellow wild flowers. Shortly after entering the meadow, Jane dropped to one knee, put a finger to her lips, and motioned for me to also go down. Then she pointed to the far end of the lea where a herd of mule deer were standing still, ears strait up, looking at us, but they didn't flee. We sat behind a fallen log, maybe 150 yards away, and watched them in wonder through binoculars I recently purchased for animal watching.

As the deer resumed their grazing, we watched a enormous, stately buck—his antlers in the fourteen point range—patrol his harem of five does, three fawns, and a yearling; one of the does, a real beauty, and also quite large, had an unusual blond streak running the length of her throat.

We sat motionless in awe. When one of the fawns strayed; the buck quickly blocked its way and nudged it back toward its mother, the large, beautiful doe. In a hushed voice, Jane started giving me a lesson on mule deer:

"Their scientific name is Odocoileus genus. That buck will probably weigh over 300 pounds by fall. With his size and antler rack, he will jealously protect his harem. The does often mate with two or more bucks, giving them a better chance of impregnation, but I don't think these will; I don't think this buck is going to share them. Their gestation period is approximately 195 days. If the fawns survive their first spring and summer, when wolves, coyotes, mountain lions, and even bears will be hunting them, and if some stupid man with a rifle doesn't shoot them, they will live for twelve to fifteen years. End of lesson! I will give you an oral examination tomorrow."

Then she laughed, and gave me a kiss on the cheek. When our eyes met, silent contemplation overcame me; finally I said, "I love you, Jane; will you marry me?"

Jane smiled and nodded her head, followed by a long embrace and kiss unlike any I experienced before. Afterwards, we rose to our feet, the deer bounded away, and we continued our hike up Mount Baldy.

That year the Rocky Mountains of Wyoming, Montana, and Idaho enjoyed heavy snowfall into May. All of the ski areas remained open, but since skiing at Bridger Bowl, the ski area closest to MSU, could not be considered a celebration-vacation spot for us, I decided to splurge a bit with the lottery money and make a trip to

Jackson Hole, Wyoming and the Amangani Ski Lodge, an internationally acclaimed, five-star plus resort.

I chartered a plane from Sunbird Aviation at Gallatin Field to fly Jane, Gilroy, Susan, and me to Jackson Hole, and a second plane to pick up Jane's parents in Great Falls. I booked the Governor's Suite at the Amangani with all amenities: five bedrooms, a private hot tub, kitchen with our private chief, a masseuse, a four-string quartet to serenade during two evening meals, and VIP priority ski tow tickets. I paid $68,000 for the entire package and I didn't feel even a bit guilty; this weekend, we would not only celebrate the graduation of four students who had been diligent for four years, and the winning lottery ticket, most importantly, Jane and I would announce our engagement. At this point, only she and I knew about it.

Both planes arrived in Jackson Hole early enough on Friday afternoon for us to ski for two glorious hours on slopes that were in perfect, packed-powder conditions. Afterword's, the six of us languished in the large Jacuzzi sipping French champagne—a beverage we four students had never tasted—and joked about delving into extravagance.

Gilroy quipped, "Theo, can we do this every weekend?"

"Of course not, Gilroy; only when there is snow on the ground."

The merriment continued into the candle lit dinner on an out-of-doors patio, under the stars, with the warmth of Highland propane gas heaters to keep us comfortable. At one instant I thought, *Where were those heaters when I needed them in North Korea,* but other than for that one digression, all thoughts were positive; my life seemed to be as propitious as I could dream.

After the strawberry-mascarpone trifles were served, I tapped on my empty wine glass three times with a silver spoon and stood.

"Ah, give me your attention, please. This is a very special weekend for Jane and me, and we want to thank all of you for sharing it with us."

In chorus, "Thank you Theo."

"However, unbeknownst to you, the main reason I impounded you here, is to announce...," I took Jane's hand and pulled her up to me, looked at her parents, and said, "With your permission, we are going to get married, and sooner rather than later—time and place to be announced."

Our four guests jumped to their feet and showed their approval with hugs and handshakes. All of us were tremendously happy, and, unfortunately, that was the happiest moment in a star struck marriage, one that never took place.

25

White Death

Saturday turned out to be a carbon copy of Friday, great skiing through most of the day; but late in the day high winds started blowing, and snow clouds rolled in. Heavy snow started falling just before dark and continued most of the night. After dinner, we spent the rest of the evening sitting around the massive, river-stone fireplace chatting and listening to live string music. That night— excited about the skiing prospects for the next morning—the deep powder enthusiast slept lightly; I slept well.

On Sunday morning, with twenty-four inches of fresh powder snow on the ski-runs, and with only four hours remaining before our planes were scheduled to fly us home, we rode the gondola through heavy fog to the top of the mountain. We could hear the avalanche suppression team firing their cannons into some ski slopes, dislodging snow in dangerous areas.

Just when it appeared we would not be able to ski, the sun broke through and revealed pristine snow with diamonds decorating the surface, and at the same time the cannon fire stopped. Jane and Gilroy, the powder snow aficionados, were ecstatic. They led our entourage to the top of the steepest, *Experts Only,* slope in the Jackson Hole area. A sign at the top of the slope named it *If You Have the Guts.* Minutes before, the avalanche repression team had fired into that slope.

After deciding the slope presented too much of a challenge for us, Jane's mother, father, Susan, and I decided to watch the real experts, Jane and Gilroy, ski *If You Have the Guts.* We would admire their courage and enjoy their coordinated, artistic, figure eight tracks from above.

Jane and Gilroy pushed off together, she zigzagging into a wide left turn, Gilroy zigzagging into to a wide right turn. As each got close to the trees, they simultaneously executed a turn in the opposite direction while dropping precipitously, each picking a line that would have resulted in them colliding had they not planned for Jane to pass near but above Gilroy. Their patterns were captivating and drew the attention of many spectators on the lift terminal deck.

They were two-thirds of the way down when the snow inside the top figure-eight loop—initially in slow motion—started sliding, followed by a mass of snow higher up on the mountain breaking loose and roaring down the slope. Immediately a man in an orange ski-patrolman's jacket screamed, "Avalanche! Avalanche!" Instantly he hit a large red button on an emergency warning horn, and the horn's cry echoed throughout the mountains.

Jane and Gilroy, now starting a new turn, apparently became aware of the avalanche at the same time. Both headed for the trees in straight lines, but their actions were too late, and they soon disappeared in a rumbling cloud of snow, ice, and a few uprooted trees.

Within two minutes a rescue team was descending through the trees to where Jane and Gilroy were last seen. A short time later over 100 volunteers were ascending from the bottom.

In absolute panic—and totally unmindful of the deep powder snow I dreaded—I pushed off and skied directly to where I last saw my fiancé, and when I reached that spot, I couldn't find a trace of her.

The slide had been massive, sending many tons of snow and debris down the mountain. Within ten minutes rescuers with long poles were probing the snow and two avalanche dogs were sniffing the scene. Fifteen minutes after the avalanche, one of the dogs started digging, and he was soon followed by ten or more rescuers digging frantically with snow shovels. However, it took them ten minutes to reach Gilroy—too late. Five minutes later they found Jane's body. Within a minute they were on the way to the emergency hospital at the sky area. All efforts there failed to revive them, leaving me, Susan, and Jane's parents stunned and devastated.

At the hospital, I demanded to see Jane's body even though the doctor said, "There is nothing you can do for her."

A nurse led me into a now apathetic treatment room where the Emergency Room team had worked on Jane. She was covered with a sheet, but the nurse pulled the sheet back to expose Jane's head. Her apparently sleeping face triggered me into a maniacal response.

Certain she could not truly be dead; I jerked the sheet from her body, exposing the brutal intrusions into her beautiful form. Jane's open chest gapped at me—her motionless heart startlingly visible—but I still could not believe she was dead. As the nurse tried to cover Jane with the sheet, I screamed, "Jane! Jane! Wake up! Wake up! The plane will be her soon. Wake up! Don't leave me! Jane! Don't leave me!"

I have no memory about what happened next. I woke up hours later in a hospital bed where I had been since a doctor forcibly sedated me with an injection. Jane's father sat beside my bed. Our eyes met—his red from crying, still filled with tears—but we didn't speak. Minutes later, he broke the silence in a choked voice.

"Theo, as terrible as this is, we must go on with life. We have no choice. I want us to take Jane's body and go home, and I want you to go with us."

I didn't respond immediately; finally I mustered, "OK."

After two excruciating funerals, I returned to Bozeman, followed by another week of intense mourning, a week I slept little, lying awake staring at the ceiling, walking the trails Jane and I had shared, trying to suppress the realization—*I'm cursed; people I love die because of me.*

Again, I contemplated suicide, but unlike my last such inclination, this time I took action. At a Bozeman pawn shop, I purchased a 357 Colt, magnum pistol and a box of ammunition, and from a hardware store I bought a small metal file, the kind often used to smooth the edges of sheet metal. I drove to the end of Sypes Canyon Road and hiked up the trail to the meadow where I proposed to Jane. After finding the tree trunk we had observed the deer from— just before I proposed to her—I took one round from the box of ammunition and filed a deep X pattern into the end of the bullet. After loading the gun with that one round, a round which would explode when it penetrated my brain—ending my life, my misery, my guilt— I placed the barrel of the pistol in my mouth and took up the slack on the trigger. At that instant a large doe, one with a vivid blond streak running from its throat to its stomach—a doe I had seen on the day I proposed to Jane—followed by a handsome yearling bounded directly toward me. I took the gun out of my mouth. When the deer were twenty meters away they stopped and froze, and then the yearling bounded into the trees but not the doe. She remained still for a full ten seconds, looked directly into my eyes, then jumped straight over me and into the trees.

My mind deteriorated into delusion: I surmised that the doe had to be Jane reincarnated, consistent with her Buddhist beliefs. Was she telling me goodbye? Or, was she telling me I should live? Suddenly, Jane's love for life in all living things—another aspect of the Buddhist training her mother provided—overwhelmed me. I unloaded the gun, and threw it into the trees, followed by lying in the grass and sobbing, "Jane! Jane! I love you! I love you!"

26

Escape to Hong Kong

I went through the graduation ceremony in a trance, my thoughts never straying from Jane and Gilroy. They were acknowledged during the program, and both, like me, graduated with *highest honors,* only theirs were posthumous—two chunks out of my heart.

Jane's parents invited me to live with them, but I couldn't. I left her father a check for 5 million dollars to build a *Jane R. Hewitson Veterinary Clinic.* In addition, I sent Gilroy's parents two million dollars.

The joint accounts opened in my and Jane's names now defaulted to me with a balance of approximately 169 million dollars. I had no idea what I would do with that money; my first inclination was to give it to charity. However, I restrained that inclination; telling myself, *Give it a few years before you dispose of it.* I never did.

After graduation I spent four days with Jane's parents grieving and reminiscing, but most conversations were forced; her father, like me, didn't want to communicate with anyone. Jane's mother, Bowakom, took her death much better than Jane's father or I did.

Maybe her Buddhist upbringing pulled her through the grieving; she accepted the loss of Jane with strength and grace. She told me, "Jane had good karma in her life; she will return. I know she will return! If you also lead a good life on this earth, you will be together in your next life."

I told Bowakom about the deer that stopped and looked at me in the mountain meadow. Her face lit up, "That was her; for sure! That was her! In a few years she will be another person."

We talked about my inclination to go to Asia and teach English. At that time I didn't have a particular country in mind. She told me, "Theo, I'm not sure you should go to Asia in order to run away from tragedy. Tragedy is everywhere in the world. If you insist on going though start in Hong Kong; everything in Asia filters through Hong Kong."

After withdrawing $10,000 in cash from the bank and getting $20,000 in travelers' checks, plus a cashier's check for 45 million, I rode a Trailways bus to San Francisco. With Hong Kong only an interim destination, I really didn't know where I would end up, and I was in no rush to get there. The bus ride gave me time to think.

A desultory beaten man, I walked the streets and byways of San Francisco for three days before boarding the Cristina Cruise Line's flag ship, Cristina Princes, for the twelve day voyage to Hong Kong. Jane would have loved the trip, but for me it mostly offered torture, not pleasure. I had absolutely no desire to socialize with the other passengers or make small talk at meals. After the first day, I asked for a private table in a corner of the massive dining room. The last six days of the journey, I stayed in my cabin except at night when I walked the deck and looked at the stars, looking for some celestial sign, in any configuration, that Jane was with me—I missed her so much.

When I arrived in Hong Kong, I entrenched myself in a clean, comfortable, but certainly not extravagant hotel, the Purple Lotus, for the U.S. dollar equivalent of $35 per night. The next day I started walking the streets near the harbor front and soon discovered the ferry that ran from Kowloon to Hong Kong Island. I rode it constantly for six hours watching happy tourists families; Asian, Eurasian, and Caucasian businessmen dressed in tailored suits, carrying expensive brief cases, commuting to their high-rise offices with calculating looks on their faces; beautiful women of all ilk's dressed in the finest European fashions, many going to their money generating workplaces from patrician homes; other women subtly displaying their physical assets—many generously endowed—promoting their Nancy Kwan ambitions, wanting to be the next Eurasian beauty discovered on the Kowloon to Hong Kong Island ferry by movie moguls as Nancy had been, at least in legend.

After finally getting off the ferry, I started walking the British designed and engineered Hong Kong streets looking at everything, seeing nothing, my mind still at the top of *If You Have the Guts* ski slope in the Wyoming mountains, still haunted by that terrible moment when Jane and Gilroy skied to their deaths in a cloud of snow and ice.

Eventually I sauntered up well groomed Chatham Boulevard, maybe for thirty minutes, repeatedly turning left, turning right, soon lost, a profound learning experience: Hong Kong's streets are not laid out in a grid like most of San Bernardino and all of Bozeman. It is a labyrinthine of one winding passage after another, leading nowhere specific and yet everywhere.

Exhausted and only wanting to find The Purple Lotus Hotel, I realized I had lost all sense of direction, so I followed a boulevard running downhill, hopefully, taking me to the harbor near my hotel.

Suddenly an unobtrusive street sign, *Wong Tai Sin Road*, got my attention and jogged something indefinable in the recesses of my mind that had to do with Jane. When a huge, ornate Buddhist Temple appeared immediately in front of me, I instantly made the connection. That temple, *The Wong Tai Sin Temple* and the *Lantour Island Temple*, as Jane characterized them, were "the two most important buildings I ever entered in my life."

When she was twelve, Jane and her mother visited Hong Kong for several days in conjunction with a trip they made to Burma, ostensibly to connect Jane with her Burmese roots.

Reenergized, I walked through the massive, ornate temple gates, gates framed by giant silver-back artocorpus trees, into a world of beauty, tranquility, and physical comfort. The aroma of flowers mixed with smoldering incense satiated my senses, and the shade broke the torment of Hong Kong's incessant heat. An enormous banyan tree—the same kind of tree that Siddhartha Gautama, the first Buddha, meditated under when founding the philosophy the bears his name—dominated the flora on the temple grounds, complimented by an abundance of Chinese maples, white olives, and red stern trees. Flowering ivy, chrysanthemums, wild carnations, cymatia, red and yellow hibiscus, and giant poinsettia flowers, bordered the grounds along with an abundance of lemon grass, all filling my eyes with pacifying hues. Wong Tai Sin Temple would provide a turning point in my shattered life.

As I strolled the temple grounds an Asian man in his thirties, wearing an orange robe, his head cleanly shaved, approached me. In perfect, British English he asked, "If this is your first time here, maybe I can help you?" We introduced ourselves. His name had rhythm to it, Ajahun Bhikkhun.

I told Ajahun my interest in Buddhism came from my now dead finance, a Buddhist, and that I knew nothing about the philosophy, but I wanted to learn. He told me that the temple, *wat* in Buddhist terms, had a program for those looking for an entrée into Buddhism, but I think he sensed that I also had an urgent need for some spiritual-psychological healing. So, if I agreed to abide by an exacting schedule, he would be my teacher. I offered to pay him whatever fee he wished, but he insisted: "No, I cannot accept your money, but you can make a contribution to the *Wong Tai Sin Wat* if you wish. Just drop it in the offering container at the main entrance to the shrine."

For two hours every day for the next week, Ajahun tutored me in the basic philosophical precepts first taught by Siddhartha Gautama more than 2,500 years ago:

1) To undertake the training to avoid taking the life of beings. This precept applies to all living beings not just humans. All beings have a right to their lives and that right should be respected. (Do not kill.)

2) To undertake the training to avoid taking things not given. This precept goes further than mere stealing. One should avoid taking anything unless one can be sure that it is intended for you. (Do not steal.)

3) To undertake the training to avoid sensual misconduct. This precept is often mistranslated or misinterpreted as relating only to sexual misconduct but it covers any overindulgence, any sensual pleasure such as gluttony, as well as misconduct of a sexual nature. (Be loyal to your sexual partner.)

4) To undertake the training to refrain from false speech. As well as avoiding lying and deceiving, this precept covers slander as well as speech which is not beneficial to the welfare of others. (Do not tell lies.)

5) To undertake the training to abstain from substances which cause intoxication and heedlessness. This precept is in a special category as it does not infer any intrinsic evil in, say, alcohol itself. But indulgence in any intoxicating substance could be the cause of breaking the other four precepts. (Do not use alcohol or drugs.)

These are the basic precepts for any lay Buddhist. On special holy days, many Buddhists, especially those following the Theravada tradition, observe these three additional precepts:

6) To abstain from taking food at inappropriate times. This would mean following the tradition of Theravada monks and not eating from noon one day until sunrise the next.

7) To abstain from dancing, singing, music and entertainments as well as refraining from the use of perfumes, ornaments and other items used to adorn or beautify the person.

8) To undertake the training to abstain from using high or luxurious beds. Don't sleep on soft, ornate beds.

These last three guidelines are adopted by members of the Sangha sect and are only followed by laypersons on special occasions.29

---

29   The Buddha's Advice to Laypeople · Guidelines for developing a happier life, from the Buddha; Blog at WordPress.com. · The Pilcrow Theme .

Ajahun Bhikkhun also introduced me to meditation, and as he predicted, meditation did relieve my mental anguish and suffering. Finally, on our last day together, Ajahun Bhikkhun, told me, "Theo, now you know everything you need to know to be a Buddhist. I wish you peace and good karma."

I asked, "How and when do I become a Buddhist?"

"That is up to you; you are a Buddhist when you say to yourself, *'I am a Buddhist'*. There is nothing in Buddhism that dictates the timing of that decision; it is strictly up to you."

I acknowledged his direction with my best *way*: clasping my hands together, touching my fingers to my forehead, and bending slightly from my waist.

Before I departed, I dropped a check for $10,000 in the Wong Tai Sin Wat offering box, but the next time I visited Ajahun Bhikkhun, he returned the check, and told me, "Only businesses are allowed to make a contributions of more than $100."

After I left *Wong Tai Sin Wat* on my *graduation* day, I walked to Victoria Harbor, sat on a bench facing the water and contemplated my next action related to Buddhism. In order to appreciate and understand Jane and her mother better, I had gone through a week of training. If I immediately declared myself a Buddhist, would that be too much of a reflex action, or would it simply be recognizing I needed the Buddhist way of life. If my mother and father, both Catholics—mother had converted to Catholicism three years after marrying Papá—could advise me, what would they say? If Jane sat by me now how would she feel? I came to the conclusion that Mother and Papá would caution me about jumping into a new religion too soon just because I had an immediate need for its support. Jane would be very happy I went through the training as a way to better understand her, but she probably would say, "It is totally your decision. No person should tell another they should adopt Buddhism or any other religion." I delayed my decision.

The next week my life didn't seem to be in such a quagmire: I meditated every day; I slept better; I ate better; and finally, I tested my legs for one hour on the harbor front, the first time I had run since the disaster at Jackson Hole. The exercise felt great.

Since retreating from Bozeman, I sometime mused about the money I deposited in the Bozeman Bank of the Rockies and the neatly folded 45 million dollar cashier's check in my wallet. Also, I remembered an elective class I took my senior year at MSU, *Finances and Monetary Growth*. The poignant words of Professor Lander kept surfacing, "The financially astute person does not work for his or her money; they let their money do the work. If you have cash, don't save it; invest it, but use extreme discretion." Another of Professor Lander's maxims: "Life is a series of games, and the investment game is lot of fun—if, you don't invest money you can't afford to lose."

Finally, one evening while riding my favorite ferry on Hong Kong Harbor, I decided to invest my money, but very conservatively at first; then, if successful, I would take risks with the extra capital those initial investments might have accumulated. The next morning I walked into the British Royal Bank of Hong Kong, a reputable investment and banking institution owned by British investors and founded in 1842 during the First Opium War. I told the receptionist I wanted to deposit some money and open an investment account. She asked me to wait for a few minutes until the New Accounts Manager could serve me. After fifteen minutes—just as I decided to leave and try another bank—a dapperly attired Chinese man approached me, stuck out his hand and said, "I am Mr. Chin. May I help you?"

At his desk, Mr. Chin asked me what kind of an account I wanted to open. I told him, "In the past I have only had checking and savings accounts; however, now I also want some investment accounts."

With a look on his face that suggested a smirk, he asked, "What is the amount you have to capitalize?"

"Forty-five million dollars."

Mr. Chin sat up strait in his chair and asked, "What are those funds in now?"

I cracked my first joke in a long time. "They're in my pocket." I smiled, but he didn't.

I reached in my hip pocket, took out my wallet, pulled out the cashier's check and handed it to Mr. Chin. He unfolded it, took a deep audible swallow, nervously cleared his throat, and said, "Ah, please wait a minute," before quickly walking to a glass enclosed office a few steps from his desk. There he talked to another man briefly before coming back to me and asking, "Sir, please, what is your name again?"

"Theodore Ruiz Rogers." Until he saw my check, he wasn't interested in my name.

"Mr. Rogers, will you please come with me?"

Immediately, the British Royal Bank of Hong Kong became more than interested in my deposit. Their investment manager, Mr. Wong, did not attempt to hide his enthusiasm for my money; he politely and deftly asked me questions about my financial goals. I could feel the question he didn't ask, *Where did this young man*—I was twenty-three at the time—*obtain 45million U.S. dollars?*

"I have no specific goals for this money, but since I have it, I want it to grow and be safe. In other words, I'm not interested in any wild, speculative investments."

"If you will allow me, Mr. Rogers, I will make some recommendations for you, but I need a couple of days to research and investigate what investments would be most appropriate.

"It will take a few days for your cashier's check to clear, certainly not more than five. Is that acceptable? "

Since I had no immediate need for cash–I still had over $9,000 in my wallet and another $20,000 in traveler's checks, it didn't bother me in the slightest. "No problem. I'm sure I can find something to do in Hong Kong for a few days."

Mr. Wong asked, "Are you here with your family or some friends?"

"Neither, I am traveling alone."

With a sly smile and a sparkle in his eyes he invited, "Would you like for me to introduce you to a beautiful, intelligent girl, maybe two of them, to keep you company and act as your guides."

Mr. Wong's offer, only slightly veiled, didn't entice or interest me in the slightest. Emotionally, Jane was still the only woman I could possibly be interested in, and it would be almost a year before that would change. "No thanks, Mr. Wong. I'm doing fine."

On a rainy Wednesday, six days later, when I walked into the British Royal Bank of Hong Kong again, I received a much different greeting than the one given me on my first visit. "Good morning, Mr. Rogers. Would you like some tea? How about some water? Here, let me take your umbrella."

After being ushered into Mr. Wong's office and seated in an ornate, comfortable high-back leather chair, the niceties completed, and Mr. Wong's investment recommendations considered, I invested 10 million dollar in a Precious Metals account; 10 million dollars in Asian Development stocks; and 10 million in a jumbo certificate of deposit at a fixed interest rate of 8% for 7 years, meaning that CD would more than double in value by its due date. In addition, I added a 10 million dollar investment in Hong Kong Real Estate funds; and, 4 million in an interest bearing savings account. And last, I deposited 1 million in a traditional checking account.

With 100 million dollars in a giant certificate of deposit in Bozeman, I felt financially secure. Those investment transactions and my newly adopted Buddhist lifestyle didn't, however, give me total peace of mind or contentment. I still didn't have a purpose in life, nothing to get out of bed for in the morning, no Jane to hug and tell her, "I love you." Also, other ghosts were always lurking over my shoulder.

Fate and bad luck—and some sort of evil curse—had dominated my life since the day Rico died when I was five-years-old. That curse had been redundantly resurrected with the deaths of my biological family; of Delores, my fifth grade class mate; the mysterious killing of my Marine Corps buddy Jim Cordell; the passing of my Glover parents; and most recently the demise of my best friend, Gilroy, and the love of my life, Jane. All of their ghosts continuously haunted me, not in an overt, terrifying way, but, still, in a never-ending guilt-ridden way. That guilt was always with me, only temporarily relieved by my falling in love with Jane, and finally, softened a bit by Buddhist meditation and financial security.

The day after I set up my financial accounts at the bank, while riding the Kowloon Hong Kong Island ferry, I picked up an English language newspaper a man left on his seat when he disembarked. I stayed on the ferry, paid my fare for the return trip across the harbor and started perusing that paper.

The front page told about the new *Great Leap Forward* in China, an attempt to get the Chinese economy moving in a positive direction, but the back page had a notice of more interest to me:

Job Fair: English Teachers Wanted in Many Asian Countries. July 12-15, from 9:00 a.m. until 6:00 p.m. Applications will be accepted and interviews conducted. Bring your passport and teaching credentials. Location: Hong Kong Convention Centre, Suite 222.

27

Teaching Adventure in China

O n the 12th of July, after taking a shower, shaving, and dressing in my newly acquired business-like, linen suit, I grabbed my documents folder and headed for the Hong Kong Convention Center. I walked with an enthusiastic gate while thinking: *This is the first day of my totally new life.*

Suite 222 hummed with the enthusiasm of education job seekers, all carrying brief cases or folders, many containing newly won college diplomas, more men than women, more Caucasian than Asian, all with a similar goal: land a teaching job that paid well in an exotic Asian country, in an exotic Asian city, in an exotic Asian school, full of beautiful, well behaved and well-motivated exotic Asian children.

Colorful placards, suspended down from Suite 222's ceiling, bore the names of countries that wanted to hire teachers: Japan, Singapore, Korea, Malaysia, Thailand, Philippines, Indonesia, Taiwan, Fiji, and surprisingly, even China, surprising since China had been *closed* to the rest of the world since the Communist took over in 1949.

The applicant lines marked the countries of highest interest: ten or more people stood in front of the Japan, Korea, and Thailand placards, and at least a few showed interest in all the other locations, all except China; not a single person waited to talk with the recruiter from China, a well groomed man in his early forties wearing a dark, wool suit, an aberration in Hong Kong's tropical climate. He tried to look occupied by scribbling notes and occasionally scanning the crowd as if soliciting, "*Please, won't one person talk to me?*"

As soon as I reached the China Desk, I saw the source of the China recruiter's problem. Prominently tapped to the front of his desk, a sign read, "Applicants holding American, British, Canadian, Australian, or New Zealand passports—not accepted."

All of those countries participated in the Korean War and fought against China; technically they were still at war because no peace treaty had been signed.

Immediately, I backed away a few paces and checked my documents folder to see if I still had my Mexican passport, the one Uncle Carlos encouraged me to get when I visited Mexico. Again, I obtained that passport since my father had been a native-born Mexican citizen.

I extended my hand and said, "I am interested in teaching in China. What do you have?"

While firmly and continuously shaking my hand, he said, "*[sic] Sound* American. *You* passport American?

I handed my green Mexican passport to the China recruiter, "No, today I am Mexican."

Motioning with his hand, "Please, *Ching zuo! Ching zuo!*" (Sit! Sit!), Mr. Gao Guangxi replied.

Over the next hour Mr. Gao told me about the Chinese government's experiment in Yunnan Providence, located in the extreme southwest corner of China. The program being inaugurated, designed to use Western technology in agriculture, primarily in rice cultivation, harvesting, and export marketing, required

English speakers. Mr. Gao's most immediate need was at Yunnan Agricultural University (YAU) in Kunming, a city with a lot of experience with English speaking foreigners.

During World War II and immediately after, from 1940 through 1948, the American Air Force had a large base in Kunming, at first in support of the legendary *Flying Tigers30*. After the war ended in 1945, Americans stayed to support the Chinese Nationalists' budding Air Force as they fought the Communist led by Mao Tse Tung.

I finally interrupted Mr. Gao's sales pitch—one I didn't understand much of anyway—and told him, "Excuse me, Mr. Gao. If you want me, I will take the job in Kunming." Obviously delighted, he stuck out his hand and shook mine for nearly a minute.

It took Mr. Gao a week to obtain the necessary visa and teaching license needed for me to enter mainland China. Finally, he accompanied me on a four hour ferry ride, followed by two hours on a crowded bus, to the Guangzhou train station. There he purchased a first class ticket for me—which meant I would have a small, unadorned compartment to myself—and two hours later, he escorted me onto the Kunming bound train and my *first class* digs.

The four day trip to Kunming was long and would have been interminably miserable had I not continuously walked through the regular passenger cars. At first the porters were upset when I wouldn't stay in my private chamber, but finally they got tired of trying to control my every movement and ignored me.

I learned my first Mandarin words and phrases on that train, for instance: *Ni hao!* (Hello!); *Wo xiang hu edar shuai.* (I would like a little water); *Ni huai shuoa Putonghua?* (Can you speak Mandarin?) Within a short period of time I developed a love for Mandarin, and within a year I became marginally fluent, at least as a speaker.

When we finally reached Kunming a delegation of five YAU administrators met me as I stepped of the train, and a beautiful young

---

30 The 1st American Volunteer Group (AVG), commanded by General Claire Chennault, flew P-40 fighter planes in 1941–1942 and battled Japanese aircraft over southwestern China.

girl, maybe twelve years old, courteously bowed and thrust a large bouquet of flowers in my hand. My greeting, formal and cordial, but staid—obviously, a new experience for all of us, especially for the interrupter who I could not understand—lasted far too long. Finally, our entourage climbed into cars and headed for the YAU campus.

28

Love at Yunnan Agricultural University

Kunming did not resemble Hong Kong—at all! On our way to the university, I saw farmers working their fields with wooden plows pulled by buffaloes. Unlike the car and bus crowded streets of Hong Kong, thousands of bicycles and hundreds of hand-pulled carts, many loaded with large baskets of recently harvested rice, occupied the roads.

Later I learned the rice fields in Yunnan Providence were planted, maintained, and harvested exclusively with manual labor. When the rice ripened, armies of peasants cut that most edible grass with hand scythes before pounding the seeds from its stocks into large gathering baskets. The entire economy of Yunnan ran almost exclusively on manual labor. No Chinese-British culture existed here, only authentic Chinese.

YAU turned out to be an excellent place for me to start my teaching career and garner my first Asian experiences outside of Korea and Hong Kong.

Picturesquely situated in the hills north of Kunming proper, YAU also turned out to be a superb place for me to live. The school provided a comfortable, fully furnished apartment on the fourth floor, the top floor, of a building exclusively for foreign teachers and consultants, all of whom, except for me, were Russian or North Korean. Unfriendly North Koreans were offset by very friendly, but heavy vodka drinking, Russians. Three of the Russians spoke understandable Spanish and two some English. Of course, neither group knew they had an American in their midst. They all accepted me as an espanól speaking Mexican who also spoke *some* English.

The surrounding buildings housed Chinese teachers and their families, often prodigiously extended families. One of my neighbors, the Lu family, had four generations—ten individuals—represented in their two bedroom apartment. The senior Lu, a great-grand-father, became my premier Mandarin teacher. On many days, he gave me five to ten minute lessons when I went to-and-from my classroom.

Flowers proliferated throughout the YAU campus, and blooming trees softened the Spartan dwellings occupied by the students. They lived eight to a small room where they learned to cooperate and endure, usually with good humor, because during those years, 1956-57, very few Chinese between the ages of 18-24 had the opportunity to attend a university; in fact, most of the schools were closed.

Many at YAU were *rice students*. Meaning, they were able to attend the school only because their home village contributed 10% of its rice crop for their education. Usually a *rice student* became the first from his or her village to attend a university; consequently, they studied as if receiving less than the highest possible grades brought disgrace on their family and the their entire village.

When I arrived, I had one week to prepare for my classes. My schedule called for me to teach six classes, two hours each, weekly. I expected to be required to teach more than twelve hours each week, but I didn't complain.

Almost all my students turned out to be raw beginners, although thirty were labeled "intermediate," and twenty-one "advanced." Nevertheless, I prepared for my classes as if I knew exactly what I would teach to all of the students over the next month: parts of speech, nouns, verbs, etc., for the beginners; extensive vocabulary development for the intermediates; and how to write a letters of application for the advanced students. What a waste of time that turned out to be, because soon I learned there were no intermediate students and only four were truly advanced, three girls and one boy.

As I lay in bed the night before my first class—my first class in China and my first class of independent teaching anywhere—reality struck me: my teacher preparation, including practice teaching, had probably been inadequate for what I faced tomorrow. At MSU, I had been coddled by a supervising teacher who, in fact, did most of the teaching, and that to a single class of twenty English speaking, American, sixth grade students; not to those six classes of sixty, Mandarin speaking Chinese students I would be looking at within hours; I slept little that night.

When I walked in and faced my first class, ten minutes early by my watch, the students were already there, and they looked at me as if I had just exited a space ship. Quickly one student barked some instructions and all sixty students stood and said, *"Ni hao Jiaoshou. Huanyuing!"* (Hello professor. Welcome!) Since I knew that *Ni hao* meant hello, I smiled and said "Ni hao, Hello."

For my first day of teaching, and only the first day, the university provided an *interpreter,* one who spoke little English I understood. Nevertheless, obviously more relaxed than I, with a seemingly good attitude, and motivated to help me get off to a good start, her presence comforted me. After some communication between the two of us, mostly hand and body language, and her redundant use of "Yes! Yes!" she told the students what I wanted them to do: they should repeat everything I said in English—first mistake.

"Good morning, Students."

My introductory phrase drew a response that explicitly complied with my instructions through the interpreter:

"*Good morning, Students,*" the students replied.

"My name is Theo Rogers."

"*My name is Theo Rogers,*" they mimicked.

Pointing to myself and raising my voice several decibels, "No! No! My name is Theo Rogers."

Pointing to themselves, my obedient students shouted, "*No! No! My name is Theo Rogers.*"

And so it went, until my interpreter stepped in and made a statement to the class; then we all had a long laugh. The students weren't making fun of me, just enjoying the ineptness of their rookie teacher.

Unbelievably, within a week, after we started singing simple songs in English like *Oh! What a Beautiful Morning* and *Five Hundred Miles*, all my classes were making progress, and after two weeks most students could say a few basic English sentences and phrases: "*Will you be my friend? Today is Monday, and tomorrow is Tuesday.*" After the third week progress accelerated, all without any intricate lesson plans that called for teaching nouns and verbs.

With only twelve hours of teaching each week and a few hours for preparation, I had plenty of free time. I enjoyed teaching much more than I dreamed I would. My life on the YAU campus, at least in the daytime, could not have been better. When I walked through the campus many students often smiled at me and said, "Hello, Professor, Theo. How are you today?" Those words always made me feel relevant and a bit noble because they came from an often repeated classroom dialogue. Only one aspect of my otherwise unspoiled campus life tainted my existence: lonely nights, thinking too much about Jane, and my morbid anathema—the people I loved died.

Running, seemingly the only effective antidote for my night time depression, motivated me to get out of bed at 4:00 a.m. Even that early, however, I always encountered other runners, students getting some exercise before starting eighteen hours of classes and study.

An ideal four kilometer running route began at the university's back gate. The gate guards, normally very attentive identification-checkers, paid little attention to runners. The course proceeded along a wall that enclosed the campus, and up a trail that followed the spine of a ridge on *Shendengde Shan* (Sacred Mountain) to the turnaround point near a small Buddhist wat. Most runners stopped near the wat long enough to stretch their legs and take a few deep breaths. Then refreshed, and with the a lot help from gravity, they sped down the mountain, almost all of them ignoring the university's 400 meter track they passed before entering the back gate. However, a few of us did an exit left onto that track for a few laps. For me, those rounds of that oval changed my life and ultimately relieved my night time loneliness.

I started going regularly to another wat, this one between the campus and Kunming City. There I went through the Buddhist rituals, lighting three sticks of incense and placing them in the proper container, prostrating myself before the ornate Buddhist icon, and meditating for thirty minutes, sometimes more. That routine pacified my guilt, to some extent, and my constant fixation on Jane, but it didn't do a thing to relieve the loneliness; nevertheless, soon, at the track, a positive bit of fate neutralized even that malady.

After about a week of running up and back on the *Shendengde Shan* trail then onto the track, I started reliving some of my high school running glory by circling the ellipsoid a couple of times at race pace. On some of those days, I took glancing looks at what appeared to be an astonishingly beautiful girl, one with long, shining, black hair in a ponytail, exceptionally slim hips, and inquisitive dark eyes. We, occasionally, flashed a smile at each other. She appeared to be a student.

Those glances became frustrating, so one day, as soon as I saw her on the track, I reversed the traditional track-running direction, counter clockwise, so I could really get a good look at this lass. On our first head-on pass, I realized she attended one of my classes. The name Ya came to mind, but as it turned out Wong Yalin[31] was one of my few truly advanced students. In spite of the obvious taboo related to a student-teacher romance—soon she relieved my loneliness.

---

31 Family names come first in Mandarin.

On Saturday morning, that first week after I recognized Yalin, it rained so I restricted my running to the mountain road. Later that day, I returned to the track, slogged through a few muddy laps, and retired to the pull-up bars on the grass at the north end of the athletic field. Suddenly, as if she dropped from the sky, Yalin ran toward me, slipping and slogging through the mud. When she reached the curve, I looked at her and waived; her waive back set my heart racing. With a beautiful smile, she said, "Hello, Professor, Theo. How are you today?" At that instant she slipped in the mud, fell, and hit her head on the cement curb, rendering her semi-conscious.

Before I got to her, Yalin sat up on the track shaking her head; she tried to stand but went down again. When I first touched her, she was lying flat on her back in the mud blinking at the sky. I slid my arms under her, picked her up and carried her to the grass.

She felt pleasantly light and emitted an intoxicating odor, one unrelated to the mud now covering much of her body and mine. Before we reached the grass both of her arms enclosed my neck, and her head rested on my chest. When I looked down at her exquisite face, she blinked a few times, opened her eyes, and we met in a perpetual, penetrating, intercourse of blue eyes and brown. The mutual message, immediate and unretractable—*I am helplessly attracted to you*—guided us through the next eighteen months. Over a shorter term though having time together presented a challenge, but as covert CIA agents might have, we managed to harvest some at least a couple of times each week, usually two or three hours.

Logic dictated I should have felt extremely guilty. An intimate personal relationship between a male teacher and one of his female students, even if their ages are not too different—mine twenty-four at the time, Yalin's twenty-one—is unacceptable in any education venue. Quickly, nevertheless, our love became too strong for any rule of ethics or any social norm to drive us apart; we worshiped each other.

Ironically, Yalin's life and mine had moved along somewhat similar paths. Her parents died when she was seven, killed when a bolt of lightning struck them as they worked together in a rice field. All of her grandparents died of starvation during a famine in the early1950s. Raised by an aunt and uncle, she became the outstanding student in her village school, which led to her becoming the first in her hamlet to attend a university. With an excellent mind and a passion for life, she became, as she characterized it, "self-contained and motivated to rise above the peasant status I was born into."

When Chinese New Year vacation came in late January—two weeks without classes—Yalin went to her home village and spent four days with her aunt and uncle. By the time she returned, the campus was virtually deserted, her dormitory empty and only a near alcoholic Russian farm equipment engineer remained in my building. He lived on the first floor and I on the fourth. This gave us the opportunity to unashamedly cohabitate for ten days, and we enjoyed every day; those were some of the happiest days in both our lives even though I still had ghosts from my past haunting me.

I could not help but recall Jorge's words after Rico, my childhood friend, and my mother, father, and sister had died in that fiery accident, "My mother says you bring bad luck to people." It was undeniable: I had been bad luck for a string of people I loved, the last one the girl I wanted to marry, Jane. Now, I truly loved different women. What would her fate be?

With one day to go on our ten days of living as man and wife, I woke one morning just as a shaft of sunlight penetrated the giant Norfolk pine outside our bedroom window. The light hit Yalin's face at an oblique angle that perpetuated her already magnificent looks: clear, smooth skin; gleaming, black hair; a perfect nose, but at the time, I thought the most attractive part of Yalin's anatomy, her brain— invisible, but always active—enchanted me more than her looks.

Yalin, who was close to full English literacy when I met her, primarily due to her long term relationship—from the age of three—with an English speaker in her village, one who had worked for American and British aviation units as an interpreter during World War II.

When the Americans closed the Kunming Air Force Station, the Station Librarian gave the interpreter several English reference books: two comprehensive dictionaries, a thesaurus, an encyclopedia, numerous copies of National Geographic Magazine, and a few other books related to English. She passed most of them on to her favorite student, Yalin, and they became Yalin's text books—her linguistic bibles—at an early age. She brought her favorite dictionary and the thesaurus with her to YAU.

Before I knew the story about the interpreter, I would often be amazed at Yalin's knowledge of American culture. In one conversation, she told me all about Henry Ford, his development of the automobile, and how he treated his employees. I remember her saying, with a smile, "Henry Ford would have made a good Communist; he took very good care of everyone who worked for him."

When I responded, "Where did you learn so much about Henry Ford and his company?

She smiled and said, "That's my secret."

Not until we had been an *item* for over six months did she tell me about the books she had at her disposal, particularly the National Geographics, where she read about Henry Ford. Also, her knowledge of English grammar often astounded me. On one occasion, when I wrote her a note with, in my mind, a minor punctuation problem she took me to school.

My Dear Yalin, I miss you. I hope we can have a long visit on Saturday evening and maybe we can go for a walk after dark. What do you think? Theo.

Yalin's response:

My Dearest Theo, I miss you too. I like both of your ideas. However, my dear teacher, I am surprised you would write two independent clauses and fail to punctuate the coordinating conjunction 'and' with a comma. Shame on you, Teacher. Ha! Ha! I love you. Yalin

As we spent more time together in my apartment, Yalin often brought her thesaurus with her, and too often, she spent long minutes that could have been used for romance, memorizing groups of words, many I had never heard of. Sometimes she would *throw* a word at me, and say, "OK, you have ten seconds to use a word meaning *conglomeration* in a sentence."

Yalin became fully literate in English during the first eight months we spent together. The only area I really helped her with was pronunciation. However, her kindness, coupled with her academic prowess, separated her from every woman I had known, except Jane, and they mimicked each other personality wise. Although I didn't tell her at that time, after knowing her for a mere six months, I knew I wanted to marry her.

One night, a week night when we were brazen and assumed all YAU students and staff would remain at the university, we bravely walked the streets of Kunming together for the first time. After an hour of window-shopping, during which Yalin refused to let me buy her a single item, we fronted an extremely rare store in China at that time, a jewelry shop[32]; I led her in. Yalin's eyes lit up with excitement as we started inspecting diamond rings; I had explained to her what it meant when a man placed a diamond ring on his sweetheart's ring finger. When I asked her which one she would like, she responded, "They are all too expensive."

Yalin—not aware of my financial circumstance—would not dream of burdening me with what in her eyes amounted to a very expensive item. I picked up a one-carat diamond set in platinum and slipped it on her finger. Yalin shook her head "No", but I knew she would love to have it. I paid for that ring, stuck it in my pocket; then we walked to a park on the shore of Cuihu Lake, near the heart of the city.

I told Yalin how much I loved her; I proposed, and she accepted with tears running down her cheeks, but for us to get married we would have to overcome a big hurdle—the Chinese government. Marriage to a foreigner, particularly a Westerner, while not specifically prohibited by law, would never be accepted by the government. However, if we could get to Hong Kong, we would not have a problem in getting a license. That presented a different problem, getting Yalin to Hong Kong—a passport for a common Chinese citizen—impossible.

Over the next few months our surreptitious romance became more difficult to keep secret, and we became a little careless at times. One morning, when I thought we were the only ones at the

---

32 In the late 1950's, jewelry was considered a commodity for the bourgeoisie, a class that did not exist in China at the time.

running track, as we walked one lap after running hard, I hugged and kissed her, a full, prolonged kiss on the mouth. When I released her from my arms, another faculty member, one we had never seen at the track before, watched from thirty meters away. While assuming the cat had just jumped out of the bag, over the next few days I nervously anticipated being called on the carpet any minute. Luckily that never happened.

29

Trek to Laos

At the beginning of the spring semester, Li Na, the secretary for YAU's president, Mr. Ba Long, asked me to recommend a student to work in her office part time, one who could read, speak, and write English well. I only had one girl in my classes with that level of literacy, my sweetheart, Yalin; a boy in my class also had good English skills, so Li Na interviewed both of them and chose her.

Yalin started working for Li Na ten hours each week. Her job: putting English titles on documents generated by the president; she also did some article translations from the only English newspaper in China, The Shanghai News. Yalin enjoyed the work; for the first time, her English skills were being put to good use. Also, Li Na seemed happy with her. In addition, Li Na had enough confidence in her that she would sometimes step out of the office and Yalin would in effect become the secretary.

On Yalin's last day of working in the President's office before the end of the semester, in Li Na's absence Yalin answered the phone.

The man calling identified himself as an officer for the Chinese Internal Security Office (CISO), one of China's most powerful and feared autocracies in the post-revolutionary years. Even though she didn't intentionally eavesdrop, the partially open door to Mr. Ba's office forced Yalin to hear part of the conversation. When she heard the President use the term, "Mexican English teacher," Yalin's casual listening turned acutely attentive.

Along with the fact that the CISO was undoubtedly looking for me, she learned an agent would arrive at YAU the next morning to interrogate the "Misiego" (*Mexican*). In response to an apparent instruction from the man in Beijing near the end of the call, Mr. Ba responded, in Mandarin of course, "No, I won't alarm him."

Soon Li Na returned and gave Yalin a small gift for her service, thus ending her office duties for that semester; she left immediately.

After clearing the Administrative Office Building in a fast walk, she ran to my apartment and pounded on the door, rousing me from a nap. As usual I gushed with happiness to see my love, but when I tried to hug her she pushed me away and said, "We have to talk now!" The conversation that followed put in motion one of the most ironic, exciting, and challenging months of my life.

Yalin started talking so fast, in both English and Mandarin, I couldn't follow her. After sitting her down and calming her down, I started understanding her story; then, I needed calming down. That call Yalin overheard had to be about me, probably the only English teacher in China at the time holding a Mexican passport.

Our mental wheels started churning at high speed searching for options. Everything we came up with boiled down to two: We could stay at YAU and take our chances, but if the CSIO had my name, they probably had already made a connection between my Mexican passport, my U.S. citizenship, and my Marine Corps service, during which I killed more than fifty Chinese soldiers. That fact was recounted in my Medal of Honor commendation, a public document. Those details would undoubtedly—in the eyes of the Chinese government— make me a *war criminal*. Our second option to flee, get out of China as quickly as possible and to Hong Kong, obviously became our only choice.

I asked Yalin, "You do want to go with me, don't you?"

"Certainly, you can't go without me; I would never see you again. Something else you need to know, I planned to tell you next month, I think I am pregnant. If I am, I don't want my baby to be born here."

Her statement hit me hard; another wave of panic went through me. The possibility of being a father, something I had never really thought about, suddenly added more pressure to my fragile psyche. I masked my concern, took her in my arms and told her, "That's wonderful my Love; now we have another good reason to get the hell out of here—and fast!"

A celebration of some kind, at least from Yalin's point of view, would have been appropriate for the baby news, but we didn't have time to rejoice. We would bolt quickly, as soon as it got dark in three hours, and head for Hong Kong. But, how would we get there? The closest straight-line way, through Guangzhou then into Macao—a Dutch enclave at the end of a peninsula that extends from Guangzhou—then finally to Hong Kong, would be difficult.

Yalin got on the phone and learned the next bus to Guangzhou didn't leave until 9:00 a.m. the next day, and it took six days. Then she tried the train; it departed at 8:30 p.m., and that didn't make sense either since it took four days. If the CISO wanted to catch me, they wouldn't have any trouble intercepting us whether we were on a bus or train. As we contemplated that fact, Yalin said, "Since we want to get out of China as fast as possible, we can best do that by going into Laos; then we can worry about getting to Hong Kong. My home village is only five kilometers from Laos, and I have crossed that border many times to pick fruit; we can just walk across the border away from the check point."

The closest city in the direction of Laos that buses ran to from Kunming was Xishangbanna, fifty kilometers from the Laos border, 150 kilometers from YAU, and forty-five kilometers from Yalin's family home. Xishangbanna became our intermediate destination with Yalin's home to follow. At this point, we didn't consider how we would get from Laos to Hong Kong, but I knew it was out of China and close to Thailand, Cambodia, and Burma. Yet, I knew little about the geography of that tri-country region and virtually nothing about Laos.

During part of our conversation, Yalin, always the intelligent thinker, realized a long distance bus could also be a trap. Before it reached Xishangbanna it stopped at two security check points where passengers had to show identification. A foreigner, she surmised, would be required to show a passport. Consequently, the only logical thing to do was to ride short-hall, mini buses. According to Yalin, "They never get checked."

That strategy had two problems: first, those buses usually quit running around 10 p.m. and didn't start running again until about 4 a.m. For at least six hours we would need to find a place to hide and, hopefully, rest. Yalin estimated we wouldn't arrive near Xishangbanna until the next afternoon, allowing anyone really looking for us time to organize their search. Still, the short-hall bus strategy became our choice.

As soon as it was dark, Yalin and I met near the back gate of YAU. She carried a small bag with some clothes in it, her English dictionary and thesaurus, and thankfully, a small blanket, along with approximately 2,000rmb ($60) in Chinese money. When I questioned the weight of the books, she snapped:

"I am not leaving my important books. Don't worry, I will carry them."

I quickly countered, "OK, I understand. I will carry one."

"Thank you, Theo."

Now my bag contained a thesaurus, some underwear, a couple of t-shirts, and my Mexican passport. All of my other documents, including my U.S. passport, were in a safety deposit box in Hong Kong. Also, I had almost $9,000 in U.S. currency, as well as 20,000rmb ($2,431) in Chinese.

After we met and moved to a secluded area about 100 meters from the gate, I hoisted Yalin to the top of the brick wall; she helped me up, and we dropped on the other side. After walking for about fifteen minutes to get clear of YAU, we caught a tricycle taxi and headed for the south part of Kunming.

Thankfully, Yalin knew the local bus connections, and again, she was thinking strategically when she had the taxi drop us off several blocks from where we would board the first short-hall bus. She didn't want our taxi driver to be able to tell anyone where we seemed to be headed.

Our first bus, *bus* being a stretch of the term, a converted U.S. Army truck[33] with wood benches on both sides and one running down the middle of the truck bed, took us to Jinning. Another took us to Yux. I have forgotten the names of three other places we changed buses, but we were now well clear of the Kunming area and feeling a bit less anxious. We ended up spending the night a few yards off the road in a cornfield where we rolled up together in Yalin's small blanket, one too small for two bodies unless they were very communal. We rested but slept little, our minds filled with excitement and apprehension. *Could we pull this off? Yes! Yes, we had no other option.* A different question: *Where would we go in Laos?* That one kept me awake most of that night. Ironically, as it turned out, that would be the easiest part of our journey.

It was 2 p.m. the next day when we reached the outskirts of Xishangbanna, but we didn't go into the city; we went directly to Yalin's village and her uncle's home. There she felt we would be safe, at least temporarily.

After walking the last ten kilometers on off-road paths—the fewer people who knew we were in the area, the better—we arrived after dark, and indeed, we did feel safer. Yalin's aunt and uncle were excited to see her and they welcomed me despite their serious risk of having a foreigner, one unregistered with the local police, in their home.

Hungry and dirty, I felt like we had been traveling for several days, when in fact we had only been on the run for three hours

---

33   The American Air Force and Army left hundreds of vehicles behind when it abandoned Kunming in 1945, at the end of World War II.

short of one day. We ate our fill of dumplings and noodles and took a traditional Chinese cold shower before going to bed; we both slept well that night on futon like rice-straw mats.

The next morning we revised our strategy. Yalin and Uncle Wen went to the border check-point and see if anything unusual was happening. When they returned, their report wasn't good: traffic at the checkpoint was backed up for half-a-mile because every vehicle was being searched, and many PLA[34] soldiers were patrolling the area. More alarming "WANTED" flyers with my picture were prominently displayed in several places near the check-point. They read: *Wanted this man. Blue eyes, black hair 180 mm tall. Speaks English, Spanish, and Mandarin. Wanted for crimes against Chinese soldiers during the Korean War. Reward for his capture.*

The only encouraging aspect: Yalin wasn't mentioned on the flyers; authorities apparently hadn't made a connection between the two of us.

Alarm spread quickly within Yalin's extended family, and naturally they wanted us to move on as quickly as possible. As soon as darkness fell, Yalin and I departed Menglongo; now, however, I wore the authentic attire of a coolie, and what skin that showed, hands and face, were smudged with dirt. My black hair stuck out from the edges of my grass coolies' hat, and that hair was matted with dirt, giving my look a strong element of authenticity, like a man who had been working in the rice paddies all day, but my blue eyes couldn't be disguised. We also exchanged my leather bag for a cloth bag, the sort locals often carried going to and from rice fields or local markets.

Our simple plan: go southeast to leave the Menglongo area, then track dead-south, using trails, staying away from roads and even small villages. Naturally, we wanted to get into Laos as quickly as possible. It looked like the night would be clear so I could set our heading by the stars.

For about four hours we trekked southeast through the jungle, sweat pouring from me while Yalin remained amazingly dry,

---

34 People Liberation Army

and mosquitos feasted on me while ignoring her. Then we turned directly south as planned into Laos, and after another hour, we stopped at a small stream and washed our faces. Yalin put her arms around me, gave me a peck kiss, and happily exclaimed: "This is the first time I have ever crossed into Laos with no intention of going back to China."

China lay behind us by several kilometers. I should have felt comfortable, but I didn't; I had no idea what awaited us in this mysterious country. We decided to rest for a while, and both of us slept soundly after Yalin rubbed my skin with lemon grass juice to keep the flying critters away.

Just as dawn broke, Yalin shook me, her index finger across her lips, telling me not to speak. The rhythmic thump of big animals, as it turned out elephants, moving on the trail we used during the night, approached us. When we could see them, Yalin smiled and jumped to her feet. She knew the mahout[35] on the first elephant in a train of six, all apparently loaded with trade goods. Later, Yalin told me that her former childhood playmate hauled Chinese goods into Laos and returned to China with Lao goods, things used to conceal their real cargo, their money maker, opium.

Yalin and her friend had an animated conversation with constant glances in my direction. Finally, she asked me, "Can we pay them about $100 US to take us to the Mekong River? There Jing says he can arrange a boat to take us down the Mekong as far as Vientiane, the capital of Laos. He says there are many Americans in Vientiane."

I handed her 200 U.S. dollars, and she made the deal. Her friend seemed happy. He yelled something to his companions, and they all gave a little cheer, *"Han how! Han how!"* (Good! Good!)

Another mahout placed me on the third elephant in the caravan and Yalin on the fourth. Since all of the mahouts carried automatic weapons with large ammunition clips, I suspected this leg of our trip might not be benign; it wasn't.

---

35 Elephant trainer and driver

Two hours after we boarded the elephants the sounds of the jungle quieted, the cacophony of insects became silent, birds flew instead of constantly squawking, and the relaxed atmosphere of the forest became tense; you could cut it with a knife. The lead mahout, Yalin's friend, held up his hand and we instantly stopped moving. With further hand signals, he directed all but one of the animals into the jungle about fifty meters off the trail to the right; the sixth elephant moved to the left and quickly stomped into the thickness, leaving a noticeable trail, made a wide U turn and returned to the caravan further down the trail. Quickly all six mahouts cut limbs from the undergrowth and covered the tracks to our hiding place. Immediately the animals were forced to reclining positions, and the mahouts took cover behind the elephants with weapons at the ready. I crawled to Yalin and held her hand; obviously danger approached.

The clatter of military equipment: rattling water canteens, ammunition belts clapping against weary thighs, whispers of soldiers ready for combat, brought back memories of my days as a Marine. Finally, an officer barked a command, bodies hit the ground, and automatic weapons started firing. None, however, were pointed our way. All the firing saturated the area where the one elephant had entered the jungle leaving a track. The ruse worked, and obviously the commander of those soldiers didn't want his men going into the dense bush.

Yalin presumed we had encountered a Chinese Army patrol looking for opium runners. They had little respect for the border since the Lao Army didn't contest the area. Soon the Chinese patrol moved on toward China.

Ten minutes later, we started moving at high speed as the mahouts prodded their beasts, and we kept up that pace most of the day. That night we camped in a clearing near a stream, cooked monkey meat over a mosquito suppressing fire, and drank coconut juice. A logical question one might ask, "How did the monkey meat taste?" Since we were really hungry, not bad at all.

The next day at about noon we arrived at the Mekong River. Many small boats, a few with outboard motors, more without, lined the banks. Soon Yalin's friend *contracted* a boat for us—one without a motor—and the two said good-bye. All the mahouts waived to us before disappearing back into the jungle.

A few minutes later, we climbed into a canoe along with a woman, her two children, two large bags of potatoes, and six piglets. We four adults would paddle when necessary, which turned out to be a lot considering we went downstream. It would take two days and two nights to reach our first destination, where the family lived, Longprabong, Laos. To Vientiane would probably take three more days.

The next two evenings we went ashore, built a fire, and purchased food from Laotians selling their wares along the river. After a couple hours of sleep, we continued our journey.

Both mornings Yalin bandaged my hands, now full of blisters from paddling, and I bandaged hers. With each passing hour I felt more confident we would eventually reach Vientiane; that turned out to be a false assumption but with a positive result.

Mid-morning on our third day on the Mekong, about one hour from Longprabong, a Laos Border Patrol boat suddenly approached. I didn't think they were looking for me, but still, I didn't have a visa to enter their country; Yalin could easily pass for being Lao. But we were not going to take any unnecessary chances. Quickly, Yalin had me lie down on the bottom of the canoe. She and the lady dumped the two twenty-five kilogram bags of potatoes on me, about fifty pounds each, and the piglets were turned loose to romp on the potatoes. Until then, she had them secured on short, bamboo leashes.

Mildly frightened, panting like a man not wanting to make any noise, with the river breeze cut off, very high humidity, sweating profusely, my back hurting from lying on a boat spur; for about ten minutes, I experienced maximum discomfort. Just as the inspectors pulled alongside, the woman gave the piglets something to eat, and their squeals, as they rooted through the potatoes, turned out to be great camouflage. The inspectors laughed at the piglets and only stayed long enough to look at the boat owner's permit. Everyone on the boat, including me, laughed when I came out of the potatoes, splattered with a little pig feces and a lot of urine.

Supposedly so we would not attract unwanted attention at the Longprabong boat dock, we were dropped off on the banks of the Mekong about one-half-mile from town. The boat owner promised to pick us up as soon as he delivered the lady, her pigs, potatoes, and children. That gave us the opportunity to jump in the water, wash the pig excrement from my body, and refresh ourselves. We both splashed happily, feeling we had overcome the major hurdles on our way to Vientiane, but our optimism became moot when our boat captain never returned; we waited two hours for him.

Attempting to look like countryside farmers or poor tourists, we walked into Longprabong and immediately started looking for a place to rest our weary bodies. It had been seven days since we fled YAU.

Now it was mid-day as we sauntered along a tree shaded boulevard on a bluff overlooking the Mekong. We started seeing small hotels. Tired and hungry, we sorely needed a place to rest and eat. A hot bath or shower would also be a nice complement to the dip we took in the muddy waters of the Mekong.

Some hotels displayed signs in English and French; the one we chose, appropriately named Mekong View Inn, provided both food and lodging. Fifteen US dollars purchased the best room available, and indeed, it turned out to be a great place for us to lie down in a real bed for the first time in more than a week.

After taking a long shower, eating a great meal of shrimp, eggplant, and rice, followed by a long nap, we decided to explore the city. Late in the afternoon we strolled into Longprabong proper. Its ambiance surprised us: magnificently cultivated tropical florae blanketed the town, including an abundance of hibiscus, monopodia orchids, and several varieties of banana plants[36]. We also saw seemingly happy and enthusiastic, uniformed children going home from school, often hand-in-hand, as they passed ornate Buddhist

---

36 Inspite of the popular perception that bananas grow on trees, they do not. Banana plants are herbs.

wats. All of those shrines were trimmed in gold and occupied by a crowd of monks whose Buddhist chants echoing throughout the city.

Compared to what we expected and what we were prepared to face, we seemed to be in an ideal haven. Longprabong looked like it could be our Shangri-La. Conversely, beauty and apparent tranquility are often clandestine cloaks for intrigue; such was the case with Longprabong

Longprabong's population of about 25,000 souls covered a small area between the Mekong and Nam Khan Rivers. That relatively small number of citizens disguised the city's historical importance; it had been the capital of the Royal Laotian Kingdom from 1707 to 1975, when the Communist took over and moved the capitol to Vientiane.

Surprisingly, many Westerners mixed with Asians, the majority well dressed, browsed along the main thoroughfare. As one would expect in a tropical location, in the cool of the evenings is when most people walk for enjoyment and when social and economic intercourse takes place in Longprabong—along with the gathering of intelligence by foreign agents.

It seemed like everyone on the street was dressed far superior to us, many of the ladies in splendid Asian dresses and the men in linen trousers and colorful open neck shirts. Quickly, it became evident that the Laos form of Communism functioned much more relaxed in Longprabong than China's did in Kunming.

Yalin loved shopping, but at this juncture in our journey only jungle-river type clothes were appropriate. So we outfitted ourselves at one establishment in high end jungle garb. When we left that store, we felt highly affluent and very happy. My U.S. dollars—I still had well over $8,700 in my new fabric *satchel*—seemed to buy a lot more in Laos than they did Hong Kong.

As night fell, we continued walking along the primary boulevard until we sighted two large hotels facing each other. One looked new and elegant, and on the opposite side of the street, the other a bit old and slightly shabby.

I took Yalin's hand, a gesture that always made her a bit uncomfortable in public, and led her to the Royal Laotian Hotel. It was the first splendid hotel she had ever seen in her life. As is the custom in China, she let go of my hand and insisted on walking behind me as we stepped onto sparkling clean, white, marble floors, floors reflecting soft light coming from a mammoth, crystal chandelier extending down from a doomed ceiling, one bordered with curved, stain glass windows.

As we approached the hotel's Main Desk, attended by two Chinese men immaculately attired, I pushed Yalin in front of me and told her to ask about the room rates. Since I had enough money, why not upgrade our accommodations? Somewhat sheepishly, she asked the question in Mandarin. However, the man ignored Yalin, looked directly at me and told me in perfect English, "Our minimum rate is thirty U.S. Dollars per night; however, we are currently booked through the next three days." He handed me a colorful brochure about the hotel and said, "I hope we can have you as guests in the future." As we walked away, I said to Yalin, "This is an elegant place, but I wouldn't stay here even if it were free; I hate snobbish businesses."

30

Getting to Hong Kong

We crossed the street from the Royal Laotian Hotel and walked through the swinging front doors of World Traveler's Inn & Bistro. The building had a slightly musty smell of Southern Asian humidity and ancient teak floors. The front desk and hotel activities seemed to be on one side of the large entrance room, on the other, a bar, several booths and tables holding mostly heavy drinkers doing some lite eating: Brits drinking stengha while snacking on fish and chips; Russians drinking vodka and munching pieroshki[37]; Chinese drinking pejiao[38] while ingesting miantao[39]; others drinking and eating whatever someone bought for them—all in a loud blather of various languages underscoring the establishment's imitation convivial atmosphere.

I smiled at Yalin and said, "I like this place; it's like the real world, variety and chaos."

---

37 Russian meat pie similar to a calzone.

38 Chinese beer

39 Chinese wheat noodles

A very attractive Laotian waitress wearing a provocative, light green cheongsam with a split reaching just below her left hip, suggesting an inviting interior, approached us and asked in perfect English, "Would you like a booth or table?"

I defaulted to Yalin, and she answered while pointing, "Let's sit at that empty table in the corner. It is a perfect spot for watching people coming and going.

I had never been much of an alcohol drinker except for a few glasses of Champaign; however, on rare occasions—once or twice each year—I would drink a bottle of beer, absolutely never more than two. Yalin had never tasted beer so I asked for a, "tall, cold, bottle of beer and two glasses."

"You want Lao, German, Chinese, Russian, Japanese, or American?"

That question told us about the diversity of clientele that visited World Traveler's Inn & Bistro, truly a place for drifters from around the world.

I had never tasted Japanese beer but once, that being while recovering from my Korean War wounds in Japan; Lieutenant Wilson had secreted some beer into our hospital ward one night, so I answered, "We'll try the Japanese."

A couple of minutes later, the waitress returned with a cold bottle of Asahi beer and two frosted glasses. I poured Yalin about an inch and filled my glass. She sipped and immediately got a painful look on her face as a shiver ran through her shoulders, and she said "Blaa!" (*I think we all detested that first taste of beer. Didn't we?*)

Just as I started roaring with laughter, three Caucasian men walked through the swinging front doors, a medium sized man walking with a observable limp, flanked by two much larger men, both wearing tropical suit jackets with bulges under their breasts; obviously armed bodyguards, their heads on swivels, quickly looking from side to side as they scanned the entire room. The limping man in the middle looked straight ahead as he walked with his impaired but quick pace toward the elevator. As he passed within a few feet of us, I noticed his left ear; the lobe was missing—shot off near the Chosen Reservoir, in North Korea, on a terrible night, November 29, 1950—he was Lieutenant Wilson.

I jumped from my seat and ran toward him, shouting, "Lieutenant Wilson! Lieutenant Wilson!" My arms were extended for an embrace, but one of his escorts blocked my way and immediately pointed a 45 caliber pistol at my head.

Lieutenant Wilson spun around as Yalin screamed. Initially his puzzled look alarmed me, then he started laughing, pushed his bodyguard aside, put his arms around me and gave me one of the most welcome hugs of my life.

Tears of happiness streamed down our cheeks as he said, "Theo! Theo! I can't believe it's you." He pushed me an arm's length away, "You don't look like my eighteen-year-old hero now."

One of his bodyguards whispered into his right ear, and Lieutenant Wilson, said, rapid fire, "Let's get out of here; follow me."

"Wait," I responded, "I have to get my sweetheart."

Yalin stood a few feet away with an astonished look on her face. I grabbed her hand, Lieutenant Wilson grabbed my arm, and one of his guardians ushered us into a service elevator.

We went to the 8th Floor, the top floor, totally occupied by *Water Resources Management Company (WRMC),* which I later learned was a front organization for the CIA. Soon we entered a room that revealed the nature of Lieutenant Wilson's current profession. One side of the room was filled with radio equipment, both receivers and transmitters, where two men with headsets on apparently monitoring radio frequencies, obviously concentrating on their task, scarcely gave us a glance. The opposite wall held unlocked racks contained M-15 automatic rifles, hand grenades, flare guns, and various other armaments. Lieutenant Wilson quickly led us through this outer room and into his private, windowless office, one cooled by a wall air conditioner and a large ceiling fan.

As soon as he closed the door, with the two bodyguards stationed outside, Lieutenant Wilson took a step back, looked at me, and said, "Theo, I simply cannot believe you are here. How in the hell did you get to Longprabong? Where did you come from? Who is this beautiful lady?"

When I started to tell the story of our epic journey with: "Well, Lieutenant...,"

He interrupted me, and emphatically told me, "Listen, Theo, please never call me *Lieutenant* again." As I found out later, all of the twenty-five agents working directly under his supervision called him *Timothy* or *Tim*. He added, "Our Marine Corps days are long gone."

We spent more than two hours exchanging information. I told everything except the details concerning the deaths of people I dearly loved; only my original family was discussed. Yalin listened attentively. When I got to the lottery-money issue, another tale Yalin didn't know about, Tim—as I would now address him—said, "Are you shitting me? I'll be god-dam! What are you doing teaching English in this part of the world when you have that kind of money?"

I explained, "I love teaching English, and I needed to get away from the United States, at least for a few years. All the money in the universe could not give me the joy I get from hearing my students develop their English skills.

"Actually, Tim, I think I have only made two or three extravagant expenditures. One, a weekend ski celebration in Jackson Hole, Wyoming that turned out to be a heart breaking disaster, and the other is Yalin's diamond ring, which, incidentally, she only wears when we are in private. At YAU she concluded, correctly, that nothing could be more of a dead giveaway that she had a relationship with a foreigner than a one carat diamond ring on her finger."

After we all laughed, I put a smile on Yalin's face when I explained that as soon as we got to *civilization*, before I married her, I was going to buy her a another ring, one she would be comfortable wearing in any circumstance. Finally, I asked Tim, "What are you doing here? All of that fire power in the other room suggests you have more than an interesting job."

Tim became tense and guarded, only saying, "I will tell you about all of that later"

"How are your leg wounds, Tim?"

"I have more stainless steel than bones in my left leg; my right leg has some hideous scars, but thanks to you, I still have two legs." Again, we laughed, while Yalin got a puzzled look on her face; Tim noticed.

"Maybe you don't know it, Yalin, but your man is a real hero in the United States, and for me personally he is my savior; he saved my life in Korea, and he saved my legs."

Then the discussion turned to our situation on the lamb, trying to get to Hong Kong but having no idea how. The Chinese government was undoubtedly looking for us with execution for me and prison for Yalin in mind. Yalin didn't have a passport or visa of any kind; and, we thought she would have our baby in about seven months, but we didn't know for sure since a doctor had not confirmed her pregnancy.

With a ferruled brow and fretful eyes, Tim asked, "Have you checked into a Hotel?"

As soon as I mentioned the Mekong View Inn, where we rented a room, his expression turned grim. "We have to get you out of there immediately. This town is full of Chinese agents. In fact I spotted two when I came in downstairs. If they aren't looking for you now, they soon will be. You stay here. I will have three of my men take Yalin to the Mekong View Inn, pick up all of your things, and come directly back. You are going to bunk here on this floor in a secure room. After we get you set up, fed, and rested, we will figure out what to do next. This is *payback time,* Theo. I am not sure how, but I am going to see that both of you get to Hong Kong and hopefully not by swimming."

As soon as Yalin and her escorts left Tim's office, he immediately started talking about things not appropriate for Yalin's ears:

"Theo, I am the CIA Station Chief for Northern Laos. I have twenty-five agents that work with me, ten Americans and the rest indigenous men and women. Four of my men fought with the French at Dien Bien Phu before the French were tossed out of Vietnam last year with their tails between their legs.

When Pongbong, a village about thirty clicks[40] east of here, became a staging area for Ho Chi Minh's army, the one agent we had here at the time, another former U.S. Marine, told his superiors in Washington that the coalition of North Vietnam and China often used Laotian territory, and the backs of Laotian men and women, to haul their supplies into South Vietnam. He told them the situation would probably lead to a war the U.S. would have trouble staying out of. Nevertheless, the bureaucrats in Washington generally ignored him, but the CIA did beef up this station. Consequently, they sent this crippled ex-Marine here, supposedly to gather information and try to keep the lid on in Laos. Frankly, it isn't working, and, now we are a lot closer to that war, and my CIA superiors in Washington know it, but the politicians don't. Interesting? Yes! Fun? No!

"We are in a precarious, sitting-ducks situation in this hotel, but until our new compound is finished, hopefully in three more months, we just have to deal with the dangers of being quartered here.

"Still, we have managed to develop some intelligence resources that are providing important information. The leader of the elephant caravan you rode with is one of our assets."

At that point, Yalin and her escorts returned with our few possessions. Tim told me we should get some rest and be his guests for dinner later that evening.

Our room in Tim's hotel compound, large geometrically but windowless—very comfortable physically while at the same time mentally confining—became our sanctuary.

That evening and the next day, we talked extensively with Tim and his staff members, listened to music, watched movie videos, and worked out in the CIA's well equipped, air conditioned exercise room. On our second day, Yalin ran for almost two hours on a treadmill and I for one.

On the morning of our third day, Tim asked us to come to his office. Two men, one American, Richard Manwaring, and one an English speaking Laotian, Moo Rang Sut, plus a Chinese-Lao

---

40 A click is roughly equivalent to one kilometer.

woman, Dow Jingwen, were there. Tim got right to the point. Obviously taking on his professional role as a CIA Station Chief, he started a monolog:

"I have an option for you, one that is more radical for you, Yalin, than Theo. If you will agree to let us interrogate you as a Chinese intelligence sources, I can get you out of Laos, through Dong Tam, Vietnam, and on to Hong Kong.

"The downside for you, Yalin, is that we will probably never allow you to return to China and your family. At this time, however, you are undoubtedly facing many years in prison, maybe torture and even death if you return to China. The Chinese Intelligence Service has undoubtedly determined that you escaped China with an *American war criminal*, Theo.

"Theo, your risks are minimal, but we will still debrief you. You may think you don't have any information of intelligence value; however, I assure you that is not the case. At present we have so few windows into China that any information is valuable. The operation of the school you taught at, the conditions students live and study in, your general and specific cultural observations and opinion are all important.

"Yalin, you can give a more in depth look into Chinese education from a student's perspective, very valuable information. Jingwen will be your primary interrogator, but Moo and Richard will also be involved.

"If you agree, the process will take several hours, probably six or seven, maybe more, and, if you are on-board, it will start this morning. Do you have any questions?"

I asked, "How is this connected with me getting Yalin to Hong Kong in a way that will allow us not to be looking over our shoulders for the Hong Kong immigration authorities to arrest her?"

"Good question, Theo. With the interviews, I can designate you ISIDs, Intelligence Sources in Danger[41], and give you appropriate pseudonyms. You are, indeed, in extreme danger. With that designation I can fly you on a Water Recourses Management Company's

---

41 intelligence sources in danger

(WRMC) chopper to Dong Tam in Vietnam, and from there to Hong Kong about two days later. Why don't you go back to your room and discuss my proposal."

I looked at Yalin. She looked directly into my eyes, a mode of communication we often used, one more authentic than words. With misty eyes, she looked at Tim and emphatically shook her head while saying, "Yes! Yes! Thank you! Thank you!"

I added, "We want to go with your plan, Tim."

Looking at Yalin, "Are you sure you want to do this, to be interrogated, Yalin? If you do, everyone in this room needs to hear you say so."

"Yes, Tim, I want to be interrogated."

"Ok, before we get started, let me give both of you an AKA."

Tim opened a safe and extracted a green, hardbound notebook. "Uhh, Theo, your pseudonym will be 'Tonto.' Yalin yours is 'Pocahontas'. We will use your pseudonyms on all interrogation documents, messages, radio or telephone conversations, and correspondence. By the way, mine is 'Red Panther.'"

With Yalin's affirmation, she and I were taken to separate rooms, she initially with Jingwen, and I with Richard Manwaring. After two-hours of recorded questioning, we took a break, switched questioners, and went on for another hour. After lunch we each had another session, and yet another shorter one, more of a review and confirmation, that evening.

The next morning, Tim spent an hour in private with Yalin and later thirty-minutes with me. We had earned our designations as ISIDs. That evening, we signed sworn affidavits agreeing to secrecy and to the accuracy of the manuscripts generated by our interrogations.

The following day, our fifth in Longprabong, we took off in a WRMC helicopter from the roof of Tim's hotel compound, Yalin's first flight on any kind of aircraft. As the props revved up and the aircraft vibrated, she squeezed my hand and asked, "Are we OK now?"

My answer, "Yes, I think so." I gave her a kiss on the cheek fol-lowed by a thumbs-up and a smile. Fretfully, she half-smiled back.

Just before we left, Tim told us we would be in Dong Tam for about three days, not the two as he previously stated. This would give him a little more time to coordinate with the agencies in Hong Kong that would be critical to our unobstructed arrival, and to in-sure we could live there as long as we wanted—unencumbered.

Our stay in Dong Tam gave me insight into just how involved the United States already was in Southeast Asia, Laos and Vietnam in particular. Helicopters bearing the WRMC logo were constantly landing and taking off, their occupants always adorned in jungle appropriate clothing, carrying automatic weapons and packs suit-able for the transport of communications equipment. Once each day a WRMC marked Caribou transport airplane landed around noon-time loaded with food, water, and boxes of equipment, and three or four men, presumably CIA agents.

At 2 p.m. the same plane took off with two or three people as passengers. This turned out to be the logistics and supply conduit between CIA Headquarters in Hong Kong and the CIA's activities in both Vietnam and Laos. Tim's station in Longprabong was logis-tically downstream and served on an as-needed basis.

What appeared to be U.S. Special Forces troops—their clothes bore no names or ranks— provided the security for the compound. When I tried to engage them in conversation, while polite and pro-fessional, they provided no information.

Dong Tam occupied about one-half square mile of jungle space with a six foot high berm enclosing the perimeter; one unimproved road exited the compound and led to Mi Toe, a large village about ten kilometers down the Mekong.

On the south edge of the WRMC compound, a sizeable dock stood with river craft constantly coming and going during the day-light hours. What appeared to be reconnaissance teams, all armed, often arrived and departed in low draft, but high powered, river boats.

All personnel on Dong Tam lived in sandbag protected, prefabricated buildings without windows; all had air conditioners, and each building had a large water tank—probably capable of holding 200 gallons of water—on its roof. A small field hospital with one doctor and three corpsmen provided medical services.

Since we had been cooped up in the World Traveler' Inn for five days, it was liberating to be able to walk under the puffy white, cumulus clouds of the Mekong Delta; however, Dong Tam was a man's place. During the three days we spent there, the only woman present, Yalin, who just happened to be a beautiful woman—even in her bush garb—constantly turned men's heads. Apparently many of them had not seen a woman for a while.

On our third day, a man with a serious expression on his face, wearing a yellow T-shirt with WRMC stenciled on it in blue, handed me a piece of yellow paper, one stamped in red with *"SECRET**SECRET**SECRET—BURN AFTER READING—REPEAT—BURN AFTER READING."*

Then he said, "Red Panther sent this message to you. Please read it closely two times, or more, and memorize it; then I will burn it for you. I will wait."

The message read. "Arrangements made for Tonto and Pocahontas : You will leave tomorrow on the WRMC currier flight to Hong Kong. You will be met on the tarmac in Hong Kong by a WRMC driver who will take you directly to the Hong Kong Special Entry Department. Go to the third floor. Ask for Gloria Chalmer; she will be waiting for you, and she will ask you for your case file code and quiz you to substantiate your identities. Your case file code is WRMC-Red Panther-IRID 13. IMPORTANT!: Memorize your case file code.

"Give me a mission report within 24 hours after your arrival in Hong Kong. To do that, go to Water Recourses Management Company at 2347 Kings Road, Hong Kong. Give your case file number, again, WRMC-Red Panther-IRID 13 to David Gathers. Tell him 'Yes' for mission accomplished, 'No' if you have problems.

"Keep David Gathers informed about where you are living. DON'T TALK TO HIM. Write any information for David on a card or piece of paper <u>while you are standing in front of him.</u> He will read it and destroy the paper. Don't worry, he has a great memory. I will communicate. Good Luck. *Red Panther.*"

31

Freedom in Hong Kong

T im, AKA *Red Panther*, had made slick arrangements for us; all his plans worked perfectly: the WRMC driver met us as we stepped off the plane, and within fifteen minutes a clerk led us to Gloria Calmer's office in the Hong Kong Special Entry Department. She stood as we entered her office, and without extending her hand, looked me in the eye and said, "And, who might you be?"

"I am Tonto and this is my wife-to-be, Pocahontas."

"You can call me Gloria," then with a knowing, half-smile, "What can I do for you two?"

"We are here concerning WRMC-Red Panther-IRID 13," I replied.

Gloria asked, "Is Red Panther still in Bangkok?"

"No, he is in Longprabong, Laos," I replied.

"I understand you and Red Panther had some experiences together in the Philippines in 1949," said Gloria.

"No, our experiences together were in North Korea in late 1950."

Turning to Yalin, Gloria asked, "How long have you been teaching?"

Nervously, and in a shaking voice, Yalin answered, "I have never been a teacher, only a student."

Gloria asked Yalin another question, "When you went into Laos from Cambodia, what was the color of the horse you were riding?"

Yalin looked at me in panic, but then her eyes lit up. "We didn't go into Laos from Cambodia, and we didn't ride horses. China is where we came from, by walking and on elephants."

Gloria then smiled and extended her hand to Yalin first, then me, while saying, "Welcome to Hong Kong. We are going to make your travels a little easier."

One hour later, after photos and fingerprinting, Yalin received a Hong Kong passport; now she was a Hong Kong citizen, giving her the full protection of the British government and the freedom to travel without a visa to many countries in the world, including the United States. As we left Gloria's office, Yalin carried her passport with pride and a sense of liberation; only a few days earlier, it would have been senseless of her to even dream of obtaining that document.

When we left the building, the WRMC driver was waiting for us, and he immediately drove to the Water Recourses Management Company at 2347 Kings Road into underground parking, stopped in front of an elevator, and said, "Take your bags. Go to the Fifth Floor."

We exited the car, and the driver drove off.

As the elevator opened on the Fifth Floor, two armed guards stopped us, one a tall Eurasian male, the other an attractive Caucasian female. A third imposing guard stood across the hallway with an automatic weapon at the ready. The tall man said, "Leave your bags here, and stand with your hands against this wall, feet spread. You are about to be searched. If that is a problem for you, let us know now."

"No problem," I replied, at the same time glancing at Yalin who seemed terrified. I gave her a smile, and said, "It's OK. Don't worry."

After passing the search, we were ushered through a large, steel, electronically coded door into a Spartan-like office. As soon as we walked in, an unsmiling, but not intimidating, man entered the room from a back office. Immediately he said, "I am Gathers. Do you have a message for me?"

Sticking to the script, I said, "WRMC-Red Panther-IRID 13; Yes!"

David Gathers turned out to be an efficient secret agent extraordinaire. That first time I saw him, without speaking, he wrote on a piece of paper and pushed it to me. It read:

You will have unobtrusive security for six weeks, more if we think you need it. If you believe you recognize a person as one of our agents, do not speak to them or try to communicate with them in any way. They will know if you are in imminent danger. If you need to communicate with me, call the number on the card I am about to give you. Simply state IRID 13. One of our agents will contact you immediately. This message will be destroyed as soon as you finish reading it two times.

I read the message twice and handed it back to Gathers; he immediately fed it into a shredding machine, handed me a business card—ostensibly from a Hong Kong Florist—turned his back and walked into his inner office.

We were escorted out of the building's front entrance, and to a smiling Chinese driver, one driving an unmarked, white sedan. He said, "Welcome to Hong Kong. My name is Chang; I have been instructed to take you to any hotel you want. What are your names and where to?"

"I am Tonto and this is Pocahontas."

The driver laughed, "Really?"

"For now, really."

Then I asked, "Is the Peninsula Hong Kong Hotel still one of the best in the city."

"Indeed it is," responded Chang. "It is the most expensive too."

"That's OK. We are going to splurge for a few days."

I wanted Yalin's first experiences in Hong Kong to be positive and memorable; I booked us for two weeks into a premium penthouse suite at the Peninsula Hong Kong Hotel.

Due to our unsavory appearance—we were still wearing the same jungle clothing we purchased in Longprabong—the Front Desk Manager was somewhat taken aback when I told him, "We want the best suite of rooms you have available, one with a good view of Victoria Harbor."

Undoubtedly, not too many jungle or river rats frequented the Peninsula Hong Kong Hotel. As his eyes scanned our bodies from head to toe, you could tell he was thinking, *What opium smuggler's boat did these people get off of?* Nevertheless, I presented my Mexican passport and registered us for the first time—even though we were not yet married— as Mr. and Mrs. Theodore Ruiz Rogers. Room cost per night: 15,000 HKD[42] ($2,000 US). I paid $6,000 in cash with the tacit understanding I would pay the balance when we checked out. I also told the manager we would probably be charging a significant amount to our room. Since this was my first stay at his hotel, he asked me for a bank reference. I quickly rummaged through my documents folder and found a card with my British Royal Bank of Hong Kong account information. That was sufficient.

An immaculately uniformed Chinese porter with a distinct British accent led us to our elegant, temporary home, one with fantastic views of Victoria Harbor and Hong Kong Island. He gave us a tour, showing us how to work the entertainment center, the electronically controlled floor to ceiling drapes, and the water controls for the exceptionally oversized, spa-like bath tub.

When the porter departed, Yalin immediately took me by the hand and led me to the king size bed where she pulled me down. My immediate thought was: *Wow! This new first class setting has activated her sexual desires.* Not so, at least not at that moment.

Yalin put her head on my shoulder and said, "Theo, I can't believe we are here; that I am with you; that I have a Hong Kong passport; and, that I will be your wife and have your baby. My friends and family would not believe what we have been through and where I am at this moment. I am not sure I believe it." Then she put her

---

42 Hong Kong dollars—in 1960, 7.5 HKDs equaled approximately 1 USD.

arms around my neck, kissed me and added, "Thank you My Love; thank you for everything."

All I could say was, "I love you, Yalin, and I want nothing more than for you to be safe and happy." Then, the physical expression of our love for each other did overwhelm us.

For a fleeting hour, I was as happy as I had ever been in my life; then, it hit me: *I love Yalin so much, is she going to die like the other people I loved?* Soon, however, my thoughts turned to more rational and practical issues.

We were still wearing our jungle clothes, and we were anxious to get out of that garb and into something more appropriate for Hong Kong.

Two blocks from The Peninsula Hong Kong we walked by a large store with immaculately attired male and female manikins in the windows. Yalin lit up. "Here, let's go in here; I saw a picture of this store in a magazine girls looked at in my dormitory. *Lai Chi Kok* stores are famous in China, but there is no place to buy from them; besides, wearing their clothes would not be allowed."[43]

After two hours in *Lai Chi Kok*—the first five minutes spent convincing Yalin and the salesmen not to consider prices—Yalin's lifetime clothes-shopping-famine came to an end. With my continuous goading, she selected three pairs of linen slacks, with complimenting blouses; three casual silk dresses; two full length chiffon dresses, one black and one white; athletic shorts and shirts, and four pairs of shoes, one pair for running, a variety of lingerie, and several accessories, including beautiful strings of natural, black and white pearls with matching earrings.

For me, the enjoyable part of this process was watching Yalin in front of the body length mirrors, turning her body, tilting her head, often smiling, and exchanging recommendations and opinions with the two Chinese salesmen. Their conversations were in rapid fire Mandarin, so fast I could only understand an occasional sentence.

---

43   In China during the 1950s, 1960s, and early 1970s, no one in China was allowed to wear Western clothing; men and women only wore simple blue or grey trousers, shirts, and jackets. Administrators and Communist officials wore blue; workers wore grey.

While some of Yalin's apparel was being measured for altering—all of our purchases would be delivered to our hotel room that evening—I bought everything I needed: some running shoes and shorts, a linen suit, one silk dress shirt and tie, two sports shirts, two pairs of slacks, some underwear, and sox.

We dressed ourselves in some of our new clothes and walked out of *Lai Chi Kok* looking like high-end, casually garbed, ecstatically happy, Hong Kong residence. We were!

As we exited the store, for the first time I had the sense that we were being followed, a valid nous considering our "unobtrusive security" promise. For a couple of minutes, I thought about the possibility of a Chinese agent following us. Then a noticed a Caucasian man walking slightly behind us on the other side of the street. As he read a newspaper, he glanced at us, and when we turned the corner, he also turned but still on the opposite side of the street. After that, I took no notice of him. I felt we were safe and free.

We further enjoyed our newly won freedom from intense stress during a walk planned for one hour, but it turned into three hours of strolling arm in arm along the waterfront of Victoria Harbor; riding the ferry to Hong Kong Island and back; window shopping; and each of us eating three French ice cream cones.

When we finally walked back into the hotel the concierge intercepted us, "Mr. Rogers, I have a message for you from our hotel manager." Obviously a call to the British Royal Bank of Hong Kong inspired the manager to write:

Dear Mr. and Mrs. Rogers,

Welcome to the historic Peninsula Hong Kong Hotel. I am delighted you are staying with us. If there is anything I, or my staff, can do for you, don't hesitate to let us know.

Our limousine and all of our other services, including multilingual guides, are at your service without remuneration. We are here to oblige you.

Please allow me to emphasize; I am available to you 24 hours a day. If you have a problem or a concern, just contact the Main Desk, and I will quickly return your call.

Enjoy your stay at The Peninsula Hong Kong Hotel.

Reynolds B. Farnsworth
VIP Service Manager

I thanked the concierge for the message, and asked him, "Where is the best place to buy a special dress for my wife and a suit for me; we are going to a wedding?"

Yalin gave me a sharp, inquisitive look. "Whose wedding are we going to; we don't know anyone here?"

"I'll tell you when we get to the elevator."

The concierge replied, "If you want the best, *La Maranga*44 has a clothier in our hotel. Just take that (*pointing*) vestibule toward the pool and you will see it on the right."

Moments later, in the elevator, "Theo, what wedding are we going to?"

"Ours! Aren't you anxious to get married and be my wife?"

"Certainly, but we haven't even talked about when that should be."

"Well, that's why we are talking about it now."

With a huge smile, "Theo, I want you to purpose like I have seen men do in Western movies. By the lake in Kunming was great, but I want to hear those words again, here in the free air of Hong Kong."

We stepped out of the elevator and into our penthouse suite. As soon as I closed the door, I led Yalin to our balcony overlooking stunning Victoria Harbor; there the conversation became romantically serious. I took her in my arms, "I love you dearly, Yalin; I want you to be my wife. Will you marry me day after tomorrow?"

---

44 World famous and prestigious Italian design-fashion company, founded in 1935 in Milan, Italy.

With tears oozing from her eyes, "You know I will, Theo, because you are the only man I have ever loved."

The next day we prepared for our wedding: she wouldn't let me buy her a custom, expensive wedding dress, preferring instead the white chiffon dress from *Lai Chi Kok,* so I didn't buy another suit. The one I purchased earlier would be my wedding attire. Later that evening, we went to a jeweler recommended by the hotel and bought my soon to be wife the ring of her choice. In spite of my lobbying for a larger diamond, the ring she chose had a smaller diamond—one-half carat—than the one I bought for her in Kunming.

The morning of our wedding, I stopped by my bank to retrieve my U.S. passport from my safety deposit box, and then we went directly to the Hong Kong Bureau of License and Vital Statistics where we procured and filed or marriage license. Officially, we were now man and wife; still, of course, we wanted to have a wedding ceremony.

That afternoon, with Yalin looking movie-star beautiful in her white dress, with matching pearls, and me in a white linen suit, both of us wearing pink carnations, we had a Buddhist type wedding[45]at *Wong Tai Sin Temple.* Ajahun Bhikkhun, my Buddhist tutor, three of his colleagues, and five apprentice monks attended. Ajahun and his compatriots melodiously chanted their best wishes, and Ajahun anointed us with incense and ceremonial water.

It was a happy day but not one without trepidation on my part: my concern for Yalin's safety and health kept clouding my mind. The thought of possibly losing her to accident or illness was terrifying, but I kept hammering those delusions from my conscious mind, driving them down into my paranoia conservatory—my subliminal.

For two happy and romantic days we shopped and walked the thoroughfares of the magnificent, exotic city of Hong Kong. We took redundant boat and ferry rides around and across Victoria Harbor, visited the Animal Park, and the Royal Gardens, constantly aware that we were being escorted by one, sometimes two, men

---

45 There is no standard Buddhist wedding. It is a secular event where a monk might chant for the couple, if they employ one.

for our security. We never spoke to them, nor they to us, but it was comforting to know they were always present. On the other hand, I really didn't feel like we needed their attention; I always felt safe in Hong Kong.

A week after our wedding a pediatrician examined Yalin to determine if she really was pregnant, and to her delight and my resignation, he confirmed our suspicions, probably three months along. Because of the hectic travel, diet, and the living conditions we experienced over the past month, she had not gained the weight one might have expected, but the doctor said she and the fetus seemed to be in fine condition.

That same week we visited my bank and reviewed my accounts. Since I previously directed the bank to hold all of my account statements, the bank officer brought me up to date, and did everything short of openly gloating when he informed me that the balance of my accounts had increased twenty-five percent in less than two years, now totaling fifty-six million U.S. dollars. The next day I had the 110 million—10 million more than I had originally deposited—still in the Bozeman bank transferred to Hong Kong, most of it to be invested in blossoming Asian companies. To be honest, I wasn't giving my investing a lot of rational thought—I would years later—since I knew I could lose more than half of my money and still have enough for my family to live on comfortably for the rest of our lives.

At this point, I thought no further in the future than the birth of our child; however, since Yalin was now a Hong Kong citizen, and we would be living there for the indefinite future, we agreed that we should purchase a home.

At that time, Hong Kong had few Western style, single family homes, ones with independent roofs and two car garages. In contrast, the preponderance of homes existed in high rise condominium complexes. The British Royal Bank's Real Estate Office advised us to take a look at a new, highly acclaimed development on Hong Kong Island overlooking Victoria Harbor, its name: *Harbor Victoria Manors*.

Almost all of the homes in *Harbor Victoria Manors* had been sold and occupied; yet, a top floor unit with approximately 4,000 square feet of living space, available at a price of 80 million Hong Kong dollars (approximately 10 million U.S. dollars), became our focus. Since I would pay cash for the home, we could move in in one week.

One of the alluring selling points: we could have a *yard* and *garden* on the quarter of the rooftop we would own. As I told Yalin the second time we looked at the property, "I can see you living here with a cook to prepare or meals, a maid to clean our house, a Bentley and a driver to take you around the city, and a roof top, yard-like-garden."

Yalin's only response, "That would be nice. Let's talk about it tonight."

When we returned to our hotel to dwell on the decision, a card under our door simply read, "See David Gathers at your convenience. DON'T TAKE A TAXI OR DRIVE. Take Bus 654 on Lancashire Road; get off at the LaSalle Road stop. You will recognize our building on the corner. You have mail from Red Panther."

Immediately, I went to David Gathers office at WRMC where he handed me an envelope. He instructed me, "Sit here at my desk. Read the letter. When you finish I will shred it. Write a response if you want, and I will send it back to Red Panther in the secure pouch."

Hello, Tonto,

I am happy you and Pocahontas made it safely to Hong Kong. I requested unobtrusive security for you for six weeks. 'Unobtrusive' meaning, the agents protecting you should not be visible to you or interrupt your daily routine. If you think you need security longer, let David Gathers know; he will arrange it.

It is hard for me to explain what seeing you meant to me. Over the past two years I have been so involved in and devoted to my job that I had forgotten how important you are to me, actually to my very existence.

Give Pocahontas, my love. She is a special woman; all who talked with her here were astounded by her intelligence, English language skills, and her ability to describe what life as a Chinese university student is like. And, I don't need to tell you, she is a beautiful woman.

Please let me know how things are going. Your devoted, buddy, Red Panther

I responded:

Dear, Red Panther,

Great to hear from you. Pocahontas and I were married two days ago,, and now we are in the process of buying a home, one I hope you will visit on your next trip to Hong Kong.

I don't think we need the security, although during our first days here it was nice to know we had it. It can stop today as far as I am concerned, but I will leave that up to you.

Pocahontas is definitely pregnant and we are thrilled that we will soon be parents. It's a little scary for me though.

Even though many years have passed, our time together in Korea is a memory that will never die. You were a great officer, and I am sure you are just as good in your current position.

Hoping to see you soon, Tonto

That night, Yalin and I discussed our plans to buy the high rise home on Hong Kong Island. I did most of the talking, and I think she tried hard to share my enthusiasm about the idea of living in a sanctuary for the affluent and practicing the wealthy lifestyle: expensive cars, a yacht, servants, cooks, drivers, rich friends, and, of course, a nanny for our baby. Yalin fell asleep while I rambled on about how comfortable and enjoyable our lives would soon be—after we moved into our perfect home and after she delivered our perfect baby.

Sometime after midnight, Yalin shook me awake. "Theo! Theo! Wake up! We need to talk."

Forcing myself awake, I responded, "OK, Sweetheart, let's talk."

"Please don't misunderstand me, Theo, I love you dearly; I love who you are; I love the things you have done in your life; I love the way you got me out of China and to Hong Kong, but to be honest, there are some things that are starting to drive me crazy."

"I'm sorry, Sweetheart," I said. "Go on, tell what is bothering you."

"You have to remember, Theo, I spent most of my life living in a farm house where our biggest worry had to do with eating our next meal. Fancy cars, homes, servants, and living a life like a movie star never entered my mind. Those kinds of things weren't practical for me then; they aren't practical for me now, and I don't really think they are right for you.

"I don't want to live in a home where I can't take care of myself and you; I don't want someone to cook our meals. I want to cook for us. We don't need a 4,000 square foot home when half that would be great. And, I don't care to rub elbows with rich people. I just don't think we would be happy living that kind of life."

Yalin's statement shocked me, but it immediately rang true, and I suddenly realized I didn't want the amenities of the affluent either. She made me realize that my intention of grasping the wealthy lifestyle was solely to impress her, not to make us happy and reinforce our love for each other.

"Please, Theo, let's not be in such a big hurry. Why don't we look at some other possibilities? Let's start by visiting the Temple Wat and meditating about our future."

When Wong Tai Sin Wat gate opened the next morning at 6:00 a.m., we were the first to enter the grounds. I took Yalin on a tour of the wat surroundings that had so impressed me, actually changing my life, two years previously. I should have given her that tour before our wedding; she had only seen the main temple during our ceremony.

We only walked a few yards before Yalin took a deep breath and said, "Theo, this is absolutely beautiful, I am so glad we came here today."

A few minutes later, we entered the wat and performed our obligatory Buddhist rituals. I had never committed myself to being a Buddhist, never made the statement, or the philosophical commitment—I am a Buddhist. Yet, doing my three bows when I entered the wat on this day, after a stressful, emotional night, definitely gave me a feeling of liberation. I said to myself, "I am a Buddhist."

Then we went hand in hand to the sacred Bodhi Tree. There we meditated together for about thirty minutes.

As we left the wat and walked down a side street with the idea of exploring that part of Hong Kong, a portion that seemed much more tranquil than the Kowloon area where we resided in our hotel, we noticed several Western style homes. One had a moving truck in front where a crew was loading furniture. A woman standing in the front yard holding a young girl's hand smiled at us as we passed. Yalin and I stopped, walked onto the lawn and introduced ourselves. As it turned out, the woman, Margarie Bossier, a French Embassy employee in Hong Kong, returning to France, had lived with her family in that house for, in her words, "six great years."

As it turned out the house didn't fit their criteria when they rented it; but the nearby Buddhist wat and the tranquility of the neighborhood captured them. When we told her that we were house hunting, she immediately invited us in and gave us a tour.

The house, with about 2,500 square feet of floor space—big by Hong Kong standards—had four bedrooms, and with the exception of the kitchen and two bathrooms, all the floors were of highly polished teak; the kitchen had a large island, and one of the three bathrooms had a large spa-like bathtub and a separate shower. A one car garage sat unobtrusively in the rear of the property, separated from the house by a flower garden and two large queen crape myrtle trees adorned with large purple blooms. A stone path led through an ironwood gate, and a redwood fence surrounded the backyard, definitely an inviting place to read, a place to play with our children and eat family meals. Immediately, we were totally sold on that home. As we walked away Yalin looked at me and said, "Theo that is where I want to live."

After talking with the owner, we signed a six month lease. After living in the house for one month, I made him *an offer he couldn't refuse*, and it was ours.

We loved our house, a cathedral of sorts that Yalin turned into an impeccable place to live. She decorated the house with the skill of a trained interior designer, purchasing individual pieces of Chinese furniture—many would justify the label *antique*—to fit a particular place, like the rosewood dining room table which she enhanced with pure gold candle sticks. Typically, we sat on the same side of that big table where touching each other didn't require the moves of a gymnast.

As Yalin's shape changed from the flat stomached, narrow hipped, girl I fell in love with, our relationship grew stronger with each fraction of an inch the baby added to her now pear shaped form. We constantly talked to our unborn child as if it sat on its mother's lap. I would cup my hands, place them on Yalin's stomach, surround her navel, and say ridiculous things: "Wake up in there. Talk to us. Aren't you lonely; come out and play." Yalin would laugh so hard she would beg me to stop.

With about two months to go in the embryonic process, I could distinctly see and feel movement. That spurned us to plan for the baby's arrival: Where should our baby be born? Where would Yalin receive the best care?

I thought back to my father insisting that my sister and I be born in the United States; his idea being that American citizens are blessed with advantages most people in the world never enjoy. In 1932, my father was absolutely correct, and he still was in 1961.

After some research and consultation with our Hong Kong pediatrician, Doctor Jordan Lee, who recommended his medical school colleague, Doctor Benjamin Rush—he had delivered President Kennedy's children—we choose him to deliver our baby at Cedars Sinai Hospital in Los Angeles. We would have an excellent doctor and U.S. citizenship all in one package.

With her Hong Kong passport, and British citizenship that went with it, a visa for the United States would not be necessary. All we had to do: make a reservation and be on time at the airport; it would be easy.

For the next two months, our lives centered on our coming child. We also visited the wat each day to meditate; we exercised, in part together, first walking as man and wife, then running for me and more walking for Yalin. In short, we enjoyed a good life, romantically, physically, and spiritually.

With only two days to go before our departure for Los Angeles, we were packed with the efficiency only the hands of a woman like Yalin can provide, the only task remaining—board the plane. But the afternoon of that day, I received a strange message from David Gathers, *"Please*—a word he never used— *come to my office immediately."*

When I arrived at the WRMC's headquarters, for the first time David Gathers ushered me into his inner office.

"Theodore (*an alarm went off; he wasn't using my pseudonym*) I have some bad news for you, and it has been devastating for all of us at WRMC. I know you and Tim Wilson (*not Red Panther*) had a special relationship, but Tim is dead. I sniper shot him in the head as he left his hotel in Longprabong, ironically, on the same day he was moving to his new office in a more secure compound."

I stared at David in disbelief. The apotheosis of an indestructible man, Tim could not be dead; it had to be a mistake, an erroneous message, faulty identification, or a ruse to confuse the many enemy agents in Longprabong. "Are you certain? Who identified his body?"

"I had the same doubts you have about Tim being dead, too strong to die, too intelligent to get ambushed or picked off by sniper, but it is true. I saw his body an hour ago; it is definitely Tim."

32

Timothy Wong Rogers is Born in the U.S.A

Totally depressed, I walked the ten miles home in a mental fog, unbelieving, followed by forced acceptance, my curse of death foremost on my mind. When I gave the news to Yalin, we combined our grief with prolonged hugs and tears. We had lost our *savior*, our friend. We didn't eat that night, and both of us slept fitfully, but the next morning Yalin proclaimed, "Theo, we must get on with life. Tomorrow we leave for America; we need to be strong; we need to be ready."

We arrived in Los Angeles on January 15, 1961, at 3:30 p.m., at the beginning of the afternoon rush-hour traffic. During the thirty minute taxi drive from the Los Angeles Airport (LAX) to Santa Monica, Yalin squeezed my hand off and on, "Theo, look at that car. Look at that building. Where are all of these cars going? Will you be driving here? I think it is too dangerous; I don't want you to do it."

When we exited Interstate 405 and turned toward Santa Monica, the traffic decreased noticeably, and Yalin relaxed. As soon as we reached our apartment fronting Santa Monica Beach, we gave our temporary home a cursory walk through and headed for the water; Yalin had never seen an ocean or a beach.

The weather was unseasonably warm for January, near 80°; consequently, the beach was full of surfers and sun worshipers. Yalin had no idea what a Bikini bathing suit looked like, and she was understandably shocked to see statuesque girls attired in suits not quite covering the more interesting parts of the female anatomy.

We walked on the same beach and dipped our feet in the same surf I had with Mother Rogers on the day she died. A wave of fear swept through me as I clutched Yalin close to me. My death ghosts were following me, haunting me, eroding what should have been a glorious time in my life. Still, Yalin and I walked that beach every day, including the day Timothy Wong Rogers was born.

Before that epic event, however, I gave Yalin Southern California tours that included, the Glover home in San Bernardino—Uncle Ned lived there now, and we had a good visit—*Old Town* in Pasadena and Colorado Boulevard where I received my inspiration to become a Marine; Grumman's Chinese Theater in Hollywood; the Getty Museum; Disneyland; Santa Anita Park in Arcadia; and the Asian Museum in Pasadena. Yalin asked hundreds of questions, some I could answer, and she didn't seem bothered by those that I couldn't. Visiting, and walking through all of those places, should have been a daunting task for a lady whose stomach was getting larger and dropping lower by the hour. Obviously, however, she was very happy, and at night she slept like a baby; I wanted to be happy with her and also sleep well, but my constant reminiscing about Tim wouldn't allow real happiness, or slumber.

Late in the afternoon on February 7, as Yalin and I walked the beach admiring a teasing, setting sun—it seemed to hang on the horizon—I commented, "That sun will soon be coming up in Hong Kong and China."

"I know that, Theo, but in how many hours?"

I guessed and said, "twenty."

Yalin started laughing vigorously, maybe too forcefully, as she corrected me, "No! No! No! You have always told me the Hong

Kong was on the other side of the world from California. So if that is true it should be coming up now, but that isn't quite true; actually the morning sun is shining on our house in Hong Kong this very minute."

Then, just after I gave Yalin a teasing kiss on the cheek and said, "Thank you Professor," she got a strange look on her face, glanced down at her legs, then in a whisper said, "My water just broke. Look!" Sure enough, blood streaked liquid ran down her legs.

During our last visit to Doctor Rush's office, only a week previously, he said, "Yalin, you are getting close. If your water breaks, and that could happen before you feel any labor pains, get to the hospital as soon as possible."

I sat Yalin down on a bench near a closed lifeguard stand, ran up the bluff, and got our rental car. In less than ten minutes, I navigated our Cadillac Seville onto the Pacific Coast Highway and parked about 100 yards from where Yalin waited. I recruited some beach volleyball players to help me, and shortly we had her in the back seat. Immediately we were on our way to Cedars Sinai. All the way, Yalin repeated, "It's coming! It's coming!"

The Cedars *Emergency Room* nurses sensed urgency in my voice when I said, "My wife is having a baby! Right now! In the car!"

Without hesitation two nurses grabbed a gurney and ran with me to Yalin. One hour later Timothy Wong Rogers—combining the name of my hero, Lieutenant Timothy Wilson, and Yalin's family name, Wong, with Rogers—came into this world.

When I first saw Timothy, swaddled in a white blanket on his mother's stomach, emotion overcame me, and all I could do was blubber, "Oh, God! He is so beautiful; are you ok, Sweetheart?"

Yalin smiled and nodded as I kissed her forehead, her nose, and lips.

The next day, alone, for over an hour I looked at Timothy, an experience filled with undulating and conflicting emotion: happiness, intense love, doubt, questioning that I could be a good father, and concentrated fear, fear that the curse following me would be placed on my child or his mother; I loved both of them so much.

Before we left Santa Monica, three weeks after Timothy's birth, during our last visit to Doctor Rush, he gave both mother and baby a clean bill of health, but the last subject he addressed, *SIDS*, injected me with a heavy dose of intense anxiety. In the long run, my psyche would not be able to cope with that fear, and eventually it destroyed our family.

Doctor Rush explained that *sudden instant death syndrome,* better known as *SIDS*, somewhat of a medical mystery, infrequently killed babies between two and eight months after their birth. Dr. Rush cautioned, "Don't overdress your child or put too many blankets on him; don't put anything over his face, day or night, that might inhibit his breathing; and, most importantly, don't let him sleep on his stomach."

As we left the doctor's office, Timothy soundly sleeping in his mother's arms, Yalin had a beautiful smile on her face as if she had no fears or concerns; she didn't. However, I left with *SIDS* and my death curse foremost on my mind.

33

Retreat to Philippines

During the flight to Hong Kong, thirteen hours and thirty minutes, mother and baby slept most of the trip, but I didn't sleep one minute; I couldn't get the *SIDS* thing out of my thoughts. Repetitively, the same questions kept troubling me: *Should I be present during those critical eight months—the most dangerous SIDS period—after our child's birth? Could I take that risk? If I truly loved him, and unequivocally I did, would I dare be present during that period?*

Timothy grew quickly, nearly two pounds during our last three weeks in California; now he weighed eleven pounds. In addition, according to me, he smiled when I talked or sang to him. Yalin insisted that he didn't smile. "When he is twitching his mouth and nose, gas bubbles are going through his stomach."

Before we left Hong Kong for Los Angeles, I hired a lady to thoroughly clean the house, care for the many flowers and plants Yalin planted in the yard, and put cut flowers in every room of the house for our return. Bringing Timothy into a safe, pleasant environment stilled my fears for his well-being, but only temporarily. More significantly, I should never have started reading the *Hong Kong Times*, an English daily newspaper.

When I read the *Times* in the past, I focused my attention on the *Sports Page*. The United States basketball and football scores were my primary focus, and I enjoyed following my investments in the *Financial Section*, but the *Obituaries* became my bane.

Before I started reading the *Times*, I had never been interested in how many Hong Kong citizens died the previous day or the ages of the deceased. Nevertheless, with *SIDS* on my mind I looked for some evidence that infants rarely die. That, however, wasn't the case: almost every day, five or more deaths listed as *infants*—rather than a numerical age—appeared on the list, and sometimes as many as ten. The name of every infant on the page distressed me. I could feel the pain of their parents and the destruction of the dreams they had for their baby, and often disturbing images flashed through my mind. When I dwelt on those images for more than an instant, I imagined little bodies being placed in the cold ground or pushed into a crematorium; then I became nauseated. Furthermore, if I thought of one of those babies being my son, I quickly lapsed into mental paralysis.

Yalin often asked me, "Theo, why do you seem so sad? Doesn't little Timothy make you as happy as he makes me?

"Are you having nightmares? You were moaning in your sleep last night. I can't sleep when you are doing that. Is something wrong?"

How could I answer those questions? How could I explain the details of all the death that had surrounded me during my lifetime, beginning at the age of five? How could I explain my fears for Timothy? I should have tried then, but I waited; I waited much too long.

A few days after we returned from California, I visited the British Royal Bank of Hong Kong and setup a 10 million dollar investment trust fund for Timothy—mostly in Asian real estate—with the following stipulations: The money would be used for Timothy's education. Fifty percent of the fund's balance increase each year could be invested in other securities. What remained in the fund when Timothy finished graduate school, or turned thirty years of age, would be paid directly to him. I also deposited 10 million dollars for Yalin to be used as she wished.

When Timothy reached two months, the pressure I put on myself over *SIDS* started manifesting itself in bizarre ways. In one dream, after reading the *Hong Kong Times*, I saw Timothy's name at the top of the obituaries. Yalin woke me up while I screamed, "No! No!"

In another repetitive dream, Timothy gasped for breath under a pile of baby blankets and neither Yalin nor I could find him. In still another nightmare, our family was on the ferry to Hong Kong Island; Yalin had Timothy in her arms. The ferry sank, and I couldn't find either of them. While I stood on the shore a policeman kept asking me, "Why didn't you save your wife and baby?"

Finally, I started looking for some way to get away from my family, in my twisted mind, in order to save them. I tried to think of a way to explain to Yalin the intensity of my paranoia concerning death and Timothy without alarming her, without having her think she was living with a real nut—even though obviously she was. Every rationalization I came up with turned hollow. The only recourse, telling her the history and truth, became my course of action.

As we sat in our garden, with Timothy sleeping nearby in his bassinette, surrounded by nothing but peace and tranquility, I told Yalin about Rico and the penetrating stare of his mother's eyes; about the death of my family; the unpredictable death of Delores from a rare disease; Father Glover's death; the mysterious killing of Jim Cordell in Korea by a sniper we couldn't find; the incident on Santa Monica Beach when Mother Glover died; about the deaths of Jane and Gilroy in the avalanche at Jackson Hole; and finally, the recent death of Lieutenant Wilson. I explained, "There is only one thing all of those dead people had in common—me; I loved them all."

I went on to tell Yalin about my fixation on the *Hong Kong Times Obituaries* and the infants I see listed every day. Up until this point

Yalin had been silent, occasionally reaching out and touching my arm, but our eyes never met. When I told her, "Sweetheart, I feel like I must get away from Timothy until he is out of this critical period as a possible *SIDs* victim. She shook her head several seconds in disbelief. We finally looked at each other, "Theo, you know how much I love you and our family, and I believe every word you say, but it is hard for me to believe that you had anything to do with the deaths of all those people. Still, if getting away for a few months gives you any relief from your fears, I won't tell you not to go. If you do, I will miss you terribly. But first, don't you think it would be a good idea for you to talk to a psychiatrist?

"Yes, I agree. I will. I will."

With that we embraced. I sobbed, "I love you too." As if on cue, Timothy woke up and started crying.

Over the next two weeks, I met with Doctor Reginald Lee, one of Hong Kong's most acclaimed psychiatrists, four times, but as he said, "Psychiatric treatment is a long term, often a lifetime, process. Do not expect relief from your problem over the short term."

I couldn't wait through a long term. With me there, I believed Timothy could die any day. My bazar dreams were not going away. My love for my wife and son demanded—in my mind—immediate action.

34

Charlita the Mermaid

While I received treatment from Doctor Lee, I continued to search for a temporary place to live, and I found one through an ad in the Hong Kong Times:

Immediate Opening for an experienced English teacher. Must be a native English speaker, U.S. or UK citizen preferred. Dumaguete, Philippines. Call 63-797-4500 for more information .

I called that number, faxed my credentials to Dumaguete University of the Southern Philippines (DUSP), and ten near-sleepless days later, after three weeks of psychiatric treatment—I didn't receive more for many years, but I should have—I caught a plane for the short flight to Manila and a shorter one to Dumaguete.

Three things struck me on my first day in the Philippines: I already terribly missed my family; I called Yalin within an hour after I arrived in Manila. She put the phone to Timothy's ear while I repeatedly said, "I love you Timmy; I love you."

Second, the flora looked like Laos; third, almost everyone spoke at least some English, but few spoke it well.

DUSP helped me find a very nice furnished apartment on the north edge of town only ten minutes from the university. The beautiful setting, surrounded by tall coconut palms, banana plants, and a cornucopia of flowers somewhat soothed my longing for Yalin and Timothy. Within a matter of hours I hired Juana, a forty year old mother of three, to do my housekeeping, cooking, and laundry. She also accompanied me into the city to buy some additional furniture and a washing machine. I didn't want to see her going through the toil of washing my clothes by hand.

Two days later, I started teaching again, picking-up the classes of a British English teacher who became seriously ill with hepatitis, evacuated to Manila and then flown to London.

My four classes met four times each week for one hour. One of those classes, Creative Writing, became a source of joy and inspiration. Many of my students, while not yet great writers, demonstrated imaginations par excellence. Love stories, adventure sagas, humorous tales, epics that made me laugh or almost cry, but none of those writings inspired me the way a paper by Charlita Sabino did. Charlita's story detailed her activities between school terms and on weekends, specifically her adventures as a professional SCUBA diver:

The Underwater World
by Charlita Sabino

When I slip into the underwater world of the open ocean near my home on Apo Island, I am reminded of just how lucky I am. Few people have shared my experiences amongst the creatures and coral reefs that surround Apo Island in the Vasaya Islands, part of the Southern Philippines.

As an infant, Mother regularly put me in the pristine, turquoise waters of the Philippine Sea, only steps from the nipa hut we called home—I learned to swim before I learned how to walk or talk.

Later, Father taught me that our ocean water was as precious as the clean air we breathed; the warm sun lighting our glorious day and the white sand that cushioned my falls, also added to our virtuous and exultant lives. As he often said, "Those blessings of nature are more important than gold; they cannot be replaced, so never besmirch them."

Before I lived ten years, I sometimes cried when I saw tourists visiting our island throw trash in the water, saturate the air with huge beach fires that didn't cook food, and even defecate in sand—the same sand where my friends and I played—rather than walk up the cliff to the toilets. Many of them had absolutely no respect for the environment, or for those of us who lived on Apo. Distressing as those abysmal deeds were, our family made its living from the perpetrators of those crimes.

One day, when I was three, my older brother, Rizal, taught me how to snorkel, and I gloried in the peace and quiet I experienced for maybe a minute at a time under the water's surface. There I swam with the fish and collected beautiful sea shells that I took to my room. I placed them in a small glass bowl of sea water where I admired, studied, and drew pictures of them for hours. Then I carried them in a wet, cloth bag while I ran back to the sea and returned them to their homes.

Later, Rizal, who made his living teaching Americans and Europeans how to use the equipment necessary for staying under water for an hour or more, taught me how to SCUBA dive in the deep water, along the vibrant, coral reefs that encircle much of Apo Island.

On my fourteenth birthday, Rizal gave me all of the equipment I needed to go with him when he taught the foreigners how to dive and guided them under water. Soon, I became—as he introduced me—"Charlita my beautiful, intelligent, highly qualified assistant."

It took me years to believe those words of commendation, but when the day came when I did, at least in part, I knew that I too could make money as a professional SCUBA teacher and guide. Now, when I am not in school learning the skills of a highly qualified business woman, (I am a business major here at Dumaguete University.)I make money from my clients in the ocean, saving most of it for the day when I open: "Charlita's Dive School and Underwater Tours."

I revel in teaching and showing visitors, whose normal habitats are the cement jungles of Western cities, the wonders of inner space, introducing them to the inhabitants of that sacred place: the fish, large, small, and tinny, the sharks, sometimes even a whale, and the *panorama of coral reefs. Of course, I also get a great deal of satisfaction from the money my clients pay; I really enjoy building up my bank account for the day I open my own school.*

Some may wonder, "What does Charlita do when she is not guiding or teaching in the ocean?" Believe it or not, I still go to the ocean, but in a way I would never, never, let my students even think of doing. Against all safety regulations and mores, I dive alone. On those occasions I am liberated from the stresses of accumulating money; satisfying others and protecting them from the inherent dangers of the ocean; always trying to mollify others with a smile on my face; and, wondering what my life will be like in twenty years.

On those dives, I swim among the most "vicious" sharks, occasionally great whites, without fear or hindrance; I ride the tails of threshers, and pet the snouts of whale sharks, some fifteen meters long, weighing more than 10,000 kilograms. In contrast, I rub my fingers together in "clouds" containing millions of tinny sapphire fish; they kiss me with their miniscule mouths, and I laugh into my face mask as they nibble at the hair floccules on my arms.

For those private forays, I choose the most remote, inaccessible sites available, places the underwater tourists never see, places I would not dare take them, through ship wrecks over 150 feet deep, much deeper than any diver holding a Deep Sea Divers' License would want to venture. Why do I take these "risks?" For me, I am risking nothing—I am simply living.

Charlita's essay astounded me. She not only schooled me on the environmental challenges of Apo Island—only thirty minutes by boat from Dumaguete—but she exposed her philosophy for living: never risk the safety of others, but to enjoy our own lives sometimes we need to face perils in a meaningful way.

After reading Charlita's writing, I lay in bed that night, alone and lonely, guilt ridden and afraid, I knew I needed something new in my life. Could ocean diving be that something? Maybe I should consider approaching Charlita for advice, but I didn't until I returned from a trip home.

Over the spring vacation, I flew back to Hong Kong. I hadn't seen Yalin and Timothy for almost four months, and I missed them terribly.

It's interesting how one can sense a change in a relationship before words are spoken, a prescient feeling. When I hugged Yalin, the *electricity* expected from her never came; our kiss, while not cold, didn't transmit that impulse of love and affection our kisses always had in the past. My anticipation and need begged for more, but she gently pushed me away; I felt like I had kissed a manikin, not my loving wife.

Yalin didn't bring Timothy to the airport, another disappointment; I had so looked forward to seeing him. Yalin explained, "Timmy is taking a nap. He should be awake when we get home."

I felt like Yalin had picked me up at a grocery store after I had been shopping.

During the one hour drive to our house, Yalin told me, with considerable enthusiasm, how much she enjoyed her classes at the *Hong Kong School of International Business,* the dancing classes at the *Fu Ning Exercise and Health Club*, her mediation sessions at Wong Tai Sin wat, and pushing Timothy in a stroller around the neighborhood.

When we arrived home, a maid/baby sitter had Timothy in his stroller in front of our house. I rushed to him with my arms out, unreasonably expecting him to reach out to his father, but the opposite happened; he started crying and reached for his mother. A couple of minutes later, Yalin attempted to put him in my arms, but Timothy totally rejected the idea of me holding him. What did I expect from a five month old baby who had not seen his father for four months—too much. Over the next four days I continuously attempted to connect with my son, and emotionally with his mother, but neither happened. Like a visiting uncle, one paying his obligatory semi-annual family visit, I felt unwanted. And, our meals, sightseeing, and conversations didn't make me feel better. All three of us seemed to be looking forward to my departure. Timothy seemed to want the *stranger* out of his house; Yalin, understandably, seemed fed up with my paranoia; and, I felt pressure every minute. Still, the question and statement I anticipated, and so wanted to hear, never came, *"Theo, when are you coming home to stay? Please don't leave."*

Back in Dumaguete, I felt as if I had returned from a funeral, my family's burial. Lonely, lost, and looking for solace, I decided to put all my energy into teaching and exercise. I started treating each student's writing papers with the acumen and analysis appropriate for an entire class, and I started running six miles each morning and eight to ten in the evening, leaving me exhausted and able to sleep. Still, I had an occasional dream depicting Yalin and Timothy in a crises.

My never ending schedule of student interviews and writing critiques—to praise, encourage, and make suggestions—took up over four hours each day. I tried to fill every day with a schedule of meaningful activities, be they related to teaching, exercise, eating, or sleeping. My disciplined and mechanized way of living went well. Finally, I had a critiquing session with Charlita.

As she sat across from me, for the first time I looked at Charlita as someone other than a student; her beauty drenched me: flashing chocolate eyes, pearly white teeth, smooth, sepia skin, and a voice projecting a soft huskiness that made me look forward to her next comment.

I praised Charlita for her candid, insightful writing—always related to her activities in the ocean—and told her she inspired me to at least consider open-ocean diving as an hobby. I asked, "Do you have any recommendations in that regard?"

"Certainly!" she responded. "My brother's dive business offers introductory dives. He furnishes all of the equipment, an instructor, in your case me, a thirty minute underwater dive in a pool, followed by a critique where I will say, 'You can be a great diver if you purchase a package from our dive shop.' We normally charge twenty-five dollars for that dive, but since you are my professor, and I want to stay on the good side of you, it will be free."

We both laughed, and I told Charlita it would be inappropriate for me to accept a freebie from one of my students. Nevertheless, we scheduled the dive for 8 a.m. the next Saturday.

As I expected, Charlita turned out to be an excellent teacher. First, she had me demonstrate my swimming strokes, both free-style and breaststroke. I swam the length of the pool and back four times, about 100 meters. Next, she laid out all of the equipment in the order I would put it on, explaining the purpose of each item:

"The rubber boot-sox will protect your feet from hot sand or debris on the beach before you enter the water and they will keep your fins from causing blisters; the wet-suit, which isn't really neces-sary for the eighty degree plus water temperatures we have in the Philippines, will protect you from sharp coral, jelly fish stings, and some fish bites; the diving watch will let you know how deep you are in the water and how long you have been at a particular depth, a detail that is essential for safe diving. The flotation device will allow you to stay on the surface when you want to, let you descend when you bleed the air out, and bring you to the surface when you are ready to ascend; and last, the oxygen tank allows you the breath under water."

By the time I got it all on, including the oxygen tank, the equip-ment must have added forty pounds to my body weight. I waddled to the edge of the pool, Charlita helped me put my fins on, and I fell in.

We spent forty minutes in the swimming pool where Charlita introduced me to the basics of SCUBA diving, and I enjoyed every minute. Getting out of the pool turned out to be an unexpected challenge; I could not get my fins off without her help.

Charlita's debriefing turned out to be more business-like than I expected: "You can be a good, safe diver, but you need to improve your swimming strength. There is nothing wrong with your tech-nique; however, if you want to get the Open Ocean Diving License, you need to demonstrate you can swim 200 meters, in choppy ocean water, away from the calm waters near shore. Right now you could undoubtedly swim that far, but it would leave you exhausted. You need to be able to comfortably swim that distance in rough water with energy to spare."

"OK, I will work on that for a couple of weeks, then we can talk again," I responded.

Charlita said, "Let me give you something to think about: In two weeks the semester will be over. There is a thirty day holiday until the next semester begins. That would be a good time for you to get certified, and as much as my brother would like to have your money, there may be a better option. If you can afford a little more expense, the island of Boracay is a great place to start diving. There are about thirty dive schools there, and one, the one I will be working at for this vacation period, is the best. It is the Calypso Diving School affiliated with *National Geographic Magazine*. Their facilities are the best, and the instruction is good. Also, they only use the best equipment."

"Wow! Let me think about that. Where would I live?"

"Boracay is full of hotels from five stars to zero stars. You can pay $1,500 a night or $5, whichever is your pleasure."

"Where do you live when you are there, Charlita?"

"All of the Calypso dive instructors live in a nipa village, not the kind of place for foreigners with money."

I responded, "OK, let me think about it. I will see what my wife, Yalin, thinks about the idea."

Charlita's furled brow signified disappointment at the mention of "*my wife.*"

The next day, when I talked with Yalin in our three-times-a-week call, I mentioned the idea of me going to Boracay and taking a diving course rather than going directly back to Hong Kong at the end of the semester. Much to my surprise, and disappointment, she said, "I think that is a good idea, Theo. You need to do something just for your enjoyment. Maybe you can get some seashells for Timmy and me."

I didn't want to face a doomed marriage, and I tried hard to put that disturbing conversation out of my mind—I couldn't. It spawned two difficult questions: Had my paranoia about the deaths of people I cared for destroyed my appeal as a husband and father? Had I simply become too difficult to live with?

Since she seemed more comfortable without me, obviously, Yalin must be thinking about her future and Tim's. What were those thoughts?

I discarded my first inclination, to call Yalin back and directly confront her about the issue. I opted to write her a letter; I simply could not bear to hear her voice tell me she didn't want to be with me anymore.

In that three page, rambling letter in which I mentioned our China experiences and the birth of Timothy, I didn't ask the litmus test question until the last paragraph:

"Yalin, what do you think the future holds for us? What do you see us doing ten years from now?"

Because of the mail process in the Philippines, I didn't expect a reply for ten days or so, but seven days later Yalin's letter arrived; she had answered me quickly.

The letter came in a thin envelope, indicating a curt reply; it was, and it hit met me like a thunderbolt:

Dear Theo,

You know I love you deeply, and I always will, but it is impossible for us to live together, at least right now. The demons from your past, maybe your combat experiences, make living with you an ongoing nightmare. Ten years from now, I think we will have gone our own ways—we probably should do that sooner—and, hopefully, we will all be happier than we are now.

I don't want your money, Theo; I am capable of making my own living and supporting Timothy. Of course, you are welcome to see him anytime you want, but right now he does not realize you are his father, and you scare him.

I love you Theo. Yalin

I put the letter down and cried, a deep rumbling of pent up emotion erupting so loudly a neighbor knocked on my door to inquire about my welfare. An hour later I went to the small Buddhist wat I rarely visited since arriving in Dumaguete, and stayed there for two hours going through the motions of meditation; however, mostly, I engendered self-pity. Needless to say, I didn't go to the dive school in Boracay, but that did happen later during our next school vacation.

Seven months after receiving the rejection letter from Yalin, we divorced. The conditions, few and contentious free, included:

Timothy's trust fund of 10 million dollars, now to be administered by his mother, kept intact. The 10 million I had deposited for Yalin would be retained by her. She wanted to return it, but I refused. And, lastly, Timothy would retain his name, Timothy Wong Rogers. The name demand on my part, perhaps an ego soothing maneuver at the time, insured Timothy would eventually want to know about his biological father.

The day I received those final divorce papers turned out to be the emptiest and most depressing day of my life—at least until years later when I tried to swim from California to Thailand. On the other hand, I experienced a strange sort of relief from that divorce: no longer did my curse threaten my son and Yalin.

For the next month, I went through my highly methodical schedule in a mental haze, my only relief from that malaise, swimming and running long distances as well as teaching English, did little to relieve my agony; however, respite finally did come at the end of one of my writing classes. On a Friday afternoon Charlita tarried when the other students departed.

"Mr. Rogers, several students in our class are going to Apo Island in the morning on the ferry. We will come back in the evening. We would like for you to go with us. Will you?"

Still wallowing in my self-pity, I wanted to decline outright, but out of respect for the invitation, I parlayed the question into one of my own. "What would I do there? Don't you think I would inhibit your fun?"

"No! Everyone likes you. You can see my home, meet my family, and snorkel. Apo is one of the best snarling islands in the world."

The next day as we rode the open ferry, only a piece of retractable canvas protected the riders from the elements, the wind blew through my hair and salt spray stung my face. Jumping dolphins paralleled our course, and the high spirits of my students infected me with a new feeling, one of hope, hope for a more rewarding life, hope for some meaningful interaction with another woman, and hope for the happiness that had eluded me.

My day on Apo Island turned out to be great, actually an epic life altering experience: Everyone around me laughed, played, snorkeled, and some SCUBA dived, something you could do directly from the shore on Apo Island. Charlita's parents and brother, Rizal, accepted me like family. When the sun went down, we ate roast pig, barbecued chicken and fish, tropical fruit, and *pan de sal*, delicious Philippine bread rolls. After eating, two guitars and dancing students entertained us by the quixotic light of a small bonfire. That morphed into a sing-along that even I, normally a non-singer, joined. Most positively, I experienced the rare feeling of happiness.

At 9:00 p.m. the ferry picked us up for the trip back to Dumaguete. As soon as I got off the boat Charlita approached me, and said, "Mr. Rogers, I hope you had a good time."

"Charlita, thank you so much for inviting me; I had a wonderful time. My morale has been low lately, but today raised my spirits."

For the first time Charlita and I touched; she reached out and briefly held my hand, sending a quiver through me, as she simply said, "I know, Mr. Rogers. I know."

How did she know? Did she have some innate sense that made her aware of my isolation and loneliness?

That moment contaminated our teacher-student relationship, but it stimulated a Theo-Charlita liaison; when we looked into each other's' eyes, subtle messages of romance filled the space between us. Nevertheless, almost a year passed before we acted on our attraction—beyond momentary touching of hands or a kiss on the cheek—in a sexual way.

Finally, I traveled to Boracay and attended the Calypso Diving School with other apprentice divers, including a man from France and a young couple from Germany, all English fluent. Five groups-of-four, ours the "blue" group, began the week-long-training together. When the twenty of us and five instructors first met, the instructors drew colored cards from a hat to marry the teachers with a group. I stifled my cheer when Charlita drew the blue card.

When it came to being a dive instructor, Charlita's age and beauty belied her expertise. She challenged us at every step of the program, a regimen that led to our Open Water Divers License. The first step, the 200 meter swim in the ocean, not intended to be a race, became one when Charlita, even though starting well after the rest of us, passed everyone at the 100 meter turn-around point. Marcel, who later told us he swam for his university team, tried unsuccessfully to keep up with her.

Prior to each of our six ocean dives, Charlita explicitly briefed us on what to expect, safety precautions to be taken, time at our maximum dive depth, our plan for resurfacing, and the procedure for the boat pickup.

Even though we would not need it until our graduation dive to 100 feet, Charlita had us do at least one intermediate stop on each assent to teach us how to deal with the diving hazards of *nitrogen narcosis(NN)* and *decompression sickness (DCS),* more commonly known as *the bends,* a painful and potentially deadly hazard of diving. To combat the onset of DCS, the more dangerous of the two, she taught us that our absolute ascent rate must never be more than thirty feet per minute. To reinforce this issue, on any ascent below thirty feet, she trained us to stop for one minute for every fifteen feet as we came closer to the surface.

When our graduation dive came—to that magic depth of 100 feet— Charlita had us well prepared. The four of us enjoyed thirty minutes at that level marveling at the variety, color, and dexterity of the inhabitants of the inner world. Our eyes feasted on tinny blue fish that swam in clouds of millions and kissed our fingers when we reached out to them; some fish were large enough to swallow hundreds of their smaller cousins with one gulp; two sharks had teeth capable of taking a diver's arm off in one bite; the 300 meter long coral reef had colors that the most skilled artist could not visualize, let alone replicate. We traversed the length of that reef on a subsurface current, allowing us to navigate smoothly without using much energy.

That one dive gave me a greater appreciation for our planet, particularly the oceans, and all planet life. It gave me a better understanding and gratitude for the Buddhist axiom: *never kill living things.*

That evening I invited all of the divers, the five instructors, and the ten other Calypso staff members to an extravagant graduation dinner party at *Shangri la Boracay,* the cream la cream of Boracay resort hotels. That great party, with a moderate amount of beer but a prodigious amount of food, went on until the wee hours of the morning. We sang and danced from the beach pavilion into the water with no regard for clothes or hairdos.

When Charlita came out of the water in front of me, her pastel pink, sheath, cotton dress clung to her body like skin, revealing every mountain, valley, and plain of her lithe physique. Many eyes, male and female, followed her until she flopped in a beach chair and covered her *landscape* with a large beach towel. When the party started breaking up, I found Charlita and asked her to walk with me on the moonlit beach.

We walked. We talked. Soon, however, she drew me out, and our dialog mutated into a near monolog. The bottom line: I spilled my guts to her, telling her everything about my history, my phobias, my divorce, my son, my Medal of Honor, I covered everything except my lottery adventure and my financial status; however, the lavish party I had just hosted suggested I wasn't indigent. I only hinted, "I have a comfortable income from investments," a true statement.

The Boracay class, Charlita's last for that school vacation, ended on that romantically, infectious walk on the beach. From that time on, we would spend as much time together as we could—always trying not to expose to others our magnetic attraction. Yet, we left Boracay together, but in separate rooms, on the Inter Island Ferry and arrived back in Dumaguete late the next evening.

We shared a taxi with the stated idea that Charlita would get out at her studio apartment and I would go home—alone. However, she invited me in for a snack and as soon as the door closed, the electromagnets of attraction drew us together, and nearly an hour passed before, with difficulty, we pried our bodies apart. Finally, she said, "I don't want to stay here alone tonight. I want you to stay with me."

We stayed in bed the next morning participating in a variety of activities—even talking—before we had breakfast. Afterwards, Charlita insisted on taking a *busman's holiday* to show me one of her favorite dive sites, an hour by boat from Dumaguete to a very remote spot near a miniscule, uninhabited island, Piquet. There, we got up close and personal with a pair of large whale sharks, magnificent beasts that weigh many thousands of pounds, with tail fins that extended six feet or more above their massive bodies.

Charlita spotted them first, tapped me on the shoulder, and signaled me to stop. She removed her breathing mouth piece, pursed her lips, and forcefully exhaled, sending a river of big air bubbles racing to the surface. The sharks immediately drew closer. After a few breaths from her oxygen tank, she repeated the exhaling three times; and eventually, the massive sharks faced us a little more than one arm's length away. I was petrified as Charlita slid her hands down the head of a creature that, I thought, could have devoured her in a second. Later I learned that whale sharks are bottom feeders that primarily live off of plankton; also, there has never been a recorded incident where one attacked a human.

Charlita motioned for me to follow her lead, and I did so reluctantly, lightly placing my hand to the shark's side. Soon more comfortable, I started to approach the second shark. When Charlita sensed my intentions she put up her hand up, signaling me to stop, but my movements upset the ambiance, and both sharks sped away.

After we surfaced, I asked Charlita what spooked the sharks. She laughed, "You might have difficulty believing this, but sharks, particular whales, are monogamous, and they get jealous. Stroking the male didn't incite any jealousy, but when you approached the female, the dance was over; time to take the lady home."

Charlita could truly live among the beasts of the ocean; she was fearless. Later I observed her—always from a comfortable distance—approach great white sharks, giant stinger rays, swim through school of jelly fish, ride dolphins, and coil seas snakes around her arms, all without fear or injury. Charlita became my mermaid, a *fish-woman* I came to love dearly.

During the next semester—Charlita's last before graduating—teaching became *excruciatingly wonderful*. Each time I saw Charlita I wanted to take her in my arms, an impossibility, since teachers and students never embrace—at least not in public. Nevertheless, on all of those occasions a comfortable feeling of secure, unfettered love went through me.

35

Lawrence is Born—Charlita Dies

Two days after Charlita's graduation— surrounded by her extended Sabino family and neighbors, palm trees and the ocean for a backdrop—we married on Apo Island, and the next day we embarked on an open ended honeymoon, and we didn't plan to return to Dumaguete and Apo Island until we felt like it. At my insistence, Charlita's brother, Rizal and his wife Reana went with us. My goal: taking the three Sabinos to dive sites they had always wanted to visit but never quite got to, turned out to be a rewarding and romantic experience. In addition, at one of our stops, Brooke's Point on Palawan, we had a beach fire conversation that eventually affected, positively and negatively, several lives—more about the efficacy of those conversations later.

For the first leg of our trip we took a ferry in first class accommodations from Dumaguete to Cebu and another from Cebu to Malapascua Island. A small power boat took us from the island to a spot called Monad Shoal, ten miles out in the Philippine Sea, surrounded by water depths of over 5,000 feet but with some underwater mountain peaks almost reaching the surface. There we had an incomparable experience with thresher sharks[46], some of the ocean's most magnificent and private creatures.

We knew that it might require several dives to find any threshers, and the first time we were on our way out to Monad, Charlita warned me, "Some peoples have been looking for threshers for years and still have not seen one. But, of course, they didn't have my brother, Rizal, guiding them." True to form, we didn't see a thresher until our third dive, that during our second morning of diving from Malapascua.

While navigating in about forty-five feet of crystal clear water, prowling parallel to a Monad coral reef wall, Rizal suddenly became very animated, giving the hand signal to STOP, quickly followed by pointing, jabbing motions to the top of the reef, about ten feet above us.

At first, I saw nothing; then the movement of a Thresher's massive *caudal fin*[47] caught my eye as it stirred slowly along the opposite side of the coral wall at about the same pace we were moving; the thresher seemed to be hunting.

Rizal led us to the end of the wall where we cautiously made a 90° right turn, followed seconds later by another 90° right turn. The second turn brought us face to face with one massive thresher, perhaps twenty-five feet long with a caudal fin to match; two much smaller threshers followed.

We stopped moving but the threshers did not. Rizal signaled us to stay in place as the sharks, now only about fifty feet away and apparently unimpressed by our presence, continued to move toward us. My pounding heart jumped to my throat until the comforting touch of Charlita's hand grabbed my arm. I turned toward her and immediately saw her reassuring smile, framed by her mask, and a thumbs-up.

---

46 Olopias Vulpinus

47 The caudal fin on a Thresher is approximately the same height as the length of its body, 20 or more feet. It is a powerful tool used to stun prey by slapping the water. It one case it was reported to have decapitated a diver.

When the sharks were about twenty feet from us they changed their trajectory and went above us, roughly ten feet, where they started circling while slowly opening and closing their intimidating mouths. Later, Rizal explained, "The oxygen bubbles generated by four divers fascinated them."

The show lasted for maybe a minute; then, apparently bored with the passive activity of devouring oxygen bubbles generated by homosapiens, they turned and gracefully disappeared.

After returning to Cebu, we flew to Coron Island—the first airplane flight for the Sabinos—and checked into the five star El Rio y Mar Resort where our first class accommodations, food and amenities ran up a bill of approximately 100,000 Pilipino pesos, about $2,000 U.S. at the time. Charlita almost chocked when she saw me paying-up four days later; her expression alone warranted the cost.

Near Coron we dove into Japanese ships sunk during World War II. We made three dives to the *Taiei Maru,* a ship over 540 feet long. Those dives turned out to be among my most intriguing diving experiences.

Because of the strong currents, the *Taiei Maru sleeps* in very clean water, her decks and interior compartments are relatively free of corral but provide excellent refuge for thousands of fish, some small, some very large; one a groper, over seven feet long, must have weighted over 1,000 pounds.

The only time I ever saw Charlita recoil from sea life came as we wove our way through the *Taiei Maru's* interior. As Rizal led with Charlita trailing him, and me following her, a giant eel, about five inches in diameter and over six feet long, with razor sharp teeth, sprung out of its lair and took a large bite out one of Rizal's fins, not a body penetrating bite mind you, but a sizeable snap that removed a large chunk of rubber, one more than four inches long and five inches wide. As Charlita sprung back, she grabbed my arm and directed me and Reana away from the eel's grotto.

We spent many hours in the *Taiei Maru*. Its intrigue not only came from the sea life inhabiting it but also from its history: Almost 2,000 Japanese sailors died when she went down suddenly after being attacked by U.S. Navy dive bombers on September 24, 1944. As we talked about it later, all four of us felt like the ghosts of those sailors watched as we navigated through their tomb.

From Coron Island we took an outboard motored canoe to a remote part of Palawan Island, the southernmost major islet, one of the more than 7,000 that make up the Philippines. In contrast to the luxury of the corporate owned El Rio y Mar Resort on Coron, for the next two nights we rented five dollar per night nipa huts at Brooke's Point from a coconut farmer. This non-resort, remote location, Remote with a capital R, provided the kind of privacy that stimulates long conversations. For two nights we visited and talked for hours next to a fire while we roasted and ate fish wrapped in banana leaves. I don't think any of us dreamed that one of those exchanges—about the prospect of having a child early in our marriage—would come back to influence us the way it did.

Rizal asked, "Do you two want to have a baby soon?"

I wasn't sure who he directed the question to, but Charlita quickly responded, "No, not soon. Not until I am about thirty. I want Theo and I to enjoy each other for a few years. I know a baby changes everything between a man and a woman, not necessarily for the bad, but a baby does change things."

A period of moderately embarrassing silence followed, until I opened my big mouth and said. "Rizal, how about you and Reana, are you planning one soon?"

Rizal put his head down, and Reana said, "We have been trying for almost ten years, but it hasn't happened. Rizal and I were both tested, and the doctor said we would probably never be able to have a baby."

Rizal snapped, "My sperm's no good."

Sensing Rizal's anguish, I tried to make light of his problem: "Well, if we have one, we will wrap it in red ribbons and give it to you for Christmas." Rizal smiled, but Charlita and Reana remained stoic.

Charlita spoke seriously, "I don't think that will happen. I am very careful about taking my temperature and plotting my fertile periods."

Now I became less flippant, "I thought you probably used pills since I have not been using any protection. Why haven't we talked about this?"

Then Charlita scolded me, "Theo, you know that our family is Catholic. It would be a sin for us to use any kind of birth control, except for timing."

"I know Sweetheart. That is fine with me." But it really wasn't; my pain over Timothy, too fresh, too intense, still bothered me tremendously. Here I was speculating about having another baby when I only took care of Timothy with money; he received no emotional support from me.

We ended our talk that night by planning a dive into a river cave the next morning. We would go in at high tide when the currents would not be too strong. That dive turned out to be unique; we observed many large salt water fish feasting on the fresh water varieties that ventured too close to the confluence of the river and the ocean. That evening our conversation took a completely new bent—business and money.

Charlita often talked about Rizal's dive business and how she hoped to start her own someday. Although Rizal and Reana considered his business successful, other than for an occasional day off, always due to undiveable weather, they had never taken a vacation until now. This one became possible when I insisted on paying all of the expenses so they could help us celebrate our marriage.

From the early conversation that night, I surmised that Rizal was significantly undercapitalized and unable to make needed improvements, such as purchasing an oxygen compressor to fill tanks and the latest dive gear; therefore, he was not competitive with other Dumaguete dive businesses. As I listened silently, but sympathetically to their business talk, an idea took root. *Why didn't I finance him?* I had money, actually over 250 million dollars by that time, sitting in the Royal Bank of Hong Kong helping no one but the bank and my growing portfolio.

After listening to Rizal try to dissuade Charlita's business ambitions in a conversation slowly growing a bit contentious, I interrupted and said, "Why don't I finance your business, Rizal? How much do you need?"

To this point, I had not told Charlita about my lottery winnings and how much I had in investments. Again, I had only told her truth, "I have a comfortable investment income."

The Sabinos looked at me in stunned silence. Without further comment, I got up and went to our nipa hut and retrieved a small writing pad and a pen. When I sat down again near the fire, Charlita said, "Theo you shouldn't say things like that if you don't mean it."

"I do mean it. Let's look at some figures. What do you need for your business that you don't have now, Rizal?"

Rizal, unresponsive, looked at Reana then Charlita. Finally Charlita started spitting out an equipment list: quality dive suits to rent to customers, training books, a better place for pool activities—Rizal currently paid a hotel to use their pool—some business and direction signs. We added an oxygen tank filling compressor to our growing list. Previously, Charlita had mentioned the high price they paid a competitor to get oxygen tanks filled. Suddenly, Charlita stopped talking. Rizal was staring at her as if to say, "That is enough. Shut up!"

I asked about a dive boat like the Calypso Dive School used in Boracay, and training aides, underwater recording cameras and TV monitors. I added those to the list. Then it suddenly hit me, Rizal didn't really have a business building. He operated from a store front where he shared the space with a Chinese noodle shop.

To this point, Rizal had not taken part in the conversation; in fact, he looked offended by it: his eyes continuously flirted from the fire to the ocean, frowning unequivocally; he walked to the water's edge, then returned and sat in the sand at an oblique angle to the rest of us—extremely negative body language that said it all. He was embarrassed, and suddenly all of us were uncomfortable.

Finally, I put on my semi-aggressive hat. "Rizal, don't you care what we are talking about?"

"Sorry, Theo. Something just seems wrong about all of this."

"OK! I can understand that, but it boils down to this: If you want to have a better business, you need to let someone with some money, a bank, a friend, or a relative like me, help you. Do you want to stay in the dive business? If you do I am going to finance you and not partially, but all the way."

Rizal looked down; looked at the surf; looked at his wife, but didn't say a word.

Charlita said, "Talk to Theo, Rizal!" But still no response.

At this point, I lost my temper, jumped to my feet and shouted, "God Damn it Rizal, talk to me! Do you want my help or not?"

With tears welling, he looked at me and nodded his head, "Yes."

"No, Rizal. That won't do. You have to tell me."

"Yes, Theo, I will let you help me."

That broke the tension. For the next two hours, under the light of a wood fire and two flash lights, we went through equipment lists and contingency strategies that called for the total restructuring of Rizal's business, soon to be called *The Sabino Dive Academy and Guide Service*.

The plan called for the construction of a company headquarters on Dumaguete's waterfront near where tourist—many of them divers—disembarked from the ships that came from Manila and Cebu, the two largest cities in the Philippines and the only two where foreign visitors arrived by airplanes.

The business complex would be designed with an adjacent, large dive-training pool, classrooms, dressing rooms, two large Jacuzzis, showers, massage rooms, a dive equipment store, and a large roof-top observation deck with ocean views attached to a restaurant, one specializing in diver friendly food and drink.

Since Apo Island would be the prime dive site, we would also construct a facility there connected to the Dumaguete company headquarters by radio and video transmitters. The final items added to the facilities-equipment lists, two boats, both diesel driven, one for small groups, six or less, and one large enough for fifteen divers and all of their equipment. And last, separate oxygen compressors would be installed at both Dumaguete and Apo.

When I asked for a rough estimate of how much it would cost to fulfill our wish list, Charlita, the best mind in our group, said, "The construction and equipment probably about 45 million pesos, about 1 million U.S. dollars. To buy the waterfront land might cost about that same amount."

Then I made a suggestion on Charlita's behalf: "I have a proposal for you, Rizal. I think it would be a good idea if you let your sister become your business partner. She has a good mind, enthusiasm, and thanks to you Rizal, she knows the dive business; I don't think you could ask for a better partner, also she just earned a degree in Business. If my hunch is right, your business is going to expand a lot and quickly. You will have a dire need for her expertise.

Rizal immediately said, "That's a great idea. I had planned to turn the business over to her someday anyway."

"You never told me that Rizal. That's wonderful."

Now we had smiles all around the fire. "OK, I will hire an attorney as soon as we get back to start the legal paper work. In, addition, I am going to deposit two million U.S. dollars in your business account next week and another two million in an interest bearing instrument to be used as contingency funds."

When Rizal asked what my involvement would be, and what the interest rate would be on the money I loaned The Sabino Dive Company, I told him, "My involvement will end when I deposit the money in your accounts. As for an interest rate, it will be zero, but you or your sister must pay me back within 150 years. And, here is our contract." I stuck out my hand and we all shook; Charlita gave me a kiss, and the deal was done.

Buying the waterfront land didn't turn out to be a big problem. All of the businesses on the lots we wanted were family owned, and since we made more than fare offers, not a single problem arose; in a little less than two months we started construction. After that, the weeks went by at warp-speed in a bustle of activity. I tried to stay at arm's length from what was going on but Charlita drug me to the construction site two or three times each week; of course, I was highly interested in all the building activity.

On one of those visits, as I admired Charlita's concentration while she bent over the architects' blue prints, she suddenly put her hand over her mouth and rushed for the toilet. When she returned, she took my hand and led me away from the blueprint table, looked me in the eye and said, "Theo, My Dear, I think I am pregnant; in fact, I am pretty sure of it."

A bolt of fear went through me, but I immediately put on a happy face and took her in my arms for a congratulations kiss. Charlita had mastered the art of disarming me, and, outwardly, I became a happy, expectant father—again.

Over the next few months Charlita and I drew closer; our love had always been strong, but now it took on a new degree of togetherness, one almost indescribable: If we were apart for more than an hour, I missed her. And, sometimes, with me at home and she at the construction site, she would call and say, "Hello, My Love. I just wanted to hear your voice and see if you are OK."

"No! I'm not OK; I miss you."

By the end of September, 1963, we were on our way to Los Angeles and Doctor Rush's office at Cedars Sinai Hospital. At the end of two weeks, a period filled with a flurry of examinations and tests, Doctor Rush expressed concern about Charlita's pelvic structure; she had an "aberration" that might make her delivery problematic. He suggested a caesarian delivery, but Charlita adamantly rejected that idea. So he advised that we stay within one hour of the hospital.

Since we were renting a house overlooking Big Bear Lake—to satisfy Charlita's desire to experience Northern Hemisphere fall weather on the shores of a pristine mountain lake—I made arrangement with Mountain Flyers, an aviation company with helicopters, to fly us to Cedars Sinai when the critical time came. The flight from Big Bear to the helicopter pad on the roof of Cedars would take twenty-five minutes, faster than the trip would take from most places in the Los Angeles area by car. I timed that trip twice when I paid the pilot to give me two preview flights.

Early on the morning of October 9th—still a couple of weeks before the predicted delivery date—Charlita and I went for a walk near the lake. Even with the now heavy load in her stomach, she loved walking the pine scented, mountain trail. When walking with Charlita, I often reflected on a comment I once read in a magazine article about love: *The essence of true love is often revealed when two people are walking together in silence.* Charlita and I often walked for as much as fifteen minutes holding hands, with no dialogue, not only comfortable but emotionally united; we treasured those moments.

As soon as we returned to our lodge, Charlita laid on the couch in front of the fireplace while I massaged her feet and legs; for several days, her feet had been giving her some discomfort after we walked.

Charlita's head lay on a mutton covered pillow, framing her light-brown skin, shinning black hair, perfectly shaped nose, and full lips—what a gorgeous woman. Suddenly her painful scream broke the peacefulness. "Theo! Theo! It hurts so much," the last words she would ever say to me. She continued shrieking in agony, and I immediately knew we had an emergency to deal with.

I called Mountain Flyers and asked them to get a helicopter ready. Ten minutes later, we loaded Charlita—now on a medical stretcher—into the helicopter, and we took off, and I asked the pilot to call Cedars Sinai. We landed on the roof of Cedars about twenty minutes after we took off, thirty minutes after her intense pain started, well within the one hour Doctor Rush recommended.

Charlita, silent and breathing shallowly, looked very pail. While fighting total panic, I held her hand continuously and kissed her periodically. The ER doctor who met us on the hospital roof immediately covered her face with an oxygen mask, and he and two nurses rushed Charlita to an elevator with me walking frantically beside them.

When they wheeled Charlita into a surgical room—not a delivery room as I expected—I knew the situation was serious. A nurse directed me to a nearby waiting room where I sat in agony, alone, for almost two hours. Finally, Doctor Rush approached wearing a light-green surgical gown and a grim look on his face; I stood and spoke first:

"Is my wife OK? How is she?"

In a soft but clear voice he answered, "No, I am very sorry, Mister Rogers, but your wife expired before she could deliver; she lost too much blood. We delivered the baby by cesarean. He is a healthy boy."

"No! No! No! It can't be!"

I collapsed in a chair in disbelief, yet in another instant the truth sank in. I had been *here* before—my curse had returned.

A few minutes later I looked at Lawrence Sabino Rogers for the first time. That should have been a glorious occasion, but with his mother dead less than an hour, no joy was possible. Yet, immediately, I felt strong love for him.

Two weeks after that, with Lawrence nestled in my arms and the body of his mother in a refrigerated luggage compartment— she had been in a cold vault since her death—we boarded an Air Philippines flight for Manila and another to Dumaguete.

The next day, we buried Charlita in a grave Rizal and I dug at the highest point of Apo Island under a solitary palm tree, steps away from where we were married. There is nothing positive I can say about her burial. By that time my emotions—dull with grief, agitated and angry about my death ghost reappearing—were at the bottom of the deepest emotional abyss.

The only positive about remaining in Dumaguete, Reana, Rizal's wife, started taking motherly care of Lawrence. A few days later she asked if she could try to nurse him. I didn't know that a woman who had never had a baby could produce milk, but sometimes they can, and she did. Soon it became obvious to me that Reana, at least subconsciously, now had the baby she always wanted.

Since Lawrence nursed as much during the day as he did at night, I only held him for short periods each day, and when I did, he would sleep for a while, but soon he would start crying. I had nothing he wanted, but Reana did. Every time I saw her nursing

Lawrence, I had visions of Charlita sitting, holding him close to her while they exchanged the love and affection only a mother and her child are capable of. Then I would come to my senses and realize my vision—an impossibility. The results were depression and paranoid thoughts of death, even suicide.

I always considered people who committed suicide to be the worst kind of cowards. As I often thought: *They didn't have the guts to face reality.* Now it was tempting; the pain too much, the same way I felt after Jane died. They only thing that stopped me this time: sometime in the future, I didn't want my sons to be told, *"Your father killed himself?"*

After teaching one more miserable semester at Dumaguete University—a semester during which my teaching failed to inspire my students, or me—I knew I had to get out of the Philippines, at least temporarily. Watching Lawrence bonding closer each day with Reana hurt. My time with him simply filled an obligation and had little substance; he cared nothing for me and undoubtedly didn't recognize me when I held him. Still, I loved him deeply.

Before I left Dumaguete, I opened a trust fund for Lawrence at the Philippines Nation Bank, one identical to Timothy's, 10 million dollars in conservative investments, stipulations: maintain the Rogers name, and spend the money on Lawrence's welfare and education, and after five years, if he still lived with his aunt and uncle, Rizal would become the executor.

When I told Rizal I planned to return to Hong Kong, he immediately told me, "Theo, how can I do all of these things alone. There are so many things to do to get the business going; I can't do them by myself. And, now that Charlita is gone, I don't know if I want to be in the dive business anymore."

"OK, Rizal, I will help you for a few months; we have to do this for Charlita. Your dive business was her dream and yours too. We have to get through all of this grief and pain together. Agreed?"

Rizal took my extended hand; we shook, "OK, Theo, I agree. Let's do it."

For the next six months, Rizal and I were busier than I had ever been in my life, outside of combat of course. We both were at the construction site before six every morning, and neither of us left before nine in the evening. Consequently, the project progressed rapidly. If we didn't know the answer to a problem, be it construction material, design or decoration, I had an expert flown in from Manila to consult with us.

Since we ended up with a more property than we needed, I talked Rizal in the adding a small hotel-guest house, one that could accommodate up to twenty-five guests. Reana got enthusiastically involved with that part of the project, especially when it came to the interior design, something she had absolutely no experience with but was more than willing to learn. I hired a highly experienced British interior designer from Hong Kong and flew her to Dumaguete to work with Reana for two weeks.

Nevertheless, Lawrence was Reana's priority; she carried him with her almost every minute. When he wanted to nurse, she sat down wherever she was, and regardless of who might be present, and *served* him.

I saw Lawrence every day, and every time I did, the pain of his mother's death stabbed me, but it was comforting to know he had a *mother* who cared for him dearly; Reana loved him as much as I did.

Finally, the end was in sight for the construction of the Sabino Dive Academy and Guide Service, and a grand opening was scheduled, one that would last for an entire week.

For some reason, I didn't want to be there for that event. I wanted to get away from Dumaguete, away from the ghost of Charlita that followed me everywhere.

On my departure day, Reana, Rizal and I exchanged hugs. Afterwards, I took a sleeping Lawrence in my arms and kissed him several times. Finally, one of my tears fell on his face, and he came awake with a wince and a cry; quickly I handed him to Reana who immediately put a nipple in his mouth. Almost instantaneously, he slept again. The three of us laughed.

As my plane departed Dumaguete Airport, I felt those now familiar feelings of guilt and abandonment, but I also had a sense of some abstract relief, relief from the pain of Charlita's death. I knew I couldn't totally leave that agony behind, but maybe getting away from the place where she totally dominated my life might provide some relief. As soon as the plane took off and banked, giving me a picturesque view of the pristine Philippine Sea, I felt a hand on my right arm, forcing me to look at the *empty* seat beside me, but it wasn't empty; a mist like image sat beside me, my love, Charlita. She smiled at me, kissed my cheek, and said, *"I'm OK, Theo. Try to be happy."*

As the plane headed for Manila, my spirits rose; I knew Charlita was with me, and she *stayed* with me for many months.

36

Thailand Remedy

Back in Hong Kong, I spent some time with Yalin and Timothy but, understandably, now there was another man in her life, Charles Farning, a British investment attorney. Painfully, when Timothy, almost three at this point, said "Daddy" he was talking to Charles.

A year later I agreed to let Charles adopt Timothy with three conditions: First, his name had to remain, *Timothy Wong Rogers*. Second, Timothy's trust fund investments would not be altered for five year. At that time, Yalin would become the executor. Third, the education plan calling for him to go to college, and maybe graduate school, both in the United States, would not be changed. I didn't feel good about these paperwork actions, because they didn't change the fact that I abandoned my son and turned the quenching of his need for fatherly love, security, and guidance over to another man.

While in Hong Kong, I went to Wong Tai Sun Wat several times, meditated for hours, and visited with Ajahun Bhikkhun, my Buddhist tutor from five years back. I poured out my guts to him, and his only advice: "You need to find peace within yourself," didn't improve my state of mind. However, his suggestion, "Maybe a visit to Thailand and its Buddhist culture would serve you well."

A week later I landed in Bangkok with a pocket full of U.S. dollars but no plan or inspiration to justify staying there. For one day I tried to be an interested tourist, visiting the Royal Palace, the Emerald Buddha[48], and the chaotic night market. The next day I roamed the streets until I passed a building with a sign that read, "Thailand Department of Education." I entered, found the office responsible for recruiting foreign teachers, filled out an application to teach English and received an interview. The bottom line: if I would present my credentials, take and pass a physical examination, and be willing to sign a contract for the remainder of school year—about six and a half months—I could have a job immediately in Northern Thailand, specifically, in Chiang Rai Providence, at a small university, Maelao Commerce University (MCU).

While meditating that night, a vision of Charlita surfaced. She gave me a short message: *"You are a good teacher, Theo. Take the job; it will make you happy."*

The next day I passed the physical, presented my papers and received a bus ticket for Chiang Rai. Little did I know that a new adventure, a rejuvenated outlook on life, and an element of contentment awaited me—at least for a few years—in Northern Thailand.

When I arrived at MCU, I expected to be confronted with bureaucratic mandates: detailed curriculum guides, examination requirements, and where I must live, etc., but those things didn't happen. Totally unfettered, and free to use my imagination, I based my oral English classes on American music lyrics. We read and hand-copied songs, sung them, and often danced to them. In short, my classes rocked; I loved it; the students loved it, and their English, particularly their pronunciation, improved rapidly.

---

48 The Emerald Buddha, actually a jade figure decorated with gold, is the *palladium of Thai society*. By generally accepted myth, it watches over the nation. Its origin is 43BC, and has been displayed at the Pavilion of Regalia in Bangkok since 1874. There the author visited and observed it.

MCU had a large English department staffed by Thai English teachers who, generally, spoke little English; however, they knew English grammar better than I, but they simply didn't speak our jargon. Many of them came to me looking for a magic formula to improve. Consequently, with the blessing of our department head, Mr. Thanasukolwit, I started teaching an English class for Thai English teachers. Unexpectedly, that class turned out to be a lot of fun too, not to mention, that is where I met my third wife, Suchanat Buakhieo.

When I arrived at MCU, Mr. Thanasukolwit gave me the option of living on the campus rent free, or receiving a stipend to pay for my living arrangements. I chose to find my own place, and I found it in Ban Sop Way, a village only twelve kilometers from MCU, and in a house only fifty meters from the *Ban Sop Nam Wat* complex.

That wat was much larger than what one would expect for a village of 250 families. In addition to the temple, a community building, a primary school, an out of doors cafeteria, and two dormitory like buildings sat adjacent to a giant Bodhi tree, just like the one Siddhartha Gautama, the founder of Buddhism, meditated under while seeking enlightenment. That tree became my place for meditating; however, unlike Siddhartha Gautama, I wasn't seeking enlightenment. Selfishly, I only sought peace and tranquility. By the way, that same tree, according to the local mythology, had been growing at that spot for over 2,000 years. I doubted that chronology until I did some research and learned that Bodhi Trees often live for more than 3,000 years.

The day after I moved into my nipa home, I started meditating under *my* Bodhi tree daily, and soon I enjoyed some relief from guilt and the intense grieving associated with Charlita's death. When I eventually left Ban Sop Way, I sorely missed that tree.

With a lady to do my washing, cleaning, and cooking, the only acquisition needed— to make my new home safe and comfortable—were mosquito nets to cover my bed and a hammock I often napped in. *Not buying them immediately turned out to be one of the major mistakes of my life: two years after arriving in Ban Sop Way, the agonies of malaria clobbered me.*

The owners of my new home, Moo and Bee Buakhieo, unbeknownst to me the aunt and uncle of Suchanat Buakhieo, my wife to be, grew rice, bananas, and rubber trees. Behind their house, in a combination mango, banana grove, sat the small, traditional Thai home I rented. It had an outdoor shower and a stone floored patio where I ate most of my meals, knapped, and read each day as I swayed in my bamboo hammock while cooling breezes washed my body. Hibiscus and other flowers grew close enough to the house to smell night and day, and there was an abundance of lemon grass plants, a flora that theoretically keeps marauding insects, like mosquitoes, at bay. As I painfully discovered, lemon grass doesn't always work as an insect repellent, particularly on Thailand's mosquitoes.

The Nam Maelao River ran through the village, and by walking north from my home for five minutes, I crossed that river and entered an area filled with endless miles of jungle trails, teak forests, and moderate mountains framing numerous valleys, all became mine to explore. From high on any ridge, the valley floor below looked like a different-shades-of-green checker board. Systematically, Ban Sop Way farmers grew two crops of rice each year on those *boards*. Running on the raised paths separating the family rice plots became pure joy; each path packed by bare feet for hundreds, if not thousands, of years.

The environment could not have been better for me, including the precise 5:00 a.m., unhurried, melodic "bong, bong, bong, bong, bong" emanating from the wat when a monk struck a traditional, gargantuan Buddhist bell with a large teak mallet, telling the villagers it was time to bow and pay respects to Buddha before eating and going to the fields. Those gongs also inspired me to venerate the culture of Ban Sop Way. From my knees, I always bowed three times to the Buddhist icon and meditated for fifteen minutes or more before I started my morning run, one that took me across the Nam Maelao and into the areas I loved: through the rice fields,

into the teak forest, and onto the jungle trails. On those adventurous runs, birds provided a chorus of unsynchronized calls—some
melodious, some warning of an intruder. If the birds were silent, as
they infrequently were, I sardonically imagined a tiger stalking me.
That, however, never happened; fifty years had passed since one of
those magnificent beasts last visited the Ban Sop Way area.

After about six months in Ban Sop Way, one night I came awake
for no reason—except—Charlita *stood* near my bed in a misty image.
She looked down at me and said, *"You are OK now, Theo. I am going
to leave you. I love you."* I never saw or heard from her again, but she
remains in my heart to this day.

On an epic full moon lit Saturday evening, while swaying in my
hammock, admiring the moon beams filtering through the mango
trees, and listening to instrumental Thai music seemingly coming
from a neighbor's home, Moo Buakhieo, my landlord, walked onto
my patio. By hand and body language—he didn't speak English,
and I only knew a few words of Thai—he invited me to come to his
house. As it turned out, the music I heard came from a large patio
in front of his home.

On Moo's patio, several of his extended family members and
friends ate, drank, and danced. I immediately recognized one of the
dancers, Suchanat, the twenty-four year old English teacher. She
danced with two other ladies; all dressed in form fitting, cheong-
gsam dresses. While the Thai music didn't really sooth my ears, the
dancing ladies definitely gratified my eyes, particularly Suchanat;
her arms, legs, her entire body flowed in precise, delicate harmony
with the music. That Thai traditional dance, while not intended to
be sexual, became very much so as I watched; I no longer heard the
refrains.

When Suchanat finally sat down, I kept staring at her until our
eyes finally met. We both smiled, and then she walked to the table
where I sat with her aunt and uncle who invited her to sit down
next to me, and that triggered a conversation that continued until
the only ones remaining at the table, she and I, decided to go for a
walk along the river. Ahh, what a walk!

A Thai wedding followed four months later on the banks of the Maelao, a traditional Thai affair with colored paper *balloons49*, lifted by the heat from candles, decorating a sky already adorned with another full moon. Also, by Thai tradition, during the dinner that followed at the best restaurant in the *Chiang Rai* area, I presented her parents with a cash gift clothed in an unobtrusive, red envelope. I feared the $100,000 (3 million Thai Baht) I gave them, far more than Thai norms call for, would distract from the wedding, but it didn't; they didn't open the envelope until they returned to the privacy of their home. Weeks later, they started building the home they always wanted on a hill overlooking Ban Sop Way. I never regretted that gift.

After a weeklong honeymoon in Singapore, we were exhausted but happy. Singapore might be the cleanest city in the World; it seemed to be scrubbed clean for us: no cigarette butts, no spit on the sidewalks, no open trash containers, no smog from polluting vehicles, and no graffiti, but since Singapore is practically on the Equator it is HOT, so walking there can wear you out quickly. However, its infrastructure pacifies the heat somewhat. The subway lines have stations completely inside the many grand shopping centers and larger hotels. We shopped to Suchanat's content, visited all of the tourist's sites, and took three boat rides, one a dinner cruise at night around the beautiful Singapore harbor. It was a great week.

When we returned to Ban Sop Way, we started construction on our own home, one designed to be a bit pretentious, but hopefully, not to a degree it would offend the villagers.

Building can move fast in Thailand because there is plenty of labor, and high quality materials are readily available. In less than seven months we were furnishing our home with the best available cherry flooring and teak furniture in Thailand; magnificent fabrics from Singapore, and appliances from Japan, including—one of the most significant acquisitions as far as I was concerned—an industrial strength air conditioner installed on our roof.

---

49 These are not balloons in a Western sense but thin paper, shaped like boxes, with a candle suspended underneath.

We anticipated that from our elevated, wraparound veranda sunrises and sunsets would be superb; they were. Finally, only eight months after construction began, we invited all of Ban Sop Way and my MCU colleagues to an opulent housewarming, the highlight of which turned out to be the *taxi* service we provided.

Our new abode, a mile and one-half from the main part of Ban Sop Way and on top of a steep hill, would have been difficult for the elder villagers to navigate, and I didn't want to see them coming in the back of pickup trucks, often the mode of transportation for the elderly in northern Thailand. I talked to Moo about hiring a bus to shuttle people, but he came up with a better idea: Moo had a friend who operated an elephant touring business, one that primarily gave tourists scenic elephant rides along the river and on the nearby jungle trails. He suggested that we hire his friend and his animals to provide the *taxi* amenity. A great idea! Six colorfully decorated pachyderms shuffled to and from the village for six hours, a big hit with our guests.

That night another full moon—we timed all of our *special* events with the moon cycles in mind, further stimulating the festivities—lighted the Mea Lao meandering below, producing a scene a French impressionist artist would savor. The moonlight turned the flowing water pastel orange for much of the evening. Suchanat and I went to bed that night totally fatigued but happy.

Soon Suchanat's extended family and friends started visiting regularly. Obviously, all enjoyed the closeness they shared, and no one liked those evenings more than my charming wife.

We hosted one impromptu party after another; people showed up uninvited and unannounced—sometimes twenty or more—usually bringing large amounts of food and drink to be consumed late into the night. Again, Suchanat loved those occasions, but all of that activity didn't fit well with my pace of life and desire for tranquility. As a result, I had a back bedroom remodeled to be my sanctuary, one with a private exit into our garden, and from there, a path led into the teak forest that extended to the top of a steep hill. On a small picturesque clearing on the summit, I had a gazebo built with an electrical line running from our house so I could install an electric insect zapper; it worked great; I *roasted* thousands of flying critters with that magnificent device. When Suchanat's relatives and friends came, after a few minutes of small talk and courtesies, I usually fled to my room to read or *hid* among the teak trees *cooking* mosquitos.

Too soon, Suchanat informed me she thought a baby would join us "in about seven months." Overt surprise and covert disappointment, combined with disingenuously acting happy—I had practice performing that act—marked the day. I had religiously been using birth control, the latex kind, and I could only remember one time when that presented a problem; a night when a condom ripped. *It only takes one.*

I had already fathered two children, both of whom I wasn't serving well—except financially—and I knew money could not replace daily interaction with an attentive father. Still, we didn't consider, or even talk about an abortion, leaving another delivery at Cedars Sinai the only viable option.

An obvious question: Why would I take Suchanat to Cedars Sinai after Charlita had died there delivering Lawrence? The simple answer, I didn't hold Doctor Rush or the hospital responsible for Charlita's death. He told us there could be a problem with her giving natural birth, and she rejected the caesarian delivery he strongly recommended. And, his reputation, along with Cedars Sinai's great repute, extended to Asia. Numerous affluent Asians used Doctor Rush and Cedars Sinai, not only for their medical acumen, but like my birth in Brownsville, Texas, also to obtain the American citizenship their child would be entitled to if born in the United States.

With three months remaining to the anticipated delivery date, we leased a comfortable home in Beverly Hills only ten minutes from the hospital, and that turned out to be a wise choice because only one hour after her first labor pains, Suchanat delivered a beautiful baby girl.

Isn't it ironic that two of my three wives had babies very easily, but the third, Charlita, died in the process.

Sara Buakhieo Rogers came into this world on February 28, 1966. Two weeks later we flew back to Bangkok and on to Chiang Rai. The entire village of Ban Sop Way celebrated our arrival, and within a few days most of the 615 residents got a look at the black haired, almond eyed, apple of her father's eye; I loved that little girl so much. Of course I felt the same way about Timothy and Lawrence when they were born, but there was something unique about Sara. Maybe her size, much smaller than either of my boys, made her seem so vulnerable, demanding my love and attention. Timothy weighed ten pounds; Lawrence nine-a-half, while Sara came into this world at only six, and her full head of hair made her body look so small and helpless. She grew fast though, and within three months she doubled her birth weight.

Shortly after her arrival, I opened Sara's 10 million dollar, trust account, identical to Timothy's and Lawrence's, at the National Bank of Thailand. I deposited another 5 million in an account for Suchanat.

I held Sara more than I did either of the boys, sometimes holding a bottle for her even though her primary source of sustenance, her mother's breasts, produced all she needed. Quickly I bonded with Sara; we were comfortable together, and ironically, with her I didn't experience the death paranoia I had immediately after Timothy and Lawrence were born. Maybe my daily meditation visits to the wat had something to do with that, or maybe it was Charlita's ghost telling me I was "OK." Also, my wat routine seemed to have helped me enjoy a peaceful state of mind, one I had not experienced since I was a high school student living with Mother and Father Glover.

Unfortunately, the tranquility and equilibrium didn't last. Eighteen months previously I slept for a few nights without a mosquito net; now I was going to pay the price for that stupidity.

I woke in the middle of a night shivering and with a headache, one like I had never had before; I assumed a cold or even the flu bug had bitten me. Soon the chills turned into sweating and a high fever, classic indications of malaria, that terrible tropical disease that annually kills millions worldwide. Suchanat quickly recognized the symptoms because malaria mosquitoes invaded her village regularly. A doctor from the Mea Lao Medical Clinic came to our house, gave me some medicine, chloroquine, and took a blood sample, and sent it to Bangkok for analysis. Seven days later, the test came back positive for *plasmodium vivax*—one of the more deadly strains of the disease—and I became another statistic for Chung Rai Province malaria sleuths to investigate.

"Have you been protecting yourself from mosquitoes?"

"No, we don't have mosquitoes up here on this hill."

"Don't you ever go down to the village?"

"Yes, but I don't recall being bitten."

"Never?"

"Maybe many, many months ago when I first came to the village, I didn't have mosquito nets for a few days, and sometimes I would wake up with bite welts, particularly on my legs."

Investigation over: The investigator left shortly after that conversation but not before giving me a look that meant, *How can you be so stupid? Sleeping without mosquito nets, near a river and rice paddies in Ban Sop Way, a village with a history of malaria, is inviting the disease.*

Two months after I recovered from the initial intense symptoms, I still felt ill and weak. Alone, I got on a plane and flew back to Los Angeles and Cedars Sinai Hospital for a complete medical checkup, one that revealed I had high concentrations of parasitic *plasmodium falciparen* in my blood. That diagnosis differed from the *plasmodium vivax* diagnosis I received in Thailand. There, I had been treated with a drug that was not the optimum for my infection.

My epidemiologist at Cedars Sani, Doctor Richard Craig, gave me a dire warning: "The *plasmodium falciparen* must be eliminated from your blood or you risk death."

When I told Suchanat about that diagnosis, she immediately responded, "Sara and I will come to Los Angeles. We can live there until you are totally cured."

A week later my family arrived, and after further consultations with Doctor Craig, who suggested I plan on at least two years of treatment, we decided to buy a house in Arcadia, one that sat high on the slopes of the San Gabriel Mountains. That abode, in a beautiful oak tree shaded neighborhood where deer visited most mornings, and on rare occasions a black bear, became our very comfortable home.

At first, Suchanat seem to enjoy the new environment and the process of buying the household furnishings needed to make our home exactly what she wanted. She found an Asian furniture store in Pasadena, one that stocked all the Asian furniture a person might want, including many polished teak and cherry wood items.

Suchanat selections would put any professional interior home designer to shame. She seemed to have an innate talent for the proper use of space with furniture and colors that blended harmoniously, making our home a great place to live. Vivid memories of Yalin decorating our house in Hong Kong were more entertaining than painful. I often laughed to myself about the coincidence, how all of my wives—Charlita had those same talent—were aficionados when it came to decorating a home.

I seemed to be getting stronger in Arcadia, and little Sara, now almost two, thrived there. For the first time I heard the words, "Da, Da," and received kisses from one of my children; she loved me, but not nearly as much as I loved her—impossible.

Suchanat also seemed happy, but I knew she missed her family and Ban Sop Way where all of her lifelong friends lived. So I encouraged her to call her family, or a friend, early every morning—evening in Thailand—and talk for as long as she wanted, and sometimes she did so for hours.

After about nine months in Arcadia, Suchanat started asking, "When can we go back Ban Sop Way."

Doctor Craig didn't think I should be making any trips, so I suggested that Suchanat and Sara go back for a month long visit. My wife put her arms around my neck, gave me a kiss, and said, "Thank you, Theo. I miss my family so much, and Sara and I will miss you when we are in Ban Sop Way."

I thought I knew her well; it never entered my mind she would not want to return to me and our home in Arcadia after that one month. However, that is exactly what happened.

One morning she called and asked if it was alright with me if she stayed one more week, a week later, "Can we stay another week?" Another month passed quickly then two more, and I started intolerably missing my wife and daughter.

Two days before Suchanat's and Sara's *definite* scheduled return—after I had front yard, living room, and bedroom signs made welcoming them—when she called hours earlier than our usual talking time I knew something was wrong:

While chocking back crying, my wife said, "Theo I have some terrible news..."

My chronic paranoia exploded, "What's wrong with Sara? What happened to her? What happened to her? Tell me now!"

"Sara is fine, Theo. It's my mother. She had a terrible stroke last night. She might die."

With both relief and guilt, "Oh, I hate to hear that; I'm so sorry. Where is she?"

"In the Chiang Rai hospital, but they are going to fly here to Bangkok tomorrow if her vital signs can be stabilized and if she is still alive."

Obviously, and understandably, I was not going to see wife and daughter for some unknown period time—so disappointing.

As time dragged by, one month, three months, and eventually, six months—now I hadn't seen my family for nine months— Muntauta's, Suchanat mother, vital signs slowly improved. However, when they brought her back to Ban Sop Way, she was totally incapacitated; she couldn't walk, she couldn't talk, and she had absolutely no control over her bodily functions. Alarmingly, her eyes did not move when Suchanat or the doctor tried to communicate with her. In short, she was in a vegetative state. During that time our daily phone calls changed to twice weekly and eventually they diminished to one on Saturday mornings.

The loneliness and pressure continued to build until finally, one day after one of our phone calls, I had a relapse with malaria. The familiar fever, chills, and sweating put me in bed for three days. When I recovered to a small degree, I went to see Doctor Craig at Cedars Sinai. He put me through the same series of test related to *plasmodium falciparen*. As expected my blood still carried the *sporozoites*, but in a lower concentration, not as low, however, as he predicted for this stage of my battle with the disease.

Doctor Craig asked me, "Have you been under any unusual pressure recently? Pressure is often a precursor to this type of malarial recurrence."

My short answer was, "Yes! A lot." Then I fully explained my family situation, followed by an important question, "Do you think it would be ok for me to make a thirty day trip back to Thailand."

His curt answer, "No, that would not be advisable."

Although I was now in a constant state of depression, I tried to use an optimistic voice and put a positive bent on our conversations when Suchanat and I talked. "I know your mother is going to get better. We just have to give her time."

From Suchanat's end, she too tried to be positive, and she always had an antidote to tell about Sara: her first unassisted steps, her first words, the fact that she liked oatmeal and bananas like me, and sometimes she would put Sara on the phone to say things like, "Da da, I lub yu."

Finally the day came when I had to ask, "When do you think you can come back to Arcadia?"

That turned out to be an agitating question, "Theo, don't you understand? My mother is never going to walk or talk again. You know I can't leave her like this. I think a better question is, when are you coming back to Ban Sop Way?"

I didn't know how to answer that other than to say, "Dr. Craig doesn't think I should travel."

I should have told her about my recent bout with malaria, but I didn't. Our conversation ended a short time later. When she didn't call the next week I called her, and a man answered the phone.

"Allo, thes es Dooctor Gulfrey."

"This is Theo. Is my wife there?"

"Noo, she as gonn to de markeet."

"Please tell her to call her husband when she gets home."

"OoK, I weel do dat."

There was something about that call that set off alarm bells, but I tried to discount that warning as part of my tendency to be suspicious of people I didn't know. Still, the aroma of subterfuge lingered. It wasn't until the next day that I reached Suchanat. Immediately I asked about *Doctor Gulfrey*. She called him by his first name, "Luke."

"Luke has been very kind to Mother and me. Since it is very difficult for me to get her to his office, he comes here and examines her."

"What about yesterday? You weren't there when I called, but your doctor was."

"When he comes to treat Mother, he sometimes watches Sara a little while so I can get away from this house."

That conversation did nothing to calm me, and she obviously didn't want to talk long. We said our good-byes and hung up.

It wasn't until two weeks later that we had our next conversation; it turned out to be our last for many months: "Tell me, Sweetheart, is something going on with you and the French doctor?

"We are friends, Theo. He is kind to Mother, to me, and to Sara."

"You know, Suchanat that is not what I am asking. Is there more to it than friendship?"

A long, silent pause came next; that gave me my answer, finally followed by, "Theo can we talk about this later. I have to help Mother."

That statement didn't take a high degree of precognition to get the message; the *lance* penetrated my heart first, then my mind totally collapsed.

From that instant, until I became lucid six months later in the psychiatric ward of a Veterans' Administration (VA) hospital in Sepulveda, California, I have absolutely no memory. Later, Doctor Justin Ramsey, my attending psychiatrist, told me that I had been picked up two miles off of Santa Monica Beach by a Coast Guard boat—a patrolling helicopter had reported me—while I was swimming west. When questioned, my only response, one I kept repeating, "I am going to Thailand to see my wife and baby."

My trousers, found on the beach, contained my wallet and driver's license and eventually identified me as Theodore Ruiz Rogers, a Marine veteran. Consequently, the police turned me over to the VA.

During my stay in Sepulveda VA Hospital, I suffered another attack of malaria. I vaguely remember that episode.

Months later Doctor Craig ran me through another series of Malaria tests. At our consultation session he admonished me, "Theo, you have to construct your life in a way that does not expose you to intense stress. If you don't, you will end up back in a mental institution, probably further debilitated by another bout with Malaria. In addition, you already have some kidney damage from the disease, and if it gets much worse it will be life threatening."

A month before leaving the hospital, I called Suchanat and found her concerned, sympathetic, but unyielding in her decision not to return to America. After talking with Doctor Craig and learning I faced at least two more years of treatment to eradicate the *plasmodium sporozoites* from my blood, I had to accept that my family was gone—at least for two years.

I tried living alone in Arcadia, but that turned out to be impossible; everywhere I looked I saw Suchanat and Sara. I knew that I was facing another mental breakdown if I didn't abandon that home. I turned it, with all of its contents, over to a real estate broker; then I consulted with a Navy[50] mental health physician in San Diego.

Navy Captain[51] Steinhoff, a psychologist with twenty-five years of Navy service, suggested I request an apartment at the Marine

---

50 The Navy provides all medical care for the Marine Corps.
51 A Navy "captain" is equivalent to a Marine Corps "colonel."

Corps Veterans' Retirement Home (MCVRH) located just outside of Washington, D.C. That is where I am writing from—thirty-one years later. That temporary get-myself-together stay mutated into an eternity.

Eighteen months after entering MCVRH, the Navy finally declared me malaria free. Suchanat and I talked regularly during that time, but when I told her I was now free to rejoin my family in Thailand, she said, "Theo, I am very sorry; I don't want to hurt you, but I have a new husband, and he is a good father for Sara."

"You can't do that to me. You are still my wife."

"Theo, I'm sure you don't know, but in Ban Sop Way[52] you can just quit being married. You don't need any divorce papers."

The details of my life for the next six months are too painful to write about, but obviously I survived.

During all the years I have been here, I have only been absent for one two-week period. Two years after being declared malaria free, I took a trip to Hong Kong, Dumaguete, and Thailand to see if there were any surviving pieces for me of the three families I spawned in Asia.

My first stop was Hong Kong where I verified that the trust fund for Timothy was being administered properly. In fact, it had grown substantially, more than doubling to over 30 million dollars. In Dumaguete, Lawrence's balance was 19 million; and in Thailand, Sara's had accumulated 14 million, indicating that all the funds were being well managed. I only made two changes to their portfolios: from all three, I invested 5 million dollars in *Emerging Markets companies* and 5 million in *Developing Technology companies*. Potentially, those investments would make my children affluent for the rest of their lives.

I met Yalin at a bay front restaurant where we mostly discussed Timothy and his future. At the age of ten, he was an outstanding student, already with aspirations of becoming an attorney like his

52 Until 1935, rural marriages were unregulated. After 1935, many villages held to the traditional marriage mores. In some locals those old ways of getting married or divorced are still practiced. (www.divorcethailand.com)

adopted father. Yalin now owned her own investment management company.

She asked me if I wanted to see Timothy, and of course I did, but not in a manner that would confuse him. The next day I sat on the bleachers with tears streaming down my face as I watched my son play soccer for his school's team. Later, Yalin gave me some pictures of Timothy in his Hong Kong English Academy uniform.

From Hong Kong I went to Dumaguete. The Sabino Dive Academy and Guide Service was now the preeminent dive company south of Manila.

Rizal attempted to repay half of the 2 million dollars I *loaned* him, but I declined. After some contentious negotiating, we agreed to use that money to give Filipino citizens ocean diving experiences—fully paid scholarships to the Open Ocean Diving Course. Very few Filipinos were divers; they could not afford the equipment or the instruction.

I saw Lawrence—also an excellent student—and along with his *mother and father,* we had dinner together. He didn't know I was his natural father, and to hear him calling Riana and Rizal *"Mother"* and *"Dad"* hurt. On the other hand, he seemed to be well adjusted and happy. Rizal gave me pictures of Lawrence in his snorkeling gear; he so resembled his mother, long legs, confident smile, and eyes that projected curiosity and intelligence. My experience in Thailand didn't turn out as well.

Suchanat met me in Bangkok. She was pleasant and polite, and redundantly thanked me for the money I had deposited for her, but when it came to Sara, she would not allow me to see her, even if only from a distance. In my absence, Suchanat had married Luke, the French doctor who treated her mother. She said he treated her and Sara wonderfully, and she didn't want to take the chance of diluting that relationship by "presenting" me to Sara and having her talk about me in front of her step-father; maybe he was a very jealous man. She did give me some pictures of Sara that brought a lump to my throat.

For the first time, I told Suchanat about setting up the 10 million dollar education trust fund for Sara with the First Bank of Thailand at their Chiang Rai offices. She knew, of course, about the 5 million I had deposited in The First Bank of Thailand in her name. Again, she was very thankful. Ten years later, I made her the trustee on Sara's fund. It had trebled during that period.

Before we parted, we took one last look into each other's eyes. She kissed me on the cheek, and that was the last time I saw her.

37

Life in Marine Corps Veteran's Retirement Home

I returned to the United States trying to come to terms with a dichotomy of emotions: while being acutely aware I had failed my children, I felt somewhat reassured since all of my children seemed to have good parents and were apparently doing well. Still, no matter how I tried to rationalize, the conclusion was clear—I had abandoned them. Nonetheless, my life had to go on, but how should I conduct it, and where?

When I originally took up residence at MCVRH, I had no intention of staying longer than a year, only time enough to get my mind to a place where I could function without ruminating too much and being periodically overcome with paranoia, guilt, pity, and depression.

I thought about buying an expensive home in a local for the rich and famous, living a lifestyle typical of a multi-millionaire. I had the money, but would I really be comfortable living ostentatiously, something I had rejected years before in Hong Kong with Yalin. On the other hand, when I came back to MCVRH, I found solace in my comfortable, but unpretentious, apartment. Conclusion: I wanted to end my nomadic existence; I needed stability and permanence, a pleasant place to live where I could meditate, exercise, sleep in a comfortable bed, and eat good food I cooked. Nothing else required. The MCVRH governing board allowed me to upgrade my apartment, at my expense of course, and it is now a much more comfortable place to live than I deserve.

Living in the Washington D.C. area had the advantage of good news sources, TV and newspapers, and good public transportation: I never really liked the burden of having my own car, stopping for gas, checking the tires, monitoring the necessary maintenance, were all tasks I did not enjoy.

During those periods of lifestyle contemplation, I often thought of the simple, unfettered régime Buddhist monks live—not that I wanted to be a monk—but they seemed contented. Consequently, I decided to stay at MCVRH for one more year, and then reevaluate my inclinations. That year turned into another year, which flowed into another and another...Now I have been here for thirty-one years, and I have absolutely no desire to live elsewhere.

Here I read a lot, write a little, play chess some, and visit a wat in Alexandria once each week. In my room I also have a Buddhist icon I pay homage to daily before meditating for 30 minutes. I have a few friends, but none so close that I will be devastated when they pass away. Occasionally, when I read in the *Washington Post* about the unfortunate plight of a person or family, I send them some money, usually one or two thousand dollars, but on a few of occasions, I have sent ten-thousand dollars; and on one, I sent a family that had lost their home in a fire—without adequate insurance—$300,000 to rebuild. And, about once each month, I get out the pictures of my children, peruse them and shed a few tears.

So this has been the story of my life. It has not always been a pretty and comfortable life, but in retrospect it has not always been as tedious as it seemed during those times of stress and anguish. After all, how many people are fortunate enough to be awarded the Medal of Honor by the President of the United States; be married to three wonderful women, all of whom mothered exceptional children; win a multi-million dollar lottery; experience the joys of teaching in three different Asian countries, and get picked up—rescued from certain death—in the middle of the ocean while crazily trying to swim to Thailand. Believe it or not, now I can actually laugh about that idiocy.

Still, I too often think of those who died under the spell of my *death curse*, be it real or imagined: Rico my four-year-old playmate; Mother, Papá, and Rachel, my little sister; Delores Hand, my best friend in elementary school; my Marine Corps buddy, Jim Cordell; Mother and Father Glover, my step-parents; Lieutenant Wilson, who helped Yalin and I escape to Hong Kong from China; and, Charlita, my near perfect wife.

I don't have debilitating nightmares any more. I think of my three wives and my children often, trying—not always successfully—to concentrate on the joy each of them brought to my life.

OK! It's time to wrap this up; it is already too long and way too self-indulgent. TRR

PART III

The Attorney's Speak

38

Dad's Autobiography

"Sara, this is Timothy. Did you receive the copy of Dad's autobiography I sent to you?"

"Timothy, how can you call that man 'Dad'? As far as I am concerned, he gave up the rights to that title when he deserted us."

"I know! I know! But please listen to me, Sara. Maybe he didn't desert you. You are an attorney; you know there are always two, sometimes more, sides to every story. Our father's life has had multiple sides, and you won't understand any of them, particularly those which apply to you personally, if you don't read his writing. As your loving big brother, I am asking you to read it. Please, do it for me."

"Has Lawrence read it?"

"Yes, after reluctantly starting at my request, Lawrence finished reading it last night, and he called me about an hour ago. What would you guess he said?"

"Timothy, I have no idea. You tell me."

"The first thing he said was, 'Has Sara read this? If not, she simply has to. I finished it an hour ago, and I feel like after forty years in prison, I have just been released; it is liberating; it is sad; it is an incredible piece of writing, and I think we should get it published for him.'"

"OK, Timothy, I will read it for you and Lawrence but not for our father. How much of my time will it take?"

"Well, if you are like me, it will take about five hours. I started it at four in the afternoon, and after the first two chapters I couldn't put it down. I called my wife, and told her I would be home late, and at 9:30 p.m. I walked in the door of my house smiling; like Lawrence, I felt liberated."

Two days later, the three Rogers attorneys had a conference call where they agreed that their father's story, incredible and almost unbelievable as it was, should not be the end of his narrative. They decided to try to get him to move out of the "old soldiers' home" and move in with one of them. All committed to making that offer to him in person.

They also discussed having a family reunion at *The Mark,* a five star San Francisco hotel, inviting their mothers and step-fathers and all of "Dad's grandchildren," expenses paid by his children.

39

The Family Reunion That Was Not

After talking for two hours in the sitting room of their father's apartment at the Marine Veterans' Retirement Home, the family reunion proposal finally came up. After Timothy, Lawrence, and Sara all made their pitch for the event, Sara said, "Well, Dad; what do you think?"

Theo gazed out the window into the Arlington National Cemetery one mile below, then beyond the Potomac River and into Washington D.C. There he could just see the spire of the Washington Monument and the dome of the Capital Building. He was stalling, trying to think of someway to respond to a heartfelt idea—one intended to heal a splintered family logically and compassionately. After almost five minutes of thick silence, he spoke:

"I don't disagree with your motives for wanting to bring all of us together; I have those same desires. Yet, I don't think it is fair to Timothy's and Sara's mothers—both of whom I loved very much when you two were born—or your *parents* Lawrence, who were standing with me when we buried your mother on Apo Island. I'm sure if you ask them, they would probably agree to come, but do you really think any of them want to dredge up the painful past? They all know, and you all know, for reasons I still don't totally understand, I abandoned all of you, and there is nothing any of us can do to change that.

"Seeing you and knowing you are successful is an extreme pleasure I don't deserve, but still, I cherish it and I am thankful."

After more silence, Sara said, "Is there anything we can do, Dad, to change your mind. We think our families; including our mothers and adopted fathers, would love seeing and visiting with each other in one big, fancy room in the best hotel in San Francisco. Please, give the idea more consideration."

"I second that," said Timothy.

Followed by Lawrence's "Here! Here!"

Finessing to another subject, "I deeply appreciate that all of you have invited me to live with your families, but to be honest, I can never do that. As scientifically illogical as it is, I still have this fear that I am an angel of death; that obsession is never going away.

"I do want to see you when it is convenient for you, and I would love to see my grandchildren on day visits. Still, we can't risk me getting too close to them emotionally; it might be dangerous in a paranormal sense."

With a smile on his face, Theo had a proposal of his own. "As you know, I have several billion dollars in investments sitting in the British Royal Bank of Hong Kong. I have tried not to become parsimonious with those funds, but obviously I have. If you need any money, I will give it to you, but I assume that all of you are financially comfortable and don't need the cash any more than I do; still I intend to *will* each of you one-billion dollars.

"By the way, I intend to live here where I am comfortable and unstressed until the day I die. When that day comes, in Buddhist tradition, I want to be cremated, and you can do what you want with my ashes—with a smile on his face—maybe one of your gardens will need some fertilizer.

"Please excuse my self-serving side track. Here's the idea I am asking the three of you to help me with: I want to start a foundation to provide education scholarships for children in Asia whose American fathers or grandfathers deserted them; I know there are hundreds, probably thousands, first or second generation offspring of men who served in the Korean and Vietnam wars, also business men and teachers. My plan is open ended, but I envision a child from a poor family, one with academic desire and promise, would receive help as early as the elementary school years. I know this foundation would not be able to educate every poor, fatherless child in Asia, but I think it could serve many.

"If you three will be the overseers of this foundation, under your direction, the investments might do better than they have under me. For the past ten years I have usually glanced at the statements the bank sends me. Periodically, I look at them closely; I did study one a couple of weeks ago, and I was shocked to see how well the Microsoft and Apple Computer stocks I purchased on their IPO's in the mid 1980's have done. Those two investments alone are now worth billions. I also learned from that statement that my total assets are a little more than sixteen billion dollars."

"Wow! Are you serious? Great job, Dad,"

40

Theodore Ruiz Roger's Legacy

Six months later *The Theodore Ruiz Rogers Education Foundation* was founded, and quickly, the foundation awarded its first twelve scholarships: four each in China, the Philippines, and Thailand. Altruism, although not a word Theo would use to describe himself, clearly defines his legacy.

On April 18, 2012, Theo's kidneys suddenly quit functioning. As confirmed by an autopsy after his death, his battle with malaria many years before apparently the precursor. Physicians told him on April 20, that he needed to undergo kidney dialysis twice each week in order to stay alive until a suitable kidney could be found for a transplant. Even after his children visited him and volunteered to undergo testing to see if their kidneys would be acceptable, while legally lucid and still capable of making his own decisions, Theo unequivocally refused dialysis or a transplant. Even if a suitable kidney became available, Theo contended, "A younger person should have that kidney."

On April 24, 2012, Theodore Ruiz Rogers died at the age of seventy-nine. His last words to his children—an indication his paranoia and guilt still existed, "Tell all of your mothers I am sorry. And I am so sorry I treated all of you the way I did. I loved each of you on the day you were born, and I will never stop loving you."

Moments later he lapsed into a coma and died at 8 p.m.—his regular sleeping time for the past thirty-two years.

On April 26, his ashes were interred at Washington Nation Cemetery. His children, Timothy Wong Rogers, Lawrence Sabino Rogers, and Sara Buakhieo Rogers-Givens—and Theo's six grandchildren—attended the ceremony along with the Commandant of the Marine Corps, General Samuel M. Jackson. A Marine Corps honor guard fired the traditional salute to dead heroes—three salvos of rifle fire.

The legacy of Theo Ruiz Rogers lives on. As of January 1, 2013, his foundation, *The Theodore Ruiz Rogers Education Foundation*, under the management of his three children, has awarded over 400 scholarships to Eurasian children.

About the Author

William "Bill" Foulk was born in Benton, Illinois. His mother was a saintly woman and his father a former professional baseball play, high school coach/teacher, and, ashamedly, a card carrying member of the Ku Klux Klan.

Unlike his older brother and sister, both outstanding students, Bill accomplished little academically in high school, but his production on the basketball court was prolific. Despite his bad grades, several universities, including the University of Kentucky, recruited him as early as his sophomore year in high school. But rather than matriculate, he joined the Marine Corps before graduating.

Following Boot Camp and Combat Infantry Training, Bill boarded a troop transport bound for the Korean War. On the way, the USNS William Wiegle stopped in Kobe, Japan for fourteen hours, just long enough for Bill to have a tryst and fall in love with a Japanese prostitute, an enigmatic memory he carries to this day.

Sandwiched between his military duties in Korea, Bill took his first steps towards becoming an author by recording his experiences in a diary; however, the Marine Corps confiscated that chronicle but not before he realized he enjoyed writing.

Over the following decades, Bill played professional basketball—not in the NBA—became an Army paratrooper, served eight years in the Air Force, and returned to the Army as a warrant officer. During a tour in Vietnam, he was awarded the Bronze Star.

After retiring from the military, Bill became a highly successful teaching tennis professional. Among his many celebrity clients were Johnny Carson, Elton John, and Joan Kennedy. Eight years after becoming *a celebrity by association,* a status he became extremely uncomfortable with, he retired from tennis to seek a better education. Still without a high school diploma, Bill attended Montana State University (MSU) for an undergraduate degree, *with honors*, followed by graduate work at both Dartmouth College and MSU. He has a master's degree in Education Administration.

During his professional tennis years his recreational athletic interests turned to running. At the age of forty-eight he became a member of the MSU track and cross country teams. The Nike Company had him under contract for twelve years, during which he won eleven national championships and became the first runner over fifty to finish in the *Top 100* at the Boston Marathon, winning his age group (50-59) and finishing *93rd* overall out of approximately 30,000 runners.

Throughout most of his running career Bill taught junior high and high school. Later, he became a school principal in Idaho and Alaska. During that same period he became a licensed pilot with an instrument rating. Later he would become a licensed Deep Water SCUBA Diver.

Another short retirement became a precursor for education jobs in China, for seven years; the Philippines, for two years; and three years in Thailand; there he also owned and managed a small banana plantation. In all—military and civilian—Bill lived in Asia for over fifteen years.

Now in Arcadia, California, Bill devotes himself to his wife, Yalin, and to writing about his experiences, mostly those in Asia. He has three children—Melody, Thomas, and James—eight grandchildren, and six great-grandchildren

He recently published <u>A Grain of Sand: the autobiographical adventures of William Foulk</u>, available on Amazon.com.